PRAISE FOR *A CURSE UPON TIDES*

"*A Curse Upon Tides* takes readers on an emotional journey they will not soon forget. With expertly woven prose, Daylin gives us characters that will surely break all our hearts—and put them back together again. A sweeping, epic sequel to *These Hallowed Binds*, this book reaches deep into the characters' hearts, weaving profound arcs through hope, pain, and a kind of faith that is only found in the fire."

—HANNAH GAUDETTE, AUTHOR OF THE DESTINED DUOLOGY AND THE ONE LIGHT TRILOGY

"Masterful storytelling, epic world-building, powerful themes. This tale will tug at your heartstrings and dare you to believe again. *A Curse Upon Tides* is a beautiful reminder that we don't have to face troubled waters alone. All we have to do is look up."

— MELODY FAITH, AUTHOR *THESE MENDING HEARTS* AND *BIRDSONG*

"A.M. Daylin has built upon the rich foundation of *These Hallowed Binds* to take the Empyreal Guardian Saga to brilliant new heights. With greater adventure, deeper tension, entertaining banter, and heartfelt moments between loveable characters both new and old, *A Curse Upon Tides* will bring you on a harrowing journey that will leave a lasting impression on your heart and your spirit."

— NATHAN KEYS, AWARD-WINNING AUTHOR OF THE EPIC OF
MARINDEL

PRAISE FOR A. M. DAYLIN

"*These Hallowed Binds* by A.M. Daylin is the story YA fantasy fans have been searching for. With an immersive world and characters you can't help but follow page after page, the clean romance and intricately woven plot will capture your heart and mind. Daylin does a fantastic job of exploring dark and emotional themes while still managing to leave her readers with a sense of hope. Don't miss this stunning first installment in The Empyreal Guardian Saga."

— SARA ELLA, AWARD-WINNING AUTHOR OF THE WONDER-
LAND TRIALS, CORAL, AND THE UNBLEMISHED TRILOGY

"*These Hallowed Binds* pulled me in from the start and didn't let go. A.M. Daylin's story is richly crafted, masterfully written and laced throughout with Christian symbolism. The fantastical world of Silvirdia is a feast for the imagination, full to the brim of guardian beasts turned hostile after a dark curse mars the land, a secret battle to set the world to rights, well-written,

interesting characters on top of a unique and well-developed magic system. With a story of finding one's destiny, a bit of found family and an entertaining love triangle, *These Hallowed Binds* is a wonderfully enjoyable read. Daylin's talent promises the makings of a spell-binding series and I can't wait to find out what happens next!"
— KELSEY CHAPMAN, AWARD-WINNING AUTHOR OF *UNMASKED*

"A.M. Daylin keeps you on the edge of your seat while you discover the truth behind the disappearance of Norielle's father and the world. The banter and discoveries are expertly woven on the pages. Readers of fantasy will love this Lord of the Rings type of adventure."
— CANDICE PEDRAZA YAMNITZ, AUTHOR OF *UNBETROTHED*

"A. M. Daylin does *not* disappoint with the unique world and lovable characters of *These Hallowed Binds*. With a world on a steady path to collapse, a cast of amazing characters that captured my heart from the beginning, and an explosive ending full of twists, turns, and surprises, *These Hallowed Binds* had me gasping, tearing up, cheering, and everything in between. Daylin has crafted an absolute rollercoaster in the best way possible, and *These Hallowed Binds* is a can't-miss if you love fantasy with golden-hearted protagonists, a unique and well-built magic system, and characters you can truly invest in!"
— TOMMIE MICHELE, AUTHOR OF THE DRAFTED DUOLOGY

formed by the Light. This is a story that has never failed to bring me to tears, and is guaranteed to be enjoyed over and over in the years to come!"

— BRIGITTE CROMEY, AUTHOR OF *THE GUARDIAN'S OATH* AND *THE SHATTERED ONES*

"Pulse-pounding and emotionally resonant, *Where Darkness Cannot Follow* seized my attention from the first page and held it captive throughout. The allure of a character-driven narrative is undeniable, and A.M. Daylin masterfully doubles the impact with two exquisitely realized point-of-view characters. Ezro and Vaeryn are a dynamic pair—each moment of their inner conflict, their forged alliance in the treacherous Canyon, and their desperate battles against netherbeasts and other lethal entities, is crafted with precision and depth. Every thread of the narrative gripped me like I was thick in the tension with the characters.

Where Darkness Cannot Follow is a rich tapestry of raw emotion and harrowing adventure, pulsating with the lifeblood of its protagonists. The anticipation for the next chapter in Ezro and Vaeryn's journey is at its peak—I want more of their story!"

— STEPHANIE COTTA, AWARD-WINNING AUTHOR OF *THE CONJURER'S CURSE*

Also by A. M. Daylin

The Empyreal Guardian Saga
These Hallowed Binds

The Luminors Trilogy
Where Darkness Cannot Follow

A Curse Upon Tides

A CURSE UPON TIDES

THE EMPYREAL GUARDIAN SAGA

BOOK 2

A.M. DAYLIN

MOONCREST PUBLISHING

MOONCREST PUBLISHING

To anyone who is afraid to let themselves be loved.

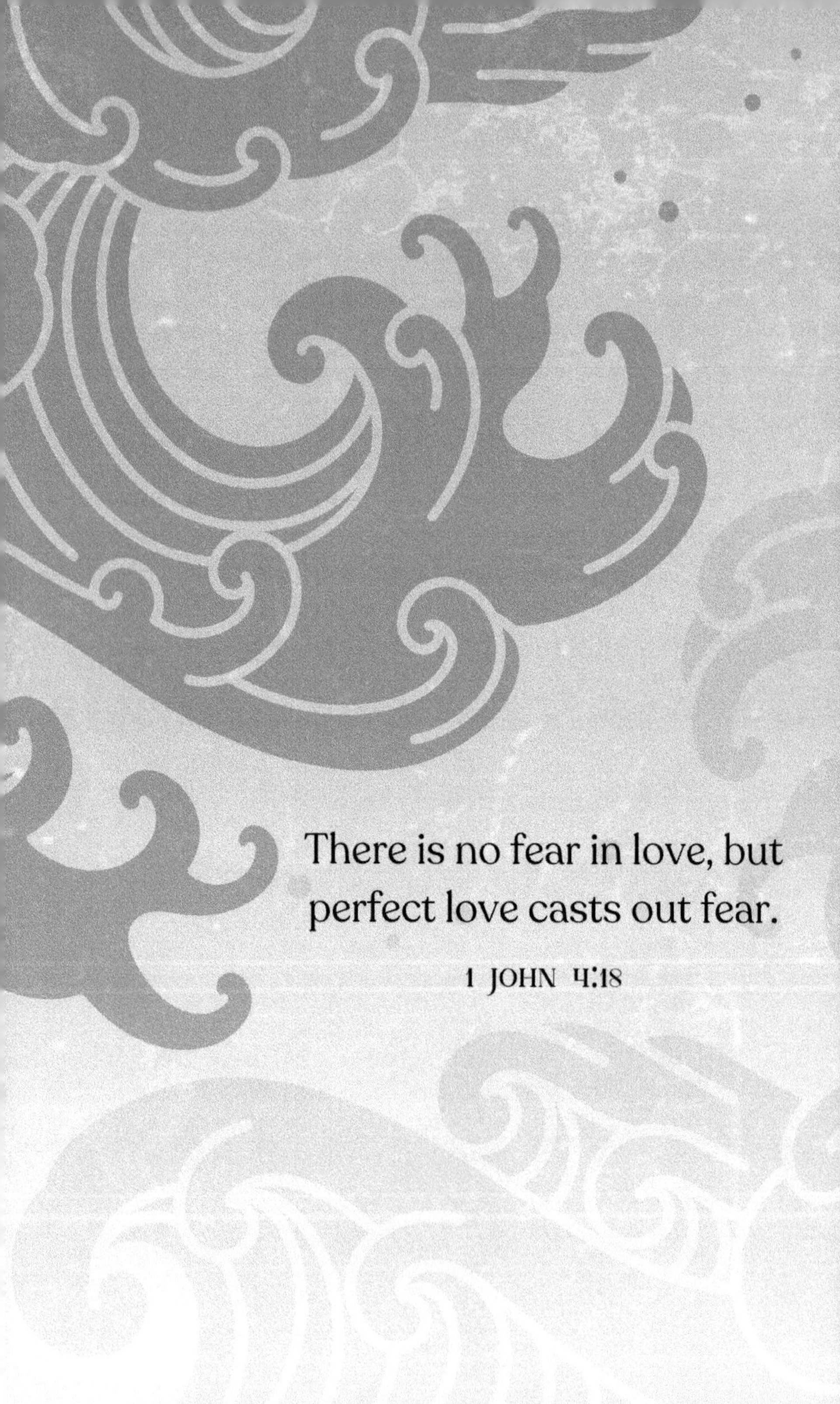
There is no fear in love, but
perfect love casts out fear.

1 JOHN 4:18

We do not find the meaning of life by ourselves alone—we find it with

ONE ANOTHER.

THOMAS MERTON

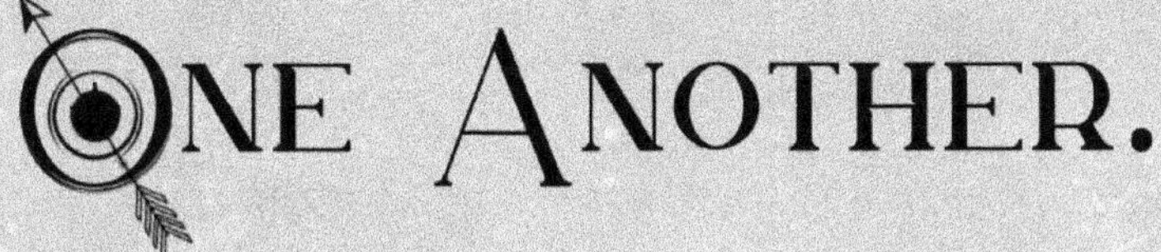

CALDEN

I fled. I failed.

The only words I've recalled from Toaph Elbara echo through my being in every silence. Yet, try as I might to remember more, only a vague memory of swarming dust ever accompanies the words.

Still, our true Empyreal Guardian lives, and with him, our world's hope to survive.

If only I could break through the barriers in my mind to find him.

I press my elbows against the cool stone railing of the citadel's communal balcony. A damp breeze flicks the loose sleeves of my robe and tickles my ears beneath my hood. I breathe in the refreshing aroma of a dozen waterfalls. Their steady *shush* fills the otherwise still evenfall—a noise which usually soothes me, but tonight, it feels as though the weight of the water pounds against me.

The longer I take to gather the information we need about Toaph Elbara's location, the more lives will be threatened by

Ta'Nathel's curse upon the world of Silvirdia. And what if I never find it? What if the dust is all I ever remember?

How then will we find him before it's too late?

The soft whimper of old hinges peels my focus from the tree-dotted courtyard below and toward the balcony door. I prepare to excuse myself and return to my private chambers, but my words dissolve when I see the intruder.

Norielle? What is she doing out here the night before her induction ceremony?

I push my hood back.

"Do you mind if I join you?" she asks, still clutching the door handle.

The sound of her voice after three days apart trades all my prior concerns for new ones. With how hard I've been trying to make contact with Toaph Elbara, I feel more dangerous than I ever have, like another violent, unconscious episode might overtake me at any moment. And the thought of her seeing that, even now that we know it's not a curse—

Would she ever seek me out again? Or would things be as they were with the last woman I favored, who acted unconcerned by my episodes until she witnessed them?

I shake my worries from my overburdened mind before my thoughts of Corene can invoke the memories of her death—her death that is so tangled now with Norielle's rescue that the longer I look into Norielle's hazel eyes, the more I can't help but envision Corene's.

I bow my head, hoping she misses my lengthy hesitation and the slight lie in my voice. "Not at all."

She steps outside, and a cool evening breeze flutters the ruffles on her cornflower-blue dress. "Rhys told me you would be out here."

My brows lift as she shuts the door behind her. *Did he?* Yet I specifically asked my attendant to keep my whereabouts clandestine for the night.

"Is something wrong?" I ask.

"Must something be wrong in order for us to talk?" She poses the question mildly, yet hurt still frays the edges of her words.

I should have visited her at least once in the three days that we've been here at the citadel, but the heaviness in my spirit has made even simple conversations nearly unbearable with anyone—let alone *her* with all the complex emotions her presence elicits in me.

"No, no. Of course not." I gesture for her to come closer.

She crosses between the array of potted plants and perennial flowers, her every step increasing the tightness in my chest. When she stops beside me, I fix my eyes down on the courtyard, scanning the shadows. What if, by some chance, Elias stood down there and saw us? What pain would spotting Norielle and me alone up here provoke in him?

"I apologize for my distance." My hands tighten on the balcony rail, as if bound to it by Snare Wards. "There's been... much for me to process."

She nods like she understands what I mean—Corene's death, the news about Toaph's survival, and, of course, the discovery that my "curse" is truly the result of an Empyreal Guardian speaking to my mind.

"Rhys told me you are settling in well," I add to change the subject before I sink back into my thoughts. "And that you've found yourself a nice collection of books from the Seer's library."

She tucks a long strand of chestnut hair behind her ear. "You have your attendant keeping tabs on me?"

"He keeps tabs on all matters within the citadel for me," I say, and her smile falters. "Have you been studying wards?"

"Mostly. I want to understand them before my endowing at the ceremony so I'm more ready for my training."

"A wise use of time."

"Your mother isn't allowing me to do much else, anyway." She shrugs. "I've already been introduced to every person she deemed important for me to meet right away and, otherwise, the most excitement I've had is answering questions about what food I want served at my induction ceremony." She cocks her head. "How grand of an event will that be?"

I consider all of Mother's tedious preparations. Two stories beneath us, her attendants are likely still at work putting together flower arrangements and polishing the ballroom floor. "Sure to be the grandest. You are the first outsider to be summoned into a Bind, not to mention the great news you've brought us. Mother wishes to announce it at the ceremony."

A snake of apprehension slithers up my spine at the mere mention of it. How will the Wardens respond to the message Norielle carried here? Will they believe us that Toaph Elbara lives after twenty-five years of the Guardian's absence, or will they disregard the message upon hearing we learned it from the Blood Wardens?

From Corene.

I fight another frown as her black-painted face flashes in my mind.

"Well, that's good," Norielle says, so innocently unaware of my troubles. "I'm nervous enough. Maybe the news about Toaph Elbara will distract people from noticing me too much."

I furrow my brows. *Is she that concerned about being in front of everyone?*

"I'm sure it will provide a significant distraction," I say.

Her chin lowers, and I realize how that must have sounded—like the news about Toaph is more important than the person who carries it. Even after how she suffered on account of it.

"Have you remembered anything more?" she asks before I can amend my statement.

Her question drops onto my shoulders like a cloak made of woven iron.

"Nothing," I say toward the treetops below. "It's like there's a wall in my consciousness with only the slightest crack to peek through. And it shows nothing of where he might be or in what state. All I can fathom is that he's injured or trapped somewhere, but that's not exactly helpful."

"Has he tried to communicate with you again?"

"Not that I am aware of, even with me trying to hear from him." I scratch the stone rail with my thumbnail. "Seer Josiah thought I may be able to converse with Toaph through meditation, now that I know what's happening. He hopes I will be able to control my episodes, even. But either because of the noise in my mind or Toaph's unresponsiveness, it's been a vain pursuit."

She faces me, leaning on the rail. The subtle moonglow against her youthful skin reminds me of when I first saw her in person—when I retrieved her from the bottom of Lake Daleia. "Is that what you were doing out here?"

"It's all I've been doing."

"Well, maybe what you need is a break from it? You've never been able to force it before, have you?"

A break. While islands sink and entire kingdoms lie in flames.

"I've never wanted to." I lower my voice. "I suppose I still don't. Curse by name or not, it still feels like one. I can't imagine that knowing what's happening will change the way it affects me—what it does. Perhaps my fear of it is the issue." A long sigh blows from my nose. "You're probably right. My mind could use a rest from the constant trying."

A smile rounds her freckled cheeks, as if my agreement was a pat on her back for the suggestion rather than a submission to my own defeat.

"El-Alam doesn't seem to be in much of a hurry," I add half-heartedly. "He's still not revealed our fifth Bind member."

"Do you suspect they'll be called from the outside also?"

"If they were among us, I don't know why El-Alam wouldn't have called them already."

I look toward the apartments beyond the courtyard, where steady gold flames illuminate a mere half dozen windows. The remaining lanterns have been extinguished by early sleepers, or sit darkened in now-vacant residences, leaving a somber display reminiscent of a cemetery.

So few Wardens remain compared to how many there were before my time. Mother said there was once a day when they hardly had enough space for everyone. But that was before the Hunter-led massacres wiped out a quarter of our forces, and the Blood Wardens' leader, the Oracle, led another third of what remained into defection.

"Regardless, our mission can't wait," I say. "We must begin searching for Toaph Elbara, even if I produce no further information to guide us."

The gravity of my last words blooms a silence between us, and eventually, Norielle inches toward the door.

"Norielle," I say, suddenly recalling something I meant to impart to her. She halts. "I should warn you. My mother may have gotten a tad carried away with your gown for the induction ceremony."

Her hand curls against her collarbone. "My *gown*?"

"Well, yes, there is a formal ball following the endowing of your power. It is a celebration, after all."

Pink swarms her cheeks, apparent even in the dim light. Strange. I expected her to be excited for the ball, at least. The last time we held the ceremony, the inductee practically took the party into his own hands.

Then again, that was Elias.

She masks her bashful reaction behind a measured response. "That was supposed to be a surprise, wasn't it?"

I chuckle. "Something told me you'd prefer the warning."

"I do, actually," she says, then her gaze sweeps over me, something thoughtful in it that she keeps to herself.

Is she wondering if we'll share a dance at the ball?

But the *clink* of the door handle draws our attention before I can say anything more. The door peels back, revealing my mother's tall figure, and anxiety leaps into my chest.

Norielle dips into an immediate curtsy.

"Norielle, I didn't expect to find you out here as well," Mother says. Her voice carries a warm contrast to the chill in her glare when she turns to me.

Norielle rises, eyeing me, as if to ask what to say.

I fix my slouched posture and adopt a formal tone. "I'm sorry to have kept you with my ramblings about Toaph. Please, get some rest."

Norielle's befuddled expression raises Mother's brows.

I nod Norielle toward the door with an apologetic smile that won't help my case with Mother, and she rushes away after a quick "goodnight" to each of us. The door closes at her heels, and my heart sinks toward my stomach as Mother strides across the platform to my side.

"One might wonder what you two were doing out here," she says, laying a hand on the rail. Her wedding ring glints in the moonlight, still polished despite the two decades it's been since the Sovereign's passing. What little of him I recall, he was often as heavyhearted as Mother is now. Though legend has it,

Mother was once a cheerful woman, but that was before the responsibility to reverse the world's imminent doom perched on her shoulders.

If only my father were here now. What I wouldn't give to have his wise guidance.

"I was having a discussion with a member of my Bind, Mother."

Mother inspects our surroundings, her gaze slowing over pastel flowers, sparkling waterfalls, and a hanging half-moon. "Of course you were. A private conversation under starlight."

"This is simply where I was when she asked Rhys where to find me. And it's hardly private when anyone could join us at any moment."

She lifts a brow, as if to remind me that she is no fool when it comes to matters of the heart. If only I could say the same about myself, then perhaps I wouldn't be so confused every time I pause to peek at the troubled thing between my ribs.

Mother lays her hand upon my shoulder and lets the subject of Norielle thaw in her long pause. I lean my head toward her hand, the gem of her ring pressing into my unshaven cheek. She's one of the few people who'd dare offer me an affectionate touch these days, especially when my distress is so apparent. Most everyone else seems to fear that a simple touch might trigger me into another devastating episode.

Yet even Mother will retreat at the first sign of trouble, calling for her guards to wrestle me to the ground with Snare Wards.

"I wish I'd heard from Toaph," I say, looking down at the apartments again. Another lantern is doused behind a window, its golden glow fading in the night. "I'd like to tell everyone where he is. Assure them that there's more to this than a hopeful idea."

Mother retracts her hand, meeting my gaze with a somber expression. "How little regard you give to hope, my son. Is the news as it is not enough to celebrate?"

I grapple for a pleasant reply or even a smile to offer her, but stress holds my lips flat. "It doesn't quite feel the same when I'm the one responsible for delivering the anticipated result."

"You fear you'll fail them?"

An image of Corene lying in a pool of her own blood resurfaces in my memory, quickly followed by flashes of Norielle dying in bonds, Alani fighting for her breaths after my episode nearly ended her life, and Corene's brother, Corwin, cursing at me as I surrendered him to Mother after his defection.

"I fear I'll fail all of Silvirdia," I confess. *Just as I've already failed each person who's ever been placed into my care.*

Mother seems to consider her response for a whole rotation of the world before delivering it. "El-Alam wouldn't have chosen you if He knew you would fail."

I retract my hands from the railing, cool air racing to dry the sweat on my palms. "Or did He choose me because—somehow—I am the only person who has even the potential to succeed?"

The hanging jewels on Mother's headdress jingle as she shakes her head. "Then what great fortune it is that the person with that potential is you, who I know will wield it to the utmost."

"Of course, Mother," I promise, as though her words were a command rather than an encouragement.

She smiles at me, light twinkling in her dark eyes like the stars overhead. "Though it may be worth considering whether or not you should be trying to do this all alone, or if, perhaps, El-Alam thought to give you a Bind for a reason."

I return her smile before she adds, "And a heart. One that might be strengthened by another's if only you'd stop being so afraid."

I squint at her, trying to discern precisely what she's implying. Does she mean romantically? And does this relate to her finding Norielle out here with me?

"Though maybe not by a girl in your Bind," she whispers, confirming her meaning in a lightly spoken rebuke. "Such things are forbidden, as you are well aware."

I force my expression to remain stoic. "I will not threaten another's life by allowing them so close. You needn't worry about that."

"Or is it that you will not risk a recurrence of what happened with Corene?"

I open my mouth to reject this, but Mother carries on before I have the chance.

"There are ways to protect others from your episodes that do not involve cutting yourself off from everything that makes life worthwhile."

My argument evaporates, pulling me into a long silence before I think of a decent response. "Thank you, Mother. But right now, finding Toaph Elbara is my sole focus. Perhaps once that has been achieved, I will have no need to worry about such matters."

Mother absorbs my words with a slow nod before submitting to my dismissal of the subject.

"You will find him, my son," she says, cradling my cheek with her warm palm. "And you will see the days when Wardens are honored again among kings."

She presses her forehead against mine, then her hand slips from my face.

"Goodnight, son."

NORIELLE

"**S**hall I prepare a bath for you, miss?"

I push the wardrobe door partway closed so I can see my personal attendant, Rhiana, standing at the door moments after I chimed the bell. "No, actually, I called on you for something else."

"Oh? How may I assist you?" she asks, her luminous brown gaze lowering to the supple leather boots already laced over my feet.

"I was wondering if you could take me to visit someone."

Her head slants, ringlets bobbing from her loose bun. "On the morning preceding your ceremony? We must get you ready..."

"It's not until this evening," I say, disregarding my sense of responsibility. "One of the scouts is an old friend of mine. Elias Auden. I heard he's back from his errand, and I've been wanting to talk with him—in private—so I'd rather not save it for tonight."

"Oh. *Elias*." She butters his name with special emphasis. "Sure. I can take you to see your *friend*."

My grip tightens on the wardrobe door. Is she another of his—apparently many—admirers? Or is she assuming I mean something more than a friend?

I shake off my confusion and return to sifting through the seven different choices for cloaks in the wardrobe. My fingers brush one with a floral embellishment that reminds me of Ila's designs. The thought that this could be one of the Aldrian safehouse keeper's creations comforts me, as if wearing it is like receiving a hug from the grandmotherly woman. I pluck it out and hold it toward the distilled light of my grand window, admiring the soft velvet's pleasant shade of green and the silver-threaded flower adornments along the trim.

Rhiana rushes to help me place the cloak over my shoulders, as if, upon arriving here, I forgot how to dress myself. But I've learned not to argue with her. She's only six years older than me, but she has a mother's heart. Or is this what it's like having an older sister?

The thought draws my lips into a frown. *I miss being an older sister.*

What are my little siblings doing now? It feels like a lifetime since I left, and yet, it's only been a few weeks. Is Milo still waiting to meet this *Kieran*?

What would Cassia say if I told her I found him after all? Would she discard the romantic notion of the prince who rescued me and swept me into an adventure in favor of childhood love?

"Let me fix your hair," Rhiana says, snatching my brush and a ribbon from my vanity.

But I hold up a hand. "Please, it's fine. We have to make this quick, anyway."

"Of course." Rhiana sets the brush and ribbon aside, assessing me with slight disappointment in her gaze before gesturing to the door. "Shall we then, miss?"

I keep stride with Rhiana's quick pace as she leads me along a winding path toward the short but sprawling apartments across the southern courtyard of the citadel. Morning sunlight dapples the paved walkway, yet a gray cloud approaches from the east cliffs. A spry wind flutters my cloak and hair, and the scent of fresh, flowing water mixes with the pungent scent of wet earth—rain somewhere beyond the cliffs that enclose the citadel.

What would a storm be like here?

"You should pull up your hood," Rhiana advises as we near the apartments.

I look at the patch of blue over our heads. "Is it that far to Elias?"

She chuckles. "Not for the rain. For the *questions*. People will want to talk to you, and you don't exactly have time for that."

"Right." I tug the hood over my head.

Rhiana told me on my first full day at the citadel that wearing a hood is a request for privacy here, and it's disrespectful to talk to someone if their hood is up. Pity we didn't have a system like that in Behria. I could have avoided many unwanted interactions with the tyrant, Landon, and his friends.

Not that they'd have bothered with respecting the hood, anyway.

I follow Rhiana to a building that reminds me of a military garrison. The flat-topped roof stands two stories above, riddled in moss like the citadel. Rhiana grips the discolored copper door handle, but before she can tug on it, a voice hollers after us.

"Nori?"

A misty gust lashes my hair into my face as I turn to find Elias standing on a side path.

When I holler his name back, I expect a smirk to twist his face into the roguish man I met at Ila's house, but a genuine smile lifts his eyes. His quick strides bring him closer to me until he's standing near enough to reach for. He stops there, looking me over like it's our first encounter in years all over again, though it's only been a few days since we parted in the main courtyard.

I draw back a step, a flush burning across my face as I inspect him. His loose shirt flutters in the wind, his attire so casual compared to how I got used to seeing him in the tunnels. No armor. No sword. Just a man only a few months older than me, probably out here watching the storm as it blows in.

The familiarity of his dark eyes lures me to linger. They're about his only feature that hasn't changed since I last knew him as Kieran.

"Miss?" Rhiana sidles up next to me, glancing between Elias and me with a poorly repressed smile. "Shall I return to the citadel, or would you like me to wait nearby so I may escort you?"

"I'll see she makes it back," Elias says before I can respond.

She flits away without my approval, and I turn back to Elias. "What if I wanted her to stay?"

"What? You still don't trust me?" A hint of his smirk returns. "That hurts, Nori."

"She's *my* attendant. You can't just send her away."

He indicates the distance between us and her with a wave. "Apparently, I can."

I scowl at him, but my laugh quickly disrupts my foul expression.

"Shouldn't you be getting pampered right now?" he asks, nodding toward my casual attire—if a velvet cloak with silver embroidery could be considered *casual*.

"I wanted to talk to you first."

He scratches his freshly trimmed beard. "What about?"

"About what happens after today... when everything is *official*."

A low rumble in the distance pulls our attention to the thickening clouds overhead. Elias motions me toward an ornate pavilion, where I spy his daily essentials—his lyre and a piping hot cup of tea—propped on a stone bench. *So that's where he was.* I follow his lead, and we settle beneath the shelter of the small pavilion's round roof, though, with the rising wind, I doubt we'll stay dry if it rains. *Rhiana and the beauticians will have their work cut out for them after this...*

But this is important.

Elias picks up his lyre and aimlessly plucks at a string, watching me with an expectant gaze. The string's low *twang* steals my focus, summoning an alternate reality in my imagination where there isn't anywhere else for me to be today. Would I stay here as long as Rhiana allowed me? Sitting with Elias beneath a beautiful structure with waterfalls flowing in our periphery, and a lively wind ruffling through the grass and trees? Would I let him play me song after song, delighting in the comfort of a long-lost friend who, in so many ways, is like a part of Papa's heart brought back to me?

Or would I—even given the opportunity to remain out here—still choose to keep this visit short and neglect the possibilities?

The distant thunder growls again, reminding me that time is limited for more reasons than just the ceremony. I renew my focus.

"I want you to know that I have thought about everything you said to me... you know, right before the defectors captured me." My throat dries at the memory of the Blood Wardens attacking us. If I think of it too long, I can still feel the brute's shoulder digging into my ribs as he hauled me away and the fiery pain across my body from the crypt crawler venom. "I understand the dangers I'm accepting tonight when I am endowed with El-Alam's power—when I fully become part of Calden's Bind. And, honestly, I'm—I'm scared."

His thumb stills, and the string buzzes a moment before quieting.

"But I know it's the right thing to do and what Papa would want to see come of all this." I shut my eyes, ever haunted by the sight of Lake Daleia dragging Papa down. After a slow breath, I open my eyes again to see Elias looking at me, as if made ill by my words. "I just want you to know before tonight that I haven't brushed off your concerns about the dangers that await when I accept El-Alam's plans for me, and I appreciate you voicing them. It means a lot to me that you still care so much about me after all these years."

Elias lowers his gaze, his dark hair flapping across his forehead. He lays the lyre flat on his lap, resting both arms against it as he seems to absorb my words and all their implications. A gust flicks a cold spray of moisture against my cheek in his pause, and my muscles tense at the brewing storm. I shouldn't stay out here—for the sake of the women in charge of dealing with the aftermath. But I at least need to hear his reaction...

"Of course I still care, Nori," he says, wind-thrashed drizzle smattering his skin with tiny droplets. "You're one of the few things about Behria I never wanted to forget."

I tuck my chin to hide how his statement makes me smile.

"And I wasn't trying to dissuade you from becoming who El-Alam has called you to be. I just wanted you to be careful about..." He winces like he doesn't want to complete the sentence.

"About Calden," I finish for him. "You're afraid of me getting closer to him."

He shrugs.

"Well, if it's any comfort to you, so am I." I recoil at my admission, unsure when I decided that. Was it when I realized Calden's episode delayed him from rescuing me sooner? When I realized I couldn't count on him the way I thought? Or when Alani recounted the event, detailing how even Corene and her accomplices—who'd all seemed so fearless—fled the moment Calden's episode was triggered?

"You're too brave for that to be of any comfort to me, Nori," Elias says, drawing me back to our conversation before he slaps on a spiritless smirk. "And you know what else you are?"

My stomach flutters, but I remain quiet, curious to know what he might say.

"*Late*," he says with a nod toward the citadel. "And wet. And probably about to get me in trouble with the Lady Sovereign for keeping you on the day of your ceremony."

"That's it?" I ask, leaning toward him. "That's all you're going to say?"

He gives me a dumbfounded look as he tucks his lyre into its case. "No. It's all I'm going to say *right now*."

My heart pounds as he stands and faces me, gaze sinking into mine for so long that my imagination concocts an image of him reaching out to touch my cheek. But he abruptly turns toward the citadel. I hold in a sigh, unsure whether I am relieved or disappointed.

"Come on, Nori, let's get you back to your palace, so the Lady doesn't wring my neck." He steps from the pavilion's covering and into the light rain. "Besides, I've got some work to do on myself. I can't show up to your party like this."

I enter the citadel, panting and damp from my long sprint in the rain. At least my hood kept my hair from getting completely tangled in the wind. Still, Rhiana looks over my wet clothes with an aghast expression, as if she shares Elias's concerns about the Lady Sovereign's reaction.

No wonder Calden is so stressed about his mother all the time. The Lady Sovereign holds even the smallest affairs within these walls in a white-knuckled grip, and Calden's life seems among the most precious of those affairs to her.

I clear my throat and give Rhiana an apologetic smile. "I'm... ready for that bath."

Rhiana glances at the door, an impish expression on her face. "I hope whatever just happened was worth the griping we're about to endure from the ladies, miss."

My face heats, but the quick turn of her heel spares me the need to respond, and we rush back to my room.

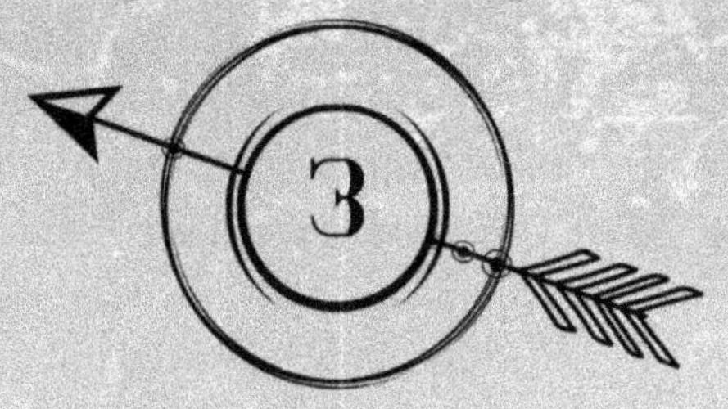

NORIELLE

"You look stunning," a warm voice says from my chamber door.

I turn, finding the Lady Sovereign beaming at me as if looking upon her daughter—not that I can compare to Lady Odessa. My one brief interaction with Calden's sister was enough to show me I have no place standing beside these royals of the underground. And to think she's also a member of our Bind...

At the Lady Sovereign's approval, Rhiana and the three beauticians who've spent half the day scrubbing at my skin, fashioning my hair, and dabbing makeup on my face all stand taller. I'm yet to see their work, but based on their hours of effort, I must look like someone else.

"Just one last step before the gown, my lady," the eldest of the three beauticians says, tilting a bottle of oil. A dense gold liquid gulps as she pours it into her palm, a nutty aroma permeating the humid air. She strokes it through my long hair, smoothing the frizz. Her fingertips gently run along the braided locks which are secured away from my face with a jeweled clamp. Keeping my hair partially down was my one request. If somehow Papa can peer down from the Empyrean,

I'd like him to see how long it has grown, since he loved my hair so much.

It's the smallest way I can honor him today.

The Lady Sovereign's eyes glint thoughtfully as she looks me over once more. Rain taps at the windows in her silence—a constant noise since this morning—and I wonder if any part of the Lady Sovereign is cursing it for intruding on her perfectly planned day. At least she seems unaware that I spent part of my morning outside, being lashed by the beginnings of the storm.

A sudden jingling swings our attention to the door as a woman rolls my gown into view on a mannequin. My lips part at the sight of the extravagant plum-colored dress, shimmering with glowing gold shards of crystal. A floral waistband gleams, as if sewn with threads of warm starlight above the belled skirt, and a matching floral hem lines the rippling, off-shoulder sleeves.

"I hope you like it," the Lady Sovereign says, stepping closer to the gown to touch the silky fabric. "My son told me purple and gold were the colors of your soulcast flower."

Is that why Calden handed me one in the field outside the Rimrook Mountains? Simply to report my colors to his mother?

A shadow creeps over the memory that I once used to comfort myself in the hour of my near death, and the recollection drains of its luster.

The Lady Sovereign carries on, "After what you endured on your way here, today is the very least I can offer as thanks." She steps toward me. "I want you to know I am deeply grateful for the way you held on to impart this world-changing news to my son. The very sight of you from this day onward will be a sign of hope to my people and to myself."

"All I did was relay a message, my lady," I say. "Your son is the true face of hope."

She absorbs my words with an unreadable expression, but a smile wipes the moment away. "Let us get you dressed. It's almost time."

My pulse throbs in my fingertips as Rhiana leads me toward a side entrance to the ballroom. She guided me down empty back halls, keeping me from sight like a bride on her wedding day. And in some ways, I feel like that is precisely what I am heading into—a marriage. But not with a man, with El-Alam and His purposes for me. For from this day out, my life entirely belongs to Him and what He calls me to do.

If I dare speak the vows.

Rhiana opens the door and gestures for me to enter before her. I hesitate, listening to the noises within. Voices echo inside what sounds like a massive, empty room. I discern a chipper voice as the Seer's, then catch the Lady Sovereign's rich timbre, then—

My breath hitches.

Calden's voice. He's already in there. Why must that make me so nervous?

My eyes plead with Rhiana, but for what, I don't know. The thought of walking into everyone's view in this shining gown with my face glittering with makeup and hair bedazzled with gems and fine oils makes me lightheaded. Why does the Lady Sovereign assume I even *want* to be honored like this? I'd rather spend the evening in the Seer's library listening to him ramble about his favorite books.

"Would you like me to go in first to announce your arrival?" Rhiana whispers.

I wince. "No, no. Let's not make a big deal of it."

Rhiana suppresses a giggle. "There's nothing about this that won't be a big deal, I'm afraid."

I briefly shut my eyes, filling my heart with courage before I step forward. My wedged heels click against the polished moonstone floor as I enter a ballroom flickering with lightning from the storm outside the three massive windows. Rain sparkles against the glass panes, reflecting light from the warmly glowing chandeliers and what little of the sunset makes it past the dreary clouds. Around the window, pine garlands hang, speckled in shining crystals like my dress. The woven evergreen limbs fill the room with a bright aroma that harmonizes with the sugary smell of fresh flowers.

My gaze darts past pristine purple-and-gold floral arrangements to a raised platform in the back where several finely dressed figures stand. The Warden Elders, I realize, recognizing their faces as they gradually turn and notice me with welcoming smiles. Seer Josiah. The Lady Sovereign. Lady Odessa, who looks like a younger version of her mother. Then Atlas, the overseer of education, and Gatlin, the warrior captain.

The last man turns the slowest, his combed blond hair giving him away before I meet his vibrant—even from this distance—blue eyes.

He smiles at me but looks away hardly a second later, and my heart sinks.

Is something wrong?

"My! Look at you!" the Seer exclaims, rushing down the steps with his gold-trimmed robe flapping behind him. "What fine work, my Lady Sovereign," he says with a nod toward her before turning to grin at me again. "You, my child, look like you've descended from the Empyrean."

An awkward chuckle escapes my lips before he snatches my arm and walks me toward the platform. His peppery cologne tickles my nose, and I fight a sneeze. When the itch passes, I steal a glance toward Calden again, but he's pivoted back to Atlas and Gatlin. Beside him, Odessa looks me over, as if bored, before turning her attention to the flashing windows. Not that I should expect anything more. She hasn't bothered to talk to me since our initial introduction.

"I assume, by your presence here, that you have indeed chosen to accept El-Alam's path for you," the Seer says, and I meet his dark yet jubilant eyes.

I realize I'm still not completely sure what El-Alam's path for me entails. The Creator hasn't offered more details besides that I am to help Calden locate Toaph Elbara, and we are to do whatever the Empyreal Guardian then requires of us.

"Yes," I say, regardless.

I barely get the word out before Seer Josiah exclaims, "Excellent! Most excellent!"

We reach the stairs to the platform, and he leads me up the wide steps to join the others. I exchange a quick greeting with everyone, saving Calden for last. When our eyes meet this close, I catch a twitch in his brow.

"Norielle." Though gentle, his resonant voice seems to flood the entire ballroom. "We're so glad you're here."

The Lady Sovereign's voice rings out before I can reply. "Let's all get into our places."

The Seer leads me to stand beside Calden at the center of the group, and all of us face the vacant ballroom.

The Lady Sovereign scans each of us, her brows suddenly cinching together. "Where is Alani?"

Calden lifts his Bind Mark. One large arrow points to me, a small one without a shaft signals Odessa on his left, but the third, equally small arrow points outside the room.

I squint at the mark. Why is mine the only full arrow and so much larger than the others?

But after a moment, my arrow shrinks and the shaft dissolves, whereas Alani's grows into full size. This arrow, unlike the former, seems to pinpoint Alani's exact location.

So, is that how it works? He chooses who to track closely?

"She's coming," Calden says.

A second later, the door opens with a loud, "I'm sorry! So sorry to be late!"

Alani rushes in, wearing a turquoise gown that embodies the waves of the sea. She gasps when she notices me—or my dress, rather—and skitters toward the platform with a series of compliments. The Seer helps her up the stairs and leads her to her place beside me before he takes his own near the Lady Sovereign.

"I can't wait to see their faces when you tell them the news," Alani whispers.

My shoulders jump. "When *I* tell them?"

"Let them in!" the Lady Sovereign orders before Alani can explain. Two attendants open the wide double doors, and within minutes, every Warden available to attend the event occupies the sprawling space below us. They stare at me like they already know what news I've brought.

As the Lady Sovereign delivers her formal welcome and begins a rather dramatic retelling of my journey to the citadel, I scan the faces in the crowd. I spot Rhiana and her older brother, Rhys, relieved of their duties for the evening so they may enjoy the event, and a few other citadel workers I've met. But amid the series of faces I vaguely recognize, I can't find the one I truly know.

Where is Elias?

The Lady Sovereign's account ends without giving away the news about Toaph Elbara, and she announces the next stage that Rhiana informed me of—the vows. The Seer steps forth, his fatherly expression encouraging me to join him a few steps ahead of the other Elders.

I swallow, reminding myself that this is easy. All I must do is say "I pledge" a dozen or so times, and it will be over.

The Seer unfurls a scroll and reads aloud the first vow. "Do you pledge to keep all passages, entries, havens, safehouses, and other such whereabouts of the Wardens a secret from common society?"

I wet my lips and glance at Calden for strength, but his attention is on his subjects below us, and instead, it's the Seer's subtle shake of the scroll that prompts me to speak up.

"I pledge." A rumble of thunder accompanies my declaration.

The Seer beams and moves to the next. "Do you pledge to use wards in a manner pleasing to El-Alam and to never utilize any other methods of acquiring power, such as Blood Wards?"

I lower my chin, recalling the horrors of my time as a captive of the Blood Wardens. The utter depravity and the lack of humanity they showed are reason enough for me to wish to never see another defector again, let alone become one.

My voice is resolute when I speak. "I pledge."

The Seer continues down the list until I've sworn my loyalty to the Wardens and El-Alam in every way. He furls the scroll, seeming to war with his own mouth to keep from expressing his apparent excitement. He subdues it to a proud smile, one I imagine Papa would wear right now, then he steps aside.

The Lady Sovereign takes his place, addressing the crowd. "Now, I normally perform the endowing myself, but I believe it is only right to allow my son the honor of endowing the latest member of his Bind."

Calden's eyes widen, as if this is news to him as well. *Does no one give warnings around here?*

The Lady Sovereign holds up a small glass vial that shimmers beneath the chandeliers. Calden steps forward, taking the vial in hand with a long, questioning look at his mother. The woman only smiles and ushers him toward me.

He holds the vial against his chest, maintaining my gaze through a long pause. The entire ballroom falls silent with anticipation.

Calden faces the audience. When he speaks, the cadence of his voice reminds me of who he truly is—the future Sovereign.

"This vial"—he raises it for all to see—"contains the very tears of El-Alam Himself. Tears of both joy and sorrow over His creation. In these tears is the blessing to access His power, granted to those whom He has called, whose hearts are open to His purposes in protecting His creation. Norielle Damaris of Behria has accepted His call and devoted herself wholly to serving El-Alam alongside us." His attention returns to me, and his tone shifts from one merely repeating a script to one speaking the words from the depth of his heart. "It is with great honor that I endow you with this blessing of power and welcome you into your new family."

He pulls the stopper on the vial, a small *pop* seeming to echo from wall to wall in the wide ballroom. I remember just in time that I am supposed to kneel for this, and I drop to a knee, my massive skirt bunching against the ground.

The entire world seems to freeze in this moment, and a sudden awareness awakens in my spirit. For all the distractions about the ceremony, announcement, and ball, I've taken little time to consider the full implications of what is happening until now, with Calden's brief speech echoing in my head.

El-Alam, the Creator of the universe, who upholds every world from one end of the Empyreal Skies to the other, has chosen *me* to grant His power to. *Me* to call into His purposes.

Me to help save this world from the brink of death, as Calden did for me in the crypt.

The realization strikes me in a way that makes me grateful I'm already kneeling. What have I ever done to deserve an honor like this?

The liquid sloshes inside the vial just before Calden's fingertips dab the Creator's tears on my forehead. Yet I hardly feel aware of whose fingers touched me, for an image swells behind my closed eyes of a man made of pure light stroking a tear from his own eye and laying it against my skin. Without an audible word from Him, knowledge enters my spirit—knowledge of the pain of the world and my responsibility to be His vessel in subduing it, of my unmistakable belonging here amongst the Wardens, but most of all, of the Creator's love for me.

The latter knowledge floods my being like when Calden healed me, spreading warmth across my body, as if sunlight has fallen directly over my kneeling form.

And in that alone, I understand the rest, even though it feels incomprehensible.

I am here, not for anything I've done, but because El-Alam wanted me here. Here, and not swallowed by Lake Daleia. Or suppressed into silence in Behria.

"Rise when you are ready, Norielle," Calden says, softly enough that only I may hear it.

I open my eyes, looking up at him, but I don't yet stand. The feeling in my spirit dissolves, and my awareness returns to where we are as if nothing happened—as if what I saw and felt was part of nothing more than a dream. The only indication that anything has changed is a subtle sense of glowing from within my spirit, like a candle just lit within me.

Calden helps me to my feet and raises my hand over our heads like I've won a battle. The Wardens cheer with shouts of celebration and praises to El-Alam. The noise rings out for what feels like years. All the while, I search the many faces for Elias, but I still can't find him. Did something happen to him? Is he angry with me for something I said this morning?

Calden lowers my hand, and the room settles.

"Thank you, Sovereign Prince," the Lady Sovereign says.

Calden releases my hand and steps back. His mother returns to my side. "My friends," she declares, "there is another significant cause for celebration today. I left out a key detail in the story of Norielle's journey here."

Every face in the crowd turns up.

"While a captive of the Blood Wardens, Norielle obtained information that brings great hope to the outlook of our world." A hint of personal relief tints her words as she continues. "This information renders what we believed to be a curse upon my son, your Sovereign Prince, a great and hidden key to redeeming our world from destruction."

The people perk up even more, but the Lady Sovereign turns to me, igniting fresh the fear Alani kindled. "Norielle, would you please tell them your discovery?"

My lips quake. *Me, tell them?*

How I wish she'd at least warned me—

I glance back at Calden, whose expression is both apologetic and encouraging at once, then at Alani, who seems too excited to notice my apprehension about speaking to a crowd. The Seer meets my gaze next with equal enthusiasm to Alani, but a hint of empathy softens his eyes, like he senses my unease.

I fill my lungs, pivoting to face the Wardens. My mouth feels as dry as the scorched deserts of Raevre. If I open it, will a word even come out?

I try it, but my lips only hang agape, leaving the rain thrumming against the windows and splattering against the flooding ground outside as the only sound.

The pressure to speak builds within me, seeming to clutch my throat and strangle any attempt to do so. I know exactly what to say. Just one simple line, yet with all these eyes on me, it feels like an entire speech, and one I've never rehearsed.

But then a subtle movement at the far side of the ballroom draws my attention to someone slipping through the crowd toward the platform. My tension dissipates as I recognize that someone is Elias, and by the time he stands at the front, unhindered by anyone else, a relieved smile spreads across my face. I draw in a breath, taken aback by my indulgence as I observe the way his rich green coat hugs his strong form and contrasts with his tan skin, which gleams like the gold buttons and embellishments on his shoulders.

He *is* here. But where has he been?

"Miss Norielle," the Lady Sovereign prompts quietly. "Please, share the news."

Elias reassures me with a wide smile and a wave of his hand. I keep my gaze on him, feeling the same bolstering to my courage that he brought me in our youth, and finally, I speak.

"Our Empyreal Guardian, Toaph Elbara, is alive."

My declaration incites a chorus of gasps through the crowd. Soft whispers slowly scratch away the silence, rising into an uproar of disbelieving voices. My nostrils flare, the familiar feeling of being doubted spiking my nerves. I thought people would celebrate—

"Our Empyreal Guardian fled Ta'Nathel's attack," an assertive voice says from behind me—the voice of the future Sovereign. My shoulders relax as he steps beside me, redirecting all the focus onto himself. "I have heard from him myself."

Another wave of gasps.

"What we have believed to be a curse upon me is Toaph Elbara attempting to communicate with me—mind to mind, spirit to spirit." Calden continues, seemingly unfazed by the Wardens' alarmed reactions, "I have seen visions. Heard the voice of Toaph Elbara speaking to me. The information Norielle received is true—as confirmed also by Seer Josiah." His arm sweeps toward the Seer, who gives an elaborate bow. "Our Guardian lives, and my Bind's task is to locate him and offer whatever aid he needs in order that he may resume his proper position over Silvirdia."

Calden pauses, and I expect this to be the moment applause erupts from the Wardens, but all goes quiet.

"I understand there are many questions, all of which we shall soon address," Calden adds, lightening his tone as he raises his hands. "But for now, let us celebrate! The hope of our world is at last restored!"

Finally, a loud handclap breaks the silence, and my attention snaps back to Elias.

"Praise El-Alam!" he shouts, clapping harder, as if to urge the other Wardens to join him.

Slowly, the applause propagates like a flame being spread from wick to wick, until a full roar of cheering breaks loose, rivaling even the storm outside the walls.

Elias winks at Calden, then his focus flicks back to me, and he smiles wider than I've seen since we were children.

"Let the celebration commence!" the Lady Sovereign announces. Immediately, a flute twitters, swiftly followed by the strings of a grand harp. As people turn from the platform, the Lady Sovereign pulls Calden away from me, whispering something I can't catch.

The Seer approaches me, offering his arm. "Come with me, child."

He leads me down the steps with his chin raised high. His gaze skirts the crowd before Elias steps forward, his hair groomed into managed waves and wearing attire suited for royalty.

The luminescent shards of crystal on my dress speckle Elias's dark irises with stars as his gaze runs from the bottom of my belled skirt to my eyes. It takes a moment—and another partial sweep of his gaze—before he extends a hand with a smile that stirs a tickle in my stomach.

"It would appear there's no need to ask if you'd like to accept this dance," the Seer says with a chuckle. He releases my arm and steps away.

A swirl of motion as people begin dancing breaks my trance, and I reach for Elias's hand. His palm encases mine, warm, like he'd just held it toward a fire, and he reels me two steps closer.

"I almost thought you didn't come," I say, my voice nearly a whisper.

"You were looking for me?" His smile stretches wider as his free hand finds my waist and rests against the floral embroidery on my bodice. My heart flutters again at his touch. "I'd never miss your party, Nori. I was just"—his smile twitches—"staying out-of-sight. I figured you'd want to start your night with... someone else. Didn't want to make it awkward."

Someone else being Calden, I register but choose not to say. I swallow a wad of regret for making Elias feel like he had to hide—like he was secondary to Calden.

Yet he was my first true friend.

His nervous chuckle breaks our silence. "But I couldn't leave you standing up there like that. So, this didn't go as planned."

I wade through responses, struggling to find the right one before I settle for, "I'm glad you came up front."

"Then, so am I." His dimmed countenance relights, and he leads us into a simple dance. His gaze remains locked on mine, so fulfilled, like he's waited his entire life for a moment like this. And honestly, so have I. Only little Nori didn't have the audacity to imagine we'd end up in a place like *this*. The way she imagined it, she and Kieran danced between trees in clothes permanently stained by mud and fishy lake air.

I blink my eyes into focus, grounding myself in the present with the touch of Elias's hands as we move to the music. But my feet can hardly remember which way to step when holding his admiring gaze, so I lower my focus to the gold adornments on his coat.

"Ila made it," he says. "It's what I wore to my induction ceremony."

My brows purse. Why didn't I consider that he had a ceremony, too?

"Mine wasn't nearly as... grand... as this." His smile suggests he's proud on my behalf, not jealous.

I make the mistake of peering around us, and despite the swooping and swaying of other dance partners, everyone either blatantly stares or steals glances at us they think will go unnoticed. A knot forms in my stomach.

"Everyone is watching us," I whisper.

"Of course they are, Nori. Eyes are drawn to beauty." He leans away enough for me to see his smile twist into a smirk. "They've been staring at me since I got here."

I snort, a most unladylike sound in such a setting, and give him a light shove. He laughs, releasing my waist to usher me away for a spin. The motion and the way my dress chimes provoke a girlish giggle from me as he draws me back.

"It's the dress they're staring at," I say as our gazes rejoin.

"It's definitely not just the dress."

Heat blooms across my cheeks at his boldness. Whatever happened to the days when he used to snivel when Mum or Papa said I looked pretty? Or the times he'd smear mud across my face—surely to receive a face full of it in return?

"Honestly, Nori, I think about every eligible man in here is hoping to steal a dance with you," Elias says, scanning the faces I'm trying desperately to pretend aren't there.

Guilt awakens in my core at his suggestion of *every eligible man*. Does that include Calden, considering how he healed me? Is he watching us now, jealously awaiting the right moment to ask for a dance?

I glance at the platform, only to find Calden still locked in conversation with his mother, paying me no mind at all.

"Do I have to accept if someone requests a dance?" I ask, trying to salvage my conversation with Elias.

His head tilts at my question like he's forgotten I've never attended a ball—or anything formal, for that matter—in my life. "No, a lady may refuse. You don't have to dance with anyone you don't want to." His grip fastens a little tighter on mine. "You can stay with me as long as you want."

My heart skips a beat, only to feel a sting as it occurs to me that there is only one other person I'd want to dance with, and he doesn't seem to have any interest in so much as stepping out onto the ballroom floor.

You're not going to have time anymore. You'll be too important. Elias's words to me before we arrived at the citadel replay in my mind, but now they're twisted into a new meaning where I'm the disregarded one.

Even at my own induction ceremony.

"What's wrong, Nori?" Elias asks, and I suddenly notice how we've slowed with the music.

I try to restore my smile. "I just... I wish people would stop watching us."

Elias, clearly not fooled, flashes a look toward Calden and back to me. But his mouth curves upward again, as if deciding he'd rather run with my lie than broach that subject here.

"They won't," he says, eyes blaming me in the most complimentary way possible.

"Not that you mind," I jest.

His brows lift. "I'm used to attention. Doesn't mean I like it as much as you think."

I give him a befuddled look, but he leaves my silent question untouched.

"You just have to ignore them. Think of something else..." His thumb rubs the back of my hand. "Do you remember when we spent all day in the field near Auberfall trying to find a three-eared rabbit?"

I wrinkle my nose. *What a weird memory to bring up.*

"Yes, I remember Landon finding it rather laughable when he realized we'd believed him enough to go search for one."

"*I* didn't believe him." Elias twirls me in unison with the other women around us, then reels me in even closer than before. "But *you* did."

"You believed. You were twice as determined to find it as I was."

His gaze slides sideways. "I'm good at playing along."

"Well, why didn't you tell me you knew it was a lie?"

"Because then you might not have spent all day with me."

My knees threaten to buckle. How naïve was I back then to not realize that's what he was doing?

"Can you imagine Landon's face now? If he saw us here, looking like this?" he asks, as if aware that I can't take more of his soft side.

"No," I confess after a moment of trying.

He chuckles. "Me neither. Haven't seen him since we were twelve."

"He hasn't changed much."

Elias smiles, easing our dance to a slight pivot from foot to foot. "Neither have you."

"Is that a good or bad thing?" I ask before I can think better of it. Because I know what it is—bait, a request for him to say all the things I've always wanted to hear him say to me.

"It's neither." He stills as the music shifts again to a peppy tune, and we're left standing in the middle of whirling gowns and laughter. "Because there's not a version of you I wouldn't want to know."

His response steals my breath, but right as he finishes giving it, his attention lifts to the platform, and even the reflection of my gown seems to be doused in his eyes.

Is it Calden? *Is he coming to dance with me?*

I resist the compulsion to look for myself.

"Elias," I say, raising my voice enough to jerk his focus back to me, but I don't know what I wish to express until it slips out, unfiltered. "I'm so sorry for the way I've been."

He gives a dramatic look to each side before returning his smile to me. "Is this really the time for an apology?"

"Is there ever a bad time for one?"

"Only if it's uncalled for."

"I've hurt you, Elias, I know that." I cut myself off before I can mention the evidence.

"Then we're even, aren't we?" The sudden seriousness on his face nearly deafens my ears to the music. "We both know I'm the one who should be apologizing."

"You already have." I frown, recalling how small he sounded when he apologized for his inability to heal me from the crypt crawler venom.

"I could never say sorry enough for that."

His sincere gaze holds me captive until a sudden laugh burbles out of me. "You know, I don't think I can remember ever hearing Kieran apologize for something."

He snorts at my obvious exaggeration. "Guess you never will."

I bite my lip, for once seeing a shed part of Kieran as a good thing. In how many other ways has he matured for the better?

The people and music around us suddenly seem miles away, even Calden and his mother. As if, for this one moment, Elias and I are completely alone, and I am seeing him—truly—for the first time. He's not Kieran, but Kieran is part of him. And all the arrogance he wore around him when we first met again was nothing more than armor protecting his very deep and vulnerable heart.

"Nori?" Elias asks, alerting me that we've ceased all efforts to dance. "Are you sure you're all right?"

I nod, feeling a sting in my eyes. "I just can't believe you're here."

"Same to you." He draws me closer again, so I feel the warmth of his chest against mine. "I'm scared for you, Nori. But I want you to know I'm also proud of you. So, so proud of you."

I smile, a tear sneaking onto my cheek when his arms shift to hug me rather than dance. My body melts against him, and I wrestle to keep the rest of my tears in. "I'm proud of you, too," I whisper.

He squeezes me, then draws a step away with a playful smile despite the glossiness in his eyes. "You're not supposed to bawl at a ball, Nori."

I chuckle. "Then stop making me cry."

He beams at my comment before stepping us back into the rhythm of the song.

CALDEN

Mother leaves me at the bottom of the stairs, taking Seer Josiah's extended hand. I scratch my forehead. A widow and a widower, not awfully far from each other in age. Both are of near equal reverence and importance. It makes sense.

Their mirroring smiles as they step into an elegant waltz keep me watching for another long moment before a shadow creeps to my left.

"It's not polite to stare, brother," Odessa says, not bothering to be quiet. Her jewels and celestial-themed gown glint in my peripheral vision.

"Since when did they take to each other?"

"You're just now catching on?" Odessa laughs, patting my shoulder like she's petting a dog. "I forget how clueless you are sometimes."

I grimace, which only encourages Odessa more.

"Well, you're not prying that child out of Elias's hands." Odessa nods toward the single women on the sidelines. "You might as well give someone else a chance."

That child. My scowl deepens at her reference to Norielle, but she walks off without seeing it, quickly accepting a dancing partner for herself—a young man who I believe serves as an intercessor in the prayer chapel.

She has mentioned requiring prayer often since I've returned…

A couple of months back, it was a need for archery lessons. And before that, a sudden thirst for the Empyreal language. She makes moving on seem nearly as easy as Alani does.

I shake my head and scan the perimeter for someone to dance with, if for no other reason than to avoid Mother's griping later. The young women on the sidelines acknowledge me with a concoction of bashful smiles, nervous fidgeting, and paled countenances. Prince or not, I'm dangerous, and all of them know it. Even those who dare hold my gaze for more than a few seconds are likely hoping I stay far away, regardless of the declaration about what my episodes are.

Yet the last induction ceremony was so different. I spent the entire evening with one woman—Corene—admiring her gracious manners and carefree spirit. The women still watched me then, the content of their whispers so easy to guess. *Will she be the next Lady Sovereign?* And though there were only hints that night that our friendship might become something more, beneath these same chandeliers, I can't help but conjure up the memories of how my heart hoped in a way it may never hope again while holding Corene in my arms.

But I was a fool. I so desperately wanted her love and companionship, I put her in danger by letting her close—all the while assuring her of her safety, as if I could control my episodes. It was no wonder that when she finally witnessed the unbridled destruction I can cause, she withdrew, nipping our once budding love back into careful friendship.

But now she's dead.

The woman I last danced with is dead.

And the man who had to kill her is now dancing with another girl who has captured my attention. *What's wrong with me? Why am I even here?*

I pivot toward the door. It would be better for us all if I left everyone else to their fun. It's not as though Norielle would even notice. Or Mother, at that—

"Pardon me, my prince, but may I have this dance?"

I jump, whirling toward the voice with a heap of apologetic denials at the ready. But my mouth shuts as I notice the woman before me, donned in a turquoise gown that draws out the vibrancy of her upswept ginger hair. She smiles, sparkles glimmering on her rosy cheeks.

"Alani." I sigh, discarding my idea of escaping. How improper that would be, anyway.

"Thought I'd save you," Alani says. "If you don't mind sparing me the embarrassment of standing alone for a while, too."

Standing alone? Hasn't anyone asked to dance with her?

I reach for her hand, gaze sweeping the crowd with the expectation of seeing a man eyeing her somewhere, maybe working up the courage to ask for a dance. Instead, I find Elias beaming as he twirls Norielle again. A blur of light trails around her dress like flittering fireflies.

What must it be like to be Elias? To have hardly a responsibility looming overhead and no expectations or episodes of madness to prevent him from just *being*?

The thought coats my tongue with a bitter taste, renewing the same jealousies I felt along the way to the citadel every time I caught them close to each other. It's unfair—completely—that I am denied such simple things as the right to fall in love freely, to hold someone close, to dream of a future that isn't marked by loneliness, without fear that I'd harm whoever dared get so near.

And yet the sacred texts claim El-Alam cares about the desires of our hearts.

"I see your lady of interest is preoccupied," Alani says, and I return my attention to her sympathetic gaze.

"You mean your gentleman of preference."

Her eyes widen, as if she didn't expect me to notice whom she hoped to steal a dance with. But unlike with Mother, Alani's interest is impossible to miss with the way she ogles every eligible young man who comes within her vicinity. Not that anyone could consider Elias eligible anymore with how his heart has fixed on Norielle. Is she the reason he's returned none of the affections of his many admirers? Was some part of him holding out for Norielle, as if El-Alam had promised their reunion to him?

Did He?

"Calden?" Alani says, drawing me back to the present moment.

I hesitantly lay my other hand against her waist and guide our steps in a formal waltz, much like Mother and Seer Josiah. A proper dance for a future Sovereign, if far less exciting than Elias and Norielle's display.

"It's nice to see you again," Alani says, as casually as a shopkeeper might. "It's been a few days since you've shown yourself. Are you all right?"

"Something like it. And you? Are you well?"

"Quite." Yet her fingers fidget against my back, exposing how nervous she is about our proximity. "Though I am missing the sea."

"You may be back to it soon." We turn, and Elias's elated smile comes into my line of sight again. Envy and some amount of happiness for him produce a numb feeling in my chest, and I struggle to finish what I intended to say next. "I... have a feeling Toaph is not in Alémor."

Alani's gaze follows mine, and our conversation falls flat. When she looks back, her brows are tight, and her eyes display twice as much concern as before.

"Well, go ask her to dance, won't you?"

"Norielle?"

"No, Calden, your mother." Alani chuckles. "Yes. *Norielle.* You keep looking at her."

I force my feet to keep up with the song. "I'm not. It's Elias I was looking at."

"Elias?" She nearly chokes on his name. "My goodness, aren't you a wretched liar? As if I'd believe you're wanting to dance with *him.*"

I can't find it within myself to laugh. "Empyrean, no."

"Then what is it?"

I shake my head, hoping to dismiss the entire conversation, but Alani's steps resist our dance, as if threatening to stop moving until I give her a proper response.

"It's nothing," I mutter, but finding that no more successful than my former attempt to drop this discussion, I relent. "I'm just thinking how much simpler life would be if El-Alam made me a scout rather than a prince. And a cursed one, at that."

Alani raises her brows at "cursed" but doesn't correct me. "You're jealous of him."

The shrill notes sung by the flutes buzz in my ears like mosquitoes. "Never mind, Alani."

Her eyes narrow, as though she wants to press the matter again, so I quickly add, "Besides, you're only trying to get me to dance with Norielle so you can claim Elias."

"I have a prince; what do I need Elias for?" Her amused tone and smile wilt as she reluctantly adds, "It's not like he'd let her go for me, anyway. That's how it always goes."

"What do you mean?"

Rapid blinking warns of her suddenly brewing tears, and she tilts her face away. "I've just never been looked at the way he looks at her."

"You mean by Elias? They've—"

"I mean, by anyone," she cuts in before I can finish reminding her of Norielle and Elias's past. "It's not really Elias. It's every man I've ever even briefly considered. There's always someone else more interesting. More beautiful..."

"Oh."

She slips her hands from me, dabbing at tears with a quiet complaint that they'll ruin her makeup. All the while, she smiles, shaking her head, as if to dismiss the evidence of her pain.

"Alani." I say her name again with more conviction than last time. "You're absolutely lovely, you know that?"

Her hands slowly lower from her eyes as she turns to look at me like I've spoken a riddle.

My throat suddenly feels dry, but something—compassion, perhaps—inclines me to keep going. "It is to others' disgrace if they don't notice it."

She blinks another dozen times before replying, "That's very kind of you to say that. Even if it's only to make me feel better."

I open my mouth to tell her I didn't say it out of pity, but then Elias laughs again, and my words dispel like a wisp of smoke carried adrift by a breeze, returning me to my own pathetic feelings.

"Really, Calden. I'm not falling for this nonsense." Alani recoils another step. "Go ask Norielle to dance. I know you want to."

Her eyes convey her unspoken rationale: *You healed her. You can't hide how you feel about her.*

But before I can correct her assumptions, Alani twirls away and strides across the polished floor, heels tapping as she dodges dancers on her way to Elias and Norielle.

I grit my teeth, wishing I'd had the sense to snatch her back and convince her to leave them alone. Norielle and Elias stop, and I watch, unable to hear their exchange over the trilling flutes. Elias shoots me a look of utter betrayal before pressing on a smile as he seems to submit to the interruption. I swallow hard, hoping he at least saw the apology in my eyes.

Then Norielle's attention shifts to me—standing here with the look of a scolded dog—and her smile shrinks.

With a sigh from the depths of my soul, I reduce the space between us and offer my hand. "May I?"

NORIELLE

I look back at Elias, heart still thrumming from our energetic dance together. The feeling of his hold on my hand lingers like a glove, but his gaze is anything but warm as he glares toward Calden, seeming to miss my backwards glance. He says something to Alani, who offered herself in my stead, then strides for the door, disheveling his hair.

Is he leaving? Or just stepping out for a moment?

Regret tugs at me with every step he takes. I should have rejected this offer to trade partners, especially with how Alani presented it.

My arms feel heavy when the ballroom doors close at Elias's heels, and Alani looks around, alone. To my partial relief, Calden's attendant, Rhys, loses his dancing partner at nearly the same moment. He approaches Alani like an older brother, rescuing her in time to spare her the awkwardness.

"I didn't mean to interrupt..." Calden's demure tone jerks my attention back to him and his outstretched hand.

"You didn't. Alani did."

He flinches at my admonishment. "What did she say?"

"She told Elias that your mother wanted to make sure you and I danced." I fight to keep the hurt and confusion from my voice. "Apparently, it's poor form for you to not dance with a female newcomer—a member of your own Bind, at that."

Calden casts an exhausted glance toward Alani. "My mother said nothing of the sort, and had she, I'd question which is of worse form, neglecting my princely duties or taking you from where you seemed most happy." He smooths a rogue strand into his otherwise well-groomed hair. "It seemed a shame to interrupt."

I stare at him, an icy feeling in my chest. "Well, whatever the reason, you could have at least asked us yourself."

My words come out more feebly than I intended, like a half-hearted swing of a sword. Yet the pained look he gives me suggests they hurt no less than a calculated strike.

"I wasn't going to ask at all," he says gently, yet the implication that he has no desire to dance with me stings, nullifying everything he says next. "Alani strode off before I could tell her to leave you two be. I *am* sorry. Truly."

I steal a glance back at the door, as if Elias might step through so I could return to someone who actually *wants* to spend the night with me. Is this why Calden has said nothing about how he healed me? Does he not care for me the way it seemed?

Then how was it even possible?

I'm tempted to ask, but the growing sorrow in his eyes weakens my resolve. *How* he did it and *why* doesn't matter nearly as much as the fact that he *did*. He bore my pain to save my life. What right do I have to be irritated with him about anything?

"Never mind. It's okay," I say, placing on a smile, as if he'd disintegrated the tension between us with his Master Talent. "I was hoping to spend some of the party with you, anyway. I wouldn't have made it here without you. And honestly, Elias was wearing me out a little. He has way more energy than should be allowed one person."

A corner of Calden's mouth lifts. "Well, rest assured, I am a far less exciting dance partner. One might label me downright boring. You may even steal a nap against my shoulder, if you're lucky."

Regret flickers on his face as soon as he finishes speaking. *What is he thinking?*

"I would offend your mother if I fell asleep during her party, especially before dinner was even served," I jest to break a long silence. But a quick glance at the enchanted way the Lady Sovereign and Seer Josiah dance together suggests she'd be oblivious.

"She'd be none the wiser," Calden affirms.

He extends his hand a second time, and I finally take it. With slow steps, he leads me beneath the golden glow of a crystal chandelier and claims my other hand. We begin a basic waltz, making it a mere two measures along with the song before I feel his palms sweating against mine.

"Norielle..." he begins, glancing at his mother, the door Elias left through, then back to me. His lips remain parted, like he means to say something more, and my pulse quickens. Why has he been so distressed today? Was there a development with Toaph he needs to share?

Or could he be mustering the courage to approach the subject of how he healed me?

He stops the dance we've barely begun, seeming to get lost in my eyes. Though, it's not in the adoring way Elias did, but almost as if he's seeing something he's afraid of.

"I—" he starts again, but before he utters another sound, he staggers back a step, releasing me.

"Calden?"

He covers his forehead, like an immense headache has suddenly struck him. His eyes squeeze shut, unresponsive to me even when I repeat his name twice more.

Oh no.

My breath comes short. *It's happening... Toaph.*

I look to each side for someone I know, someone I can ask to help, yet every familiar face suddenly seems hidden. *I need to get him out of here.* But when I turn toward him again, two glowing white eyes have replaced his. A shriek escapes my lips, but the fear-pinched sound is lost in the loud music and roaring storm outside.

With a few aggressive blinks, the light douses, returning his eyes to the pleasant blue I recognize. Yet his face blanches when he looks at me again.

"Norielle," he whispers. "I'm so sorry."

Before I can reply, he rushes toward a side door. My feet pivot to follow him, but then I remember my promise to stay away. "E-Elias," I stutter, twisting back to where he and I once danced, only to recall he left. "Alani!" I try instead.

I spot her and Rhys and fumble through a series of oblivious dancers until I'm close enough to draw their attention. They freeze, smiles falling as they notice my expression.

"It's Calden—he—" I don't get any further before Rhys releases Alani.

"Where?" he asks.

I point at the side door, and Rhys lurches past me, breaking into a jog.

"Alani..." Her name is a whimper on my lips as fear replaces my adrenaline. What might Calden have done to me if he hadn't been able to stall the episode?

"It's okay," Alani says, pressing on a smile that doesn't reach her trembling eyes. "He's going to be fine. This is what he's been waiting for... it just can't happen in here." She gestures around at the filled ballroom.

"His—his eyes," I stutter.

"Terrifying, I know. Imagine meeting those alone in the tunnels." A nervous laugh sputters from her, but my ears hardly hear it after her statement. I very well could have met them in the tunnels, and how much more terrifying would it have been if I didn't know what it was? And what if, like with Alani, he hadn't stopped it? I'd have been defenseless. Yet it took over a week of us traveling together before he confessed his secret.

Compassion and alarm previously stole my ability to feel offended by that, but here, coming so close to experiencing something akin to what Alani did, I can't help but feel a spark of anger. He could have hurt me. I might have never made it to this ceremony—all because he wasn't willing to be open with me.

Alani pulls me from my thoughts and into a tight hug. I sink into her safe embrace, like I'm Cas and she's me.

"It'll be all right, Norielle," Alani assures me, releasing me. "You only get one of these parties. Best to enjoy it while it's here."

I frown but turn my back on the door, trying not to feel sick as I face my party again.

6

CALDEN

Tendrils of lightning sprawl across the black sky, and a ferocious crack of thunder shakes the ground beneath my feet. The waterfalls pour from the cliffs in a heavy gallop rather than their usual canter, gushing into the lake below. With their excess, and the water spilling off our elevated island, the lake will flood the ports beneath us within the hour.

I step onto a stone overhang, looking across the obscured landscape as water seeps through the thick fabric of my dress coat. The seven bridges that stretch from the citadel's island to the tunnel entrances vaguely pierce through the fog and downpour, lit by dim crystals along the piers. The lake, at least twenty feet below me, is but an abyss, only visible when the lightning flashes.

I tilt my head back, shut my eyes, and let the rain fall across my face. The sensation invigorates my senses as I plead for Toaph to return. I saw nothing besides dust while in the ballroom, but I had to resist it. Norielle was right there. Norielle and at least fifty other Wardens. Running off is bad enough, but wrecking her entire celebration? Possibly hurting people?

"My lord," a man hollers from behind my perch.

The storm obstructing his voice hinders my recognition of him until I spot my attendant behind me with a lantern lit by a Glory Ward.

"Go back inside, Rhys," I order alongside a rumble of thunder.

"That is a command I am afraid I will not be obeying," Rhys counters, stepping nearer to me. "Especially when you choose to stand on the edge of the island over a twenty-foot drop in a storm, as if there are no safer places to be."

At the next flash from the sky, I look down at the rocks jutting up from the dark water like fangs. I briefly consider stepping further inland, but Empyrean knows Toaph prefers to speak to me when I am under some threat of danger, so perhaps this will help me.

"My lord," Rhys repeats. "Come away from the edge."

I ignore him, not wishing for an argument to distract me from Toaph again after all these days trying to hear from him. Rhys falls quiet, but the light of his lantern crawls closer until I sense he's right behind me—a foolish thing to do should my power erupt. But this is Rhys, who has served as my personal attendant since my boyhood. He isn't ignorant of the signs that suggest he needs to get away.

I return my focus to the matter of Toaph Elbara and the world, homing in on my responsibilities and all that will be lost if I don't hear from him. My imagination floods with visuals—these bridges cracking, the waters below coming alive like Lake Daleia and swallowing the citadel, the people I most treasure sinking helplessly beneath it. Then I picture that devastation expanding—reaching the very ends of the world until the cries of the people are the only noise to be heard.

The end of all things. That is what awaits us should things remain as they are.

Yet the alternative is even worse—the Blood Wardens could find Toaph Elbara before I do. They could break through the barrier and deliver Toaph's location to Ta'Nathel. And then the corrupt Guardian would find and slay Toaph Elbara so he could fully attach his soul to our world. Doing so may preserve Silvirdia—but for what fate? For Ta'Nathel to torment humanity for his good pleasure?

The throbbing of my pulse in my ears joins with the storm's ruckus. My nails dig into my palms, ready to pierce the skin, and if not for the cool rain, I'd be sweating. Yet I see and taste no dust, as though the other mind hadn't come over me at all. Why did Toaph reach out to me while I was surrounded? Why couldn't he attempt his message during the times I've spent readily prepared for it?

Instead, he interrupted a celebration—the first break I've taken since Seer Josiah confirmed the information about our Guardian's survival—as if to further remind me of my enslavement to my mission.

Am I not allowed to have one bit of happiness or reprieve until I've given everything I have to this cause?

A bellow erupts from my throat, drowning in the rain and thunder. The recollection that Rhys is right behind me is all that holds the rest of my shouts inside, but I direct my inner cries toward Toaph, no less. *I never asked for this. This isn't fair. Why can't you speak to the Seer? Or to Mother? I'm not even the Sovereign yet—and I wasn't supposed to be. Why must you curse me in both your silence and your voice?*

"Calden..." Rhys's rare use of my real name almost turns me around, but I feel too heavy to move an inch.

"I missed it." Rain sputters from my lips. "I missed my opportunity to hear from him."

"There will be another."

My eye twitches, and before I can think better of it, I twist toward him, all my anger spilling out like the water gushing off the cliffs. "I don't want to wait for another. I want this to be over, Rhys. *Over.* For twenty-five years, I've lived as though cursed, and now, finally, there seems to be a way out, but it's still out of reach. How much longer must I wait to be free?"

The rain slows in the long pause after my outburst. In all our years together, I've never shouted at Rhys. Not even as a child. Yet he bears it with the calm of a seasoned father, and a compassionate smile covers the trespass before I can even contemplate an apology.

"What were you thinking when the episode triggered?" he asks, his tone steady and collected.

I grapple with my regret for a long minute before I remember what happened in the ballroom. I was trying to express my gratitude to Norielle for accepting her place in the Bind, even after the pain she endured to get there. But like last night on the balcony, gazing into her eyes only awoke my memories of Corene, like mirrors reflecting the pain I've buried beneath constant distraction. My mind filled with visuals from when I last saw her—the horror on Corene's painted face flashing between visions of dust. Her hands, casting attacks that I narrowly dodged and never returned. Her blood spilled around the ruby pendant I'd given her at the last ball.

That ball was two months before the Blood Warden incident, which cost me my two closest friends. Still, my failure to rescue Corwin from the defectors is not what stifled my romantic relationship with Corene. That happened mere weeks before then, when she finally witnessed one of my episodes. *My curse.* The same thing that ruins everything. Every chance that I have to experience the simple joys of being alive.

El-Alam placed me in this world as a living martyr. To die in every way except with my physical being. Or will that, too, be taken from me in due time?

I sigh, finally turning to Rhys with an answer. "My life has never been my own," I say, my voice hardly audible even in the quieting rain. "That's what I was thinking right before it happened."

Rhys absorbs my words slowly, but he shares none of his usual wise responses. Though, I trust even Rhys's silence is a display of his wisdom—knowing when to speak and when to listen.

"All my life, we've been searching for a cure for my curse, a way to stop it," I add, accepting his unspoken invitation to continue. "I've managed it to the best of my abilities, but it never ceases to stand like a wall between me and the things I desire. Now here we are, discovering the curse isn't a curse, and the cure is so simple, yet so evasive. If I can just locate Toaph, then surely these episodes will stop..." I smooth my hand across my drenched hair. "At least, I hope they will stop."

"And then your life will be yours," Rhys says.

I lower my chin, water dripping off my brow. "Yes. And there will be a world to live it in." I meet his lantern-dotted gaze again. "But Rhys, I *have* to find him. I—I cannot live like this much longer."

The pity in Rhys's eyes almost makes me wish I hadn't spoken so candidly. I rarely do so with anyone—not about anything personal, at least. The last time I had a conversation where my heart poured from my mouth like this, it was to Elias about Corene defecting, and that was as much of an accident.

Rhys squints, an expression that foretells he's about to share something I've not contemplated myself. "Might I make a suggestion?"

"Please do."

He hesitates despite the eagerness in my tone. "You might consider getting away from the citadel for a time. I'd guess your desire to protect others from so much as witnessing your troubled state may be what causes the hindrance. Perhaps if you are somewhere more isolated, you may have a better chance of letting down your guard that you've worked so many years to uphold."

I perk up at the suggestion. His words ring true, as always. He's absolutely right. As I told Norielle last night, my fear of my episodes is the issue. I can't trust what will happen once the other mind takes hold, even knowing what it is.

"But where shall I—" I cut myself off, the answer manifesting in my mind before I can complete the question, and a restored hope ignites in my spirit. "You've just given me a brilliant idea."

"Have I?" Rhys asks with a twitch in his brow.

I smile, albeit roguishly. "You're not going to like it."

ELIAS

A knock at the door slows my hands as I'm trimming the excess end from the new D-string on my lyre. I consider the door with a glance before turning back to my instrument. Whoever it is, they can wait. They probably have the wrong door, anyway.

With a snap of my cutters, the curled metal clipping falls aside. I tweak the tuning pin, then pluck the string to check the pitch—

A harder bang at the door pounds over the note.

I roll my eyes, my lyre ringing as I set it on the floor against my squeaky wooden chair. *Some patience wouldn't kill whoever it is, would it?*

In the small space, it takes about ten steps to get from my chair in the corner to the door, but an idealistic thought stops me in front of it.

Could it be Nori? Did she notice I disappeared from the ball last night, and now she's coming to talk about it?

I rake my fingers through my unbrushed hair and check that I remembered to properly dress this morning, then I swing the door open, a smile ready to greet her. But it falls the moment

I see the hooded man looming several inches taller than where I expected to meet Nori's eyes.

What is Cal doing here?

I restrain the question with respect to his hood, and he checks both ways down the dorm hall before nodding like he wants to be let inside.

I scratch my ear. What is this about? *He* hasn't come to check on me, has he? Did he suddenly remember we were friends before Nori came between us? I almost snort at the laughable suggestion that comes to mind next. *Maybe he's come to apologize.*

I step aside, and the old floorboards whimper as Cal enters, looking around at my humble residence. He's never seen it, besides what he can glimpse from the doorway. My home is hardly any better than the havens with five pieces of furniture in total: a bed, a chair, a half-sized table, the miniature hearth, and a wardrobe barely large enough to fit a week's worth of clothes.

Cal's hood falls back as I shut the door.

"Do you mop the floors with that swamp water tea of yours?" he asks with a scrunched nose. "The whole place reeks of it."

"That's what happens when you live in a small space." I gesture toward my steaming tea on the table.

He glares at the cup like it's filled with poison before returning his attention to me. "Sorry to bother you so early after last evening, but I wanted to ask something of you."

"Of course." Air puffs from my nose. "That's what would bring you here."

"Have I done something to offend you?" He gives me a baffled look that reminds me too much of Landon whenever I dared accuse him to his father—as if Landon could never do anything wrong, even if he tried. Except on Cal, the expression is almost believable, and doubt sprouts in the soil of my bitterness.

I snip the weed.

"I wonder what," I say, eyelids lowering at his complete naivety. When he still doesn't say anything, I clue him in. "You could have just *asked* last night. I would have handed her off to you, if that's what she wanted. You didn't have to send Alani."

Cal groans. "I didn't send Alani. My intention was to leave you two alone."

"Oh, come on, Cal." An irate chuckle escapes my lips. "You sent her and had her blame the interruption on your mother. Real mature, prince."

"It was Alani's idea, which she acted on against my will," Cal defends himself, bristling more by the second. "And if you'd like to know why, it's because *she* was hoping to dance with you."

I cringe, remembering how Alani offered to dance with me once Nori turned away. But I couldn't go straight from dancing with Nori to whisking around some other woman who knows nothing about who I actually am. Especially not while thinking *my friend* sent her to take Nori away with such a lame excuse.

I told Alani I needed to use the washroom first and left to give myself a minute to calm down from the insult of how it all went down. But by the time I got back, Rhys had claimed her, and Nori had fixated on Cal like our time together had meant nothing. So, I did us all a favor and left for the night.

"I went to the washroom, and your shoe shiner had her by the time I got back," I say flatly. "I left after that, by the way. In case you were too busy to notice."

Cal sighs, as if to dismiss my jab. "Then I suppose you didn't see what happened?"

I cross my arms. "No. Sorry, Cal. I wasn't there to see you ask Nori to be your Lady Sovereign."

"*Empyrean*, Lias. I'm not in some competition with you, if that's what you think." Cal swipes a hand across his face, missing the way his statement makes me flinch. *What's that supposed to mean?* I don't get to ask before he carries on. "I hardly spent a moment with her before Toaph decided the ball was the perfect place to attempt communicating with me again."

A mixed wave of relief and concern wipes away my harsh attitude, and I uncross my arms.

Cal's disposition shifts with mine from defensive to something sullen. "I resisted it, not wishing to harm Norielle or anyone else. Then I rushed outside, hoping I'd not missed the opportunity to hear from him altogether. But he didn't make another attempt to contact me."

"So..." The seriousness of the subject weighs down the room. "You heard nothing else about where he is?"

"Not a word. And I have had no luck hearing from him since we've arrived, not by meditation or even through attempting to trigger an episode." He glances toward the door like someone might have picked the lock and snuck in while we were conversing, then his gaze returns with a concerning intensity. "But I had an idea last night."

I raise a brow, unsure whether to be intrigued or unnerved by his ideas. They almost always sound ludicrous, no matter how familiar I get with his ways of doing things. I gesture for him to continue.

"When we were in the crypt, I heard Toaph's voice. It was as though his statue was speaking to me. And now I wonder, if I were to go back to it, would I hear him again?"

He falls quiet, letting me infer the rest.

"You want me to lead the way."

He nods.

"Back into Blood Warden territory, even after what happened?"

His sideways glance suggests a hint of uncertainty.

"Nori's not trained yet. She's barely just been endowed—"

"She's not coming." He takes another step closer and lowers his voice. "I was hoping only you and I could go. I don't... I don't want to involve the others."

"Your Bind."

"You're right about Norielle. She needs to stay here and learn her wards. Alani can help her. And I would prefer not to mention this quest to Odessa yet. Mother needs her support here, handling all the regular affairs, and I fear Odessa might..."

"Tell your mother if she knew." I scowl when his wince validates my assumption. "So, what you're saying is, the Lady Sovereign wouldn't want you to do it, but you're going to anyway, and now you want to bring me into it."

"I ran it by her last night, and no, she was not approving of the idea..." Cal looks at me with the feigned innocence of a brother who pulled his sister's hair. "But she didn't forbid *you*, Lias. She forbade *me*. You can tell her I ordered you to come."

I grunt, turning away from him to sip my *swamp water*. The tangy tea does nothing to wash away the ill taste his idea brought to my mouth. "Don't you think defectors will be waiting around every corner for you now that they know that *you know* Toaph is trying to reach you? Won't they assume this means you've now gained communication with him? That you know something?"

I refrain from mentioning the danger he's putting me specifically in. The defectors would be more likely to nab me like they did Nori than go after Cal directly. But obviously, he's not concerned about my safety any more than I am. What would it matter if the Blood Wardens got me? Even if I had information to give them, I'd be dead before they could ever pry it out of me. And what difference would it make to the Wardens if they lost me?

Virtually none, if I'm being honest with myself.

Cal's gaze drops to the floor. "Lias, I don't know what else to do. I *need* to find Toaph Elbara, and that's the only lead I have to hear from him. You and I both know my mother is always going to be biased in her dealings with me—protective, if you will. But we've been here five days now, and I've gained no more information than I had when we first arrived. How much longer can the world wait?"

I rub my forehead, envisioning my glowing reputation with the Lady Sovereign being quenched like a flame beneath Cal's stubborn stupidity.

Yet...

I can't dispute the urgency of Cal finding Toaph Elbara, especially not with a job like mine, where all I hear about is all the new and exciting ways our world is falling apart or into chaos. The quest is worth the risks. My life and reputation, included. This might be my only chance to do something that really *matters* in the grand scheme of saving Silvirdia.

I sigh toward the ceiling. "It's a terrible idea, Cal."

"But if—"

"Let's do it."

My acquiescence clips his argument short, and a smile spreads across his face that would make even a good idea seem like a bad one. "Can you leave tonight?"

"I could leave right now if you wanted." I signal toward my boring residence. "Not exactly a lot going on here. Though I was supposed to start my route tomorrow. I wanted to check in on Aldrian to see if the Hunters are still hovering around out there."

"The crypts are on the way, anyway."

No, they aren't. And someone has to see you return home alive, so I'll have to make two trips.

I save the corrections and grab my travel bag from the ground. It jangles as I plop it onto my chair to pack.

Cal inclines his head toward the door. "I need to gather my things yet. Meet me at the bridge at sundown."

"Don't get caught by your mama on the way," I say as he's passing me for the door, but then something strikes me. "Does Nori know?"

Cal clutches his hood, delaying raising it until he finishes speaking. "She will... after we've left."

With that, he walks out, rendering my protest unheard.

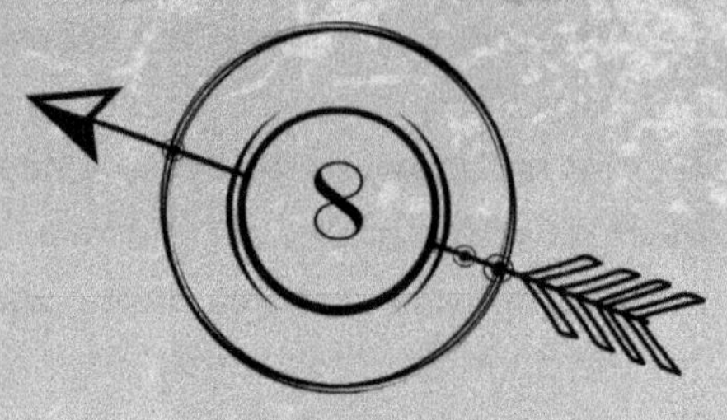

NORIELLE

I pass my ceremony gown—returned to its display mannequin—on the way out the door. The fractured crystals are already fading, looking more like dying fireflies than shards of sunlight. The sight of it revives a dozen memories from last night—the vision of El-Alam pressing a tear to my forehead, me standing over the crowd struggling to share the news, Elias hugging me in the middle of the ballroom, my dress chiming every time he whirled me... and Calden's eyes glowing white just before he dashed from the party.

Neither man ever came back, so I spent the rest of the evening with Alani—stealing glances at the doors, wondering if one of them might return and wishing I could leave myself.

I carry the reflections through the citadel hall, hardly able to focus on where I'm going between the memories' oppressive presence and my rising headache. But luckily, I've walked the lengthy path to the Seer's Sanctum enough times already that my feet know where to go, even with my mind trapped in the ballroom two stories below.

When I reach the grand doors of the sanctum, they are already open, as if the Seer anticipated me—and my handful of books. I peek in, spotting Seer Josiah in his velvet reading chair with the wall of flowing water at his back. The calming aroma of fresh water, paper, and ink greets me with a sense of refuge as I walk inside, like I'm a traveler returning home after a long journey. But the Seer remains gripped by the text he's reading until I softly clear my throat.

He jolts—maybe he hadn't expected me, or else he forgot already. "My! A girl after my own heart," he beams, laying his book face down in his lap. The wide sleeves of his robe cover it like a blanket as he rests his hands atop its leather surface. "I always find, after so much excitement, that a long day with my books is required to restore my soul."

I smile, hugging the texts I've finally remembered to return. "I've never had so much excitement"—I glance around at the shelves lining every wall except where the steady waterfall flows in the back—"or access to so many books. But I can see why you'd need that. I still feel like I'm spinning."

He chuckles as his young attendant comes to gather my books, but rather than rushing them to the shelves, the boy sets a couple aside for himself before putting the others away.

I sigh. If only I could be the Seer's attendant. Of all the roles I've seen so far, it's by far the most peaceful, and the Seer has quickly become my favorite companion inside the citadel walls, tied with Alani.

"Ah!" Seer Josiah suddenly jumps from his seat. He whirls one way, then the other, before seeming to recall which direction he needed to go. "There's a book I remembered—one you may find of particular interest."

"Oh?" I ask, watching his robes flap as he flits to a far shelf.

He stretches for a book nearly too high to reach without his ladder, plucking it out with his fingertips. "You mentioned your grandfather during your last visit. Jensen Damaris, yes?"

I nod. I'd shared with him how Papa's father was a Warden, before King Arlo outlawed Wardens. My grandfather left the society when my grandmother was pregnant with Papa, desiring a more normal life—almost as if he somehow sensed that the days of Wardens being respected were coming to a close.

But my grandfather passed away before I ever met him, so I never had the opportunity to ask him anything about the Wardens. What little he shared with Papa was only enough to kindle my insatiable curiosity about them.

Seer Josiah reduces the gap between us. "This is one of our many quest records. I do believe he's mentioned a time or two in here." Fondness fills his eyes as he passes the book to me. "I thought it may bring you a better sense of belonging, seeing that Warden blood runs in your veins."

I take the book, the murk of my self-doubts diminishing his kind words. I've often wondered who my grandfather *really* was, but now that I have a chance to learn more about him, the thought is almost intimidating. Will I measure up to the Warden he was?

I look up to thank the Seer but find him eyeing the door, twisting the curled edge of his mustache.

Before I can inquire, Rhiana appears from the stairs. She pauses at the entrance, giving Seer Josiah a subtle curtsy. "Good morning, Seer," she says. A mischievous grin forms on her face as she turns toward me. "I thought I might find you up here, Miss Norielle. A *certain scout* requests your presence before his departure."

Energy surges through my body, banishing my groggy state in one breath. "His departure?"

He just got back from his last errand...

"For his route, I presume," Rhiana says. "He asked if you'd meet him in the orchard."

"Where is that?" I ask, not recalling having seen it yet. But then again, I've hardly seen anything of the small island beyond the citadel itself.

"I'll show you to it. And I'll be prompt to leave you two be, of course."

I furrow my brows at her; not that I have any right to judge her for assuming there is something romantic between Elias and me after how we danced at the ball.

"Maybe he'd like to explain why he disappeared last night," I mumble, though I've already figured it was for the same reason he stayed hidden in the back during my ceremony. He didn't want Calden or me to feel uncomfortable with his presence while we danced. I wonder if he's aware that hardly even happened...

I turn back to Seer Josiah, who wears a curious expression.

"Thank you for this," I say, shaking the book, then I follow Rhiana out.

Purple polifruits speckle the well-groomed branches of the trees as we approach the orchard. A mild breeze sweeps their citrusy scent over to me, tempting me to snatch one once I reach them. It might do my headache some good if I did, given the caffeine in a single polifruit is equal to a full cup of morning brew.

I'm considering asking Rhiana if I'm allowed to pick any fruit when Elias comes into view from behind one of the mature trees. He pops a pink wedge into his mouth a moment before he notices me.

Well, if *he's* eating them...

"I'll wait for you near the citadel entrance," Rhiana assures me, then she takes the book the Seer lent me for safekeeping and strides down the paved path.

"Want one?" Elias asks as my focus returns to him.

I nod, and he picks a polifruit from over his head, causing the entire branch to jitter. He tosses the round fruit to me as I join him in the shade.

"You disappeared last night," I say.

He delays his response by inspecting his last polifruit wedge. A breeze flutters the loose collar on his pale shirt. The garment seems so plain after what I saw him in last night, yet he manages to look no less dashing. No wonder all the Warden ladies swoon over him. I bet they'd never guess people teased him for his appearance—among other things—as a child.

Elias fleetingly meets my gaze before seeming to find the citadel's turrets a safer focal point. "I'm sorry, Nori. I was trying to stay out of the way. I'm having a hard time finding my place right now."

"What do you mean?" I could guess the answer, but I'd rather hear his honest response.

He shakes his head. "I'm just not sure if I'm actually welcome around you, or if you're just showing me pity because you think you owe me that."

"Elias..." I lower the polifruit I was about to peel. "I wasn't dancing with you out of pity. Or because I think I owe you."

The disbelief in his gaze makes me wonder if he even remembers our time together at the ball, or if the moment Alani interrupted us, the whole night was wiped from his memory.

"I wanted to spend time with you," I add. "And truthfully, the part where you were there was the only good part of the entire ball."

His lips teeter between a smile and a frown. "Not sure whether to say *thank you* or *I'm sorry* to that." He tosses his final wedge away, like he's spontaneously lost his appetite. "Cal told me what happened."

"You've seen him?"

"Yeah, he came to see me this morning. That's the other reason I needed to talk to you."

I finally pierce the soft skin of my polifruit with a thumbnail, releasing a fresh burst of the bright aroma. "What's going on? Did Toaph tell him something?"

"No." Elias hesitates, scanning our surroundings. His voice is quiet when he continues, "He wants to go back to the crypt. There's a statue of Toaph down there. He thinks he heard Toaph's voice when he was near it before, so he's hoping that if we go back, maybe he'll hear him again."

Numbness crawls over my face at the prospect of entering the place I nearly died in. "All of us?"

"No, just him and me." He glances toward the citadel again. "Cal doesn't want anyone to know until after we've left, so keep quiet about it."

I raise my brows. "The Lady Sovereign doesn't know?"

"She doesn't approve, so Cal's wanting to slip out. But... the prince ordered me to do something, so that's between them. Cal needs me to be his guide."

My eyes blur as I stare at the barely peeled polifruit in my hands. The sticky juice leaks down my fingers, left unwiped, while I attempt to process this news. "Isn't that dangerous?"

"Isn't everything?" Elias asks before strapping on a more reassuring tone. "Blood Wardens know better than to mess with Cal directly."

"Well, they didn't seem to have any problem messing with his friends."

"We'll be careful."

His words have no effect on my rising heart rate. "Why isn't he bringing the Bind? Wouldn't that be safer?"

"It would." He rakes his fingers through his hair. "But that's not the way Cal wants to do it, so here we are. Besides, you aren't allowed to leave the citadel until your initial training is complete, for your own safety."

I return to peeling my polifruit, my motions now jerky from unease and frustration.

"We'll be gone about two weeks tops," Elias says after a moment. "I just thought you should know what's happening and wanted to at least say goodbye before disappearing on you again."

I chew my lip, a bulge forming in my throat. *Two weeks.* They will be away for that long? What about my ward training? Calden implied he was going to oversee it, but how can he if he's off putting himself and Elias in danger? And what happens if Elias is wrong about the Blood Wardens leaving them alone? What if they never come back?

"Nori, it'll be fine," Elias says. "It's not like Cal and I haven't been in dangerous places before. We've got this. And this is important. If Cal can hear from Toaph about where he is, it's worth the risk."

I blink away a sudden onslaught of tears, banishing a tidal wave of emotions before they can crash into me. "I know."

"Hey," he says, his gentle tenor drawing my gaze up to his. "I mean it. It'll be fine. If you think some defectors are going to stop us from coming back to you, you're sorely mistaken."

I smile at his overconfidence. If only that claim actually meant anything for his safety.

"And with Corene gone, Cal should be in full force," he adds, as if sensing I'm still not convinced. "The defectors probably know that, too. Really, they'd have to be idiots to come near us now."

I notice my tight grip on the polifruit and force my muscles to relax. "Just come back, okay?"

The affection that fills his gaze is almost magnetic, yet he doesn't draw any closer. "I will. *Always*."

He lets his promise hang between us for a long moment before shifting away. "I better go. See you when we get back."

I gulp down the last of my reservations. "See you then."

CALDEN

I exit the citadel gate with a quick farewell to the guards and rush onto the shadow-laden east bridge. Upon it, Elias stands with his back to me, staring at the faded moon overhead. The cliffs already block the descending sun, but a pale sky and smattering of gold-flecked clouds signal the day has yet to fully surrender to night. Still, I sense Elias's complaint before he turns around to deliver it.

"It's awfully unprincely to be late," he hollers.

"I'm not. The sun is still setting," I say, striding to reach a more reasonable speaking range.

Elias jostles his backpack by the straps as he looks over my head. I trace his wistful gaze to Norielle's chamber window on the citadel's third story, small as a fingernail in the distance. Whatever he's thinking, he keeps it to himself as he turns east.

"It's going to take your mother one blink to figure out where you went. You realize that, right?" he asks once I've reached his side.

"Yes." Metal hisses beneath my hand as I run it along the bridge rail. "And by the time she opens her eyes, I'll already be gone."

Elias groans. "Well, just so you know, I told Nori."

My feet balk at the admission. "You what?"

"I told her, since you weren't planning on it. Thought she had a right to hear from one of us directly, rather than finding out after word drips down the ranks to her."

I double my pace to catch up with him. "I left a letter."

He gives me a sour look over his shoulder. "Really? A letter?"

"I was afraid she'd try to follow us."

"She's not that rebellious, Cal. Nori respects her authorities, unless they give her a specific reason not to."

"Then she may have warned Mother?"

"Unlikely." He looks back at the citadel again. "She's more loyal than that."

I bow my head, realizing how little I know of Norielle compared to Elias. But, as if this weren't enough proof, Elias carries on in a more serious tone.

"Nori's prone to anxiety, Cal. If you're going to be her leader, you need to know that. She does better when plans are laid out for her—not carried out behind her back—even if you think it's for her good."

Again, my gait slows unintentionally. Why is he telling me this? To further show me I don't know half as much about her as he does? Or is he genuinely trying to help me understand Norielle's needs?

I decide not to ask, and instead, take advantage of the quiet to soak up the free-flowing air and the sight of an endless sky overhead. But it doesn't last for long before we reach the end of the bridge and step into the black mouth of the east tunnel.

The stone walls of the Wardens' passages seem unusually oppressive as we walk past them. I brush my fingertips against the smooth surface, contemplating if it's only an illusion, or if the shaft is in fact tighter than it was when I traveled this way on my trek to Behria. Of course, back then I was hardly paying heed to anything. The only concept my mind seemed capable of fathoming was that a young woman whose destiny was bound to mine was soon to die at the watery hands of an angry lake.

"So, what if Toaph's statue has nothing to say to you?" Elias finally asks, breaking what turned into an hour-long silence. He doesn't miss his opportunity to look at me like I'm a madman for expecting a hunk of carved stone to communicate with me.

I speak toward the ground in the hope that my voice won't travel far. "Then we return to the citadel, I gather my Bind, and we search anywhere that might be worth investigating."

"Seems vague."

"I have hunches," I say, projecting more confidence than I feel. "From what little I can recall from my visions, it seems Toaph may be in a desert somewhere."

"Because of the dust?" Elias asks after a moment.

I nod. "And the barrenness of the surroundings. Unfortunately, that hardly limits our options. There are at least nine significant deserts across Silvirdia."

"Is the Valley of the Four Winds in question?"

My brows scrunch. "What's that?"

Elias laughs like he's alarmed by my ignorance, but as his steps slow, his amusement dissipates, and his serious demeanor returns. "In Raevre, they call it *Vala dos Quaventos*. It's what the war with Raevre is *really* about. I thought the Wardens would know?"

"We've not exactly maintained great contact with Raevre in recent years because of the war, and King Arlo isn't about to slip such private intel to us." I sift through my memories, trying to recall any mentions of this valley, but nothing comes to mind. "All I've heard about the war is that King Arlo believes

Raevre is forming a weapon that could destroy all of Alémor if they don't stop them. What do you know about it?"

Elias checks our surroundings again before answering. "Well, the Raevrans discovered the Valley of the Four Winds about two decades ago, way out in the middle of the Segredo Desert. They claim winds from the north, south, east, and west meet there, causing an unrelenting vortex. The Raevrans think there is something inside the vortex—some great source of magic or the like. But the winds are too strong for anyone to pass through, and you can't see inside through all the dust."

I nearly stop in my tracks, the revelation rendering this quest to the crypt pointless. Strong winds. Dust. That sounds incredibly like what I've seen in my visions.

"King Arlo found out about it through his spies. He's always been suspicious of Queen Uxia with her... barbaric reputation," Elias continues. "Now he wants control over whatever is inside the vortex. If there *is* anything in there. I always figured it was like the vortices in the sea—just another freak occurrence in nature caused by the curse. But the Raevrans are very superstitious, from what I've heard. They're always making up nonsense about hidden power and reading into things that don't need to be read into."

"Yet King Arlo believes this enough to send his soldiers not once, but *twice*, into Raevre in pursuit of it?" I ask.

"Well, the first time he only recalled the soldiers, because that's when the wildfires started. He sent them back when he realized the fires weren't going out." Elias raps his knuckles along the tunnel wall, pondering awhile before adding, "King Arlo is obviously terrified of magic. I'm not sure if he even wants to enter the vortex or if he just wants to make certain no one else does."

I absorb the information with a long inhale. Why haven't the Wardens of Raevre reached out to us to share knowledge about this Valley of the Four Winds? Are they unaware? Or do they know there is nothing to it?

"Lias, how do you know about this?"

He stuffs his hands into his pockets. "Nori's papa was one of the first spies sent to investigate Raevre, and reports of what he saw made it to my ears."

"And why haven't you mentioned it before?"

He shrugs. "I figured this would be common knowledge to Warden Elders, and that you'd all assumed the same as me or had already confirmed the rumors are rubbish. And honestly, this is the first time that it's felt relevant to bring up. I still don't know if there's anything to it, but I thought I should mention it, since you've got nothing better to go on—unless Stony decides to talk."

I chew on the idea, still partially inclined to turn back, but I decide against it. We wouldn't be able to leave right away anyway, not with Norielle's training and while lacking our final Bind member. I might as well spend this time following a more reliable lead. The trip overseas would take weeks, and we'd have to sneak through an active war zone to reach the vortex and investigate. And what if Elias's assumptions are correct, that the vortex is only another caused by the curse? I'd be risking our lives and wasting our time in vain. Besides, surely, the Raevran Wardens have looked into it and have already written off the suspicions, otherwise they would have informed Mother.

"Hey, Cal..." Elias's oddly quiet tone yanks me from my thoughts. "If you decide to go there, I want to come."

"What's in Raevre for you?"

He grips his backpack straps, leaving a long delay before answering toward his boots. "My father's ashes."

I straighten. Elias openly sharing a sensitive detail about his past? Since when?

"Your father died in Raevre?" I ask.

"First war. Probably sounds macabre, but I've always wanted to go there. Stand on the ground he fought on and thank whatever remnant of him has joined with the earth."

The sentiment conjures a mournful image in my mind. "Honorable, Lias, not macabre."

His gaze remains fixed on the ground for a while, as if this dirt is the very ground he speaks of. But before the silence can stretch too long, he pushes a smirk back on his face. "You'll let me come then, if you go? Or am I only allowed to tag along these days when Nori isn't hanging onto your shirttails?"

I grunt as the vulnerable moment between us shatters. "What would make you say that?"

Elias gawks at me like I've asked the most foolish question in the history of speech. "You nearly refused my offer to join you two on the way to the citadel, even after the Seer's warning."

"We were nearly to Alani."

"And? What harm was one more person? A *friend*, at that." He scratches the side of his head. "Oh, wait. I know. You were afraid she'd lose interest in you if she met me, so you nearly put her in worse danger so you could shove me aside before I got any closer."

The bitterness in his tone sharpens mine and quickens my tongue. "And perhaps I *shouldn't* have let you come. After all, they abducted her on *your* watch."

Elias huffs, his strides hastening ahead of me, and my comment returns to my ears. Regret for my harshness bows my lips, but I can't dig myself from the trench of shame to apologize for it.

We fall back into silence.

NORIELLE

The buttery scent of freshly baked crescent rolls and a harsh aroma of morning brew reach my nose as Rhiana and I turn the corner for the refectory. The crystal-lit dining area sprawls beneath a raised walkway and is much quieter than it was during the days prior to my ceremony. Before, there seemed to always be at least five people in it, even outside of normal mealtimes. Today, I only spot two people sitting across from each other at the extraordinarily long table: Alani and Rhys.

I wave at them before approaching the serving counter to request one of the morning pastries, and the cook passes off a tart oozing with strawberry filling, something a much younger Elias would have sold half his clothing for.

I almost chuckle at the thought before the same ill feeling that kept me up last night strangles my amusement. Does anyone else even know Calden and Elias are gone?

I sit beside Alani, and she delivers a muffled greeting through a mouthful of cheese. Rhiana, with her matching pastry, claims the space beside her older brother. But when I meet Rhys's gaze, his formal pose turns even more rigid, and his smile twitches.

He does *know. And he thinks I don't.*

"Before you get your hands dirty," he says, digging into the pocket of his dress coat. "I have something for you from the Sovereign Prince."

My nerves spark. Something for me?

And here I was wondering if he forgot I was even here, considering how he didn't bother to say goodbye to me yesterday or inform me of his plans.

Rhys slides a small rolled parchment across the table. I snatch it, quickly unfurling it to read the words neatly etched across its white sprawl.

Norielle,

I apologize for the nature of my departure, but I had to slip out without my mother noticing. She forbade the brief quest I am going on.

Elias and I are returning to the crypt in hopes that Toaph Elbara might communicate with me again. It is where I heard from him most clearly before. We should return in roughly two weeks.

Please don't worry about us. My mother's concerns are just that—a mother's concerns. We will be safe, and hopefully, we'll be back quickly with answers about where to find Toaph Elbara.

All the best,
Calden

My mouth hangs open as I read the note a second time, then I roll the paper, nearly crushing it in my hand. Why couldn't Calden tell me this in person? Did he think I'd betray him to his mother?

Maybe I should. Maybe his mother has a right to worry.

"Does the Lady Sovereign know yet?" I ask Rhys.

He hesitates. "As soon as she realizes he's gone, she will figure out where to."

Alani offers me a reassuring smile, but I clutch the paper tighter.

"I, too, feel concern for his well-being at times," Rhys says, adopting a gentle tone. "But after nearly twenty years in his close service, I also know the Sovereign Prince is both impossible to persuade out of his ideas *and* worthy of our trust in his abilities. It's not as though he's a novice with wards. I assure you that the Sovereign Prince knows what he is doing and will return safely. In the meantime, give him the benefit of the doubt and honor his absence by focusing on your lessons."

My shoulders droop, but I shut my mouth. Rhys has a point—he's known Calden significantly longer than I have—and I can see the genuine concern in his eyes. If anyone knew when to worry about Calden, it would be Rhys. Or Alani, at that, and she hardly seems fazed by his departure. Calden must do this sort of thing all the time—disappearing without warning.

Does he not realize that some of us would like fair notice? And did he forget he implied that he would be the one to train me in wards?

I search my rose-colored kirtle for a pocket, but finding none, I stuff the note into my boot just quickly enough to hide it before a voice calls from the raised walkway.

"Miss Norielle!"

I twist to find Odessa standing at the rail, almost unrecognizable in her belted tunic and trousers. But even without her regal gown, she looks no less like a haughty queen overlooking her kingdom.

"I've been waiting for you to show yourself," she says with a tap of her long nails against the mahogany banister. "My mother asked me to oversee your ward training in my brother's stead, considering he has more important things to do."

I fight a frown. Even though I know it's true—finding Toaph Elbara *is* more important than Calden investing his time in my training—it still stings to hear it said so bluntly.

"Lady Odessa, if I may." Rhys rises to bow to her. "The Sovereign Prince requested that Alani be placed in charge of Norielle's ward training. She, too, is a Master, and therefore eligible to train a new inductee."

Odessa arches a brow, her exquisitely beautiful features unmatched by anyone I've seen at the citadel—or possibly anywhere. "Well, then I've wasted my time."

She turns without a fight, as if this news is actually a relief to her.

"He does, however, wish that you would spend some time in the arena with her, my lady," Rhys adds, and Odessa halts.

Arena?

"He says she can wield a sword well, but he'd like to see that she gets more practice while she's here and considered it may be beneficial for you two to spend time together, since you are both in the Bind."

Odessa smiles, but in a way that tastes as sour as Alani and Elias's mullenberry leaf tea. "How very thoughtful of him to recall that I, too, have a place amongst the Bind."

I glance at the others, searching for an explanation. Does Calden regularly leave her out? I thought Odessa herself was the one who didn't seem to care about being part of the group.

All I can gather from my companions is a storm of mutual annoyance brewing in their eyes.

"Meet me in the arena in twenty minutes," Odessa says, turning again to leave.

I shoot a questioning gaze toward Alani, but she only shrugs. Who are we to argue with the Second Lady of the Wardens?

A sigh blows from my nose. "Yes, my lady."

CALDEN

The steady squeak of a wheel fills the silence of our shaft—a supplier tending their route up ahead. My boots pound the cart's tracks in the dirt. The bright ceiling highlights the imprints, as well as Elias's persistent scowl. He hasn't wiped off the expression since our conversation last night, not even when we stopped to rest at a haven.

"Lias," I say, dragging out my steps to match his slower stride.

He doesn't look at me.

"I'm sorry."

The apology dangles in the air, unacknowledged for so long that a desire to rationalize the harsh words I spoke yesterday rises and almost escapes. Luckily, he looks up in time to stop me from making it any worse.

"For what?" he asks, as if it isn't obvious.

"For what I said yesterday about Norielle's abduction." Guilt lowers my voice to hardly more than a rumble.

"It's not like you're wrong." His focus sharpens ahead, as if to blur me from his peripheral vision.

"Right or wrong, I shouldn't have said it."

He only shakes his head.

Our footsteps and the squeaky wheel up ahead become the only noise again, and a heaviness fills my spirit at the way things have shifted between Elias and me since Norielle came between us. Until her appearance, I considered Elias my closest friend, even above Alani and Rhys. But now what is to come of the times we once shared? Our sparring in the arena, battling with both weapons and wit? Or our adventures when I'd enlist his aid more for his company than because I had need of him? Or the moments like when I bared my heart to him about Corene—when I felt for a rare occasion like I could fully peel off my princely mask and show someone the flawed and uncertain man underneath without fear?

Are those times now past? And was it my doing after the unfair way I reacted when he asked to join Norielle and me on the way to the citadel?

"I shouldn't have hesitated to accept your offer, either," I add, realizing I've yet to apologize for that. His gait slows behind me. "I confess I wasn't thinking properly."

"So, then I'm right." The stony walls amplify his quiet voice. "You were trying to keep me away so I wouldn't mess up whatever you two had going."

I take a slow breath, recounting my concerns and rationale. Though now, after everything that's transpired, it all feels distant—almost as if my mind and heart now belong to someone else.

"I didn't know who she was to you," I say, a dull feeling washing over my chest. "And I was savoring too much the presence of someone who knew me not for my curse or for my title. I..." My throat suddenly feels parched despite the humid air. "I don't know what I was thinking, Lias. I suppose I wanted to keep feeling like I was a somewhat normal Warden for a change, and her coming in from the outside, being so naïve to everything—it gave me that."

We walk another five or six strides before he asks, "And what did that have to do with me?"

I shake my head, struggling to form an answer that doesn't sound foolish, but given how unwise my actions were, I find myself cornered by my own stupidity. "I fancied the idea of someone just seeing me as I am—in my heart, that is—and perhaps growing fond enough before discovering my curse to not fear me when it finally showed. And with how brave she is..." My words trail off again. The more I hear them, the more ridiculous they sound. First, because I endangered Norielle by keeping her ignorant. And second, because I know better than to believe anyone could ever overlook my curse and the threat it would bring someone close to me. "I regret it. Every part of it. I should have warned her from the first night we camped together and accepted your offer without hesitation. I wronged you both, and for that, I am very sorry."

A long silence follows my apology, and after a time, I look back at Elias. His knotted fists and tense steps suggest I've not sufficiently restored the lost ease between us. But by his low-cast gaze, I sense it's more than just me he's angry with. It's himself, as well. Otherwise, he'd be firing a sharp comment my way or making light of the situation for the sake of ending the awkwardness.

"You know, Norielle would have died if not for you, Lias," I add, though it irks me to admit it aloud. I wasn't enough. I couldn't have been, not with Corene no longer just haunting my memories, but coalesced into an inescapable nightmare before my eyes.

Elias glances at me, as if confused.

"You did right by Norielle in every way that you could have."

He waves me down. "I don't want to hear it. We all know why she's alive, and it has nothing to do with me."

"Elias, it's not what it seems—"

But right as I'm saying it, our path turns, and the man pulling the noisy cart comes into view, much nearer to us than I'd assumed. I fall silent, knowing neither of us want this conversation to be overheard by anyone, and quicken my pace.

As we approach, I hear the supplier grumbling under his breath, as if unaware of our presence. Elias coughs to get his attention, since the path is too narrow to pass him easily, and the man glances back. The supplier grunts, not bothering to greet us or shift his cart to the side. But a moment later, he does a double take, and he halts in his tracks, as if suddenly registering my face.

"Sovereign Prince," he says, failing to bow as other Wardens do.

I hide my uncertainty about him behind a polite smile. "Good afternoon, friend. Is"—the man grimaces, and I almost don't finish my question—"everything all right?"

The green-blue crystals on the tunnel walls light his intelligent gaze. "When was the last time everything was all right in this Empyrean-forsaken world?"

I glance at Elias before responding to the supplier, "Sir, did you miss the ceremony the other night?" *Surely, with such an attitude, he didn't hear the announcement.*

But the man's expression darkens. "Oh, I was there."

"Then you should know that things will return to normal soon enough, if not better than normal. Just as soon as I find Toaph Elbara."

The man only looks at me. I start ahead, readying to side-shuffle past the cart to get away from him, but Elias and I don't take more than a step closer before the man speaks again.

"Twenty-five years..." The roused anger in his tone stills me. "He's been trying to communicate with you for twenty-five years, and you only just now found that out? *From the Blood Wardens?*"

My mouth doesn't form a quick enough reply to the sudden accusation, and he goes on.

"How do you know that the Blood Wardens haven't somehow deceived you? Or that this isn't Ta'Nathel's work? I know what happens to you... sounds like you've been touched by Ta'Nathel's curse, not like Toaph Elbara is trying to communicate with you."

"The Seer has confirmed what it is," I say.

This only wins an aggressive sneer across the man's reddening face. "And of course we can trust *him*. As well as we can trust the rest of you."

"How dare you speak to the Sovereign Prince like that," Elias cuts in, sounding more like a personal guard than a scout I appointed as an escort. I face him, surprised he'd defend me with the tension between us, but his stance is resolute. "You think you know better than the Elders?"

The man glances at him before his glare returns to me. "Excuse me, Sovereign Prince. A quarter century of watching the Warden leadership fail to redeem Silvirdia has made me skeptical. Particularly of a boy being charged with deciding the world's fate."

Air floods my chest at the insult toward my mother and the other Elders, not to mention me. Yet the guilt of our failure stalls my response once more.

"I lost my entire family in the massacre," the man adds. "And do you recall what the last Sovereign did? He dared not even address King Arlo to defend our integrity. He let us shrink into obscurity, ordering us to keep protecting the very people who would kill us. Served him right to be killed by Hunters.

And the Lady's done no better. I'm sure we could hardly expect any different from you."

"Enough," Elias snaps. "This is your Sovereign Prince. Show him some respect."

Another sneer cracks on the man's lips. "I'll show him respect when he proves he's worth it." He turns his scrutinizing gaze on me. "Until then."

He waves, as if to dismiss the conversation, and starts on his way—which is, regretfully, the same as ours. I prepare to let him go so we can lag behind, but Elias seizes his shoulder and jerks him back around.

"*Lias—*" I spew, but it's too late. The insolent man is already drawing his sword in defense.

Elias flaunts his own weapon and a smirk that is just as sharp. "You know what you sound like?" He leaves his opponent with no space to reply. "A man on his way to join the defectors."

I expect the man to deny it readily, but his hesitation suggests Elias's quick assumption isn't as far-fetched as I hoped.

A man considering abandoning the Order—abandoning El-Alam—because of his doubt in *me?*

The supplier's sword swooshes in response, clashing with Elias's, but before either party can attempt another strike, I ignite a pre-drawn Vitality Ward on my arm. A blue-tinged sphere of energy launches from my palm and between the two men. They leap to avoid it, and the energy collides with the tunnel wall with a loud crack in the stone.

"Stand down, Lias," I order. "Let the man think what he wants of me. Time itself will prove which of us is right."

Elias's chest rises and falls before he finally sheathes his sword. But the man doesn't follow his lead.

"Put away your weapon," I command. "Or I will disintegrate it from your hand."

The man runs his tongue over his teeth—so much contempt in his gaze, one might think we announced we are handing the Wardens over to Ta'Nathel's authority.

But finally, he tucks his weapon away and retracts a step.

I eye him, half anticipating him to attack us the moment we turn our backs, but he settles against the wall, as if to show he will hang behind until we have a strong lead.

I clench my teeth as we shimmy past his cart and press onward. How many more Wardens like him are out there? Questioning the leadership of the Elders? Doubting my ability to make good on all I've promised? Would they risk eternal punishment in the everlife due only to their perception of folly in those leading them? Have they no loyalty to El-Alam Himself? Or has their faith already shattered in all the places where mine has cracked?

"Don't take it so hard, Cal," Elias mutters beside me. "I've seen him around before. That's just how he is."

"Do others feel that way about our leadership?"

He walks for a while before answering. "Not many."

Yet his delay suggests otherwise. I swallow that reality before asking, "What do they say of me?"

"Most people would sooner write your name in the *Book of Legends* than accuse you of anything, Cal." A smirk creeps onto his face. "You're El-Alam's gift to the Wardens, remember? The answer to the Lady Sovereign's prayers? Our Empyrean-sent hero?"

The pressure builds in my chest with his every declaration. "I'm not sure which is worse. To be doubted or to be held to impossible standards."

"They're only impossible alone," Elias says, and as if sensing his words are inadequate at relieving my stress, he continues, "You've got your Bind. You've got El-Alam. The Elders. Idiots like me who'll follow you into whatever pit you decide to go into, no matter how annoying you are. Don't listen to the one voice that makes you feel small, Cal."

I smile but give him a skeptical side-glance. "An hour ago, you were telling me to shut up. Now you're defending me."

He shrugs. "Consider it me accepting your apology."

NORIELLE

Steel clashes against steel, sending a vibration into the hilt of my dull training sword. I tighten my grip, my heel scraping the packed dirt of the citadel's arena as I slide back a step. But I'm not quick enough to escape before Odessa whirls her weapon from parry to strike. The unsharpened tip of her blade jabs into my abdomen. My leather cuirass reduces the impact, but the force still sends me staggering back, winded, as if punched in the upper stomach.

Odessa offers me no mercy, seizing the opportunity to lay her blade against my throat. Even without a sharp edge, the sensation of cool metal against my sensitive skin raises goosebumps down my arms.

Odessa laughs and retracts her blade. "Not terrible, but needs work."

I let my muscles relax, dangling the sword at my side while I catch my breath. It feels like we've been dueling all day, though judging by the sun's placement overhead, it's only been one hour since we made it to the arena. A light wind cools the sweat on my forehead as I look around at the sprawling training yard. The fenced-in field supplies no shelter from the sun besides a flapping tarp canopy over a set of wooden benches, and the arena is vacant besides Rhiana, who's taken the time outside as her chance to practice shooting arrows at one of the painted targets on the other side of the yard. From what I can tell by the number of arrows on the ground, she's not faring well with the breeze. Not that I would do any better with a bow.

"You said your father taught you what you know?" Odessa asks.

"Yes. He was a soldier." I retrieve my flask from a bench and take several gulps of water before meeting Odessa's piercing gaze. "I haven't practiced much in this past year since he's been gone."

Odessa nods like someone already filled her in on what happened to Papa. "Well, I am impressed. If that's you when you're rusty, then you should be ready to take down Hunters in a few weeks."

I can't help but smile, though I feel prouder of Papa, who taught me, than of my skill. With Papa's talent, I'm surprised King Arlo never attempted to recruit him as one of the elite Warden Hunters. Though Papa never would have accepted such a role, not for all the wealth the king could offer, and King Arlo already took advantage of him as one of the original spies sent to Raevre.

"Let's meet here again tomorrow," Odessa says, returning her training sword to the weapons rack beside the benches.

Metal clunks against the wooden bracket as I add my sword to the vacant space next to hers. When I turn around, she's already striding down the long path back to the citadel.

"Hey, wait!" I holler, and she stops. "You know where Calden went, don't you?"

She glances at her Bind Mark and jabs her thumb in the direction of its arrow. "Somewhere that way."

"He's going back to the crypt," I say, expecting her to flinch or frown—something. All she does is stare at me like I said he went to take a nap.

Actually, that would be more alarming at this point.

She considers me for a moment. "How do you know that?"

My mouth opens to tell her that Elias imparted the information to me, but I think better of it. Instead, I fish Calden's letter out of my boot and hold it up. "He left me a note."

"Considerate," she mumbles. "That's more than I received. I found out from my mother once she figured out he left."

"Aren't you worried?"

"For Calden?" Odessa rolls her eyes. "No. The Blood Wardens are smart. They won't do anything to him unless he attacks them directly—which is not his goal. Everybody knows he's my mother's precious darling. If they killed or captured him, Mother would send every Warden she has into defector territory to avenge him, even if it would kill us all."

Why hasn't she done that already?

I fidget with a strand of my hair, tempted to ask, but she speaks again before I have the chance.

"Don't worry about him. The only thing you should be worried about right now is improving with your sword and learning wards so you can pass your initiation test. My brother can handle himself. It's you who needs to learn how to do the same."

I frown, and she stops herself mid-turn, as if reconsidering the way she wanted to leave me.

"You're at a severe disadvantage, is all I mean to say," she adds, her tone a touch softer than before. "I never would have expected El-Alam to call an outsider to join this Bind, especially now knowing what our purpose is. You'll need to work hard to keep up... for your own sake."

With that, she marches off to return to whatever business the Second Lady is responsible for.

My shoulders sag as I turn around, finding Rhiana hurrying to meet me with her bow and quiver already returned to the rack.

"How long did you say it takes to learn wards?" I ask once she's close.

"Most people have a decent understanding of the standard wards within two to three weeks, but generally speaking, new inductees spend a full month practicing before they test." She smiles despite the grimace pressing my lips together. "However, your friend, Elias, passed his test after only two weeks of training, if I recall correctly. The Lady Sovereign was highly impressed. Practically everyone heard about it."

My heart twists at Elias's name. Odessa only assured me about *Calden's* safety, and if my experience in the crypt proved nothing else, it's that Elias is right to worry about the people Calden keeps in close company.

I force levity into my voice, hoping it will lift my spirits. "No wonder Elias is so arrogant these days, with the Lady Sovereign praising him like that."

Rhiana snickers before urging me toward the path Odessa took. "We should ready you for your lessons with Alani. If you're to beat Elias's record, you'd best get started."

Alani rushes into the courtyard ten minutes after our agreed meeting time, shouting apologies from the door until she reaches my side beneath a blue astria oak. She wags her gleaming stylus at me as she stops in the tree's shadow. "I had to go back for my pen. Would be awfully hard to draw wards without it."

She giggles, but the smile I return is tense. I have two and a half weeks at most to learn the standard wards, and Calden paired me with someone who has no sense of punctuality or urgency.

Maybe we should have let Odessa teach me…

"I should be honest with you; I've never trained anyone. And, well, I'm not exactly sure where to start or how. My mum taught me as a little girl, and I hardly remember it at all, I was so young." She stops to smile at Rhiana, as if she's just noticed her, then she presses the clear crystal end of her illuminated warding pen against her lip. The inexhaustible ink within the stylus—as I've learned in one of the many texts the Seer lent me—is said to be El-Alam's tears over creation, the same as what Calden used to endow me. Only someone who has been bestowed with power from El-Alam can use a proper warding pen, and only wards written with the blessed ink inside hold any magic, unless using the defectors' corrupt means.

But I won't receive my pen until I pass my initiation test, thus proving my trustworthiness and ability to use such power.

"Is there a particular ward you'd like to try first?"

"Calden seemed to think the Purification Ward was a good starting point," I say, recalling that evening at Ila's house when he showed me how to draw the ward, even though he wasn't allowed. I should have taken that as a warning that he would make a habit of doing forbidden things under people's noses. But it felt different then, when no one was in danger.

And it wasn't *my* nose it was being done under.

"Hmm," Alani hums, her posture wilting. "That's a boring start, I'd say."

"That's where most lessons begin, isn't it?"

Alani's lips twist sideways, but eventually, she nods. "I suppose you're right. Starting you with a Vitality Ward might be a good way to put a hole in the citadel."

"Let's avoid that," I say with a soft laugh.

Alani's attention flits from me to a ceramic fountain in the center of the courtyard. Its scalloped tiers spill with water like the cliffsides surrounding the citadel, but the gentle trickle is nothing compared to the constant roar of the waterfalls.

Alani prances toward the fountain, her voice bobbing with her steps. "Perhaps I should explain a bit more about how they work first? Then I'll show you how to draw the Purification Ward?"

I seal my lips, thinking better of disclosing how many times I practiced drawing the Purification Ward with Calden at Ila's table. "Sure."

She fidgets a moment before her eyes light with intention, and she peels her ruffled sleeve back, revealing a series of glyphs on her arms. "You've probably figured out that we can draw them anytime we want and activate them later, yes?"

"Y—"

"Most of us keep a few 'on hand,' so to speak," she carries on over me. "But I wonder if you've noticed something..."

I decide against trying to respond and wait for her to continue.

"Besides permanent wards like the Omen and Bind Marks—notice how those are called *marks* rather than *wards*—wards have a limited number of uses. A new Warden can only use a ward once or twice before having to redraw it, but as your skills develop, you'll be able to use the same ward multiple times." She holds up her hand, and a ward resembling the sun lights on her forearm. A second later, a blue sphere launches from her palm, buzzing past several trees before fizzling out in midair.

"See, the ward remains," she says, shoving her arm closer to my eyes. "Now, if I do that a few more times…"

Six more balls of energy shoot from her hand in close succession, all dissolving in the distance before she turns back to show me the bare patch on her skin.

"Gone," she says with a childlike smile, though her eyes suddenly appear wearier than the last time she looked at me. "I'm quite proud of seven. That's almost as many vitality spheres as Calden can fire with one ward."

"How many can he do?" I ask.

"Last I heard, thirteen."

That's nearly double what she said…

I withhold my comment. "Is that the record?"

"Actually, no." Alani tosses her hair. "Technically, Odessa has done nearly twenty. But she cheats."

"Cheats?"

"Her Master Talent allows her to sap vitality from living things—plants, enemies—and use it herself, but around here, we don't consider that fair."

"So, she could… drain someone's life?" My face tingles at the thought. "*Completely?*"

Alani giggles. "No, it still costs her energy to sap energy. So, while it boosts her, yes, she runs out of her ability to use the Talent before that happens. At least, that's the case for larger life-forms, like people. It mostly just weakens her enemies while lengthening her own endurance."

"Oh." I shove the information to the back of my mind before it can make me any more intimidated by Odessa than I already am. "So, what would you say is an average number of vitality spheres for us normal people?"

"Three to five. As you can imagine, it's a bit of a sport for us Wardens, trying to see who can outperform the other with such things." She laughs, seeming to get lost in a memory that I assume must have to do with her many brothers before she refocuses. "But all you need to worry about for now is launching one. You'll get stronger as you practice, and then maybe we can revisit the subject of competition."

I smile, envisioning what fun being a Warden would be if not for all the responsibilities and danger. Was there ever a time when the only things a Warden had to worry about was how to make their wards outlast those of their peers? Will there ever be a time like that again?

"Now, the Purification Ward, that's the one that looks—"

"Like a sprout."

"Ah, I see you've been studying," she says, and I opt to let her think that's all I've been doing. "Here, I'll draw it on the fountain, but I won't activate mine. You draw yours next to it, all right?"

I nod, though she turns before she sees it. Her pen etches the smooth ink across the ceramic lip of the fountain's middle tier. As she withdraws her hand, I see the familiar ward—not quite as precise as Calden drew—but after a second, the lines all seem to smooth on their own, correcting the slight flaws.

Calden didn't say it would do that—

"If you draw it right, the ward will perfect itself," Alani explains, holding her pen toward me. "But if you're too far off, the ward... well, it won't recognize itself, you might say."

"As if it's alive," I murmur, taking the pen.

"The power in them is. Alive as the God who grants it," Alani says.

Her casual comment reminds me again that I'm not just drawing pictures, I'm stewarding a great and holy power that only a small percentage of humanity has ever been entrusted with.

I set the pen against the fountain with renewed purpose, noticing a distinct steadiness in my hand that wasn't there the last time I attempted to draw the Purification Ward. I would credit the endowing if it weren't so obvious that the difference is in who is spectating.

When I'm done, I retract my hand and lean closer. To my surprise, the lines even out and thicken on their own, just as Alani's did.

"Goodness," Alani says with a bright chuckle. "Perhaps teaching you will be easier than I thought."

I almost admit that I practiced with Calden, not wanting her to think me too impressive, but she pipes on.

"Of course, drawing it is one thing, but igniting is another." She holds out her hand for the pen, and I return it to her. "Once you're used to it, it doesn't take much, but as a beginner, you might need to be patient with yourself."

"I'll try," I say.

She tucks her pen away. "So, all you have to do is focus on your ward and will it to activate."

I glance at Rhiana, who watches from a few paces away. "Will it, how? Do I just think it?"

Alani scans the sky, as if searching for the right way to explain the concept. "It's more than thinking it. It's... well, it's something like you have to *want* for it to activate and command it to do so at once."

"So, if I didn't *really* want to purify this water for some reason, I couldn't just demand it to be purified with my thoughts?"

"That's it," she says, then she gestures toward the fountain for me to try.

I remember this idea, vaguely, from when Calden explained the conditions of the Healing Ward to me. But I hadn't realized that it applied to all wards, though in a less complex way.

"What if I wasn't sure?" I ask, the memory of the Healing Ward's conditions making me recall something else I've wanted to consult her about. "Would it work if I felt indifferent about it?"

"No," Alani says without hesitation, but her mouth hangs open, as if at a loss for how to explain why.

"Your whole mind, body, and heart must come into alignment," Rhiana says with a cautious glance toward Alani. When Alani smiles at her, Rhiana's confidence returns, and she approaches us. "Your mind commands the energy, your body conducts it, and your heart releases it. If your heart disagrees with the action, it will not release the energy. However, it is possible to train or condition our hearts into cohesion over time for specific uses."

My brows press together, and I turn to stare up at the trees. *Odd,* I think when I notice yellow leaves speckled through the oaks. Soltûm, our warmest season, has just begun. Why are the leaves turning shades of yellow? Is that normal for astrias?

I blink the curiosity away, already having enough to think about.

"How would one do that?" I direct the rest of my question between the two women. "How do you condition your heart to do something it doesn't want to do?"

Alani and Rhiana exchange a glance, as if sensing I'm not talking about purifying water anymore, but something far more significant.

"With help, miss, and much practice," Rhiana says.

"Help?" But I realize what she means immediately after saying it. "From El-Alam."

Rhiana nods. "He conditions the heart, should the heart be willing."

I want to ask ten more skeptical questions about that single answer, but my interest clings to something else. "Does this apply to the Healing Ward? Could someone condition their heart to heal despite bitterness, unforgiveness, or apathy?"

Both women's gazes center on me, but Rhiana answers first. "The Healing Ward is in a category of its own, miss. As a Conditional Ward, it retains the same stipulations as all wards, plus the added requirements. Bitterness and unforgiveness inhibit the heart from releasing pure love, which is the energy required to heal. That is why it is necessary that you hold nothing against the person you are trying to heal. Of course, this is infinitely easier said than done, unless someone continuously trains their heart to release the negative inhibitors when needed."

"So..." I take a moment to collect my theories before finishing. "Does that mean someone can get better at healing with practice, like with other wards?"

"Yes, that's true for all wards," Rhiana says.

"You're asking because Calden healed you, aren't you?" Alani butts in, and heat floods my face.

No sense in denying it.

"Yes."

"The Sovereign Prince is one of the most powerful healers we have," Rhiana says offhandedly.

Is there nothing he doesn't excel at, besides personal relationships?

"But that's not what you're getting at," Alani says, smiling wider. "You want to know if he's fallen for you."

I flinch at her boldness. "No, it's... it's just that we haven't known each other for very long. How could he feel that strongly about me? To bring me back when I was nearly dead?" *And why couldn't the man I knew as a child not do so instead?* "Is Calden simply that well-practiced?"

They leave my questions dangling until my pulse thuds in my ears.

"Calden can heal strangers," Alani answers at last. "Like myself, when the *incident* happened. While he couldn't complete the healing because of the severity of my injuries and our lack of time together, he mended me considerably for someone he barely knew. And now he has another year of experience."

"So, his magic is just that powerful?" *Not his feelings for me?*

Then what was that warm sensation inside when he healed me? The feeling I took as his care washing over me? Was it only magic?

Rhiana adjusts her rippled shirt collar and meets my eyes. "There is a way to heal in greater measures than our hearts are presently capable of, but I cannot speak for the Sovereign Prince to say if he used it. It would be better to ask him, miss, so that he may tell you himself how he healed you. Anything else I'd say is mere speculation."

"But what's the other way?"

Rhiana shakes her head at Alani, seeming to caution against any further explanation, before turning back to me. "Ask the Sovereign Prince."

I toy with a strand of my hair, trying to decipher what the feeling crawling through my chest is, besides that it makes me dizzy.

"What about Elias?" I ask. "He couldn't heal me. Not even a little."

But he loves me, doesn't he? Always has?

"I don't believe he has done much healing in his few years with us," Alani says. "Inexperience could have worked against him."

I hug my core, regretting again that I didn't recognize Elias as Kieran sooner—and worse, that I made him feel inferior to Calden on the way here. It's my fault he couldn't heal me. I wounded him too deeply for him to set it aside that soon.

But wouldn't his level of hurt prove the strength of his love? Don't the ones we care the most about have the greatest ability to hurt us? Wouldn't bitterness also impair Calden if he had romantic feelings for me, considering he'd just discovered my and Elias's past and my capture took place during a private walk with Elias?

"If I may?" Rhiana asks, though even with my nod of approval, her tone remains hesitant. "Attempting to discern their feelings for you by this one event is highly unfair to all three of you. And the more important matter—as far as you are concerned—is *you* deciding your own feelings. For what does the affection of one matter, if it's the other your heart longs for?"

I seal my lips, grateful for the cool gust that blows my hair into my face like a veil.

"Do you know who your heart longs for, miss?" Rhiana presses in my pause.

I contemplate her question, recounting all my recent memories of them both, but it only adds to my confusion. I shake my thoughts out of my head. With everything else happening, which man I prefer should be at the very bottom of my list of concerns.

"Never mind. I shouldn't have even asked." I focus back on the Purification Ward on the fountain. "We don't have time for this."

ELIAS

The familiar feeling of marching down tunnel after tunnel with none but the Sovereign Prince at my heels almost tricks me into thinking we've gone back in time to the days before the Bind. Before Nori, especially.

I've lost count of how many times Cal pulled me off my route, asking me to take him somewhere or get him into a certain town. The only time I ever felt as much apprehension as I do now was when he wanted to take down Rimrir, the stone golem in the Rimrook Mountains near Behria. I spent the whole trek there silently arguing with myself. *Should I visit Nori? Should I leave her alone?* I was so close to Behria, closer than I'd been since Nori's papa sent me to live with my grandparents in the Western Isles.

At least three times during our last night camping in the mountains, I almost left to go see Nori—even if from afar. But I knew I wouldn't be able to resist talking to her, so I convinced myself to stay put. If Hunters somehow detected me and spotted us together, they might have suspected her or interrogated her for information. Then Nori, with her lousy ability to lie, would reveal her true beliefs about the Wardens, and the Hunters would have punished her.

But that wasn't all that held me back.

I was afraid—afraid that she'd forgotten about me and wouldn't care who I was now.

That was also part of why I didn't tell her I was Kieran right away. I wanted to see if she'd recognize me on her own and observe how she'd respond to the person I became. But when that backfired, I put my mask on and pretended her failure to recognize me and Cal pushing me away didn't hurt.

And, in the process, I made myself look like a scoundrel.

"It's been quiet," Cal says, and my thoughts fade.

I look over my shoulder. The aquamarine crystals cast a watery light across him and seem to illuminate his vibrant irises, even with his hood shadowing the upper part of his face. He's had the hood up since we encountered the supplier four days ago, like he doesn't want to risk someone else recognizing him after the way the previous encounter went down.

"We're off the main route," I say. "This way's faster. Just a bit more dank."

Cal wipes the condensation off his steel breastplate and looks at his wet fingertips. "I'll say."

"All the rain soaking through from aboveground doesn't help. There's been so much lately. Kinda strange for Soltûm."

Cal shrugs away my comment. "If this route gets us there faster, I don't mind."

"We should be there in a few days," I say, feeling the weight of the humidity sevenfold now that I've noticed it again. I usually avoid leaving the major routes, which are wider, more heavily traveled, and well-ventilated through apertures large and small. But as he said, *if it gets us there faster...*

We continue in silence, stepping down a staircase carved by a stone golem years ago. Those powerful Sentries fashioned most of the underground before they became the Accursed—back when they were friends of Wardens and mankind, when Toaph Elbara still reigned. But I only know that from the stories. The former Sentries became our enemies just a few years before I was born.

I lead Cal for another two hours along the fusty route until we finally reach a chamber large enough to set up camp in.

"Not a haven," I say as my boots thump into the space. "But the next haven along the route is too far, unless we want to take a detour to the one nearest to us."

"A bed isn't worth the loss of time," Cal says, checking his Omen Mark before setting his bag in the dirt.

His comment pulls me back into my memories. When I first met him upon joining the Wardens, I assumed he was like Landon. He had that look about him, the look of privilege—a smile like he'd never endured a hard thing in his life and a voice that spoke like he never doubted a word out of his own mouth. I was inclined to hate him on principle.

But a year and a half into my time with the Wardens, he showed up in the training yard while I was out there trying to prove to myself that I deserved to belong amongst these blessed people. He revealed himself to be humble despite his position as the future Sovereign, and he took me in as his mentee since I was only fifteen at the time, and him, twenty-one. We started meeting out there to spar every few days, and slowly, as I grew into adulthood, I watched his princely mask dissolve, and the sense of him being so much older went with it. Now I hardly remember the age gap between us, and reflecting on it, I'm not sure he really wanted someone to mentor as much as he wanted a friend. Especially since he lost Corwin and Corene shortly after my induction.

We set up our camp, building a fire with the stores of wood left for who knows how long in the chamber. It takes forever to kindle a flame on the moist twigs, but finally, the heat dries them and a small, steady blaze stirs to life. The trembling light throws a giant shadow of Cal against the wall, as he sits on the ground in front of the fire. I join him on the opposite side once I've arranged my prop stick and kettle.

By the time the kettle is whistling, I've replayed the entire journey to the citadel with Nori, wondered about Toaph Elbara and what Nori will have to do to further help Cal restore him, and debated if I should press Cal for his theories, but I decide against it after seeing the thousand-mile-away look in his eyes.

The trickle of me pouring my tea stirs him from his half-dead trance and wins a familiar scowl.

"You'll be happy to know I brought starroot, not mullenberry," I say, setting the empty kettle aside to cool. "Doesn't smell half as much."

Cal's grimace remains. "No, it smells *twice* as much. Can't you smell it? It's like moldy soil."

I glance around the space we occupy. While mostly stone, there is damp ground beneath us. "That's not the tea."

"Yet I didn't notice it until you brewed it."

"That's because you weren't paying attention."

Cal seemingly submits to this conclusion and drags his bag over to pick through his rations. He settles on a chunk of bread that's gone stale, judging by the crunch when he bites into it. The blank look in his eyes suggests he hardly notices it as he goes back to staring at the fire.

I help myself to my own rations and sip my tea. The blue tinge of starroot always reminds me of fellion blood, but the earthy flavor is calming at least. When I've eaten all I'll allow myself to, I turn back to Cal and see he's taken maybe two more bites in the last ten minutes, and if not for the tension dimpling his jaw, I'd think he's fallen asleep sitting up with his eyes open.

"Cal."

His entire body jerks. *Empyreal Skies.* Was *he asleep?*

"What?" he asks, then looks at his bread like he forgot it was in his hand.

"You alive?"

"Last I checked." He feigns feeling for his pulse on his neck before a lame version of his usual smile returns.

"You won't be for long like that," I say, nodding to his bread, but really, I could point out his entire existence. The bags under his eyes suggest he's hardly slept since we made it to the citadel, and there's a slight tremble in his hands—like that bread isn't the only food he's forgotten to eat recently. "You're still thinking about what that supplier said, aren't you?"

Cal seems to consider taking a bite of his bread, but lowers it back to his lap instead. "That and everything else."

"Well, talk about it," I say when he stops there.

"Mother has always said worry only grows louder when spoken aloud." Cal tries again to smile. "It's not worth giving it a voice."

I rest my elbows on my bent knees. "You know what my mum said?"

This gains his full attention, and I realize I've rarely said a word to him about either of my parents until the other day when I mentioned my papa dying in Raevre. He doesn't even know that my mum died of the same venom that nearly took Nori.

"She said if we leave our worries in our minds, we can't hear how unfounded they are when said out loud."

Cal releases a soft chuckle. "Whose mother is right then?"

"Only one way to find out."

Cal sighs, but he looks more alive than he did a few minutes ago. "I wouldn't even know where to begin. There's so much, Lias. Too much."

"What else am I doing right now?"

"Sipping the sweat of the earth and looking for ways to scrutinize me."

I finish my tea with added gusto and set the cup aside. "Well, down to one of those. Give me some fodder."

Cal returns his bread to a linen wrap. Hopefully, he'll revisit it after he spills his concerns on me.

"I suppose it's mostly the supplier's words haunting me at the moment," Cal starts, with a low-set gaze. "He's not wrong to question me. It *has* been a long time, and it is pathetic that I'd only learn this recent development of Toaph's survival now, and through defectors, at that. How could I be so oblivious?"

"I don't know, Cal. Seems like dead Guardians are trying to communicate with almost anyone these days. Hard to miss." I add a smirk in case his exhaustion causes him to overlook my jest.

"But for twenty-five years?"

"It's not like he's said, 'Hello, this is Toaph Elbara. Come find me at *X* location.' He's been a little rude, if you ask me—making you lose it on us."

A trace of Cal's genuine smile comes back, but it dies again before he speaks. "That's the other thing. If he's merely speaking with me, why—*and how*—does my power release like that? Why don't I simply fall unconscious or into a trance?" There's a pause that I can't fill with a theory readily enough before he continues. "Mother and Seer Josiah speculate that it's unnatural for an Empyreal Guardian to communicate in such a way, so in my mortality, I'm going into some sort of shock or terror state. That makes sense for the emotional reaction, but still, how could my power work without wards?"

I sit with this for a long while, suddenly feeling like my mind and body are no longer in contact with each other. But when I finally find something worth saying, I clear my throat to draw his attention.

"Maybe he's not only trying to impart a message. Maybe he's trying to give you some additional power."

Cal sits up straighter, eyes narrowing as if to say, *Keep going.*

"Just a thought, but if he is injured or trapped somewhere, he's probably going to need you to do something significant to help him—something beyond what a normal Warden can do. So, maybe he's trying to transfer some additional power to you."

Cal scratches his chin. "But why me?"

"Because you're the future Sovereign."

"I wasn't supposed to be."

"He must have known where you'd end up," I say. "Or your theories about why your birth parents left you are wrong. Maybe they never saw you freak out—you weren't even endowed with power until after the Lady took you in, right? And she never saw it happen until after the endowing. So, maybe your birth parents never witnessed an episode, and Toaph chose you after."

Cal stares at his wrapped bread, looking sickened by the sight of it.

"Then why would they leave me?" he asks, glancing at me long enough for me to see the hurt swimming in his eyes.

Always got to make it worse, huh, Lias?

"Because they didn't know you, Cal," I say.

Cal keeps his gaze averted awhile before commenting, "Your theory about Toaph is interesting."

I sense this would be a good time to shut my mouth before I say something to spoil his appetite again. I scope out the small atrium for a place to lie down for the night. Spotting it in an oval-shaped crevice, I gather my belongings.

"Lias," Cal says as I'm turning away, and I stop. "Thank you for coming."

"Thank me by finishing that bread and getting some sleep. I don't want to go back to the citadel dragging your corpse," I tease. "Your mother might think I did it. Then you'll really have ruined my perfect ledger."

Cal lifts the bread, as if in promise to heed my words, and I retreat into my nook for the night.

CALDEN

When a prolonged stillness alerts me that Elias has fallen asleep, I set the last quarter of my bread aside. My stomach churns from the little I ate—a feeling that hasn't left since the supplier's harsh words. But it's Elias's suggestion that occupies my mind now.

Could Toaph be doing something more to me than simply sending a message? Or is his small connection with my spirit enough to cause my power to surge outside of its normal limitations? Seers and Sovereigns have conversed aloud with the Empyreal Guardian before without such reactions, but Toaph has never spoken to someone's inmost being. Could that make it different?

Unable to make sense of it, I try for the hundredth time to draw the Guardian's voice to me, first with an empty mind, then with direct questions posed toward him like a prayer in my thoughts. *Where are you? What do you need from me?*

No answer. As usual.

How many lives were threatened or even lost today because I failed to hear Toaph's words? How many more will be endangered tomorrow?

Elias shifts, the soft noise reminding me of his parting statement to me before turning in. My condition must be even worse than I'm allowing myself to realize. I need to at least *try* to stay alive. I'd be even more useless to the world dead than I am now.

I find a nook, not quite as enclosed as the one Elias claimed, and force myself to sleep.

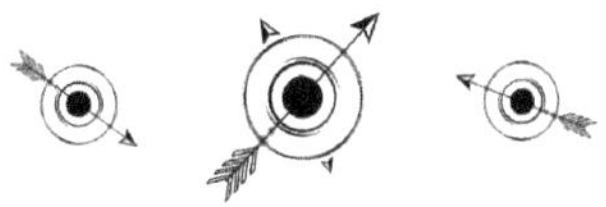

A hot puff of air against my cheek startles me awake. My eyes open, and I find myself nose-to-nose with a long, blue-black snout. I lurch away, and a low snarl rumbles from the animal. It crouches, the aquamarine glow of the crystals catching on the tips of the wolflike creature's raised hackles. Its pointed ears pull back, lips curling to reveal bared fangs.

I freeze, cautiously studying the canine's illuminated eyes. Flecks of glowing gold and silver shimmer in its fur, like sprinkles of stardust that twinkle as it heaves.

A *canyx*, I realize at last—a wolflike species of Accursed that can travel like phantoms through shadows without detection. They were once protectors in the night, said to patrol the lonely spaces outside civilization in search of lost travelers to aid. But now, they'd sooner hunt them. What is one doing down here in the passages and without its pack?

My hand twitches, and I nearly command my Conjuration Ward to activate and equip me with my swordstaff, but I hesitate. The canyx could have sunk his fangs into my throat in my sleep had he wanted to. Why didn't he?

Watching his ethereal eyes, I slowly shift into a sitting position. His head dips lower, the tone of his growl sinking with it. My throat dries, but he still doesn't lunge.

Is he... not cursed? Or is he simply afraid to attack without the aid of his pack?

An utterly foolish idea crosses my mind, and I extend my hand toward him, fingers trembling with apprehension. The wolflike creature's growl vibrates even louder.

"We weren't supposed to be enemies," I whisper.

The idiocy of my action weighs on me as he stares—an ancient creature with memories spanning to the creation of Silvirdia itself, looking upon me, whose life is but a breath in comparison. But as I fight to still my hand's trembling, his growl quiets. Then, slowly, his black lips seal his fangs away, like a warrior sheathing his sword.

I hold my breath as the canyx creeps closer to sniff my fingers. His wet snout brushes my skin. He lets out a soft whine, and his tail curls between his hind legs, as if upon smelling me, he sensed something that intimidated him. Does he know who I am? Does my status as Sovereign Prince scare him? Can he sense that I'm a Master Warden and doesn't wish to risk ending his lengthy life by attacking me?

Or could it truly be that he isn't cursed at all?

He retreats a step, and the crystals' light illuminates the matted fur on his right side. *Blood,* I realize. He's injured. That explains why he hasn't dematerialized and fled into the shadows; they can't do that when wounded enough to bleed.

But right as I'm wondering what hurt him, I hear a voice down the shaft, chased by an angry hushing. The canyx and I both turn toward the sound, seeming to forget the threat of each other at once. I glance at my Omen Mark, registering its tingle, and oddly, the way it points toward the intruders rather than the creature beside me. Normally, the arrow would favor my nearest enemy.

The canine's bushy tail tucks even further between his legs, but a deep growl looses from his throat as his moonlike gaze pierces the darkness toward what must be Blood Wardens, judging by my mark's warning.

Finally, understanding hits me. Blood Wardens captured and brought this canyx into the underground. They intended to sacrifice him, to use his magic-laced blood to fuel their corrupt warding pens.

"Hide, friend," I whisper. "I will protect you."

The statement feels almost blasphemous after a quarter century of fighting the Accursed in defense of man. But a typical Accursed would not have hesitated to attack me, which inclines me to believe this canyx has maintained his integrity—though how, I'm not sure.

The canyx recoils a step but otherwise ignores my command.

Cautiously, I turn away from him and conjure my sword-staff into my hand. The long shaft with two curved blades on each end manifests, and the canyx's growl ceases as he inspects the weapon. I almost murmur a reassurance that I don't mean to use my staff against him, but the encroaching footsteps cause me to hold my tongue.

The steps suddenly stop. I imagine the defectors checking their own Omen Marks and forming a silent plan of attack beyond the curve of the tunnel. I should have used a Shroud Ward in this chamber so their Omen Marks wouldn't detect us. Where was my head last night?

A flicker in the canyx's attention makes my gaze swerve toward Elias's nook, where he's finally easing out. His dark eyes widen at the sight of the animal beside me, and the canyx releases a warning snarl in his direction.

"Friend, not foe," I mutter to the beast, then I shake my head at Elias, hoping he understands my order to not harm the canyx.

His expression contorts, but at my signal, he turns his focus to the tunnel opening, silently drawing his sword. The sharp tip of his blade just glistens into view when two orange orbs launch toward the canyx and me.

I swing my swordstaff, igniting an energy shield from an engraved ward on the shaft. A blue wall expands in front of the canyx and me in time to block the attack, and the spheres combust against the shield. I maintain the field between us, peering through the sheet of watery energy to the two hooded figures now standing on the other side.

A subtle whir announces Elias's vitality sphere as he ignites it, but he holds it in warning across the space, awaiting my command.

I thin my shield to better see the defectors' black-painted faces. So... *young*, I realize, noticing their short heights and the juvenile softness of their features. One looks hardly over thirteen and the other, maybe three years older. Both their stances lack the confidence of defectors more advanced in age.

Could we rehabilitate these girls? The youngest, at least?

The older readies an orange vitality orb, but like Elias, she keeps it in her hand. Her nostrils flare as she looks between us. The younger girl grimaces at the canyx, confirming my theory, but then her gaze meets mine and terror replaces every trace of frustration in her round face. *She recognizes me.* Her petite hand grips the other girl's cloak, and she tugs at it with a pleading expression that the elder misses.

"What were you doing with this canyx?" I ask, though it's obvious. A canyx wouldn't fear such small humans unless they proved themselves more violent than their age should allow for.

The older girl's vitality orb flickers, almost going out. Her mouth opens, pale lips trembling, but then she flinches, and her orb shoots across the space toward Elias. He releases a small hiss of pain as the girls flee into the tunnel. Their boots thud along the dense ground, sharp breaths ricocheting down the stony shaft.

I dissolve my shield, stepping once in pursuit of them before thinking better of it. I'd have to capture them and haul them all the way back to the citadel for potential rehabilitation—that or kill them, and I've already decided against such an action. They're too young.

Perhaps Toaph Elbara can help them himself soon enough.

My swordstaff dissipates from my hold, and I check the canyx to be sure he hasn't turned on me. He eyes me with similar skepticism, but his ears are tucked back, as if to signal he means no harm.

"Lias, how bad is it?" I ask, remembering Elias's hiss of pain. "Do you need healing?"

Elias gives me a doubtful look as he undoes the top buttons of his seared shirt. He peels his shirt back enough to reveal a shining red wound across his shoulder. "Just a burn. Don't worry about it," he says, letting the shirt cover the wound again. "I see the Oracle is getting to them young."

I frown. Even the older girl seemed young to be a Blood Warden, but the other? Unreasonable. What did the Oracle say to her to lead these children into such dark ways?

Elias steps in my direction, reawakening the canyx's growl, and he halts.

"I don't think he's cursed," I say, despite the fur prickled along the canine's spine.

"Sure, he looks friendly to me," Elias sneers, and the canyx curls his lips even further back.

I extend my hand toward the dog's muzzle and speak to him softly. "I know Elias may seem questionable, but he won't hurt you. He's with me."

"Questionable?" Elias snorts.

The canyx's expression calms, though a quiet warning rumbles in his throat.

"He's not cursed," I repeat to Elias. "He's just afraid and hurt."

Elias crosses his arms, though the motion makes him wince. "You know that canyxes are known for being deceptive, right? He's probably waiting for you to drop your guard."

My lip twitches. Truthfully, I'd forgotten that detail about their nature. As Sentries, the canyxes' clever ways helped them avoid danger, especially when leading those lost in the wilderness back to their homes. Now, they use their cunning strategies for ambushes.

But the canyx meets my gaze, and I recall how we met.

"My guard was down when he found me. If he'd wanted to kill me, he'd have attempted to do so while I was asleep." I lift my Omen Mark, showing Elias how the faintly colored arrow points in the direction the Blood Warden girls went rather than at the canyx.

Elias checks his mark and holds it out. *Red* and aimed at the canyx.

"It will change," I assure him, though I have no foundation for my certainty. "Give him a moment to see you mean him no harm."

Elias raises a brow at the animal. "Yes, let's give the growling beast known for trickery a chance to see that I'm not a threat. Makes sense."

I sigh, then suddenly recall the canyx's injury. Could I heal an animal? A Sentry, at that? Might that alleviate his tension some?

Moving slowly, I kneel beside him and slip my pen from my belt. Unable to draw the ward on its fur, I draw the flowerlike glyph on my palm instead, hoping my mastery of the ward will enable me to channel the effect into the animal.

"What are you doing?" Elias asks as I tuck my pen away.

"Trying something new," I answer, then I lock eyes with the canyx. "I have to touch your wound to heal it. It will only hurt for a moment."

"*Cal*," Elias snaps, stepping toward us, but another growl from the canyx stops him. "This is probably what it's hoping for—you to heal it so it can kill you."

The canyx grunts, as if to object.

"It will be fine, Lias."

My hand tenses, but I reach toward the canyx before Elias can offer another protest. The canyx watches me astutely, seeming to understand exactly what I am trying to do.

Empyrean forbid Elias is right about you, I think toward the creature before I press my palm into its blood-sodden fur.

NORIELLE

I squeeze my hands into fists, trying—for what must be the hundredth time—to ignite the Purification Ward I drew on the courtyard fountain days ago. I failed every attempt when Alani and Rhiana hovered nearby, and eventually, Alani thought it best to move me on from attempting to use wards to simply practicing their designs and memorizing their purposes.

A dull pain presses the base of my skull when the ward still doesn't activate, and I plop onto the grass in defeat. Dawn crests the cliffsides, turning the waterfalls into golden, glowing streams—the way the fountain might look if I'd successfully ignited the Purification Ward—and spite turns my gaze to the grass. I pluck one of the blades, tearing it into tiny pieces. If only I could dismantle all my problems so easily...

"Ah, Miss Norielle, do the benches not suit you?"

I toss aside the shredded grass, registering the spritely cadence of Seer Josiah's voice behind me. The cool breeze flicks the green shards away as I rise to my feet to meet the Seer's sunlit gaze. He rubs the end of his mustache, an amused look on his face.

"I was trying to activate this ward," I say, heat blazing across my cheeks at the thought of not just another Warden, but *the Seer* witnessing my failure.

"Indeed, you were," he says with a brief glance around. "But now?"

But now, what?

His eyes prompt a response despite my confusion, and I go off my best guess of what he means. "Now I'm taking a break, because it was... frustrating me."

He walks to the fountain and stretches his hand into a trickling stream. The water splatters against his fingertips, and a smile further curls his lips. "Most Wardens have a good deal of trouble on their first attempt," he says. "It's not the easiest of tasks, aligning our whole self toward something. It always seems that one part of our being falters as soon as the other two are in agreement."

"Other Wardens make it seem so easy."

"Ah, they do, don't they?" The Seer turns to me with a gentle look and retracts his hand from the fountain. "It's like anything. The more you do it, the easier it gets, unless something poses a particular challenge."

I chew the inside of my lip, wanting to complain that I don't have time for that. I need to be ready to leave by the time Calden and Elias return. Even if they come back empty-handed, Calden will surely want to go *somewhere* soon. And what will he do if I'm not ready? Postpone our mission to save the world because of my incapacities or leave me behind?

"So much conflict," the Seer says, his gaze set on the skies. "Your thoughts are like arrows shot into a squall—tossed aside before ever reaching any destination."

I swallow. "You can hear my thoughts?"

Seer Josiah chuckles. "Hear them, no. Certainly not. *Sense* them, however? *My*. Couldn't anyone?"

I seal my lips, unsure how to take his words. Is he criticizing me? Is he right? Can everyone see I'm a mess inside?

"You don't worry alone, child," he says, kindness cradling his words. "All of us feel troubled to some extent over it all. The world. Our role in it. The man El-Alam has charged with finding Toaph." He eyes me more closely as he says the last part, as if sensing that many of my concerns have to do with Calden himself. "You feel pressured. Rushed to become who you were called to be. To be everything the Sovereign Prince needs—not tomorrow, but today. It's no wonder your mind is turbulent. And may we not forget the division in your heart."

He pauses, his gaze reaching into mine with such focus that I'm tempted to question if he's *sure* he can't read my thoughts.

"That's so very much turmoil in one young woman," he continues. "And that's not even accounting for the fact that you're still grieving your life before this and everyone who was once part of it—even if the separation is only for a time."

My heart lurches at his implication. Does he believe I'll be able to return to my family once we find Toaph?

A sudden dizziness swirls over me. Of course I could. If Toaph reigns again, the Wardens won't have to hide anymore. I could be a daughter and a sister *and* a Warden all at once. Not one over the other.

"Can you..." I hold my question, afraid to speak so boldly to the Seer even after all the pleasant conversations we've had in his library about books.

He waves me on.

"Can you see it?" I ask, more quietly than I first intended. "The world when Toaph Elbara returns?"

"My sight is limited only to what El-Alam wishes for me to see—that which He deems necessary. However, there are other ways to see the future, dear girl."

I almost mention the Oracle, but the twinkle in his eyes suggests his thoughts are not in such dark places.

"How?" I ask.

His hand cups my shoulder. "Hope."

I smile, and he slowly retracts his hand, his fingers wiggling like he's stirring up the breeze.

"While the future we see when we choose to hope can never be guaranteed, it gives us the strength we need to endure today—to help us draw closer to that potential outcome." His chin lifts, the rising sun reflecting on his face and seeming to hide any trace of age on his skin.

I fill my lungs, as if breathing the same air as this man might infuse me with his optimism and youthful spirit. It seems to work, if only barely.

"Why don't you try again?" Seer Josiah prompts, his billowy sleeve fluttering as he gestures toward the fountain. "And this time, remember, there is no hurry. El-Alam called you when He meant to. Not a minute too soon or too late."

I soak in his comforting expression another moment before daring to approach the fountain again. Now more than before, I should feel the pressure. The Seer stands by, hopeful and expectant. Yet his words swathe me with peace, calming my heart and soothing my headache.

I set my fingertips against the ward I drew earlier this week. Then, one by one, I dismiss my thoughts and worries. It doesn't matter how long I take. I have as long as I need. Calden and Elias will return safely to the citadel and with answers. The only impossible expectations hanging over me are my own.

Purify, I command the ward with my thoughts.

I cage my breath, waiting for the water within the fountain to light.

Nothing.

I force myself to remain calm, and I repeat the command from my heart, as if this were the last possible opportunity to purify the water I'll ever have.

Purify.

Light glimmers from the sprout-like symbol, illuminating it before the glow spreads to the water within the fountain. It begins with the middle tier where the ward is, then the brilliant water pours into the base and spews from the top tier until the entire fountain flows with gleaming, almost honey-like water.

I gasp through a wide smile, finding the Seer's gaze for further affirmation that this was me—*I did this.*

He returns the expression, then we watch the fountain until the purification is complete, and the glow is doused.

"A most impressive start," the Seer says, then he gives me one last pat to my shoulder and turns toward the citadel.

16

CALDEN

I clench my jaw as a sharp sting spreads across my side, like a dagger sliced me. The pain intensifies even as my hand slips away from the canyx's matted fur. Navy blood stains my skin, but the wound must have sealed beneath his coat, because the wolflike creature watches me with relief mingled with a trace of concern.

"It's all right," I tell the animal, despite my throbbing side.

The canyx whines, leaning so his muzzle gently rests on my bent knee. I smile, marveling at him until I barely feel the pain I bore to heal him anymore. A *real* Sentry. How could that be after all this time? A Sentry unaffected by the curse hasn't been seen in twenty-five years.

I cautiously bring my clean hand toward his nose to let him sniff me again, then I stroke the plush, midnight-toned fur along his neck.

"Shall you come with us?" I ask him.

Elias's glare beats against me like a hot Soltûm sun, but he remains silent.

I try to read the canyx's radiant eyes for an answer, but despite his ancient lifespan, he's still unable to communicate with me any better than an intelligent dog. But if I had to guess, his expression almost seems inquiring... as if he wants me to decide his path.

"Where is the nearest exit?" I ask, turning to Elias.

He watches the canyx with unwavering focus, like he expects him to attack the moment I avert my gaze. "There isn't one. We'd have to backtrack miles."

I consider Elias and his concerns for a moment before dismissing them. He'll see. The canyx means no harm.

My hand slips to the side of the canyx's face, and I gently nudge him to lift his head and fully meet my gaze. "Then you'll have to accompany us. At least, until we're on our way back, so we can let you out."

The canyx watches me for a long moment before standing. His fluffy, foxlike tail flicks behind his slender figure, as if in agreement.

"You're serious," Elias says to me.

"Quite." I turn to gather my belongings. "Perhaps we're wrong about more than we thought. Maybe Ta'Nathel and his curse aren't as powerful as we've long believed." I wince slightly at my own words. No, Ta'Nathel is *at least* as powerful as we believe, considering what he's done to Toaph Elbara. But maybe there are some exceptions to his curse over the Sentries. If Toaph survived, then some of them must know their true master lives and therefore they aren't subject to Ta'Nathel.

I lock eyes with the canyx again. Might he know where Toaph is?

Elias releases a dramatic sigh, as if to inform the entire underground of his disapproval. "Well, don't even think about naming it. That'll only make it that much more personal when it turns on you."

"Pity," I say, flashing a smile his way. "I've already thought of one."

The humor falls from Elias's face.

"He's a reflection of what was." I meet the canyx's luminous eyes. "So, I'm going to call him Echo."

The pain in my side subsides within the hour, and my strength fully returns. The canyx—*Echo*—trots beside me, the occasional rumble in his throat declaring Elias has yet to earn his trust. And likewise, Elias's frequent checks over his shoulder suggest the canyx has some trust to earn himself.

I spend most of our walk pondering the possibility of more Sentries still being on our side and ruing the choices of the two young defector girls. But all my thoughts seem to lead to more questions, and before long, we are stepping into a haven to stop for the day.

Echo enters ahead of us, his bushy tail twitching as he diligently sniffs every piece of furniture and cranny in the haven. Elias eyes him with continued skepticism, but I carry on as I normally would when not accompanied by a canyx. After changing and forcing myself—on account of my promise to Elias—to eat at least half of a meal, I settle on a lopsided couch in the front chamber with every intention of pursuing Toaph again. But Elias plops into a chair at the table across the space, producing his lyre for the first time on this trip.

I shift to stand, thinking I'll seek solitude somewhere else, but when Echo prances in and lies at my feet, I sink back into my seat. His ears twitch as I pet his sparkling indigo coat, but his tail gives an approving wag.

A break, Calden. Take a break, I demand of myself.

Elias tunes his lyre and gives all ten strings a single pluck, allowing each note to ring out and bounce around the stone walls. Satisfied with his work, he begins a familiar song—one he often warms up with. I half listen as he continues, more entertained by how Echo raises his head, tilting it sideways as Elias plays, than the song itself. Echo must have heard music before, considering how ancient he is, but perhaps it's been so long since he's been able to get close to a human that the sound is intriguing to him. Or calming, rather, because the canyx soon lays his head down again and falls asleep within a few minutes.

I continue stroking him, wishing I could find rest that easily myself.

Elias finishes his song before looking over with a simper. "Enjoying your new dog?"

Echo stirs at Elias's voice but settles again with his majestic head against his thick paws.

"Yes, actually," I say. "I am."

Elias taps the mahogany frame of his lyre with his thumb. "You're not taking him back to the citadel, are you?"

My fingers curl into Echo's coarse fur. "No, that would be a mistake. The guards would kill him before I could even try to explain he's safe. But I'll enjoy his company while I can."

Elias gives the canyx another cynical look. "Well, at least watch what you say around him. He could be a spy."

I scowl, particularly at the way Elias's comment draws up my own skepticism about Echo. I look around for something to help change the subject before that skepticism takes root too deeply, and my gaze lands back on Elias's lyre.

"Can I try it?" I ask with a nod toward the instrument.

Elias gives a slow blink before holding up his lyre. "This?"

"Yes, that. Just for a moment."

Elias's knuckles pale as he tightens his grip on it, but after a long consideration, he passes the lyre to me. I inspect the vine-like carving on the wood frame, twisting it to see the instrument from all angles. Then I rest it on my lap, mimicking the way I've seen Elias hold it so many times before.

"If you figure that thing out without even trying, I'm gonna kill you," Elias says.

I snigger. "My life is undoubtedly in no danger then. I have absolutely no idea what to do with it."

I senselessly pluck at a few strings, unable to make even the start of a melody but enjoying the feeling no less. Elias smirks, as if dignified by my lack of musical talent—one thing he can certainly hold over me.

If only I had time and energy for hobbies. Perhaps then I'd attempt to learn, or pick up some of my lost interests, like reading and sketching. But even once I've found Toaph, I'll have an entire underground kingdom to run, which will lend me little energy for such pursuits—unless by El-Alam's grace, the return of Toaph greatly reduces the burden of a Sovereign.

Suddenly, the feeling of the strings vibrating beneath my hands feels less appealing and the thought of lying in my room alone in the dark seems far more suitable. I paste on a smile and extend the lyre toward its proper owner. Elias snatches it.

"I'm going to get some sleep," I say, rising.

Elias gives me a farewell nod, thankfully missing the shift in my mood. At my heels, Echo stirs again from his light sleep and eyes me.

"Come with me, I suppose," I say to the canyx, resolving to trust my Omen Mark more than Elias's pessimism. Besides, I've heard dogs make good company for those with downcast souls.

Elias withholds any argument about me taking a "suspicious" creature into my room with me. I leave my door slightly ajar so Echo can leave if he wants. Then, with some apprehension, I climb into the dusty bed. Echo stares at me from across the room, eyes glowing as bright as the scattered crystals along the walls.

Please don't try to kill me in my sleep, I think, more fearful of his betrayal than the actual threat to my life itself.

Echo lies down where I can see him, like a mound of darkness-obscured fluff speckled with light. He returns to sleep within minutes, but I remain awake, listening as Elias carries on his music alone. Though he doesn't sing—he rarely does underground, or at least, not around me—I recognize the melody as one I have heard him sing before. My mind fills in the gaps, recalling the lyrics from the handful of times I've heard it.

"*Two shores, one sea,*
Will the tide bring you back to me?
I would swim, I would sail,
I would cross the waters deep."

The mournful way he's always sung it has often made me curious about who he grieves, though I never asked. But now, especially as he reaches the last measures of the song that infers this woman moved on to someone else, I realize who she is.

She's Norielle.

The bed whines as I shift, lying flat on my back to stare at the dark stone ceiling overhead. She's *his.* Even if she never chooses him, me attempting to win her over would be a death sentence for our friendship. A treason of the highest order.

It would be better if neither of us had her than for me to steal his greatest desire—and for what? A chance with a woman I barely know?

No. A pit forms in my stomach as a long-repressed admission fully rears its head. *For a chance with a woman I deemed truly brave enough to love me despite my curse.*

17

ELIAS

"What do you mean, there's nothing you can do?" I snap, balling my sweating hands. But my voice is higher than when I last heard it—younger.

Through the blur of my tears, I see Behria's top physician standing at Mum's bedside. The physician's face is as pallid as the curtains swaying over the window behind her. Sweat glimmers along her grey hairline, and a frown adds wrinkles to her chin.

Before she can answer, Mum lurches in her bed, knocking a tatty pillow onto the floor I'd swept just yesterday. She screams again—a sound more wretched and agonized than anything I've ever heard. The hoarse yell fades into a cry, then a whimper.

"There's nothing that can cure crypt crawler venom. I'm sorry," the physician repeats in a frail whisper.

My knees give way, but someone catches me. Her long, straight hair sweeps into my face, and I twist toward her small form to cry against her chest.

Nori. My Nori.

I should feel humiliated at her seeing me this way, but grief devours every other emotion until all I feel is the devastation, fear, and anger of watching Mum die—of hearing those sickening words.

There's nothing I can do.

The statement drives into my core like a flaming spear. There's nothing I can do.

It resonates so much with how I feel. So hopeless.

"Kieran," Nori says, but another wail from Mum silences her. She moves her small hands over my ears, dimming the horrid noise of my mother's painful cries beneath her palms.

I meet Nori's hazel eyes, almost turned green from the red swarming them. Tears slip down her face, streaking through her Soltûm-darkened freckles, but her steady gaze gives me the strength to gather myself. Mum needs me. For however many minutes she has left—she needs me.

I impulsively plant a kiss on Nori's forehead. She almost smiles, and I regret not saving that for better circumstances, but it was the best "thank you" I could think of for her being here with me.

Being with me through everything.

Could I even live without her?

I rise, turning toward my thrashing mum. Fresh agony tears open a wound that has barely started to heal—losing Papa to the war just months prior—as I near the bedside.

But when I look at the woman in the bed, it's not Mum's dark, curly hair or tanned skin I see. It's an older version of the girl who gave me the strength to stand again.

And she's dying. Dying in the same way as Mum.

Yet she doesn't scream, she only whimpers as tears soak her face and hair. I rush to her, suddenly taller than I was a moment ago, and slide a pen from my belt. I set it to her skin, drawing the flowerlike symbol of the Healing Ward just behind her Bind Mark. The arrow on the Bind Mark points beyond me to a man I abruptly realize is here with us.

Calden.

A bulge forms in my throat.

I ignore it, completing the Healing Ward before wrapping my shaking hand around the symbol. I think of everything Nori and I ever had and everything I ever wanted between us, hoping the love will emanate from my being and wash over her—that it will cleanse every single trace of the venom from her body. Not a fraction of me cares what will happen to me in exchange—live or die.

I just want to see that she'll be okay, even if it's the last thing I witness.

But my power feels stunted—trapped—like a dammed river.

She didn't recognize you, *whispers a voice in my head that always reminds me of Landon.* She doesn't even like you anymore.

I curse it. It doesn't matter. I don't care. I just want her alive.

The voice laughs at me. So much like the bully from Behria. If that were true, you'd be able to save her.

I banish the intrusive thoughts and focus on Nori again, reflecting on all the things I've ever valued about her—the fire well-contained inside her gentle spirit, her intelligence and love for learning, her bravery and determination. It's all still there. After all these years. But now it's no longer held within the frame of a young girl, but in a young woman whose beauty would have captivated me, history or not. And now there's the promise of so much more to her personality, so much more that I haven't had time yet to discover.

El-Alam, don't take that chance from me.

My prayer repeats again and again as I desperately seek to send my power into the Healing Ward—into Nori. But then she whines. I open my eyes again, and the sight of her weakened expression slaps me with the harshness of reality.

There's nothing I can do.

She's going to die in my arms.

No. I can't let her—

"Cal!" *I croak his name in utter defeat. I'd rather watch him steal her from my hands than watch her die.*

But he doesn't come.

"Calden!" I yelp again before turning to see he's preoccupied with defending himself against Corene, not once bothering to fight back.

I look at Nori, suddenly realizing what I need to do. I need to trade places with Cal—handle his past and give him mine.

I shift to stand.

My body judders, and my eyes open to a small haven room with blue crystals glaring from overhead. I peel back my wool blanket, catching my breath, as if I've just hiked to the top of Northspire Peak. How many nights am I going to relive this?

My clothes stick to my skin as I sit up, air cooling the thick sweat the nightmares induced. I scratch at my scalp, wishing I could scrape the memories from my mind. The one of Mum is old enough for me to numb and move on from, so long as I don't think about it too long, but with Nori—

I groan. *Empyreal Skies,* I never want to see that again.

Why did El-Alam have to choose Nori for Cal's Bind? Why couldn't He call her into the Wardens to be a scout or something like me? Then maybe all this would look different. I might have even been the recruiter sent to get her. And then I wouldn't feel angry at Cal half the time, as if he hasn't been the nearest thing to family I've had besides Ila since my grandparents died.

If only I could trade places with Nori. Not that she doesn't deserve the honor of being in Cal's Bind, but I can't stand knowing the danger she's in.

What if I lose her again? What if I lose them *both*?

I wipe my eyes and get up, unsure if it's morning yet or not. I'm awake now—might as well get ready and make sure the canyx hasn't sunk its fangs into Cal's throat. He managed not to attack him the past three nights Cal let him stay in his room, but maybe he's waiting until he's gathered more information from us to make his move.

With the bed haphazardly made, I hang the key on the hook outside the door. My booted steps thump along the packed dirt passage into the front room where Cal sits at the wobbly table, drinking a morning brew. His giant fox stands nearby, crunching on a dried strip of meat that Cal should have saved for himself. I decide not to comment. Obviously, doing so has done *so much* in the past.

"Almost there," I say.

The canyx perks up and delivers a low snarl in my direction. I growl back, and its head jerks away, as if surprised.

I roll my eyes and address the dog's all-too-trusting master. "There's only one haven after this." *The one we took Nori to after she almost died.* "Then you and your statue will be reunited at long last."

Cal sips his morning brew—how he thinks that smells better than any of my teas is beyond me. "I do hope this all pays off."

"Me too. But hey"—I jab a thumb toward the canyx—"if not, at least you saved the spy."

Cal stands, finishing his drink before passing me with a disapproving glare. "He's a Sentry," he declares again. "And perhaps if you stopped viewing him as an enemy, he might do the same for you."

I glance at my now permanently red Omen Mark.

"I'll be trying to get a head start on hearing from Toaph. Come get me when you're ready to leave," Cal says, striding toward the atrium in the back of the haven.

The canyx gives me another eerie look before following Cal. An unpleasant feeling crawls up my back as I watch its blue tail disappear around the bow of the tunnel.

The sooner we get rid of that dog, the better.

CALDEN

It's not until we reach our last rest stop before the crypt that I realize which haven it is—the one we stayed in after Norielle's abduction.

Tension clutches my neck as I look around the familiar space. A chair lingers beside the weathered couch where Norielle once lay—the place where Elias sat for nearly two days as he watched over her. The keys all hang on their hooks beside the bedroom doors, right where we left them. Even the communal dishes we forgot in our haste still sit in the washbasin.

Echo skulks by me, crouching as he inspects the haven much like he did the last. He ventures into the chamber where the firepit awaits a flame, leaving Elias and I standing in the front area, as if trapped in our memories of Norielle.

The same guilt I felt the day we nearly lost her pierces my chest afresh when I recall her pale, trembling body slumped against the pillar. She was moments from death—the girl El-Alam entrusted to *me* to protect.

Yet I failed her. And had Elias not been there, I might have failed her completely.

Elias was the one to let down his shield, risking his own life to end my paralysis when Corene challenged me to choose between him and Norielle. He was the one urging our pursuit onward while I slowed at Toaph's voice, forgetting the urgency of recovering my newest Bind member. He traded places with me so that I could heal Norielle, even at the risk of my affection for her being exposed and potentially shattering his chances with her. He's the one who carried her here and watched over her while I was too weak from grief, pain, and exhausting my vitality.

Elias is the real reason she's alive. Because of his love for her, not mine.

It wasn't even *my* love that healed her in the first place, not solely.

Elias turns, resting his hand on the chair he last occupied. I shift to follow Echo so I can leave Elias to his thoughts, but my feet are rooted to the floor, snared by a sudden conviction in my spirit.

I need to tell him—wholly face the truth for myself—and lay this matter about Norielle to rest before it utterly destroys my friendship with Elias.

And yet, to do so feels like resigning all hope that I could ever have what my heart yearns for—as if Norielle is the only woman in all Silvirdia who may be brave enough to look beyond the danger of my curse and see the man standing behind it. But even if she is, how hypocritical it is of me to esteem her mostly for that, disregarding the individual behind her bravery, as if someone's acceptance of me even with my curse is the only qualifier for a potential relationship. There is so much more to love than that.

"You should have seen her," I say at last, not knowing where else to start. "At the ball, when she turned to me. It was like watching a flower wilt."

Elias's gaze slowly peels from the couch. "What?"

"She would have danced with you until my mother shut down the party... maybe even after."

His grip tightens on the chair's backrest, but his mouth only hangs ajar, as if lost at how to respond.

"I thought you should know. It wasn't just my near episode that spoiled the evening for her. It was you not being there." I press on a smile, despite the discomfort of my next words. "So, whatever it is you thought could have happened that night between me and her, it never would have. Her heart belongs to you, as it always has. And I may be many questionable things—according to my mother—but the one thing I'm not is a thief."

A soft whistle hisses through a small aperture in the chamber, filling an otherwise lengthy silence before he asks, "Why are you saying this?"

"Because what I felt for her before discovering who she is to you was only an ember of what you feel. And I will not fan into flame a fire that will burn you, my friend." I tilt my face away, checking my heart for honesty before continuing. "Nor do I have any interest in trying to, for my own sake."

Elias chuckles, a grim, doubtful sound. "I find that hard to believe after the way you healed her."

I drop my gaze even lower, my memories conjuring the sensation of Norielle wrapped in my arms, cradled in my lap. She felt so small then, like a child—a child El-Alam tied my destiny to and charged me with looking after.

And she is so young, isn't she? She's still coming into her own. Meanwhile, I'm fully submerged in my identity and purposes. If there's anything I should be toward her, it's a mentor and leader.

...which is exactly what El-Alam asked of me. What was I doing by fantasizing that I could add anything more to His already perfect plan? As if it were a man, not El-Alam, who instructed that Bind leaders should not seek romantic connections within their Bind?

"You don't have to lie to me, Cal. I'm not stupid." Elias's voice reels back my focus. The frayed edges of his measured tone are like someone trying to sound kind whilst an arrow protrudes from their chest. "Anyone could tell you two had something started before I ever made the mistake of showing up."

"Lias—"

He waves me down and twists away like he means to leave, but stops himself. "Who Nori wants to be with is up to her, and it's pretty obvious that's not me. So, I don't see why we are even talking about this like there's anything else to say than that. You want to be with her. She wants to be with you. I've already resigned myself to the fact that Nori and I will only ever be friends. What else is there to talk about?"

"I don't *want* to be with her."

The assertiveness in my tone turns him toward me again, but the skepticism returns to his eyes only a blink later. "Just stop, Calden. She's yours. Just"—his voice cracks as he mumbles—"don't hurt her."

A sudden motion turns my attention toward the small passage where Echo peers out, head dipped low like he sensed the tension between Elias and me. Holding his ethereal gaze somehow slows my pulse and eases my breaths, grounding me even more in my stance on this matter.

As I face Elias again, my next words come out more gently. "I'm not in love with Norielle; that's what I'm trying to tell you, Elias."

Elias hesitantly looks up from the trance he'd fallen into.

"I fancied the idea of her—someone brave, maybe brave enough to look past my curse. But whether or not that is true of her doesn't matter. We aren't right for each other." I close my mouth, seeing no point in explaining aloud what brought me to that conclusion.

Though, when I blink, I can still see the disappointment in her eyes that night on the balcony and again at the ball. She doesn't understand the responsibilities of a future Sovereign or fully comprehend the weight I'm carrying. I would only continue to let her down with unmet expectations, and she would be ill-equipped to truly support me—leading only to mutual frustration. And all this aside, until I find Toaph, I'd be endangering her, whether she proved brave enough or not. To pursue her, or *anyone*, would be selfish.

Elias rubs the back of his neck, inclining himself away from me. "Cal... you healed her when she was nearly dead."

I shake my head. "Not with my affections, Lias."

"Then how?"

I suck in a breath and nod toward the table. "Perhaps we should sit down for this."

19

ELIAS

I dump my tea into the dirt and watch the bluish liquid roll across the dark ground until the earth absorbs it. Even the taste of tea turns my stomach this morning. I shouldn't feel so conflicted. I should be relieved about what Cal said to me last night. Grateful that things aren't what I thought.

Yet... I can't shake the sense that's he's being dishonest—that he's pretending to feel this way for my sake and for Nori's safety.

His bedroom door squeaks open, and my lips swivel between a grimace and a fake smile. His oversized fox prances ahead of him, stopping to growl at me the moment he notices me standing here.

I click my tongue, and the sharp noise causes the canyx's ears to twitch. "Good morning to you too, pup."

Cal steps out next, steel and leather encasing him from his heels to his sternum. He stops beside the canyx and strokes the glimmering fluff along the creature's neck.

Well, at least he's got his dog now.

Until it tries to kill him.

The canyx's growl calms, and Cal looks up, his swollen, bloodshot eyes and purple lids suggesting he probably spent the night like I did after Mum died. *Crying like a man,* as Papa would say. Quiet and out-of-sight.

A pit forms in my stomach. What would he be grieving over if not what he said last night?

I scratch at my side, uncertain if I should draw attention to his emotional state or not, but I can't even conjure a smirk to attempt playing it off.

"Nightmares?" I ask.

Cal shakes his head. "I'd have to sleep to have those."

"Then what kept you awake?"

He twists his armguard, misaligning it, only to realign it again. "Not what you think."

I glance at the fox like he might suddenly develop an ability to speak so he can explain what's going on. Not that I could trust him, anyway. "Then what?"

"I just hope I find Toaph soon, so that this burden will lift from me, is all."

I eye his twitching thumb. "No, it's not."

He gives me a grave look. "I was not mourning Norielle. I was mourning *Corene,* and the selfish fantasy I've carried since losing her that someday a woman may prove herself braver than she—or at least, her love may prove stronger."

I clamp my jaw shut, a bitter taste crawling up my throat at the woman's name. Depraved or not, that woman's blood is on my hands. And I will never unsee watching the life drain out of her eyes or the red smears across my sword as I withdrew the blade from her chest.

El-Alam, forgive me. I don't know if the deed requires forgiveness, but it feels like it does. I've never had to finish the job, not on a human. In my previous skirmishes with defectors, I've only brought them down enough to escape, but I knew

I couldn't do the same with Corene. Not with the power her mere existence held over Cal.

"Are you satisfied with that answer?" Cal asks.

For a moment, I can't remember my question, but even once I do, it takes several more blinks for me to wipe my mind clear of the image of Corene.

"I'm sorry, Cal," is all I can muster, and I'm not sure whether I mean it in regard to what he said or what I did to the woman he once loved.

"Never mind. Perhaps finding Toaph and ending all this is within reach," he says, a forced levity in his tone.

I finally muster a smirk. "Well, ready to go talk to a statue, then?"

Cal returns his focus to his new pet, as if finding him easier to look at than me. "I'd much prefer if it talked to me."

Even the dog tilts his head at this.

"It's not far," I say, hefting my backpack. *Especially when I'm not carrying an unconscious girl the whole way.*

Cal glances about, as if checking that he's remembered everything, then he turns for the passage leading out of the haven and motions for me to go ahead.

"Brace yourself, pup," I say, looking at the canyx as I pass them. "We're heading into Blood Warden territory."

I hold my breath as I creep down the steps leading to the crypt. The tunnels are eerily silent, not even a drip of water to mask our wary footfalls.

I ignite my Glory Ward as my feet hit level ground, and my lantern spills a mild light into the round space. Jagged shadows stretch from the carved stone faces of the Accursed marking the many passages, and the reek of rotting flesh crinkles my nose. There must be another slain fellion down here somewhere, or maybe another canyx from Echo's pack.

I glance at Cal. Even in the faint light, his skin looks sickly white. I wonder if he's noticing the stench, or if he's too busy fearing we'll somehow stumble across Corene's decaying corpse along the way.

His dog keeps at his side. So faithful for a traitor. Though, it makes perfect sense. The more loyal he seems, the less Cal will suspect him.

Or he really isn't cursed.

I dismiss the thought. One of us needs to stay skeptical, and it obviously isn't Cal.

"This is the one," I say, nodding toward the mouth of the passage we tried first last time. It didn't lead us to where we wanted, but if Cal's right, it may have been the place we needed to go.

I check my Omen Mark, finding it still pointed at the dog. *Useless.*

"Anything?" I ask Cal instead, waving my mark at him.

He checks his. "No."

I step onto the path, leading us through the stone channel. Soon, catacombs flank us, and the reek of death intensifies enough to make my eyes water.

The heavy caskets look the same as before, their lids askew and some with bones protruding from them. *Disgusting.* Someone would have to be demented to want to pass through here regularly. And to think these people *touch* the corpses, dismantle them...

"There it is," Cal mutters, brushing past me.

I look up, finding the sprawling stone wings of Toaph Elbara's statue. The stone figure clutches his swordstaff in both hands, like he's blocking an attack. It's odd seeing someone else hold the weapon I'm so used to associating with Cal. But Warden tradition has every Sovereign wield a swordstaff in the likeness of Toaph's.

Cal steps forward, and I exchange a look with his dog. The two of us at least seem able to agree on this: Cal's lost his mind. In every way the man can.

He touches the tip of Toaph's stone blade and locks eyes with the pupilless statue. I watch, heart quickening with every moment that passes. *Is he seeing anything? Is Toaph speaking to him?*

I want to ask, but I hold my tongue, not wanting to disrupt him.

Come on, Toaph. Help us out, I urge toward the statue, feeling half as deranged. But we're desperate. And maybe that's what desperation does—it makes people crazy.

"I'm here," Cal whispers, and by the dejected note in his voice, I can tell nothing has come of this yet. "Tell me where to find you."

Again, we enter an aching silence. Another minute passes without answer, then another. Cal hangs his head, his hand slipping away from the statue.

"I'm here," he repeats.

But this time, a resonant voice responds, "And what a gift it is to see you."

CALDEN

I jolt at the voice, my gaze leaping to the shadowy cross-roads behind the statue. A hooded figure emerges from the darkness, his magnificent cloak trailing on the ground behind his boots like an ebony river. A painted black mask outlines the harsh angles of his cheekbones, their lines meeting with his silver-streaked beard that tweaks as he smiles at me. I meet his pale eyes—their shade indistinguishable in the low light—and his pupils expand, like a wildernwolf who's just spotted his prey.

Echo's snarl ruptures the silence, followed by a whir of energy behind me as Elias ignites a vitality sphere. The blue light from his energy shines onto the sculpture of Toaph and remains, as though Elias is waiting for my response. I step back, conjuring my swordstaff and mirroring the defensive stance of the statue beside me.

"You needn't use that," says the man.

I tighten my hold on the weapon as his voice permeates my being. Something about its worn, leathery texture—both tough and supple at once—sounds familiar. But I can't recall where I've heard it before, or if I'm only imagining I have.

"I don't wish to fight you, Sovereign Prince, but I'll warn you, should you challenge me, you will find yourself outnumbered." With his words, a band of Blood Wardens step from the shadows in all directions. I risk looking around to estimate their number—twelve or thirteen? Why didn't our Omen Marks perceive them? Were they expecting us and planted a Shroud Ward on the wall somewhere?

I return my focus to the tall man, realization dawning. "You are the Oracle."

The man's lips slant into a smile, confirming my suspicions, and my next breath comes short.

"Whatever information you seek from me, I do not have it," I say.

The Oracle steps closer, seeming unfazed by the weapon in my hand or how it shifts into position to strike, should it become necessary.

"*Yet*. You haven't received it *yet*," he says once he's within my blade's reach. The light touches his aged eyes, revealing his eucalyptus-green irises.

My heart palpitates. I've seen these eyes—where? Has the Oracle approached me before, disguised as someone lesser? Or am I recalling a dream?

"But you need it—this information," the Oracle continues. "And I could help you obtain it, should you find the wisdom to listen to my proposal."

"Speak," I say, though I have no intention of agreeing to anything the Oracle offers. This is the man who has led at least a hundred Wardens from Alémor off the righteous path and spurred them toward eternal darkness. This is the one who lures the uncalled, the vulnerable, like the two girls we encountered at our camp, and tricks them into a life of senseless rebellion and brutality.

This is the man who ordered Norielle's capture, which almost claimed her life, and who fostered Corene's rebellion into utter depravity.

The Oracle studies me. "I expected at least some argument from you."

"Listening is one matter," I say. "Accepting, another."

He nods, a trace of amusement glinting in his eyes. "You have grown so much since I last saw you."

My brows draw together. *So, we have met?*

"The orphan turned prince," he carries on. "Yet you bear the title as if born with it in your blood."

"I didn't ask for your ill-intended compliments. I asked for your proposition."

The Oracle surveys me, his expression turning stoic. "Then let us waste no more of your precious, fleeting time."

My lips press together as I brace for whatever temptation awaits me.

"We both seek Toaph Elbara," he says, admiring the statue for a moment. "And you are the one he has chosen to communicate with. However, it appears that you have had no success in that endeavor thus far... is this correct?"

I answer his question with a hard stare.

"That is what I thought," he says, returning his full attention to me. "And that is why I would like to offer you my aid. I could help you hear from him."

I bite back a retort that I'd rather sift through every grain of sand in the nine deserts in search of Toaph than form an alliance with the leader of the Blood Wardens.

"I have much knowledge that has long been lost to the Wardens of the Order." He releases a heavy sigh. "I have tried to share my insights with your mother, but sadly, she refuses to reason with me. I hoped you might be wiser than that, as you do so seem. You are markedly unlike her, from what I can tell."

Regret for my continued disregard for my mother's rules and the ways of the Warden Order twists my gut. Somehow, I never considered how this could reflect on us if the Blood Wardens took notice of it—how it could mark me as a rebel, a party vulnerable to defecting.

If my allegiances were only to man.

His attention moves again to the statue, and I recognize a perfect opportunity to strike him. Yet I hold my weapon still, as he must expect. He's hinting at something, something I can't leave here without knowing more about. Which means for now, he has me in his hand.

I force myself to sound open. "And what insights do you wish to share with me?"

Elias hisses behind me, but a swift shift in the surrounding defectors' positions silences his retort. At least three of them—as far as I can see—are ready to impale or blast him with their choice of attack.

"See, I thought you were reasonable," the Oracle says, though skepticism swims in his eyes. "You must realize by now that Toaph Elbara is a weak Guardian and a coward. It is for this reason that Ta'Nathel came to Silvirdia. He wished to provide our world with a stronger source of protection; however, to do so, he needed to slay Toaph, which, as you've surely discovered, was a task left incomplete because Toaph fled."

The Guardian's voice echoes in my head for the thousandth time. *I fled. I failed.*

"The Wardens retaliated before Ta'Nathel could find Toaph, and now they hold Ta'Nathel back, preventing him from doing what is necessary to not simply restore the world but to make it better than it was before."

"Which is, of course, why he cursed it," I say with a sarcastic glaze on my words.

"Oh dear." The Oracle looks at me in disbelief. "You've been so misguided... Can you not see? It is not Ta'Nathel that has caused the world to be in such disarray, but Toaph Elbara."

Despite my best intentions to steel myself, I flinch, and my weapon drifts an inch from its ready stance.

"You of all people should be able to discern it," he says. "You've lived as though cursed your entire life. And why? Because of Toaph. Because of what he's done to your mind."

Echo's growl deepens, but I'm too frozen to look back to see why. Is it because of the Oracle's words, or have the defectors further threatened the canyx?

"Toaph Elbara is angry," the Oracle says, leaning to keep my gaze. "Angry and helpless, besides what fury he can unleash upon the world from wherever he's trapped himself. He's turned the Sentries against us. Riddled the world with all forms of mayhem. And all the while, the Wardens believe these assaults are from their enemy, whilst imprisoning our one hope for survival behind that barrier." The Oracle points a finger at my chest. "But you—you are the chief pawn in Toaph's ultimate plan. If only you could find him, he could use you and the people you will soon rule to defeat Ta'Nathel, since he was too weak to do it alone."

I ponder his words, half my mind knowing they are twisted; the other, receptive and confused. He paces around me, utterly unaffected by my weapon's presence or the threat of my renowned power.

"But should you comply with Toaph's wishes..." A mournful sound weakens his tone. "Then you will hand our world back to a Guardian who is now against us, and he will not stop this desolation until every plain, every mountain, every leaf lies in a bed of *dust*."

My head jerks back at the word.

Dust.

Just like what I see in my mind. Has the Oracle seen this too?

"Your mother..." The Oracle touches his chest, as if his heart aches. "She won't listen. I tried. So many times, I tried to convince her we'd pegged the wrong enemy..."

I glance toward Elias, needing someone else's opinion as doubt clouds my reasoning. Elias's tense expression reveals similar confusion, but he shakes his head slightly. Just enough to tell me he doesn't think I should buy into it.

And I shouldn't. The source is foul. It can't be trusted.

Yet...

"I'm so sorry to burden you with this, Sovereign Prince." The Oracle's apology sounds alarmingly sincere. "But it seems El-Alam has placed you at the center of our world's fate. Whichever way you lean, the entire world will follow. Should you choose wrong, you'll tip us toward the depths of utter ruin."

My breaths shorten, and an urge to flee rises in me. I twist away from him to stare instead at the statue of Toaph. He couldn't be the enemy. The curse on the world couldn't be from him. It's all Ta'Nathel. Everything is Ta'Nathel—

"Toaph Elbara sees your resistance toward him, you know," the Oracle adds. "He's seen and feared it since your infancy. That is why he seeks to control you, to channel himself through you with these... these devastating episodes."

I spin toward him again, eyes wide. *Lies. All lies. They must be—*

"It's just as he's done to the Sentries." He waves a hand toward Echo. "But as you can see, some minds are stronger than others. Some can still resist." He steps toward me, holding my gaze with captivating intensity. *Familiar* intensity. "You, too, can resist. And if you help me—help Ta'Nathel—you can be free of your curse. Forever."

My curse. Because if the Oracle speaks truly, that's still what it would be in some respects.

Freedom. Is there anything my soul longs for more deeply?

"Please." The Oracle sets his hand upon my shoulder, and though I wince, I don't shudder away from it—the hold of his gaze is too powerful to break. "Every day for the past two decades, I have given to this one purpose: to save you from Toaph Elbara and his plans. To break this *curse.*"

A ringing fills my ears. *Save me? Break my curse?*

Why? Why should the Oracle care at all for me? What do I matter to him?

"*Liar,*" Elias snaps, but his voice sounds like he's across the world. "You don't save people; you damn them."

The Oracle turns to Elias, eyes flashing with offense, innocence, and anger, but he restores his calm composure before he speaks. "Is that what the Lady tells you?"

"And the Seer," Elias asserts.

"Of course." The Oracle's attention pivots between us. "Yes. That is what I would tell my people if I wanted to limit and control them. What else would the Elders say to prevent rebellion against their ways?" He strokes his beard. "But you know what they say... Those who seek control are the ones who are most afraid. What is it they fear, I wonder?"

"Says the man who ambushed us," Elias counters.

The Oracle smiles. "All your prince has to do is ask, and we will leave."

"Prove it."

The Oracle turns to me, seeming to await my response. I fight for my voice, still lost in the turbulence of all his claims.

"Leave us," I finally say. "At once."

"As you wish," the Oracle says, then he withdraws a few paces. I watch as each defector disappears into the crossroads ahead of us, but the Oracle remains until the sounds of their footsteps have faded.

"Send for me when you are ready to be free." He meets my gaze once more with a victorious smile that stands in contrast to his failure to persuade me. "Then we shall hunt Toaph together... *my son.*"

NORIELLE

I spin, evading a thrust toward my underarm, and return Odessa's attack with added momentum. Our dull blades collide as she blocks me again, our gazes locking. Her smile seems approving, if a bit snide, before she pushes me back with a harsh shove of her sword against mine. I fumble slightly but re-form my stance in time to parry her next swipe. Only this time, I take a chance and will the Vitality Ward engraved onto my blade to ignite.

A blast of blue energy erupts from my sword, knocking Odessa back several steps. With her balance still compromised, I bound after her, swinging a kick to her torso, and she falls. I cringe, guilt swelling in me as I step over her and meet her wide-eyed expression. But when I press the dull tip of my sword against her throat, she smiles.

"Finally," she says between heavy breaths.

My shoulders sag with relief as I step back. I did it. I finally bested her—though it took the added use of a ward to do it. But even that is a success. I ignited the ward at the exact moment I needed it. That's a significant improvement compared to how things were going just a couple of days ago.

From beneath the awning, Alani and Rhiana applaud me as I help Odessa to her feet. Odessa brushes the dirt off her clothes and returns her weapon to the rack. I follow suit, then gulp down water from my flask, relishing the refreshment to my parched mouth. Adrenaline tingles through my body, but I already feel it dwindling and a sense of fatigue rising in its place. We've been dueling for over an hour, and the use of such a powerful ward is exhausting, even if only used once. For now.

I hope.

"Well done!" Alani exclaims, springing to her feet from a bench and prancing toward us. "You're really catching on to your wards. Whatever the Seer said to you, it seems he should be the one to train new inductees from here on out."

A tender feeling envelops my heart like a hug, and I think back to my conversation with Seer Josiah beside the fountain. Maybe she's right. Ever since then, I've picked up each new ward within a few tries.

"I've also been staying up to study," I say.

"It shows." Alani beams. "Empyrean, maybe you *will* be ready before Calden and Elias return."

I turn to Odessa for her thoughts, but when she offers no comment, I ask, "When can I test?"

Odessa smooths her hair, her breath already even, and her posture as casual as if we hadn't exerted ourselves at all yet. "As soon as you feel confident that you can pass."

"I want to try," I say. "I know the wards. No one said I had to be great at them, right?"

"We don't expect total mastery, but you need to display solid control of them." Her eyes narrow. "It's only been ten days since you started learning, and my mother's time shouldn't be wasted. I think you'd be better off practicing a while longer."

I look at Alani, then Rhiana, who remains on the bench watching from afar. Both encourage me with smiles.

"I can do it," I say, though my confidence wavers as I hear the words spoken aloud. "I want to be ready when Calden returns."

"I'd give it another week," Odessa says.

My eye twitches. "They'll be back by then. I *feel* ready, Lady Odessa. Please."

She studies me for a long while with a flat expression, but a sour grin crawls onto her face. "I don't know which man you're trying to impress, but no one has passed this early. Believe me. I've seen what pressure does to people when testing time comes. You need more time to build your confidence and control."

Which man I'm trying to impress? I try not to glower at her. As if *that* is what I'm concerned about when my training might stand in the way of us searching for *Toaph Elbara.*

"Alani?" I ask, since she's the ward instructor Calden chose for me.

"Testing *is* intimidating," Alani admits. "And if you fail, the Lady Sovereign requires at least two weeks more training before you try again. It could be a good idea to practice at least a bit more. You know, just to make it easier to pass."

I frown, the threat of delaying us an extra two weeks weighing on my confidence.

"Calden would never ask you to leave before you were ready," Alani adds.

"No, he'd leave without me, and I'd find out after you all were gone." The frustration lacing my tone surprises me, and apparently, everyone else, because all their heads slant.

"We're still waiting on number five," Odessa says. "My brother's an idiot sometimes, but he won't go on a Bind mission with two members out."

"He told me the mission couldn't wait," I counter, recalling my conversation with Calden on the balcony. "He insisted we needed to start looking for Toaph as soon as possible, and I'm not sure if he even means to wait for the fifth Bind member."

"The Elders would never agree to that. And I, for one, will not join him on any Bind-related expeditions until the fifth member is with us." Odessa eyes Alani. "It would be wise if the three of us all agreed on that right now."

Alani closes her mouth and shifts away.

Odessa's nostrils flare as she stares at the back of Alani's head, and the uncomfortable quiet occupies the arena until I speak up again.

"For all we know, the Seer could receive a vision about the final member right now," I say. "I *want* to be ready for anything. *Please*. Let me test."

The Second Lady shuts her eyes, as if too annoyed by Alani and me to look at us any longer, then she sighs. "Give it three more days, Norielle. Just *trust* me. I am trying to help you succeed."

I swallow my desire to be unreasonably obstinate and nod.

CALDEN

Mother lied to me. She lied to all the Wardens.

The man who took me in and called me his own—the last Sovereign—wasn't killed by Hunters. He defected. He turned on us—on El-Alam. And now he leads the Blood Wardens, growing his numbers by the year. To do what? Rally them against us? Against the woman he once claimed to love?

The madness of it oppresses me even three days after our encounter, as fresh as it was when the Oracle first departed with those words. *My son.*

How? How could such a righteous man stoop so low?

Yet... his arguments spread like insidious vines, constricting my sense of reality, of truth. What I endure from Toaph doesn't feel like mere communication; it *feels* like a curse, just as that supplier said. After all, the Seer hears from El-Alam mind to mind, spirit to spirit. If it were just the touch of Toaph's great power sending me into chaos, then why isn't the Seer affected by the touch of an even greater power? And why would something holy cause something so very *not*?

"There's your exit, pup," Elias says, and I jump at the sudden noise.

Exit. Pup. *Echo…*

It all registers so slowly, like someone attempting to comprehend reality after waking from a visceral dream. If only that's what this entire trip to the crypt had been, one long and agonizing nightmare.

I halt, finding Echo has already stopped a few paces behind me. His luminous eyes watch me in a way that almost feels sorrowful, unless that's my heart projecting onto him. Another connection soon to be severed. Will I always be foolish enough to get attached to something that can't last?

"I could use your help soon," I say. My steel armor *clinks* as I kneel in front of the canyx. "That is, if you happen to know where our true Empyreal Guardian went?"

Echo's ears flick forward, but he gives no other indication of whether he knows where Toaph is or not. I accept his nonanswer after a long stillness and weave my fingers into his coarse, glistening fur for what may be the last time.

"Well, I…" An awareness slinks over me of Elias watching me talk to this animal as if he were a person, and I level my tone and expression. "I hope you find yourself somewhere safe, and that there are more like you there."

Echo nuzzles my arm, and despite Elias's judgmental glare and the common sense any other Warden would have, I wrap my arms around the canyx. Warmth emanates from his muscular body and dense fur, providing a much-needed sense of comfort. I almost smile before the recollection that this is goodbye elicits a frown instead.

"Thank you for accompanying me, friend." I stand, scratching his head before stepping back to make way for him to pass me.

The canyx stares at me for a long while before glancing at Elias, who nods him toward the exit, overly eager to be done with this "spy." And finally, Echo trots past me into the sunlight haloing the passage.

"So..." Elias breaks an extended silence between us as the murmur of the underground river swells in my ears. "Is Raevre next?"

Several strides separate his question from my answer. "I haven't decided. I will save that decision for after I've discussed these matters with my mother." Bitterness seeps into my voice at the mention of Mother, but a childlike whisper inside objects. *She doesn't know. The Oracle fooled her into believing him dead.*

But the Oracle implied they've conversed since his departure. There's no way she wouldn't recognize her own husband, even with his face painted. Is he why she has never ordered us to seek out the Blood Wardens and eliminate them? Does she fear facing him in the same way I feared Corene?

"She's not the one deceiving you," Elias says, as if he's sensed where my mind fell in our pause.

I lower my head. This is why I didn't want to discuss it with him. His unwavering loyalty to the Order and undying trust in our Elders—while admirable—labels him narrow-minded. Though perhaps I could use a dose of his logic before I confront my mother like she's a villain's accomplice.

"Truth is the best foundation for lies, Lias," I counter, tasting the fresh air produced by the river when I inhale, yet my steps slow. "Not all he spoke was false, only some of it. The trouble is discerning which parts."

"All he did was tell you everything backwards," Elias says, so steady and sure I almost resent him. How is he not swayed? Even a little? Or is this feigned assurance? "He told you everything Ta'Nathel's done as if it were Toaph—as if our Guardian were the enemy. But a Guardian wouldn't curse their own world."

"Unless he turned corrupt." I stop as the rolling river comes into view, like a glimmering snake slithering through the underground.

"Turned corrupt?" Elias prompts when I don't explain.

"It is possible, isn't it? The Oracle"—I refuse to call him *Father*—"posed it as though Ta'Nathel came to help us. *If* there is any truth to that, then that would mean Toaph Elbara was endangering our world in some way that we didn't know about, and he needed to be stopped."

Elias's slack expression tells me he not only disagrees, but is utterly disappointed that I'm considering the possibility. "Ta'Nathel came to claim Silvirdia. Everything was fine until Ta'Nathel showed up. It's not Toaph, Cal. You can't take anything the Oracle said to heart."

"Explain my curse then," I say, but I step toward the canoes lining the river, as if to declare there is no other explanation and that my argument is strong enough to withstand any opposition.

Elias catches me by the shoulder and jerks me around as he did to that supplier—the supplier he feared was on the path to defecting.

"Listen, Cal," he says. "If you were the Oracle serving Ta'Nathel, what would you be doing? You'd be building an army to send against the Wardens at the barrier so you could free Ta'Nathel. And in the meantime, you'd be focusing your efforts on delaying the person who can restore Ta'Nathel's greatest enemy."

"No." My voice is sure. "I'd want to kill him, not delay him."

"Not if your master needed him."

This lowers my weary gaze to the damp earth.

"Obviously, Toaph has somehow hidden himself from even Ta'Nathel's sight, but for whatever reason, *you* are the person Toaph revealed himself to. I think that might come in handy to Ta'Nathel if he were to escape." Elias lets the idea sink in before carrying on. "And let's also consider how useful it would be to the Oracle if he could somehow convince you to turn against your mother and the Order. He wouldn't even need to use his army then. All he's trying to do is tie strings onto your hands and feet so he can puppet you into helping him give this world over to Ta'Nathel."

My vision seems to blur as his reasoning joins with what the logical part of my mind has been saying since the encounter. Yet a flash of Alani, crumpled against a passage wall not much different from the surrounding ones, clutching her broken ribs and unable to breathe, splits the foundation of these ideas. What happens to me is not holy. It's a curse. It must be a curse, just as the Oracle implied. Just like we've always believed.

"You can't tell me it makes no sense to you at all," I counter, letting the fissure spread. "We've always wondered about Ta'Nathel's motivations. Why does he want Silvirdia? Why would he curse a world he wanted to claim? And isn't it said that if a Guardian turns corrupt, their Sentries will follow? Could it be that the Sentries' only curse is that their master's soul has turned dark?" I look to Echo for reassurance before remembering he's left us. "And again, Toaph speaking to me shouldn't cause such destructive power to explode from my being, unbidden. That doesn't make sense."

Elias's jaw works as he seems to chew on a response, but I start after a canoe stowed along the riverside before he can deliver one.

"We'll see what my mother says about the Oracle," I say, hauling the boat toward the river. "That should tell me if any word out of the Oracle's mouth can be trusted."

NORIELLE

My palms sweat as I follow Alani into the arena. The usually wide-open space is now occupied by a series of markers and stations. The Elders sit on the benches, their quiet chatter ceasing as soon as my shadow crawls into their peripheral vision. Their heads turn to watch me, as they did when I approached the platform at my induction ceremony.

I pause with Alani to curtsy to the Lady Sovereign. Curiosity sparks in her eyes as I rise; she's surely wondering as much as I am if I will pass this test, given my short training time. But Mum always called me a quick learner.

I can do this.

I will not be the reason the world has to wait on our Bind. And I'm not about to let Elias keep his record, either.

Yet when my gaze passes Atlas and Gatlin to find Seer Josiah, his smile looks wary. Has he already foreseen my failure? Or is he nervous that all the trouble he sensed in me has made me impulsive?

Not that he'd be entirely wrong...

Lady Odessa's gaze catches me from the shadow of the awning where she stands, arms crossed and leaning against a pillar. She shakes her head at me, as if to remind me she disapproves of my choice to be here so soon.

Landon. She's just a female Landon, too proud to think she could ever be wrong in her estimations about someone else.

"Over this way, Norielle," Alani says, leading me to the first station, which is simply an "X" drawn into the dirt.

Once we are in position, the Lady Sovereign stands. Her dignified voice fills the bland arena with a sense of regality. "Norielle Damaris of Behria, welcome to your official testing. Should you pass, we will grant you your own warding pen and allow you the full privileges of being a Warden. Should you fail, you must continue your training for two more weeks before attempting your test again. Are you certain you wish to begin?"

I swallow. This is my chance—my last chance—to take the cautious route and not risk adding a two weeks' delay to whatever plans Calden may have for us upon his return.

"Remember, there is no hurry. El-Alam called you when He meant to. Not a moment too soon or too late."

I hear the Seer's statement again as I meet his eyes. He seems to be repeating it from his heart, and yet his fingers fidget in his lap.

"I am ready to test," I affirm despite my reservations.

Seer Josiah looks down, preventing me from seeing his reaction.

The Lady Sovereign gives a slow nod before whisking a hand toward the arena stations. "Then let the testing begin."

I curtsy to her again, then I face Alani for instructions. Her enthusiastic smile brings back a layer of my courage. At least *she* seems to believe in me.

"All right. Your first test is the Snare Ward. Draw it there"—Alani points to the marking on the ground before snatching a stake and holding it like a long walking staff—"then I'll test it with this."

I pull the pen Alani lent me from my belt, then I crouch and ready myself to draw my first ward of the test. I get one chance, according to Alani's earlier instructions. One chance to draw it correctly, one chance to ignite it, and one chance to show I have full control over the magic that follows.

My hand trembles, the Elders' gazes seeming to burn against the side of my face. *This was a mistake.* Even the image of the glyph seems hidden under their expectant observation. My nose scrunches as I force my memory to recall the look of it—a circle with spires and squiggles like chains woven together down the straight lines. Easy.

The pen meets with the packed dirt, and somehow, its magic ink perfectly colors the pale earth, as if I were drawing on paper. When I finish the glyph, the circle at the center evens and the spires perfect themselves. A long sigh blows from my nose.

Except, drawing the ward is the easy part. Now I must ignite it, then command it.

I stand, squeezing the pen, and attempt to focus on the ward. But then Gatlin coughs, renewing my awareness of the Elders' presence. Am I taking too long? Are they growing impatient? Surely, they have a million other important matters to attend to—

No, this is the most important thing, I correct myself. How could the testing of the *Sovereign Prince's* Bind member not be?

Somehow, that only makes my stomach churn.

You just have to ignore them, I hear Elias tell me, as he did at the ball. *Think of something else.*

I smile to myself, remembering the conversation that followed about the make-believe rabbit Landon convinced me to go searching for, and how Elias played along just for the sake of spending time with me. What made him think I wouldn't have spent all day with him back then? I'd have taken any excuse to neglect my responsibilities at home and laugh with him until my sides hurt.

The thought makes me wish he was here. He always had a way of making me feel invincible when we were kids. But I can imagine, at least, that he'd be making some smart comment about the time we got ourselves stuck in Alani's snares and how all I need to do is pretend it's him who'll get stuck in it.

A small chuckle breaks my protracted silence and earns me a perplexed look from Alani. When I set my focus back onto the Snare Ward, anxiety loosens its grip on my chest.

I send a mental command to the ward to snatch the first thing that touches it. Though the glyph does not respond in any visible way, I feel the small waft of energy as it leaves my spirit to enter the ward.

"Okay," I say to Alani, signaling for her to test it.

She smiles toward the Elders before staking the wooden pole into the center of the ward. I hold my breath for the split second it takes before buzzing tendrils of energy shoot from the ground like luminescent roots and coil around the shaft.

A silent squeal of relief leaps from my heart, then I rein back my focus. I still have to show I can release it.

Now let go, I order it.

It takes an extra blink before the energy vines release the pole and recoil toward the ground, where they disappear along with the glyph.

"Fantastic," Alani cheers, and I glance back to the Elders. Atlas draws something—a tally, maybe—onto a parchment. Seer Josiah's smile lifts his curled moustache. The others all watch with only the slightest hint of approval on their expressions, as if to not overencourage me.

"To the next test," Alani says, gesturing me toward a chest resting atop a small table.

A Key Ward. This will be easy.

My confidence grows as I continue from station to station, demonstrating my use of each ward just as well—and sometimes better than—the first. And soon, I find myself at the last station, the only one that comes with a target.

The Vitality Ward.

I recall the sunlike glyph with ease and draw it on my clammy palm. As it perfects on its own, I turn my attention to the target in the opposite direction of where the Elders sit. The painted red center seems to watch me like an eye. This is it, the last challenge. The hardest of the standard wards to control.

But I can do this. It's only one ward, and I've done it before—if only twice.

I funnel all my attention to the glyph on my hand and the target as I aim my palm toward it. Just one. One sphere of energy is all I must launch, and the target is a considerable size—hard to miss.

I can do this.

I repeat the assurance to myself until my full courage returns, then I turn my thoughts into commands for the Vitality Ward to ignite.

My heart pulses in my ears. One. Two. Three...

Then the warmth of kindled energy blooms against my skin, and a brilliant blue orb launches from my hand.

CALDEN

Though the river ride takes nearly twice as long without Alani's Master Talent rushing the canoe, it seems to pass in a blink with how distracted I am. Before I've decided on what I'll say to Mother first, we're striding across one of the seven bridges to the citadel. A morning sun glares over the mossy turrets, a lovely sight after spending so many days underground. But beneath them, the astria oaks are dappled in fiery shades—gold and bronze—slowing my once quick stride to a halt. *It's Soltûm, is it not?* The trees should be greener than ever.

A crisp leaf rustles across the bridge, blown by an abnormally chilly wind. It catches on my boot, and I briefly remember Elias commenting about the unusual amount of rain.

"What is happening?" I mutter.

Elias and I exchange a look, neither of us forming an answer. But the sight of the citadel looming up ahead banishes my concerns about the odd climate to the back of my mind to be fretted over another time. A time when I'm not about to face Mother.

If she truly lied . . .

My trust in her will shatter, but could she ever restore it?

My fingertips tingle as we cross the flower field and yellow-draped willows in the east yard of the citadel. I ball my fists, squeezing them as if to squash the nervous feeling, but it goes nowhere.

"Calden! Elias!"

I start at the sudden sound of Norielle's voice and turn to find her standing between a pair of twisty alela willows. She hoists up the skirt of her lilac dress to jog toward us, stopping a few steps away. "You're both okay," she says, her gaze pivoting between us before finally landing on Elias.

"As promised," I say.

I expect Elias to take over the conversation, maybe even step forward and seize her in his arms. After all, I've affirmed her affection for him and renounced any claim on her. But he stands back, out of my field of vision.

Norielle's eyes flutter, a watery sheen filling them as her gaze turns to the distance. Her lips twitch like there is something she wants to say, and the glistening in her eyes holds me still for a moment, wanting to inquire what the matter is. But my ears are already burning for Mother's answers, and I can't wait another moment for them. I need to talk to her.

Now.

"Norielle, I apologize, but we will have to catch up later," I say, feeling a pinch in my heart when she looks at me like I've splashed cold water onto her face. "There is something I need to discuss with my mother. Urgently."

"Did Toaph speak to you?" Hope kindles in her eyes, only to be smothered when I shake my head.

"It's about something else." I step back from them. "Lias, please tell her what happened."

"Everything?" he asks.

My brow twitches as I reconsider. "Tell her about the canyx and who the Oracle is."

Elias nods, and I pray he earnestly means to spare her the other details of my conversation with the Oracle. There's no sense in troubling Norielle with them—not unless I deem the Oracle's theories are right in any part.

I turn away from them both and rush toward the citadel.

An attendant informs me of Mother's location, and I head to the Seer's Sanctum, reaching the closed doors with a knotted fist. I pound the mauve-painted wood more aggressively than I intended and wait to be let inside with words flinging in all directions in my mind. As prepared as I should be to confront her, I still don't know where to begin, what to say first. Do I accuse her and see how she reacts? Or do I try to pry the truth from her gently, like picking a lock?

The door disarms with a click, sending my heartrate into a tizzy. Do I even have it in me to face her, to face the possibility she will confirm the Oracle is who he claims to be?

I don't get to answer that question before the door opens and a boy, the Seer's youngest attendant, greets me with a bow. He quickly steps away, and my attention flits past the filled bookshelves to my mother and Seer Josiah, standing near the flowing wall of water at the back of the sanctum.

"You've returned!" The relieved lilt in Mother's tone sinks as a scowl replaces her smile. "I told you not to go there."

The wedding ring still glinting on her finger catches my gaze, stoking the flames within.

"Have you heard from Toaph Elbara?" the Seer asks, as if oblivious to my mother's frustration with me—or rather, dismissive of it. He is one of the few members of the council who is unbothered by my lack of regard for the Order. If anything, he quietly celebrates my rebelliousness with smiles he tries to hide.

"No," I say, summoning my bravery as I meet Mother's eyes. She steps near enough for me to pull her into a hug, if I had the desire for it, but even the sight of her sends a blaze over my skin. "But I heard from someone else."

There's a piercing silence as they both await my news. I seize this as my chance to remember some sense of decorum.

"I'd like to speak with you alone, Mother."

Another silence.

"I am due for a meal," Seer Josiah says, a slight apprehension in his voice, though he smiles at us and gives a dramatic wave toward his space. "If you wish to borrow the sanctum, that is."

"Thank you, Josiah," Mother says, and I squint. No title?

What were they doing in here?

The thought of her taking a romantic interest in Seer Josiah suddenly reeks when considering her husband still lives.

She can't know that. She simply can't.

Does the Seer know?

Seer Josiah takes his attendant with him, leaving Mother and me standing alone in the sanctum with only the trickling of the wall fountain to fill the quiet between us. I delay, despite my impatience, and fumble one last time for the right words. But only now do I realize the problem with that. There are no right words—no right way to address this. There is simply a choice to call attention to it or not.

But the latter option would destroy me.

"Who did you hear from?" Mother prompts, brushing a thin braid of hair behind her copper-embellished earlobe. Again, the shimmer of her ring assaults my eyes.

"My father."

My answer, short and aggressive as a punch to the jaw, is not what I meant to give. *The Oracle,* that is what I intended to say. But now my words hang overhead like a blinding sun, exposing every tell of Mother's fear as it kindles on her face.

"Mother..." Compassion and love fall like a blanket over the fire I carried into this room, dousing it, but still, its smoke scratches my throat.

"Your—your blood father, you mean?" Mother asks.

I shake my head, recalling the pale green eyes and the way the man spoke of my mother. He couldn't have been my true father, not given his dark features. Though, that revelation would likely have been easier to bear, even if it meant I shared blood with the Oracle.

"I mean the Sovereign," I say.

Mother glances back toward where Seer Josiah stood, as if searching for comfort in his presence, only to remember he's left the room. When she faces me again, she looks ill, like she might faint before I can get a proper answer from her.

But is it because her husband, whom she presumed dead, lives? Or is it because she knows I've uncovered a secret she's kept from me for nearly twenty years?

I force myself to keep speaking. "I recognized his eyes, and he called me son. He lives, Mother. If only in the flesh."

At this, she closes her eyes and turns from me. The son in me wants to wrap an arm around her, but I can't move, not even my lips, to ask the question screaming in my heart. *Did you know, Mother? Did you know?*

I wait for what feels like hours for her to speak, but the next sound to fill the room is her weeping. She stumbles away from me, bracing herself on the bookshelves until she can reach the Seer's armchair, then she falls into it like it is her private reading chair in her chambers. Her hands cover her face, and all I can do is watch from afar.

I'm sorry, Mother, some part of me whispers, but I'm too afraid of what this reaction means, too confused, to voice it aloud.

"I—" Mother croaks. She lifts her head, seeming to force herself into a formal posture. "I knew I needed to tell you, but..." That's as far as she gets before she crumbles again, sobbing into her palms.

But it's all I need to hear to know the truth.

She knew. Mother knew.

And all these years, she's been covering for his corruption by claiming he's dead.

My chest heaves, ten responses seeming to war for release. I wrangle them all into silence, knowing if I speak, it will come out in a shout.

I wait until the anger simmers down from a feverish spell to a dull ache across my body. Then I approach her and speak low. "Why didn't you tell me? How could you lie to everyone? To *me*?" Another thought suddenly crosses my mind. *Does Odessa know?* He is, after all, even more her father than he is mine.

I pocket that question for the moment.

"I didn't lie," Mother says, her body going rigid. "The man he was died nearly two decades ago. The man he became is... is something else entirely."

I remember Alani's words to me in the crypt as we stood over Corene's dead body. *Corene's been dead for years.*

It was true, as are Mother's words... almost. *Truth is the best foundation for lies.*

"You said Hunters killed him," I say.

Mother looks up at me, her eyelashes dotted with tears, but her scowl makes it harder to remember the compassion that softened me a few minutes ago. "What else was I supposed to say? If I'd told everyone he abandoned the Order, that he'd found another way to wield magic that was nearly limitless, we may have lost half—if not more—of our forces. People adored him, Calden. They *trusted* him. More Wardens would have followed him into the darkness if they knew."

Her reasoning makes sense, even if I still despise it. At least, it makes sense regarding the Wardens as a whole. "But me? What about Odessa?"

"Odessa knows."

I blink, hard, as if when I open my eyes, I'll awaken in some bed in one of the havens and discover this has all been another nightmare induced by the crystal ceilings.

Mother still sits in the Seer's chair, her gaze now distant.

"Oh, Odessa knows?" I retort. "You thought to tell her—"

"Calden," Mother interjects, but I'm not ready to be stopped yet.

"What about the other Elders? *The Seer?*"

"*Only* Odessa knows."

The slightest hint of relief eases my next breath. Somehow, the insult of the Seer knowing and not slipping the information to me would have been too much to handle on top of the rest. The man has been a surrogate father to me in many ways, in place of my last surrogate. I couldn't stand to lose *three* fathers of sorts.

But Odessa. She never thought to inform me? Not even to suggest the truth, so I might grow suspicious and inquire about the matter?

"Then why did you leave me out?" I ask.

Mother tenses even more, the veins in her hands protruding. She meets my gaze again, and I see the regret in her eyes before she replies. "Because I feared you might follow him."

I step back, stricken. How could she dare think that?

She looks toward her hands as they wring each other in her lap. "I watched a noble man of great faith and virtue fall into temptation. Our leader. *My* leader." Her voice cracks. "I planned to tell you when you came of age, but you'd so often demonstrated a rebellious nature regarding our traditions, and I thought if you discovered your father—your example—had found a means of circumventing our rules entirely, you would be tempted as well. I feared that, like him, your good nature wouldn't be enough. He'd use it against you to convince you it was to others' benefit that you followed this path."

I twist, wishing for another chair to sit in because my knees feel weak. "How did this even happen? What made him turn away?"

She leaves my question untouched for so long that I almost ask it again, thinking she missed it. But when she delivers her reply, she does so with her face bowing from my sight. "I-I don't know. He became drawn to the darkness, filled with strange ideas. Then one day, he returned with the discovery that the Accursed's blood could be wielded in place of El-Alam's divine tears. He was unwilling to listen to any reasoning that I offered, and instead, he tried with all his might to convince me to follow his pursuit of this new magic."

"And then?" I prompt when she falls quiet again.

"I refused, and he disappeared."

"Why would he leave?" I ask, thinking of Elias's theory about the Oracle wanting to use my position to his advantage.

"I'm not sure. I think he may have feared the retaliation of the Elders—that, like me, they would oppose him, and his power wouldn't be enough to withstand the Elders combined. He needed to grow his forces and power, it seems."

"And you..." I take a breath. "And you just... let him go?"

"Calden, I had you and your sister to look after," she says. "I couldn't pursue him, and I was devastated, confused. How could I think rationally? In one night, I lost my husband and inherited the full responsibilities of the Sovereign. Besides, you know the heartache of losing the one you love to defection. I would never have been able to strike him down myself. Even now, I never could."

Sympathy softens my voice. "But you didn't send anyone after him? Or tell the Elders?"

"They would have killed him."

I almost argue that's what needed to happen, but I can't. It's far too easy to see myself in her place—my inability to fight Corene.

But I was at least able to step aside and let someone else do it.

You didn't love her the way Mother loved Father, I remind myself. Corene and I spent only a few months dancing around the idea of being together. I'd only met her lips once before she witnessed one of my episodes and withdrew from me. That is nothing compared to the years my parents had together, the hardships they faced side by side, and the family they started...

But even with all this reasoning, I can't fight the resurgence of my anger. It's been nearly twenty years since Father left. That's two decades for her to come to terms with his defection, grieve, and do what's right. Her heart has moved on, it seems, so why hasn't she commanded her forces to do away with the Blood Wardens and closed her eyes until it's over?

And how dare she lie to me for all these years out of a lack of trust in my integrity and my loyalty to El-Alam?

The slightest recollection of how swayed I felt by the Oracle's words, even if for a moment, crosses my mind. But I disregard it. To be tempted is not the same as giving in. I wouldn't have. Even if Elias wasn't there to intervene.

I wouldn't have.

"Well, he's plenty strong now," I say, my voice gravelly. "Who knows how numerous his followers are?"

Mother stares straight ahead. Her mouth remains sealed.

"I'm sorry for your misfortune, Mother, but now it appears we have a much greater problem on our hands than we ever should have had." Though I regret the harshness of my words, I storm toward the door and grab the handle, nearly wrenching it before I recall the other matter at hand. "I'm calling for a council."

"Calden!" Mother yelps as I open the door.

I look back to see she's leapt from the chair. "You mustn't tell them. Please."

I stall, contemplating what I *mustn't* do: hide the truth or expose it and deal with the chaos it causes?

"It's not about that," I say. "We need to discuss the search for Toaph Elbara."

Mother's entire body seems to melt with her sigh.

No, Mother, I won't expose your lie yet. But soon enough.

NORIELLE

I'm still shaking long after Elias finishes telling me about the Oracle's identity and the canyx. He remains quiet, allowing me time to process the alarming news as we walk around the citadel. Swishing trees line our path, offering their shade as the sun reaches its zenith. I track an orange leaf as it squirms loose and flutters to the ground ahead of us. Elias steps out of his way to smash it under his boot, and the deliberate assault stirs a small chuckle from me.

But a moment later, I recall the trees shouldn't be shedding right now, and the humor dissolves.

I open my mouth to ask Elias what he thinks about the peculiar weather, as if that might be a lighter subject than everything else we've discussed, but Rhiana's sudden holler intercepts me. "Miss Norielle!"

I spin around to find Rhiana and her older brother waving at us.

"The Sovereign Prince requests your attendance at a council, Miss Norielle," Rhys calls.

"Well, there you go. Off to your first meeting." Elias nudges my arm with his elbow. He reassures me with a smile, but I feel his wistful gaze lingering on me as I step away.

I reach the two attendants in time to hear Rhys murmuring something to Rhiana about Calden seeming unwell. But by the confused look on Rhys's face, I'm guessing Calden hasn't yet told him the news that Elias shared with me.

Rhys guides our trio through the citadel and into the most interesting hallway I've seen so far. Stained glass windows adorn the walls, one for each phase of the moon, and at the very end, a colorful window forms an archway around the double doors, shining a resplendent light across the entrance.

"The council room," Rhys says, opening the door for me.

I stick close to Rhiana as we enter a long room with equally dazzling windows. A thick table with intricately carved designs fills the space. The Elders already occupy most of the seats—Seer Josiah at one head, flanked by the stout and mighty warrior captain, Gatlin, and the ever-weary-looking overseer of education, Atlas. On the opposite end, the tallest chair—intended for the Lady Sovereign, I assume—is empty, but Calden sits at its right side with an unflinching stare toward Odessa across from him. His chest heaves, as if readying for battle, and a darkness taints his normally serene expression.

My heart stammers. What happened when he confronted his mother?

Rhiana steps away, and Rhys ushers me to the seat beside Odessa. I sit and wait, my body feeling made of wood. Calden's eyes look down rather than toward me, but I still catch his half-hidden frown.

An awkward silence passes before Alani, notoriously late for everything, bustles into the room. Her mouth opens like she means to apologize, but as if sensing the weighty atmosphere, she keeps quiet. Rhys pulls out the seat beside Calden for her, then he joins Rhiana and the other attendants along the back wall of the room.

A moment later, another pair of doors opens, revealing the Lady Sovereign. A waft of lilac-scented perfume parades ahead of her, mixing with the Seer's potent cologne that's already permeated the room. Her pristine makeup looks fresh and intricate braids secure her copper-ornamented hair, painting a façade of composure that her glassy eyes undermine.

Chairs scoot back, people rise, and I rush to follow their lead. The Lady Sovereign's heels click against the gleaming stone, and the party bows. Once more, I mimic them.

"Thank you all for coming on such short notice," the Lady Sovereign says, taking her seat at the head of the table, and the rest of us return to our chairs. "My son would like to speak with you."

"Thank you, Mother." Calden sucks in a breath, and his head lifts with authority. "I would like to discuss with you the latest plans for finding Toaph Elbara."

Everyone sits at attention as Calden locks eyes with each person. Time seems to slow when he reaches me, and his stoic expression flinches, as if Alani pinched him under the table. He turns his focus toward Seer Josiah, avoiding looking at Odessa or his mother again.

"Over the past two and a half weeks, I have done everything I can to hear from Toaph Elbara, to no avail," Calden begins. "I have tried meditation as Seer Josiah suggested. I tried depriving myself of sleep, fasting, endangering myself, and ruminating on subjects most painful—all things previously shown to trigger my episodes—yet still, nothing."

I squeeze the fabric of my dress. Is that why he's looked so unhealthy? He's been sabotaging his own well-being on purpose?

"I also attempted returning to the place where I'd last heard Toaph with clarity, and while this led to the same empty result, I formed a theory with the help of my escort and friend, Elias Auden."

My friend, Elias. This would make me smile if not for everything else he said before it.

"We are going to go off of what little I have received from Toaph," Calden declares. "It seems within reason to me that Toaph may no longer be speaking because he knows he's already shown me all I need to see to find him."

"And what has he shown you, sire?" Captain Gatlin asks with an intrigued glimmer in his blue-gray eyes.

"Dust," Calden says.

Several heads cock to the side, mine amongst them.

Atlas tucks his white hair behind his ear as though it made him hear Calden incorrectly. "Dust, my lord?"

"In every glimpse I can recall, I see walls of dust. It swarms in the air, clouding everything that surrounds me. It's impossible to see through—like a shroud." A passionate energy gradually fills Calden's voice the longer he speaks. "Elias informed me of a place in the Segredo Desert known as *Vala dos Quaventos*, or the Valley of the Four Winds. He said the valley is in a perpetual dust storm, and that the Raevrans claim a great power lies inside the vortex—power that has prompted King Arlo to invade Raevre. I believe this power may be Toaph Elbara."

"*Raevre?*" Several voices pose the question at once, but it's Captain Gatlin that presses it further. "You aren't proposing going into a war zone, are you, sire?"

A flicker of irritation crosses Calden's face. "That is exactly what I am proposing."

My pulse quickens as I recall the many horrors Papa shared about Raevre in between his deployments during the thirteen-year-long first war. My imagination still swims with images from the details he gave about range warriors launching clay orbs that shattered and filled the air with poisonous vapors, cutlass-wielding savages that disregarded the rules of swordsmanship, and arrows laced with the blood of redarian snakes, causing explosions upon impact. Papa considered the Raevrans' tactics to be as barbaric as they are advanced.

As if the battlefields themselves aren't enough to scare me, my uncle—rather senselessly—shared a rumor once that the Raevrans brutally torture their captives before delivering their heads as decorations for their queen's court. Papa and Uncle Dedric never witnessed this themselves, but based on all I've heard of the merciless Queen Uxia of Raevre, I'm inclined to believe the tale.

And now, on top of all this, there are supernatural wildfires that spontaneously erupt and devour everything in their path. The flames have claimed whole battlefields and cities—ruthlessly killing soldiers from both kingdoms.

Won't Raevre's navy see us and assume we're part of another fleet of soldiers coming to oppress what little of their kingdom remains? Does Calden mean to take us directly into the heart of the battle in pursuit of this rumored power inside the vortex?

"With all due respect, my lord, the Raevrans are highly superstitious. Rarely have their accounts been anything more than the stuff of legends," Atlas says. "And given the circumstances of the war, I'm not sure this is the wisest course of action. Would not the High Warden of Raevre have passed on his concerns to us if he and his Seer sensed there was something to the Raevrans' claims?"

"Perhaps they don't know of it," Calden counters without pause. "Elias's source comes from outside the Wardens—an Alémor spy."

My tongue presses against the roof of my mouth. *Papa.* In the safety of our home, Papa used to whisper classified information he'd gathered, warning us never to share it. But, of course, Kieran was an exception. I told him anything Papa didn't.

"It seems what could lie in the Valley is, otherwise, a secret," Calden continues. "And there is only one way to find out for certain whether the Raevrans' claims are true. But even if I'm wrong about the Valley, the deserts of Raevre are still the best starting place. The expedition will be risky, because of the war, but the Raevran Wardens have a hidden cove where we can access their underground from the coast. So long as we exercise swiftness and stealth, we can avoid the war on our way in, and hopefully, we can gather aid from the Raevran Wardens from there out." He shifts, gesturing toward Alani. "And fortunately, I have a master sailor in my Bind to see to the first part, which is no mistake of El-Alam's, I'm sure."

Alani beams, somehow unfazed by any of this, but sweat suddenly dampens my palms as I fully put the pieces of Calden's plan together. To get into Raevre, we'll have to cross an ocean. A massive body of water, significantly wider and deeper than Lake Daleia. Could it also come alive? Could the same malevolent energies that possessed the lake back home awaken in the deep?

Would a ship full of Wardens be powerful enough to tame a sentient sea?

"And if you find him, my lord?" Atlas's question yanks me back to the conversation, but my heart only beats faster.

"I trust Toaph himself will tell us what to do next," Calden says.

The Seer, who has been uncharacteristically quiet, finally enters the discussion. "It seems a worthwhile chance to take, if you ask me."

I follow his gaze to the Lady Sovereign. Her lip twitches as she turns to Calden.

"And when would you like to begin this expedition?" she asks.

"As soon as possible." Calden addresses the rest of the council rather than his mother. "We should begin preparations today."

I nearly shrink beneath the table at the Lady Sovereign's next words. "That may present a problem." But instead of looking at me, she directs her attention toward Seer Josiah. "You are still a member shy of having a complete Bind, and you should not attempt any mission relating to the purpose of the Bind without every member present."

Odessa shoots Alani another look, like the one she gave her in the arena when she advised us not to join Calden without our fifth Bind member. But Alani misses it, too focused on Calden to notice.

Calden's forced smile capsizes, though before he can reply, Seer Josiah juts in. "Actually, my Lady..." Every head turns toward him. "El-Alam *has* given word to me about the final Bind member. Just this morning."

What? I mouth the word as Calden speaks it aloud.

"But His message would be best shared with the Sovereign Prince in private." Seer Josiah leans toward Calden on his opposite side of the table. "I intended to tell you upon your arrival, but I've not yet had the opportunity."

"Has El-Alam chosen the final Bind member?" Calden asks, disregarding the Seer's preference for privacy.

"He... ah, how shall I say this?" Seer Josiah glances around the council, drumming all ten of his fingers against the tabletop. "Well, He hasn't provided us a name. However..."

"However?" Calden shifts like he might stand to pry the words from the Seer's mouth. "Please, Seer. There shouldn't be any secrets amongst the council."

I tense at the pointed comment and the side-glance Calden gives his mother, reminded of what Elias told me. Is what Calden feared true then? His mother lied about the Sovereign's death and wasn't deceived herself?

The Seer considers Calden's statement another moment before giving in. "El-Alam has declared that the final Bind member is yours to choose."

"Mine to choose?" Calden echoes. "Why leave it to me?"

The Seer shakes his head. "That is beyond me. It's unheard of, like your last member being called from the outside." He nods toward me. "But these are uncharted times, which do indeed call for uncharted methods, I daresay."

The Lady Sovereign's glare bores into him like he's betrayed her. I look at Calden again, now curious about who might come to his mind first. Would he consider Elias? Rhys, maybe? Or someone I haven't met yet?

"Then, there," Calden says. "It is my decision, and I will certainly make it before we leave."

The Lady Sovereign's wordless conversation with the Seer breaks off, and she faces her son again. "Are you forgetting the other matter?"

Calden stills, seeming to puzzle over what she means, but I'm already shriveling inside.

The Lady Sovereign's hand gestures toward me. "Your fourth Bind member has yet to pass her test."

Calden flinches. "Rhys said she tested—"

He stops himself, as if recalling something, and looks at me in question.

The same horror I felt when watching my vitality sphere not only *miss* the target, but fire behind me and blast a bench apart, claws at me again. My mouth doesn't provide the answer he seems to await.

"She failed," the Lady Sovereign says in my place. "Which means she needs at least two more weeks of training before she can test again, per the Order."

Calden wets his lips after a long pause. "How close was she to passing?"

"She scored nineteen out of twenty."

One point shy of perfection—the only number considered to be a passing score. My stomach suddenly roils as Calden's face fills with dismay.

I shift, wishing I'd thought to ask Rhys or Rhiana if I am allowed to speak, so I could apologize. Or better yet, ask why a single point matters that much.

"The journey to Raevre is plenty long," Calden says, a strained optimism in his tone. "She can continue her training on the ship, and test with me when she's ready."

"Calden." The Lady Sovereign straightens in her seat. "A new inductee is forbidden from leaving the citadel until they've passed their test."

Calden's sturdy form swells as he draws in a deep breath. His gaze singles me out like a pair of blue flames, blazing desperately, like he's asking—pleading—for me to take his side in this matter.

But am I allowed to say anything? *Should* I?

I nod my reassurance, disregarding my apprehensions on account of not wanting to disappoint him. After all that he's done for me, the least I can do is stand beside him, even if it puts me at odds with the Lady Sovereign.

"Well, as the Seer said,"—Calden almost smiles—"uncharted times call for uncharted methods."

But the Lady's tone only turns colder. "Uncharted methods should never include blatant rebellion against the Warden Order."

Her words loom overhead, like a cloud casting a shadow over Calden's entire demeanor. He sits, wordless, with a storm brewing in his eyes before he suddenly erupts.

"To the pits with the Order." Calden bangs his fist against the table, and I jump. "The world is falling apart. Beasts and disasters endanger innocent people every day. The Blood Wardens' forces fester in the darkness, hardly opposed. And we can't even set foot aboveground without risking our lives. The Order was formed for a time very different from now. How much longer must we uphold its restrictions? When do we realize they are part of the obstacle?"

"The Order exists to protect us." The Lady Sovereign raises her chin with dignity despite his outburst. "It was set in place so that radical ideas, impatience, and over-ambitiousness wouldn't threaten the lives of the Wardens as a whole."

"*Fascinating*." Calden's bitter tone shoots a shiver down my spine. "Because last I saw, our numbers have depleted to less than half of what we used to be. Would you consider that protected, Mother?"

"*Calden*," she chides, but she's not fast enough to argue before he continues over her.

"I am not in thoughtless rebellion against the Order. But to uphold it as though exceptions could never be made, particularly in such dire circumstances, is irrational." Calden sweeps his gaze across the onlookers, as if to ascertain their reactions. "Every day we postpone finding Toaph, we threaten not only the lives of the Wardens, but of all Silvirdia. We cannot delay pursuing this lead over some old rule that applied to a world that wasn't destroying itself."

"The world has been destroying itself for a quarter century," the Lady Sovereign objects. "We can spare two more weeks."

"Can we?" Calden gestures toward the window that stands level with the crown of an orange-leafed oak. "Has anyone not seen the trees outside?"

There's a long quiet.

"It would appear Alatûm has come three months too soon—skipping right over Soltûm. If that is the case, then plantations across the kingdom—if not the world—are about to be devastated by the untimely cold. *Famine* could sweep across Silvirdia. And what if the warmth never returns?"

The table seems to wobble in my vision. Is that possible?

"My lord, it is conceivable that we are merely experiencing an unusual cold front," Atlas says, yet his tone is unsteady. "And for all we presently know, it could only be happening right here around the citadel. We've not heard any reports come in from elsewhere."

Calden shakes his head. "*Regardless.* Schillon has lost entire islands to the sea. The storms in Ashtera are raging. Raevre is on fire. The barrier in Northspire requires more of our sentinels by the year to maintain, and the Hunters here in Alémor are ever increasing in number. We're in enough danger as it stands. We *must* act. Now."

"Then you would imperil her?" His mother's words are as sharp as the look she gives me... almost as if she wants *me* to protest.

I keep my lips sealed tight, but goosebumps sprout down my arms. How he responds should tell me everything I need to know about where he stands regarding our relationship—if I really matter enough to him for him to prioritize my safety.

"We can protect her," Calden counters after only a moment's consideration.

I cringe, as if his words were a strike to my cheek. Of course, I don't want to hold us back, but I'd much prefer *I* be arguing with *him* about my right to board the ship—not watching him dismiss the risk to me with hardly a second thought. Where is his head? Where is the protective man who led me to the citadel? The man who healed me?

Have his fears completely consumed him?

"She is not ready to face the dangers of the world, and especially not the dangers of the sea and Raevre," the Lady protests.

Not ready? Over one point? I find it even harder to hold my tongue. *All* of this is ridiculous.

"Norielle," Calden addresses me, and a spark shoots through my system. *Finally.* "Would you be willing to board the ship and complete your training with me there, knowing the dangers?"

I clamp my trembling hands together beneath the table and straighten my shoulders, refusing to let my dread of the threats ahead or my indignation toward him inform my decision.

"I'll do it," I say. *For Toaph Elbara.*

Calden, instead of looking validated by my agreement, pales, as if my reply brought him immediate regret. This, at least, calms some of my frustration with him and invokes a hint of my fading compassion. He *is* reeling from a betrayal, it seems. And even I have been wrestling with the pressure to hurry—to race against the world's destruction—which is what led me to fail my test.

Still, my understanding can't quite quell my anger.

"I was only one point from passing, I—" I stammer, not wanting to offend the Lady Sovereign, but not knowing how else to rationalize my answer and convince Calden not to back down. "I don't see how one point would make a life-or-death difference if it came to it."

All eyes turn to the Lady Sovereign, seeming to await her verdict.

"What says the council?" the Lady Sovereign asks, her corded throat squeezing out her words.

There's another pause, then Captain Gatlin croaks, "I support the expedition."

"I do not support it," Atlas adds.

"I support the Sovereign Prince," Alani chimes in, with a confident smile toward Calden. How she maintains her spirit in this room baffles me.

Odessa shuffles her feet under the table. Of all people, I expected she would fire off an opinion before the question was even declared, but she remains as silent as she's been for the entire council.

"Forgive me, Lady Sovereign," says the Seer, dark eyes twinkling as he turns to Calden. "But I support the expedition. I trust the Sovereign Prince's judgment. After all, it was to him that this mission was assigned. I do believe the Creator knows the man to whom He has assigned this."

The Lady Sovereign sighs, and I realize by a quick count that Odessa's opinion wouldn't matter now. Even if she sided with her mother, the tally already favors Calden.

"Then it is decided," the Lady Sovereign declares with a low-set gaze. "The Bind will sail for Raevre."

CALDEN

"Have you lost your mind?" Odessa hisses as she follows me into the hallway leading to my private chamber.

I spin to meet Odessa's dark gaze. "Of which mind do you speak? Because last I checked, only one is missing and the entire world's fate rests upon our finding it."

Odessa's grimace deepens. "You shamed Mother back there. Have you no respect for her? Or are you too busy trying to prove yourself to the council and that girl?"

Trying to prove myself? To that girl? How dare she—

"I spoke reason. If Mother opposed it, then she shamed herself," I say, though my heart twists as soon as the words come out. I march onward, hoping my sister will quiet herself and leave me alone before she can provoke another harsh comment from me. But her footsteps follow without pause.

"You're being reckless."

Her weak accusation feels like a pebble hitting steel armor. "Good. Maybe something will change because of it. *Careful* certainly isn't working."

"Sure, you'll get the Bind killed. What a fine change that will be."

I resist a childish urge to roll my eyes and instead quicken my pace like I might outrun her. My room isn't much farther, and it's about the only place I can slip into where no one can reach me without going through Rhys. *Wherever he is now.*

Probably with Mother, receiving orders to talk me out of going to Raevre.

"If you're trying to run away because you're mad at Mother, there are a hundred safer places you could go," Odessa says, charging after me. "You don't need to be so outrageous."

"I'm not running away," I grumble. "I'm trying to save this world before it's too late."

But even I can hear the way my denial wavers. I intended for the council to be a discussion about what to do next, not an argument for why we must sail to Raevre *now* at any cost. Yet, in the brief span of time between Mother's confirmation that she's been lying to me and the moment the council began, I decided, immovably, on Raevre—as an excuse to get us far away from this citadel and Mother.

"Calden," Odessa snaps when my bedroom door comes into view. "Stop."

"For what?" I ask, feet pressing onward still. "So, you can continue rebuking me like you're Mother's right arm?"

"No. I am actually trying to apologize to you, but you aren't making it very easy."

This pulls me to a stop. I meet her gaze, which still burns with judgment. In the embers there is remorse, faint and fading, but present no less.

"This hasn't felt much like the beginnings of an apology."

Odessa remains quiet for a moment, seeming to hold an argument inside. When she finally speaks, agitation laces her low voice. "I understand why you are angry with her and me. You have a right to be. To be frank, I wanted to tell you sooner about Father, but Mother ordered me not to. She wanted to be the one to say it, when the time was right." She crosses her arms. "But I don't think your anger at her is a valid reason to be obstinate and rash."

"Yet the council agreed with me."

"You are persuasive," Odessa says, raising her brows. "That does not equate to being right."

I look away, gaze landing on a painting on the wall—a ship, ironically, sailing amidst a squall with Toaph Elbara creating an eye in the storm for the ship to travel in. Mother once said it was a symbolic portrayal of us in the universe. What lies beyond our world is darkness and chaos, but Toaph held it back, protecting us from it. Only now, he's gone. And all that remains is the darkness. How much longer until the dark spirits beyond our world discover we are nearly defenseless and come for us too?

"So, you are against the quest?" I ask.

Odessa scowls. "You're leading us across cursed waters into an enemy kingdom engulfed in flames to enter a war zone, all the while following a voice inside your head. You can't say that doesn't sound ridiculous."

My lips press together. *She had to say it like that…*

"But to your point, we have nothing else to go on," Odessa adds, and my tension subsides a notch. "So, do I like it? Absolutely not. Do I think we'll gain anything by sailing to Raevre? No. Am I irritated with you for your bullheaded means of getting your way? Considerably. But I will comply for the sake of the small part of me that hopes you're right… on the condition that you promise to apologize to Mother and that you swear you will not follow our father into rebellion."

Heaviness presses against my chest. "Is that why you kept Mother's secret? You doubted me also?"

"You can't deny my right to be skeptical, considering your disobedient reputation."

Her words seem to pin me to the wall, inciting every doubt I have about myself at once. But with a glance downward, I see my Bind Mark and remember Seer Josiah's words. *It was to him that this mission was assigned. I do believe the Creator knows the man to whom He has assigned this.*

I meet Odessa's gaze with renewed confidence. "There is a stark difference, sister, between neglecting to follow the rules set in place by man and disobeying the rules provided by El-Alam. I am not like Father—using divinely forbidden methods. I am merely challenging the legitimacy of traditions that have potentially prevented us from doing what El-Alam has foremost called us to do."

She gives me a questioning look, as if she's forgetting what the Wardens are here for.

"We exist to protect Silvirdia, and if our man-made rules inhibit us from doing that, then the rules render us disobedient to El-Alam Himself."

Odessa smirks. "And what of His command to obey authority?"

"I will follow it insomuch as it does not prevent me from obeying El-Alam first."

Her smirk falls, and a look of genuine consideration softens her features. I smile, seeing again my little sister, who once occasionally found it within herself to appreciate me as her older brother.

"I promise you, Odessa," I say, leaning closer to her. "I will not walk a path that leads to eternal death, nor will I lead others toward it. I need you to trust me. We are in this Bind together, and I need you on my side."

I hold her gaze until she turns away. Saying nothing in reply, she walks back down the hall.

I rise at first light after a fitful night's rest and slip through the citadel's dim halls and into the quiet courtyard. In the distance, I faintly hear a sword clanging against wood. My eyes fix on the training arena as I abandon the pathway to stride over the frost-dusted grass. With my brisk pace, the chilly air gusts against my skin and sweeps away my weariness.

I push my hood back as I approach the arena, spotting Elias, as expected, near the wooden dummies. His sword thwacks against his defenseless opponent in merciless swings, reminding me of the first time I met him out here. He was only fifteen then and had not been with us for a full year yet. I'd hardly encountered him besides during his induction ceremony, where he seemed less than interested in talking to me, but that day in this very yard was when I sensed that, despite his confident exterior, he was struggling to find his worth here amongst the Wardens. So, I took him under my wing, mentoring him in hopes that I could help him see no one is insignificant in El-Alam's eyes. Not even our newest recruit.

I rap my knuckle against the weapons rack to announce myself, and Elias freezes mid-swing. He turns, and the moment our eyes meet, a muscle spasms in my chest. I fight to keep my expression flat, but the pain of all that has occurred since our quest to the crypt seems to resurface at once, as if his gaze somehow fractured the walls of my inner fortress. And now it feels like a different day here in the arena, when I confessed to him what happened to Corene—the day I realized he was more than an apprentice that I'd taken in for his sake. He was a friend I'd sought in my own time of need.

Elias lowers his weapon, sparing me his usual smart remarks, and meets me midway in the yard. His brows knit as he looks me over, surely noticing how utterly unkempt I am for the start of a day. I haven't shaved. Purple colors the skin beneath my eyes. I don't recall if I brushed my hair. And only now do I realize I've not bothered to redress since yesterday.

"She lied," Elias says after a moment.

The blunt statement hits like a cannonball, blasting another hole in my fortress. I avert my gaze and nod, sparing myself from having to see his reaction. Him—someone who's valued my mother's leadership, possibly more than I have—hearing that she's lied to everyone. Him, learning for certain that our last Sovereign created the Blood Wardens.

Elias says nothing for so long that I finally force myself to look at him to be sure the news hasn't stopped his heart. He stands with a white-knuckled grip on his sword and a parted, yet silent, mouth.

I lower my voice even more. "She claims she was trying to protect the Wardens by not telling them. She feared more might follow him... including me."

I say no more, allowing him to process what I've revealed. He stands like a shell of himself until a robin's whistle seems to awaken every bird in the molting oaks—a warning that this yard won't stay private for much longer. As soon as the light touches it, Captain Gatlin and his defenders will appear for their routine practice.

"Well, that's... disappointing," Elias finally says in a reserved tone. Yet the tension gripping his voice hints that he's confined an entire tirade to the barriers of those three words. He ventures toward the rack and deposits his sword there before facing me again without further response.

"Yes," I say, fighting to sound as measured as him. "It is. Which begs the question of how much more of what the Oracle said was truth."

Elias looks down, but doesn't give the quick retort I expected, as if this time, he's actually considering the Oracle might not have delivered a full basket of lies.

"But that's a subject for another time. There's something else I came out here to talk to you about." I take a deep breath. "I have made my decision about Raevre. We are going there to investigate the Valley of the Four Winds. I plan to leave for the coast tomorrow morning, and I'd like for you to come with us."

His brows lift. "Tomorrow?"

"Yes. That is what we discussed at the council—not the matter of the Sovereign."

"What about Nori's training? She told me she failed her test."

I glance away, uncertain what sort of response I'm about to elicit from him. But Norielle herself approved of this decision, and it was only a single point. "She scored nineteen, which I say is close enough to passing for an exception to be made. My mother isn't delighted, but the council—and Norielle—elected that she be permitted to accompany us. I will continue training her on the ship and be sure she passes before we ever reach Raevre."

Elias scowls as he dabs the sweat off his brow with a cloth. I'm still bracing myself for his protest when he twists my way again. "Aren't you still down one member?"

"Actually, Lias... We may have our fifth Bind member by the time we leave tomorrow."

His face contorts. "What?"

"The Seer heard from El-Alam, and apparently, the Creator has decided that I should choose the final Bind member."

Elias takes a long drink from his water flask before questioning me with a forceful layer of nonchalance in his voice. "So, you've already picked, then? Who is it? Rhys?"

"I considered Rhys," I say, contemplating my decision one more time to be sure I've made the correct one.

Elias's gaze narrows on me, as if suddenly realizing what I'm about to say, but he dares not suggest it.

I straighten. "Lias, I want you to be the final member."

He jerks—maybe that's not what he expected—and water splashes on his dusty boots. "You what?"

"I want you to be the fifth member of the Bind," I repeat more confidently. "You might find this alarming, but as it stands, you are the truest and most capable friend I have beyond those already in my Bind, and you've supported me through so many missions. It wouldn't make sense to choose anyone else. Not even Rhys. And you are, after all, my protégé."

Elias laughs, a disbelieving sound, and caps his flask before he can spill any more of it. "You want *me* in your Bind?"

His reaction causes a smile to break through my heavy demeanor. "Well, now, don't keep questioning me; I might change my mind."

"Cal..." Elias starts, a full range of emotions crossing his face before he gets anything else out. "Have you... asked the rest of the Bind about this?"

By the rest of the Bind, I'm assuming he means Norielle, or possibly Odessa.

"No. El-Alam didn't ask them to choose. He asked me, and that's what I decided."

He squints at me again. "And you don't want to think about it, you know, give it a few days and maybe some actual sleep first?"

I almost laugh at his disbelief. I expected him to gloat about this, even if jokingly, or at least, assume I'd chosen him before I could say it.

"Sleep? There's no time for that nonsense," I joke, but my tone turns serious as I continue. "Of course, I won't make you join if you don't want to. Even El-Alam doesn't require us to answer a call. But if you would accept this, then meet us tomorrow morning in the main foyer for our departure."

Elias stares at me like he's expecting me to withdraw my invitation, call it a prank, and spit on him as I leave.

Have I been that unappreciative of his friendship? Or does he truly think so little of himself still?

"I'll be there," Elias finally says, though his voice sounds shaky, like he might fall to his knees weeping any moment.

I smile, but find myself uncertain of what to say next, so I turn back toward the citadel. "See you then."

NORIELLE

Rhiana falls into step beside me in the hallway. Only two nights after the council meeting, I've already loaded Papa's bag onto my back, the weight forcing the straps to dig into my underarms. At my hip, Papa's sword hangs, ready for its next adventure—its return to Raevre. Only now, it bears an engraved Conjuration Ward as Odessa thought to recommend, which will allow me to materialize it into my hand, if I somehow achieve Mastery while we are away and become able to use the advanced ward.

My boots *clip-clop* down the stairs to the main foyer, joining the noise of the murmuring voices below. I look over the polished rail at the group already waiting for me. Calden notices me first, breaking from his conversation with his mother and the Seer to wave at me. His motion draws the rest of their gazes up. Odessa, the Elders—

Elias?

I stop mid-step, blinking, as if what I'm seeing is an illusion. Nevertheless, Elias stands with a bag on his back and a sword hanging from his hip like me. Is he coming? Did Calden choose him as our final Bind member?

Elias meets me at the bottom of the stairs. "At what point are you going to stop being surprised that I'm still here?" he asks, raking back his hair. I squint to see if he has a Bind Mark, but his wrist doesn't turn enough to reveal it. "I take it Cal hasn't told you."

No, he hasn't talked to me directly since the council.

"Told me what?" I ask, my glance pivoting between Calden and Elias.

Elias holds up his arm, and my heart flutters as I spy the compass-like mark peeking between the curves of his leather armguard.

He lowers his arm. "Looks like we're stuck with each other. Hope you don't mind." He winks at me, but gives a sideways glance at Calden, and his expression loses its mirth.

I follow his gaze and find Calden reassuring him with a half-hearted smile before turning back to talk with his mother and Seer Josiah.

"Do you?" Elias asks, drawing my attention back to him.

"Do I what?"

"Mind."

I bite my lip. Can he not tell by my smile? Have I been so rude to him he'd assume I'd be unhappy to hear my long-lost friend is now bound to my soul also?

"No," I say, quieting my next words so that Calden can't overhear them. "I was hoping he'd choose you."

Elias grins. "Knew you'd come around."

I do my best to scowl at him, but, as usual, I can't maintain the sour look for more than a second. "It's good to see you two are actually friends," I say, though I know it's more than that. I wanted *my* friend to be with me. Like how it used to be.

I've given up everything else to be here.

"Eh, I'd say we're *allies,*" Elias teases, and his obvious down-playing of their relationship makes me smile more. Kieran always acted nonchalant when he cared more about something than he wanted to expose.

"If everyone is ready," Calden says, his mother glaring at the floor behind him, "we should get moving. The coast is a two-day journey from here. Since she departed after the council, Alani should arrive there today and will have the ship fully stocked and prepared by the time we catch up."

"Everybody here was waiting on you, prince," Elias says.

Calden ignores his comment, meeting my gaze fully for the first time since the council meeting. His eyes seem to swirl with determination and sorrow at once—a complex combination that makes me yearn for a chance to talk to him about all that's happened. But something feels different about him, like he went to the crypt as one man and came back as another. Distant, angry. Hurting. And even more intimidating to me after watching him take command of that council and glimpsing the beginning of one of his episodes at my ball.

"Let's take our leave, then," Calden says. The attendants open the double doors, releasing us for our most dangerous journey yet, and we set out across the courtyard.

A wild wind blows, tossing mist from the waterfalls into my face as we cross one of the seven bridges. The gust stirs my excitement, and my steps bob with energy. Despite how pretty the citadel is, the regulations upheld in it have left me feeling suffocated. But this—setting out on a new quest—tastes like freedom.

Even if it is utterly terrifying.

"So, we're two days from the coast?" I prompt to get someone talking.

"Assuming no one drags their feet, and no Blood Wardens attempt to get in our way," Odessa says from the head of the group, and my heartbeat stutters. I hadn't considered they'd come this close to the citadel.

"What would that set us back by? Ten seconds?" Elias remarks, looking around at our company. Two Master Wardens from the Sovereign household, and himself, who's proven his skills sufficient against defectors before.

Odessa releases an amused hum. "Point taken, bard."

I steal a glance at Calden, hoping to see agreement shining on his face, just to further prove there's little for us to worry about right now, but he's focused on the ground. We reach the end of the bridge, stepping onto moist dirt. A tunnel mouth awaits us up ahead. In a few steps, darkness will encase us again besides what light the crystals provide. My tongue dries as we near it—the last time I was in passages like these, I almost died.

I inch closer to Elias, my heart silently pleading for his and all their protection, even with my training. The yearning feels weak and stands in stark contrast to the confidence exuding from Odessa as she marches onward. But what if I find out the hard way that one point does matter? That the Lady Sovereign's concerns were valid?

The stone tunnel amplifies my sharp inhale as we enter, and Elias turns to me. I smile away any concerns on his part and turn my gaze toward the wall. Yet he shifts even closer to me, never fooled by my pretenses.

Small white-gold crystals glow in clusters along the passage, but their dim light is barely more than that of candles. *Candles.* Like in the atrium the brute threw me into. Where I was tied up... venom searing through my body...

Light suddenly floods the space, and I blink myself out of the memory. I trace the light's source to Calden behind me, who gives a small smile. "I've never been on the sea," he says. "Have you, Norielle?"

So now he's talking to me.

"No. Only the lake."

"That's right. You'd never left Behria," Calden says. "What about you, Lias? You've been on the sea, haven't you?"

"Twice," Elias says, offering no details. But I know the rest. Once on his way to the Western Isles after his mother died, and once more on his way back after he lost his grandparents. And now, he's heading overseas to the land his papa died on.

Strange, how so much pain can hide in someone's silences.

"Well, hopefully we don't all end up seasick," Calden says.

My stomach twists at the thought of boarding a ship, and I scowl toward the ground. Nightmares of the sea awakening and dragging the ship to the ocean floor so the seaweed could strangle us have haunted my last two nights' sleep. I've reassured myself a thousand times that it won't happen—not with so many Wardens aboard the ship. The sea wouldn't dare, and even if it did, the Wardens could stop it.

But that doesn't loosen the phantom grip of weeds around my wrists.

"Why haven't you ever been on your ship?" I ask Calden, rubbing the imaginary sensation of seaweed off my skin.

There's a long pause before Calden answers, "I've never much liked the idea of it... being confined to a ship for weeks with nowhere to go. I don't care to be in one place for that long. Besides, Mother enjoys her expeditions to visit the High Wardens in the other kingdoms, and someone must watch over the citadel in her stead. I'm happy to do that if it keeps me on land. Though, once I am officially appointed as Sovereign, I will be required to make the visits myself."

"And when will that be?"

Calden's tone drops, an edge in it causing me to regret my question. "We aren't sure yet. If my father were still *properly* around, he would continue to lead until I reached the age of thirty. Then he would dub himself the Venerate, acting as my ongoing mentor and regent, as required, until his health declined. However, considering his absence, I should have become Sovereign upon coming of age, but with how bad my episodes were then, Mother maintained her post as our leader to buy me more time to either gain control over or stop the episodes. And now with the Bind mission at hand, she's felt it best to spare me the full responsibilities of Sovereign until after our mission is complete."

I chew on his complicated answer, grateful for the distraction from my unease about being underground and the dread of the sea that follows. The Wardens' hierarchy differs significantly from Alémor's. King Arlo will sit upon his throne until old age or poor health takes him, and even if that happened before his son had come of age, the prince would still have become king as a boy. Though his advisors would have run the kingdom in his name. And the king's wife, Queen Karisi, would never be entrusted with leadership as a female. Alémor's low view of women has made her into nothing more than a pretty accessory to our king.

But what great pressure the Wardens' leadership structure places on any woman who falls in love with a Sovereign Prince—knowing that they would have to truly rule beside the Sovereign or even step in for him in circumstances like these. Or is this an unheard-of exception?

"Did your mother help lead the Wardens before losing the Sovereign?" I ask, unable to quell my curiosity.

This time, Odessa speaks before Calden can get a word out. "Of course. All Lady Sovereigns are expected to help carry the load, and part of their marriage vows to the Sovereign include an agreement to step in on the rare occasion that a Sovereign dies before his successor is ready to assume the role."

I swallow her subtext—the unspoken warning to me about the feelings she's assumed I have for her brother.

"For this reason," Calden adds, so flatly that I can't tell if he's feigning neutrality, or if he has resigned himself to this reality, "Sovereign Princes are encouraged to select their wives from the daughters of the High Wardens, since they are essentially princesses beneath the stewards of other kingdoms. Daughters of the Elders are also highly regarded options. Mother is the High Warden of Schillon's eldest daughter."

I glance at Elias, whose silence has made it feel like I'm walking beside a ghost. All he offers is a half-smile before returning his focus to picking dirt out from under his nails. Oddly, the habit that annoyed me as a child now gives me a sense of home.

"Do Atlas and Captain Gatlin have daughters?" I ask, but the question feels too prying the moment it leaves my lips and earns me a perturbed side-glance from Elias, as well as a long silence from Calden.

"Corene was Atlas's daughter," Odessa fills in.

I seal a gasp behind my lips. Why hasn't anyone told me that the woman who almost killed me was Atlas's daughter? And what pain must that poor man be carrying around, knowing both his children defected and are now dead? How can he even stand sitting in the Lady Sovereign's or Calden's presence?

"Gatlin only has sons," Odessa carries on as she rounds a corner in the tunnel, "and the Seer's firstborn was delivered without a heartbeat. His wife passed shortly after that, so he is without offspring."

I lay a hand against my heart, feeling briefly the Seer's pain as if it were my own. With his jubilant manner, I'd never have suspected he'd suffered so much as to lose his firstborn and wife. I'd assumed he'd never married. Is that why he seems to take such joy in calling me his child and watching over me? Does it help fill the void inside him, much like he's helped filled the one Papa's death left in me?

Odessa's tone suddenly turns cheerful, relieving me from the heaviness of her last statement. "The High Warden of Raevre has a daughter. Perhaps this will be your chance, brother. It would be an embarrassment to be the first Sovereign to receive his position without a bride at his side."

Calden grunts. "The very last thing I'm going to Raevre for is to find a bride."

A devilish smile fills Odessa's face as she looks at him over her shoulder. "Well, you'd best be prepared, because she will be most interested in meeting you, I'm sure."

"Much to her disappointment."

Odessa laughs at Calden's retort, and the echo of her amusement is the last sound for at least an hour.

I catch the glisten of stars through a fissure overhead as we reach our rest stop, a haven much like the ones we stayed in along the way to the citadel. The scent of smoke mixed with something peppery irritates my nose and alerts me to the fact that another Warden is here before I spot one of the bedroom doors shut and missing its key.

A shiver trickles down my spine as I recall that Blood Wardens sometimes use these same havens and passages, but when I check my Omen Mark, it is black, and the arrow rests in an idle, upright position.

"This is a popular haven," Elias says to me as Calden and Odessa turn for the communal chamber to revive what smells like a smoldering fire. "I'm surprised there's even any rooms left."

At his comment, I notice there are only three rooms, and with one occupied, that leaves us only two to stay in, and this haven lacks the couch some others have had. I gulp, realizing that we'll have to double up—which means I'll be sleeping on the floor, trying to be invisible lest I annoy the Second Lady of the Wardens.

"Defectors don't come here often," Elias adds, reminding me of my former concern.

At least I'll have the comfort of not being completely alone then, even if I must feel like a dog on the floor beneath the princess's feet.

I follow Elias to the chamber Calden and Odessa ventured into, and find Odessa crouched beside the firepit, stoking fresh flames while Calden rearranges the wooden chairs into a proper circle.

Elias's bag rattles as he plunks it onto a chair and digs through it. He produces his kettle and begins preparing his tea while the rest of us settle in to poke through our food rations. I start on a soft slab of sharp cheddar cheese and retrieve a wrapped pastry that I snatched from the refectory this morning. But the moment the sugary scent wafts into my nose, I recall my thoughts from the other day about little Kieran's love for tarts.

I wait for him to finish propping his kettle over the flames, then hold the pastry toward him. "It's strawberry."

His face scrunches, but a smile crawls onto his lips. "I brought plenty, Nori. You eat it."

I extend the tart even closer to him. "It would taste better with your tea."

"You want a cup?"

"No," I half groan, half laugh. "I want you to eat it. Just take it."

He stalls before finally accepting the pastry, only to tear it in half and insist we at least share it. I concede, and Elias and I fall quiet again as I pick at my portion of the pastry. Calden and Odessa quietly exchange words about the peculiar climate, a conversation that lasts only as long as Elias's water takes to boil. And soon the only noise is our munching and the crackles from the fire.

I abruptly remember something I wanted to bring up and check around the crystal-dotted atrium before asking, "Did the Oracle say anything else to you when you encountered him?"

Calden stares down at the jerky in his hand. By the length of it, he's taken maybe a single bite this entire time. His eyes don't even glance up, as if he didn't hear me at all.

"Calden?"

His chest rises, but not his gaze. "Nothing worth repeating. The source is foul. Only that which is confirmed by a Seer is worth giving any consideration to."

"Did you... not ask Seer Josiah?" I ask.

Calden's face tilts even further toward his lap. "Seer Josiah has no answers."

"By which he means, he didn't ask," Odessa says, shooting him a scrutinizing look that he misses.

My sticky hands go still.

"I am untrusting of his discernment right now," Calden says. "He couldn't sense my mother's lies. How could we expect him to sense the Oracle's?"

"You trusted him about Toaph Elbara being alive," I counter, a chill spreading across my skin.

"That was before I realized that even our Seer can be deceived." Calden's next statement is barely audible. "Or he is otherwise good at denying truths he wishes not to face."

I lower my chin at the thought of the Seer, who I've already grown so fond of, possibly partaking in hiding this information. Would it be for the same reason as the Lady Sovereign? Would he also fear Calden might follow his adoptive father into corruption?

Anxiety turns my shoulders inward. Should I be concerned about Calden, too? Have I been too quick to accept his kindness and nobility as evidence that he'd never sway us in the wrong direction? Or is everyone else only paranoid about him?

"Besides, I'd not like to be the one to deliver the news to him that the woman he's taken to is married still to a living man," Calden adds. "There is another Seer in Raevre. I plan to inquire of her instead—someone unbiased."

With a sigh, I finally remember my pastry, but the sweet bread and strawberry filling only make me feel ill when I take another bite. I force the rest down, following it with a long drink of water before rising.

"I'd like to get some rest," I announce, hoping to steal a few private moments before Odessa joins me. My fingers twitch at the thought. "I'll leave the door unlocked... and save the bed for you."

Odessa shifts, as if she hadn't taken notice of our bedroom predicament—or maybe she expected to have a room reserved for herself with no consideration of what position that placed the rest of us in.

"Take the bed," Odessa says, but before her selflessness can alarm me too much, she adds, "I'd rather sleep on the dirt than atop a used bed. No telling when the sheets were last washed with how few suppliers we have these days."

I glance at Calden for a clue on how to respond to his sister, but he's paying no attention to us. I try Elias next, only to find him staring like he wants to say something, but isn't sure if he should. The questioning look I give him goes unanswered, so I turn back to Odessa. "Thank you, then, I guess," I say, then I retreat to steal a few minutes of privacy.

CALDEN

"Why don't you try it?" I say to Norielle when we reach the tunnel's exit after another long day of walking.

She steps away from Elias's side—her near-permanent position—then takes my outstretched warding pen. The softly lit shaft reflects on her fair skin.

"Where?" she asks.

I lift my lantern, the dim section of the tunnel making it challenging to spot the Sealing Ward placed there by ancient Grand Masters. My light spills across the stone wall, startling a cluster of moths into the air. The rapid flutter of their white wings creates a purring sound as they scatter into the dark space behind us. In their wake lies the simple yet ornate Sealing Ward, like a braided ring on the wall.

"Draw it right in the center," I say.

Norielle gives me a look that says, *I know*—reminding me that Alani has already taught her this, and that I missed my chance to be the one to train her when I left for the crypt.

She gives a partial glance at her spectators before approaching the wall. After a slight delay, she sets my pen to the stone and fills the blank space inside the ring with the Key Ward.

The symbol shimmers, correcting her wobbly lines, and I smile, remembering our lesson at Ila's table. I deliberately withheld the fact that wards will perfect themselves when drawn accurately enough. I wanted to be sure she gave it her utmost effort, so she'd be less likely to make mistakes and fail to draw a successful ward when she needed it.

There's a long quiet while she attempts to ignite the ward, and I feel the moment stretching, as if all eyes were on me. Key Wards, despite their immense usefulness, are some of the easiest to ignite. There shouldn't be any reason she can't do it now, not with how near she was to passing her test.

Norielle frowns, turning to me. "What am I doing wrong?"

"Are you afraid of what lies on the other side?" I ask.

"I don't think so."

"Perhaps it's because we are all watching you," I say, looking at Odessa and Elias with a silent suggestion for us to give Norielle her space. They both turn, but Odessa gives me an impatient glower, as if to ask why I didn't open it myself rather than leaving it to the newest Warden in the group.

For practice, I silently tell her with my raised brows. She huffs.

Norielle tries again, and after another minute, a radiance blossoms behind me. I turn in time to see the last of the door forming where solid stone once stood.

"Should I open it?" Norielle asks, beaming at her success.

"Let me go out first," Elias says before I can respond. "Make sure it's safe."

He steps ahead of her, and dirt rains from the door as he opens it. The loud buzz of insects drifts inside, no longer blocked by heaps of sealed stone.

Elias walks into the lush forest, scouting the area for dangers and checking his Omen Mark. He waves for us to follow.

Odessa and I step out next, but before I look about, I check that Norielle seals the door. At the touch of her palm, stone materializes in place of the wood, dissolving the access point.

Norielle swiftly makes her way to Elias's side, her gaze turning up toward the massive cedars looming around us. I gawp at their incredibly tall and wide trunks that make me feel as small as a field mouse. Fungus and verdant moss dress the trees' auburn bark and the deadwood logs scattered across the forest floor.

What a mistake I've made, never venturing out this way.

Dried leaves and twigs crinkle and snap beneath our feet as we follow Elias deeper into the woods, too awestruck by the size of the ancient trees and preoccupied with trying not to trip on the overgrowth to speak. After about a mile, the sun begins to sink, its brilliant rays piercing through gaps in the evergreen canopy overhead. The further it descends, the colder the forest becomes, and soon Norielle is clutching her arms and quaking.

"Need another layer?" Elias asks, already undoing the button of his cloak.

"No, it's okay. You keep it," Norielle says, every word rattling despite her own coat and cloak. "I wasn't expecting it to be this cold. It's supposed to be Soltûm."

"*Supposed* to be," Elias emphasizes, then tries again to get her to accept his cloak, but when she still refuses, he stretches it like a wing toward her. "Walk with me for a while, at least."

She hesitates, glancing at both Odessa and me before stepping nearer to him. He wraps his arm around her shoulder, pulling her flush against his side so he can cover her with the thick fabric. He smiles at her, but the expression wavers as he flicks an uncertain look back at me.

Is that guilt in his eyes? Does he still doubt what I said about my feelings for Norielle?

I turn away, only to find Odessa at my side, giving me a hard stare. But despite the judgment written on her scowl, I catch a glimmer of compassion in her eyes before she leans over to whisper. "I bet the High Warden's daughter is pretty. She's at least your age."

I grimace. The thought of considering someone solely because of their title has never appealed to me, even if I understand the wisdom behind it. It would be too much to expect someone to rise to the responsibility of leadership for marriage when such things require years of preparation—if one could ever be prepared for such a burden.

With Corene, it was more of a lucky coincidence that she was Atlas's daughter, since it was more so my friendship with Corwin that connected us.

I slow, allowing Elias and Norielle to gain a fair lead on Odessa and me before answering, "With all she's surely heard of me and my episodes, I highly doubt she'd be interested in a single conversation."

Odessa's eyes narrow, her smile turning even more devious. "So, then you'd be willing to talk to her?"

"No."

"Why not?

"You *know* why not."

"Because you're afraid you'll get hurt," Odessa fires back without hesitation.

I nearly trip on a raised tree root. "I'm afraid to hurt *someone else.*"

"As if there're no precautions that can be taken *at all* to protect her. I've been around you for over two decades. Same as Mother. The worst you've done to either of us is give us a splitting headache with all your yelling." Odessa tightens her curly ponytail, the ringlets swaying from side to side. "Well, you also disintegrated my favorite sword. I'm still holding that against you."

I clench my jaw at Odessa's blatant understatements. She speaks as though I don't remember seeing her hiding in her wardrobe as a child after witnessing my episodes.

"Really, Calden," Odessa carries on before I can offer a rebuttal. "Finding a woman might do you some good. She might at least help you be somewhat less of an idiot."

"Sure. Once I find Toaph Elbara, I will take your suggestion into consideration."

Odessa huffs. "El-Alam help you."

"*Please*," I concur as Elias and Norielle suddenly stop ahead of us.

Elias raises his Omen Mark. A patch of faded sunlight catches on the red arrow at the center, and he swivels around. The rest of us check our marks as well. Mine is still black, but Norielle's and Odessa's match Elias's.

Is something wrong with my Omen Mark?

I focus my energy on it, commanding it to show me if an enemy is nearby, but it remains colorless.

Elias squints in the direction his mark points, but dusk lays a cloak of shadows over the woods, making it hard to discern what lies ahead. I hold my breath, listening to every noise in the area—the scratching branches and quiet hum of wildlife. We remain still until Odessa grows restless. Conjuring her sword into her hand, she follows her mark into the foliage, using her long blade to push away the fanned leaves of the ferns. I creep behind her, palm splayed and ready to summon my swordstaff, should I need it.

Odessa stretches her neck to see around a massive cedar's trunk, and a sudden rustle ruptures the silence as something darts away. Leaves bob in the wake of whatever fled, and by the time they've gone still, Odessa's Omen Mark is black again. She turns around, dematerializing her sword into a vapor.

"Whatever it was, it's gone," she says, a fleck of disappointment in her tone, like she *wanted* something to fight. "It must have realized what a mistake it was making by coming near."

She returns to Norielle and Elias, but I remain, staring at the settled bush where whatever was watching us once hid. Some lonely part of me wonders if it may have been Echo, but why would the canyx be all the way out here?

"We're losing light, Cal," Elias says when I finally return. "We need to set up camp. There's a clearing up ahead."

I take one last look through the greenery, but seeing nothing, I twist to face the path with a nod toward Elias. "We'll be taking watches tonight."

NORIELLE

A tickle on my arm startles me awake. The image of an ethereal blue crypt crawler scorpion flashes in my mind before I lay eyes on what it actually is—hair. *Elias's* hair, because somehow, I stretched my arm over to where he lies, adjacent to me. I retract my arm deeper into my sleeve and beneath my blanket. Even with my coat and the fire close by, the now frost-coated forest floor emanates a cold that reaches nearly to my bones.

I curl beneath my covering, soaking in what little warmth it provides before recalling there was something in the forest earlier. Sitting up, I twist my Omen Mark toward the firelight and gasp at the deep red tinge in the center arrow. It's dark—barely visible—but still. Something is out there. Somewhere.

Did it follow us?

I look at Odessa, who lies bunched up on her side near the foot of my blanket. Asleep. Across the fire, Calden's rolled blanket remains strapped to his backpack. Is it still his watch? Did I sleep for that short a time?

I search the dark surroundings, but when I can't locate him, I check my Bind Mark and find it aimed in the same direction as the Omen Mark. My heart skips a beat, and though I try to remind myself that he's capable of handling nearly anything that could ever cross us, I can't help but rise to my feet. I pause, looking at Odessa. Should I tell her? Ask her to come with me to find Calden?

The thought of disturbing her seems about as smart as poking a sleeping bear with a stick. I turn to Elias next. Asleep, he looks more like he did when he was younger—softer. His serene expression holds me still, fanning a myriad of emotions. I shake myself out of it.

Calden. The mark. Danger.

Focus.

I draw in a breath to whisper Elias's name, but it doesn't come out. Instead, I grab my sword and tiptoe as best as my boots will allow me toward where Calden is.

The feeling of sneaking away while others sleep draws back memories of slipping from the bedroom I shared with Cas. Her tear-streaked face still haunts my sleep, and it probably will until I can see her again, smiling. How old will she be then? Will that be years from now? Or do we even have years to figure all this out? The way Calden acted at the council, I'd almost think Seer Josiah foresaw the world's doom happening within the year.

Not that Calden trusts a word out of the Seer's mouth anymore...

I banish the troubling thoughts, again commanding myself to focus as I weave through the musty forest. The light of the campfire is barely in view by the time I spot Calden's outline between the trees. He twists my way, noticing me, though I didn't make a sound. I hold my Omen Mark up, but with only the moon to light the space, I can't tell anything besides that it points somewhere just left of him.

"Are you searching for it?" I whisper.

He avoids looking at me. "Yes. With no luck, at that. My Omen Mark doesn't appear to be working."

"Not working?" I repeat, squinting to see the mark when he holds his wrist toward me.

From what I can see, it doesn't even point in the same direction as mine; instead, it rests in its neutral position.

"Yours is working?" he asks, though it's more of a suggestion than a question.

I show him my mark, and he raises his hands like he might grab my arm to pull the mark closer into his view. But his fingers curl before he ever touches my skin. A memory sparks of when he drew my original Omen Mark on me in the Rimrook Mountains... the way he hesitated to let go.

So much has changed since then. Yet out here, alone, the feelings I had along the way to the citadel stir. I've been so judgmental toward him with all that's happened lately—as if expecting perfection from him when he's just a person who is struggling to measure up to who he is meant to be.

Someone who is struggling like me.

"Norielle, I..." There's a long pause, and a small part of me sparks, wondering if he's remembering what he seemed to feel toward me once. But his tone shifts. "I think whatever is out there is not really an enemy."

"What do you mean?" I ask, staring again at the red arrow.

"I made a friend while Elias and I were away." He turns to face the area my arrow points to. "The canyx I asked Elias to tell you about. The one that didn't seem to be under the curse."

My interest piques. "Yes, I remember. Do you think he's out there?"

"Possibly." Calden scans the obscure surroundings. "Or another like him."

He takes a step away from me, moving a branch from his path. I follow at his heels.

"Is this why you took first watch? To go looking for him?"

He twists back to smile at me. A familiar twinkle winks onto his expression, reminding me even more of how he was before Corene's death and the discovery about Toaph. "That is exactly why. Only... my mark hasn't provided the best navigation."

The way he says it seems both asking and forbidding at once.

"Use mine then," I assert, holding my wrist out again.

Calden contemplates the offer for a few seconds before giving me a once-over, as if to check that I'm properly armed for an adventure. When he sees my sword, he concedes. "Stay close to me, in case I'm wrong."

Stay close. The order feels odd after how he's kept me at such a distance lately.

Still, I heed his words, carefully tracking in his footsteps and showing him my Omen Mark whenever he seems to require it. Our path leads so far from the way I came, I wouldn't know the way back to camp if Calden weren't with me to guide us with his Bind Mark. I try not to think of how Elias will react if he wakes up while we are away or contemplate how troubled I am by that idea. Instead, I watch the ferns nodding in the light breeze and remind my jaw to stay tight, so my rattling teeth don't cost us our chance of finding whatever this is.

"The trees," Calden whispers suddenly, drawing my focus upward.

In the glow of the full moon, pallid branches droop from the towering cedars. At first, it's only a few branches per tree, but as we walk, the wilted appearance seems to spread like a plague until entire trees are pale and sagging—some lacking branches altogether. Shed limbs clutter the forest floor, which looks no better than the trees with shriveled shrubs and ferns lying in mangled heaps like corpses.

How could a forest go from looking so lush to this... dead?

"What happened?" I whisper.

Calden doesn't readily respond, as if too overwhelmed by the sight of the decaying forest around us to register my question right away. "The curse," he eventually says under his breath. "It must have poisoned the forest."

My shoulders sag as I think of how beautiful the forest was where we first stepped out. Is the poison spreading? Will all this be lost someday?

Calden makes a sharp turn toward one of the cedars. The base appears nearly as wide as my house back in Behria. He lays his palm against the bark, tilting his head back to inspect its sagging limbs. A ward lights on his arm, bright enough for the glow to sneak through his thin sleeve. He closes his eyes.

I clutch the collar of my cloak, shivering as I watch the branches *move*—slowly perking up and returning to their dark green shade beneath the unobstructed moonlight. Even after being healed myself, witnessing the tree's restoration still renders me breathless.

Calden's hand slides from the trunk.

"How did you do that?" I ask.

"Healing Ward," he says, looking up to the tree with a smile that defies any pain he must have absorbed from the cedar—if healing works that way with trees.

"I thought those only worked on people?"

"So did I once," he says, approaching another tree. This one is utterly bare, besides one snapped limb that looks about ready to crumble to the forest floor. "Though I don't think I could do that too many times."

He reaches for the next cedar, and my mouth hangs open, waiting to see if he can restore a tree that looks completely dead. But nothing lights on his arm, and instead a sound like raining sand precedes my realization that the tree is disintegrating from the top down. The pale cloud billows like smoke toward me, and I shield my face, coughing in the dust. Tiny particles powder the dried undergrowth.

"Sorry," Calden says once the air is clear enough to speak again. "I should have warned you."

I shoot him a confused look.

"Using Master Talents takes less energy," he says. "I'm thinking if I separate the fully contaminated trees from those still living, it might stop the spread of whatever sickness this is."

He walks to the next barren tree, and I remember my Omen Mark and the enemy out here somewhere. But I don't mention it. I can see now that the red is not bright enough for whatever it is to be close, and the arrow points away from the direction we came from, assuring me Elias and Odessa are still safe. I stand back, watching Calden disintegrate the dead cedars in a single, sustained touch. As he travels from one to the next, he runs his hands along the underbrush, dissolving the desiccated bushes.

My breath shortens, and the awe swarming me makes me forget how cold I am. With his touch, this man can heal trees taller than the citadel's turrets or turn them to mere dust, like the power of death and life is at his fingertips. Are all Master Wardens this powerful? Is what I'm witnessing the extent of his power, or is this a mere glimpse of his full potential?

Is this why Rhys insisted I not worry about him?

A half hour must pass before Calden stops, declaring he can't do any more. In his path, a clearing separates the trees that have hope for survival from those that have none left. The one fully restored tree now stands in the distance. The ground between us is coated, as if with snow, and particles linger in the air, still itching my throat. Calden sits on a boulder, panting like he's spent that entire time running rather than strolling through the woods.

I check my Omen Mark again, finding it the same shade as before.

"That was incredible," I whisper, though it's an understatement.

Calden gives me a weary smile. "It was not enough. All I can hope is that it will slow the spread until I can come back to finish my work."

I watch the white dust drifting around us awhile before mustering the courage to share what lies in my heart. "It's no wonder Toaph Elbara chose you to speak to."

Curiosity gleams in his gaze as he looks up at me.

"You cared enough for that tree to heal it. Toaph must have seen in your heart that you would do anything for this world." I try not to consider the implications of this regarding his healing of me.

Calden's face lowers, his hands folding together in his lap. Specks slowly sprinkle his hair and cloak as he considers my words for what feels like an entire season.

"He wouldn't be wrong," is all he says before his attention suddenly snaps toward my wrist, and he points at my Omen Mark.

I hold it into the moonlight, teeth clenching as I notice it's now red as fresh blood.

Calden stands, pivoting toward where the arrow points, and I clutch my sword hilt. A second later, I notice eyes glowing behind one of the dead bushes near the tree Calden healed. I draw my sword but only get the blade halfway unsheathed before Calden's defensive stance folds.

"Echo?" he asks.

I squint, barely able to make out the wolflike shape of the animal's face, but the shimmers in his coat seem to sparkle when Calden says the name.

Calden steps toward him, but I remain back, not wanting to startle the canyx away. I still haven't decided what to think of him, to side with Calden's opinion of him or Elias's, but maybe now I'll have the chance to form my own.

The canyx creeps closer, and Calden kneels. My eyes widen at the surreal sight of an Accursed—or a Sentry, whatever he is—approaching a man without attacking him. Could it be true? Could there still be real Sentries out there?

The shimmering wolf sniffs Calden's hand, then nestles his head against his palm.

I take a step closer, but the canyx jumps back with a warning growl.

"She's a friend," Calden reassures him. "Nicer than the other one."

Elias, I realize with a laugh.

The canyx quiets, and I creep a few steps closer, but I don't get within range of touching him before he jolts, ears pointing upright. His luminescent gaze is directed behind me, and a shiver rattles down my spine. I turn, only to find Elias and Odessa standing with their globelike lanterns stretched toward us.

"Wait!" Calden says as the canyx leaps into the shadows of the forest, dematerializing from his physical form and dissolving into the darkness.

I barely catch the sparkle of his tail before he's entirely gone, and my Omen Mark turns black. My posture sags like the untouched trees as I meet Elias's and Odessa's incredulous expressions.

"This is not what I would call keeping watch, brother," Odessa chides before seeming to notice the distinct gap in the forest. "What in the Silvirdian seas happened to the trees?"

CALDEN

Apparently, tending a dying forest must be the answer to my sleeplessness, because I don't wake until the sun hangs directly over my head. Its light pulses through the bobbing branches of the great cedars around our camp, banishing even the memory of my dreams.

When I sit up, the fire is but a few glowing embers, and my companions are already packed and waiting on me. Norielle notices me first with a smile. Her long hair drapes over Elias's olive cloak that she's wearing on top of her own and spills to the log she sits upon.

A short way from her, Elias leans against a tree. "I see you finally decided to get some sleep," he comments when he sees me.

"I wouldn't say, *I decided...*" My words crackle from my dry throat.

I pivot my focus to Odessa, who is inspecting her tightly woven braids in the reflection of a blade. She turns her dagger, catching my image in the steel before rising to sheathe her backup weapon.

A wave of dizziness when I stand reminds me of how much I exerted myself last night. But I couldn't leave the forest in that state. I had to at least *try* to mend one broken thing within my control.

"Why didn't anyone wake me?"

My question is more of a rebuke, but Elias raises a brow at me. "You're really asking that?"

"We have a ship to reach." I shake out my blanket and roll it up. "We don't have time for sleeping in."

"Oh no, not *sleep*." Elias's tone fills with added sarcasm. "What a horrible thing to do... especially when you look two steps from the grave half the time."

I look at Norielle and Odessa, whose affirming expressions suggest they agree with him.

"Well, I'm up now. Let's get moving," I say, strapping my blanket onto my backpack. I sling the pack over my shoulders, casting a long look into the forest where we found Echo. Elias and Odessa convinced me not to seek him again last night, but the thought that he's out there, nearby, tempts me to try one last time. He could prove useful in Raevre, if he knows where Toaph Elbara is. Yet something tells me I'd sooner find Toaph on my own than convince a canyx to get on a ship—especially one who assumes everyone but me is an enemy.

Norielle rises, returning Elias's cloak to him despite his protest, and we begin our last trek on land until Raevre.

A few hours later, we step onto the mottled earth of the south coast, eyes fluttering at the sun glaring on water and pale sand. I barely catch sight of a ship with a Toaph Elbara figurehead looming a stretch from the shore before a young man approaches me with a bow.

"The *Celestella* is ready for you, my lord," he declares. His sun-lightened brown hair flutters in the salty breeze as he meets my gaze with irises the same hue as the bobbing cattails.

"Thank you," I say, but Alani's excited shriek drowns out my reply. Beyond the young man, she springs from a dinghy and dashes across the uneven shore. Her wind-fluffed mane could contend with that of the fellions in the Dûnori Ravine.

"You're here!" she calls. "Finally. This has been the longest four days of my life."

The man steps aside as Alani skids to a stop in front of us. Her attention moves beyond me to deliver a quick greeting to the other three, but her brows pinch when she notices Elias among us. I affirm with a nod what she is likely guessing—that he's our final Bind member. She gives me a questioning look before waving us toward the man who greeted us. "This is Willian, my first mate, and the former captain's nephew. I think his Talent will come in handy."

"His Talent?" I ask, shifting my focus to Willian.

Willian smiles, and a sudden gust of wind blasts gritty air into my face, flapping my cloak.

"I can command the wind, my lord," he says.

My brows lift. *Handy* is an understatement. "Well, between you two, perhaps we'll be to Raevre by tomorrow."

Alani giggles. "Maybe not that fast, but it will expedite the voyage some."

I glance at the other three. "Are we ready?"

"As it gets," Elias says.

Norielle flinches from a troubled stare at the water before nodding her agreement. I give her an apologetic smile, not having considered the trepidation she must feel about subjecting herself to such a large body of water. But now it only serves to remind me of my own apprehensions.

It's just a few weeks, I assure myself, and I start toward the dinghy. The party follows, and Alani rushes ahead of us. Willian quickly joins her side, and the two begin some naval chatter that I can hardly comprehend. The man, though much calmer than Alani, seems to share her light spirit, and their warm laughter fills the walk with a deceitful sense that this will be a pleasurable journey across the sea.

Fizzing waves lap at the shoreline when we reach the long-boat Alani brought to carry us to the ship. The wood creaks as Alani steps in first. Willian stands on the outside, water sloshing against his rubber boots while he assists Odessa and Norielle aboard. I eye Norielle cautiously, but whatever she's feeling, she subdues it with a tense smile and a glance that darts between Elias and me. I gesture for Elias to go first, letting him occupy the seat beside her. With a final glance at the shore, I claim the seat next to Odessa. The first mate pulls a stake from the sand and joins us in the back.

With a sweeping gesture, Alani uses her Talent to command the water beneath us to lift the boat and carry it toward the ship, as if it's held in the hand of a sea giant. Norielle's already sunburnt face pales, and even Odessa and I clutch the wooden edge of our seat, nervous that the water might drop us. Willian, however, watches Alani with a sort of childlike wonder that strips ten years off his already youthful face.

Alani lowers the dinghy so it rests beside the *Celestella*, and I gape at the ship's massive hull. Salt crusts the wooden plating along the side from its many voyages hauling my mother, father, and even my grandparents across the seas to visit the High Wardens of the other four kingdoms. Not to mention, its many treks to Northspire, delivering supplies, aid, and reinforcements to the sentinels who uphold the barrier trapping Ta'Nathel.

So much history, yet I've never so much as laid eyes on the vessel.

Metal hooks glint as ropes are lowered over the side of the ship. Alani and Willian snatch their dangling tails and attach the cords to the dinghy. A man with white hair peers over the side, and I faintly hear him issue a command to raise the vessel.

The davits squeak as the deckhands crank them, and the ropes lift our boat past two other dinghies fastened to the ship's side by wooden chocks. If my memory serves me correctly, Mother mentioned there are three other longboats on the opposite side. Boats I pray we'll not have any more use for besides to reach the Warden's secret cove in Raevre.

The dinghy stops once we are level with the main deck of the ship, and Willian climbs aboard the larger vessel. He helps the women over as Elias and I fumble onto the deck. I exchange a look with Elias before turning a full rotation to take in the sights.

Suntanned people shift all around us, dodging the three masts and various sagging ropes. Beyond the ship's large, curved body, a sheet of rippling blue stretches indefinitely until the sky and its pale reflection on the water seem to blend into one.

"Briefing on deck!" Alani shouts, the commanding nature of her tone straightening my spine.

Every member of the crew stands in attention, abandoning freshly tied knots, mops, and all other forms of tending the ship. They gather before us on the main deck, and I admire the interesting assortment of ages and perceived heritages among them. Mother claims these sailors are the best amongst Wardens, all plucked from various kingdoms across Silvirdia for their skills. And the previous captain selected each of the deckhands for their bravery and aptitude for service.

The group—I count fifteen outside of Alani and Willian—delivers an unsynchronized bow toward Odessa and me before all eyes turn to our redheaded captain.

Alani introduces us to the crew before listing off a few key members such as the other two mates, a pair of navigators, and a quartermaster, though the jargon means little to me. I do my best to pocket their names and tie a subconscious apology to each one for not remembering their role on the ship. Hopefully, by the time we reach Raevre, I'll have caught on.

With introductions out of the way, Alani shoots off a series of commands, which are swiftly carried out and declared "Ready" as completed. The white sails flap open after her last order, their wide shadows blanketing the deck as the wind catches the sheets.

Alani scans the ship, then the sparse number of crew members still left standing ahead of us. Her gaze dials in on a petite young woman with dark, reddish-brown hair.

"Zamirah," Alani says. "Come with me, will you?"

Zamirah...

The uncommon yet familiar name hangs in my mind as the young woman follows Alani to the quarterdeck. It's not until they've reached the steps that I recall why I recognize her name. Mother has mentioned Zamirah a handful of times upon returning from her own voyages on the *Celestella*. The former captain claimed Zamirah for this ship after she achieved Warden Mastery at the record age of fourteen. Though, that was at least seven years ago, and now, I can't remember what Talent she received for her Mastery.

Zamirah looks back toward us as she climbs the last step, giving a kind smile that even a mourner wouldn't be able to resist returning. Then she spins to face Alani, her gold-toned dress swirling just above her boots.

I pivot to Elias, whose attention is, of course, on Norielle, but she's too busy glaring at the sea to notice his concerned stare.

"Well, here we are," I say to break the silence. "Now all we have to do is pray we make it to Raevre without trouble."

Elias snorts like I made a joke.

"We'd do better to pray we're able to *handle* the trouble," Odessa says before striding away to do what she does best—avoid the rest of us. She retreats behind a door under the quarterdeck, where I suppose our cabins must be. As the door shuts, I notice Zamirah is already stepping down from the quarterdeck, granting me a chance to catch up with Alani. I excuse myself from the nonexistent conversation with Elias and Norielle and head toward the raised deck.

Zamirah balks as we cross paths, stretching the skirt of her dress in a curtsy.

"Thank you, but that won't be necessary," I say, returning her polite smile. "If everyone stopped to bow to me at every sighting, no one would ever get anything done around here."

Zamirah chuckles, shaking back her shoulder-length hair. Her green-gold eyes meet mine, pupils swelling the longer I hold her gaze, but her lips twitch, as if she is not sure how to respond—or if she's allowed to.

"You've been part of this crew for some time, haven't you?" I ask.

She clears her throat. "Yes, my lord. Since I was fourteen. I hope to be of good help to you, as I have a Master Talent that—"

"Allows you to send messages across the sea," I say as the recollection suddenly strikes me.

"That's it," she says, then adds "my lord" after a shuffle, as though she'd nearly forgotten to use my title.

A small laugh chirps in my throat. "No need to bother with that, either. I think, so long as we're on this ship, I'd like to just be Calden for once."

Zamirah's smile spreads, crinkling her eyes. "Wouldn't we all like to just be who we are without any expectations?"

I give her a curious squint.

"I'll try to remember," she adds when I don't readily respond.

"Thank you." I glance toward Alani before centering my focus on Zamirah again. "And thank you for being here as well."

"It is my pleasure. Truly." She sidesteps out of my path, as if sensing my need to speak with her captain, but she stops there. "Do let me know if you have any messages for me to send. I've already alerted the High Warden in Raevre that we're heading that way, as Captain Alani requested. But I'm happy to send messages of any kind, formal or otherwise. Though you'll have to catch me at shift change since Captain Alani placed me on the night crew."

"I will be sure to do so, should I think of something."

Her short hair bobs against her shoulders as she nods, then she flits away, her presence seeming to shine a light on everyone she crosses before she descends under a hatch on the main deck.

The stairs creak as I climb to the quarterdeck, where Alani stands at the helm, overlooking the ship. Her attention lingers on Willian and the white-haired gentleman who ordered our boat to be raised—the *third* mate, I recall. But his name already evades me. Willian laughs at something the man says, then turns to wave at Alani. She beams back at him, unaware that I've even approached her.

"All this time, you were looking on land," I murmur so the young man doesn't hear, yet she still squeals. "And he was on the sea."

Alani furiously shakes her head. "Don't be silly, Calden. I've only just met him."

I leave my response at a chuckle, and I return to the matters at hand. "How long, really, would you say it should take us to reach Raevre?"

Alani admires the sails while she thinks. "It's hard to estimate. A normal voyage to Raevre takes about three to four weeks. But with Willian's Talent and mine? Maybe two? Two and a half?"

"That's not bad."

"Of course, that's not factoring in any complications."

"Are there many Accursed between Alémor and Raevre?"

"Not many, but certainly some we don't want to run into. We'll have to keep Shroud Wards active whenever we want to use magic. That will help them not sense us at least. Not much we can do to prevent them from seeing us besides keeping a quick pace. I think Willian and I can see to that."

"It's nice to see you where you belong."

"It's nice to *be* where I belong." She casts the sea a loving look. "And to think I grew up wanting nothing more than to be on land."

"I'll try not to keep you tethered to the shore too much longer," I say, a strange sadness curling around my heart. "As soon as we fulfill our Bind duties, I'll have you back on this ship. Consider it your own."

Alani's shoulders seem to melt. "You really are the best of men, Calden."

"To be fair, I'm already not sure I like the feeling of the floor moving beneath my feet."

"You'll get used to it." She laughs. "But there're buckets around if you need them."

I wince at the thought, but now that I'm paying attention, I do feel something squirming in my stomach. "Noted," I say with a quiet prayer that I'll not have need of them. Empyrean knows I've done enough to damage myself lately. The last thing my body needs is to lose what little nutrients are sustaining me.

"We've made space for the whole Bind in the deckhouse below us," Alani says, confirming my guess about the door Odessa went through. "The mates kindly opted to bunk with the sailors across the way to accommodate the Bind in the stern." She nods toward the forecastle in the ship's bow. "So, make yourself at home. You'll be here awhile."

I rub my neck. *Unfortunately.*

"Um, Calden," Alani says, a concerned shift in her tone numbing my skin to the warmth of the sun overhead. "Are you doing all right? You know, after *everything*?"

I ponder her meaning for a moment before I register she is referring to the discovery about the Oracle's identity and Mother's lies. I slipped that information to Alani before sending her ahead to ready the ship, not wanting to leave her out. Though, I neglected to share with her the full conversation I had with the Oracle, just as I have kept it from everyone else. Even now, only Elias knows the details.

"I suppose," I say, lowering my voice. "Honestly, I'm not sure which is the greater offense, what my father did or how my mother hid it, even from me."

"I'm so sorry, Calden. Both are awful in their own ways."

I nod but quickly shove down the rising pain the subject brings. "Well, best I don't think too much about it for a while—not aboard your ship, anyway. I'd rather not see what happens if Toaph decides to speak to me on here."

Alani watches her crew as she seems to piece together my implications that the agony of this topic could serve as a prime trigger for my episodes. Though, how it hasn't already done so evades my understanding. If it were going to happen, it should have been in the Seer's Sanctum when Mother admitted she'd lied to me.

Cheer returns to Alani's voice. "I suppose this can be your little vacation then."

I try to smile, as if these revelations were that inconsequential. "Sure."

"Really, Calden." Her expression turns downright motherly. "Take care of yourself on here. You look ill. You need the rest—in every sense of the word."

I sigh. "Of course, Alani."

"I'll tell the quartermaster to give you a double ration." She pats my shoulder. "Promise me you'll not let it go to waste."

I muster a convincing expression and nod. "I promise."

ELIAS

The first time I was aboard a ship, I was twelve. Mum had recently died, and I'd left the only other family I'd ever known back in Behria. My *second* family, as I liked to think of them. Nori's family. The trip took only one week, but I spent most of it hurling into buckets or off the side of the ship. I still don't know whether it was seasickness or if grief had made me ill. Either way, it was the worst week of my life.

When I reached the Western Isles, I wasn't even sure if my grandparents would be there to receive me, but that was where my parents once told Nori's papa to send me should something happen to them. A lady on the ship knew my grandparents—a light leak of grace from El-Alam, or else I'd have probably never found them. She took me to their doorstep, where I had to be the one to deliver all the news. *Your son didn't come back from the war. Now his wife is dead, and you have to raise me.*

They were both so weathered-looking from the start, I should have known they wouldn't be around much longer. It wasn't even two full years later that I found myself on another ship, sailing to the mainland of Alémor with a lyre attached to my hip and a hopelessness in my heart that I never want to feel again. I set my path toward Behria, stopping in every town along the way to earn a few coins. But I never made it. The Wardens found me first, and I couldn't turn away from that call—that promise of a place to live and to find my purpose. To recover.

Now here I am, a member of the Sovereign Prince's Bind. Charged with helping him in the biggest mission ever handed to a Warden. Because Cal *chose* me.

But why? I'm still struggling to understand that, even after the brief explanation he gave. I'm not a Master. What place do I have here with such important people on the most significant task granted to man since Grand Master Kadriea and her Bind sealed Ta'Nathel away behind the barrier in Northspire?

There had to be someone better for Cal to choose.

I rest my arms against the cool rail of the starboard side, hands dangling above the sea. The dusk paints the water in golden strokes and slowly steals more and more of its blue. On my right, Nori stares at the water in silence. Her shoulders have finally loosened, as if a few hours of calm have convinced her that the ocean has no plans of awakening. Yet she's clung to my side like the satchel of my lyre since we boarded.

"Doing okay, Nori?" I ask.

She audibly gulps, but nods. "I'm starting to settle. It's comforting knowing we're at least not helpless, even if the sea woke."

"We'd put it back to sleep in a second." I suppress the urge to put an arm around her for further reassurance. "They line the keels of these ships with Peace Wards. Anything suspicious happens with the water, and they'll activate those wards to stop it."

She draws in a deep breath, then releases it from her nose. When she smiles, we fall quiet again, and my mind drifts, recalling another potential reason for Nori's distress that she hasn't brought up. In the first war with Raevre, her father was aboard a ship that was blown to bits by cannons. He survived, but his brother, Nori's uncle, never came back. He drowned, and though Nori's papa never told us the details, by the way the man would blanch at the mention of his brother, I imagine he witnessed it as closely as Nori witnessed her papa's drowning.

It was only a few weeks after the shipwreck that Nori's papa watched a Raevran soldier slice open my father's throat with a cutlass. The wildfires started soon after that, and King Arlo recalled our men.

Now I can't help but wonder if Toaph is behind those wildfires. If he *is* inside the vortex like Cal and I have guessed, then could the fires be a form of self-defense? Or is it the opposite? Has Ta'Nathel started them to prevent people from reaching Toaph, as if the impassible winds of the vortex aren't sufficient on their own?

"Are *you* all right?" Nori asks, her gentle voice drawing me from my contemplations, yet I fail to respond.

She leans forward to see my face, her hair spilling over the side of the ship like ropes.

I force on the same expression I wear whenever I'm trying to be convincing. The one that often labels me smug. "I'm fine, Nori. Just enjoying getting to slow down."

I face the horizon again, and she leans even further, as if hoping her gaze will pull mine back.

It does.

And this time, I take in her familiar features—those same hazel eyes and that smile that comforted me back when the body of water I overlooked was Lake Daleia. The honeyed light from the sunset warms half of her face and daubs shadows on the other, defining her matured features. Coming of age has made her even more beautiful, but the way she looks at me feels the same as it used to—maybe for the first time since we've met again.

It's the look of someone who knows you far too well to accept "I'm fine" without putting up a fight for the truth.

Empyreal Skies. This is why I loved her. And why I always will.

"It's a lot," she says when I still don't break open my heart and hand it to her. "The ship... where we are going... what you accepted to be here."

I hear everything she leaves out in those pauses. *The ship—like the ones you sailed on right after you lost your family. Where we are going—the land your papa died in. What you accepted—a role with unknown requirements where failure means the world's demise.*

Totally fine. All of it. Especially the part where she's here, too, in equal danger to me, if not worse, considering her training is incomplete.

"Yeah," I admit, seeing no other way out. "It is."

She shuffles her feet, and I almost wonder if she's going to come closer—put a hand on my arm or something like she would when we were younger. But she returns to her former position and mimics me as I look away again.

Behind us, the crew blabs and shouts at each other. Their noise and the constant creaking of the ship waxes and wanes in my attention as the sun disappears, as if it fell into the ocean. In its place, the moon glosses the water with a silver hue, bringing with it an added chill. Nori, who's already fetched extra layers once—if not twice—bundles her arms against her chest. How someone from Behria, where it gets at least this cold in Veratûm, can't handle the brisk weather, makes me laugh.

"Good thing we're headed to a desert," I say.

She twists toward me, the boat dipping and rising underfoot in her pause. "Good thing I brought gloves," she says, but when she sinks her hands into her pockets, they come back empty. "Except I left them in my bag in the deckhouse."

"Better grab them. It's only going to get colder."

She stalls, looking me over like she's wondering if I'll still be here when she returns.

"It's teatime," I say. "I'm heading to the galley. You want something? It'll warm you up."

"Maybe I'll just curl up inside the hearth."

I laugh. "Please don't do that."

"I'll take some tea." She cringes, but presses her smile back on before I can ask what's wrong. "Whichever you think is best, tea master."

I grin at the title and start toward the forecastle, but when I turn to ask if she wants anything else, her expression contorts again. The water rolls beneath the ship, and she covers her mouth, sealing her eyes shut.

Oh no.

Her eyes open again, gaze darting around the deck before she spins toward the side of the ship. I wince, thinking of her long hair and the way it sweeps into her face whenever she leans over.

Well, this isn't how I planned on spending the evening.

I lurch toward her and pull her hair away from her face, bunching it in my hands. Then I do my best to block out the noise and smell that follows. My teeth grit through several minutes of her stomach's upheaval, glaring away the gazes of anyone who bothers to notice. Fortunately for Nori, most of them probably anticipated one of us would hurl and hardly seem fazed.

How is Cal faring? Is that why he disappeared into the deckhouse?

When it seems over, Nori slowly peels back from the edge and wipes her mouth on a handkerchief. Her hair falls through my fingers, soft as dry beach sand, as I release it. She remains with her back to me, undoubtedly fighting a fierce blush at the humiliation of emptying her stomach in front of me and everyone else.

"So, peppermint tea," I say, recalling how it helps with nausea.

Nori doesn't meet my eyes when she finally turns around. "Please."

CALDEN

Early sunlight greets me as I exit the galley with a fresh cup of morning brew in hand and a full stomach. The salty sea air rushes against my skin while I stroll across the main deck, admiring the energy of the crew tending the ship. I wish I shared their vigor this morning. Even with the decent rest I had last night, my vitality feels drained ever since encountering the Oracle, as if he punctured a hole in my spirit and now my very life is slowly seeping out of me.

Still, it's Mother's betrayal and her reasons for keeping me in the dark that impale me most deeply. I was so young when I lost my father, too young to truly miss more than the idea of him. But with Mother... this all feels like losing her—the person I thought she was—and the belief in me I thought she had, aside from our disagreements.

"How are you taking to the ship, my lord?" a man asks.

I cease my moseying and look over to find the first mate, Willian, approaching me.

I almost remind him I'd prefer to be addressed by name, as I told him and several others yesterday after we boarded. But I discard the idea, writing it off as a mistake.

"It's not so bad," I say, slurping my morning brew. "I actually found the motion rather pleasant when trying to fall asleep last night."

"It's like a giant cradle." Willian chuckles, rocking his hands, as if to demonstrate the motion. "I've always found it soothing myself. Though, I hear not everyone in the Bind is taking well to it."

I glance at the door to the deckhouse. Behind it, Norielle is probably still sitting on her bunk, fighting to keep what little dinner she managed to eat last night inside her. And Elias is surely at her side, armed with buckets, towels, and a constant supply of peppermint tea.

"No, Norielle is not feeling her best," I say. "But she's well taken care of, at least."

Willian smiles. "Glad to hear there's some consolation. I hope she adjusts quickly, otherwise this may be a long adventure for her."

I nod, but the guilt for dragging Norielle onto this ship renders me silent.

"Your sister was looking for you," Willian says. "She's in the roundhouse now, I believe. Talking with Captain Alani. I told her I'd send you that way if I ran into you."

"Thank you, Willian. I'll head up there."

Willian smiles and departs from me, hollering the fourth mate's name. I sigh, unprepared for my morning to be spoiled by whatever conversation Odessa has in store for me, but I stride toward the Bind's quarters, no less.

When I enter the deckhouse, I'm alarmed to find that Norielle and Elias are asleep in their partially walled-in bunks. I'd expected Elias, at least, would be awake since he's always been an early riser, but perhaps the lack of sleep he had last night while tending to Norielle got the better of him.

She's blessed to have you, I think toward him as I pass. The more I see them together, the more solidified I feel in my conclusion, though my jealousy that I cannot have with another what they share only arises. But at least now I am more resolved that it was the fantasy of what I thought Norielle could be to me that drew me in, not truly the girl herself.

And fortunately so, for her sake.

And mine. *And* Elias's.

I soften my footfalls and ascend the stairs to the sun-filled roundhouse where Alani and Odessa sit at opposite sides of a meeting table wearing matching scowls. The nasty expression suits one of them far less than the other.

"Good morning," I say, tightening my grip around my mug. "Is something awry?"

"No, of course not," Odessa says, the sarcasm in her tone making my morning brew taste even more bitter. "How could anything be wrong in such *wonderful* conditions?"

I defer to Alani for a franker response.

"I was filling Odessa in on the outlook of our voyage," Alani says. With a sour look toward my sister, she adds, "And she was so kindly informing me she feels you should have left the previous captain in command for this trip rather than entrusting this ship to me."

Odessa scoffs. "That is *not* how I meant it."

"But it is how you feel about me, isn't it? You think I'm not cut out for this?"

I pull up a chair, though I'd rather be seeing myself to the far side of the ship. Their bickering is one of the reasons I never cared to gather my whole Bind together—when it was only the three of us—for anything.

"I only meant that this is a particularly complicated and dangerous voyage, and yet this is the first time you've ever officially been in charge of a ship that wasn't sailed by your brothers." Odessa turns to me, as if expecting me to repent and agree that I made a foolish choice by asking that Alani be my captain.

"Captain Theos was *asking* to retire," I remind Odessa. "And Alani is doing a wonderful job."

"You'd know," Odessa sneers. "You've been on a ship so many times, after all."

Alani rises from her chair before I can reply. The indignation on her face makes her appear like she's put on a mask, given how uncommon it is to see her so angry. "This is what I was *born* to do, Lady Odessa. I may not be perfect at it, but I know what I'm doing."

Odessa leans against her backrest, a satisfied smile on her face. Immediately, my expression goes slack with annoyance. Alani marches out, whispering an apology to me as she passes by. I wait until I hear the door downstairs close to meet Odessa's gaze.

"Why must you always provoke everyone so?" I ask.

She whisks her hand in the direction Alani went. "Because it works. Some people can't grow a backbone until someone challenges them to do so. Alani will be an even better captain after this, you'll see. She'll want to prove to herself that she's right about what she said."

"There are much kinder ways to instill confidence in someone, Odessa."

"You mean less effective ways?"

I lay an elbow on the table, rubbing my forehead. Where Odessa learned her harsh methods, I may never know. Perhaps she was born to be an instigator. Though, I can't deny her effectiveness. She *does* have a way of pushing people into finding themselves, their beliefs, and their confidence. Even if it is backwards.

"Willian said you wanted to speak with me," I say, lowering my hand back to the table.

Odessa watches the water through the curved windows along the back wall of the roundhouse. Her delay grows more disquieting by the second. This must have to do with Mother or the Oracle—or both.

"That canyx," she finally says, catching me by surprise. "You said your Omen Mark wasn't registering him as an enemy?"

I tilt my Omen Mark into view, as if looking upon it might sharpen my memories of Echo, or better still, bring him to me on this ship. "Indeed. Because he was *not* my enemy."

"Yet he was mine, Norielle's, and Elias's."

I wait for Odessa to elaborate. Instead, she eyes me, as if expecting an explanation.

"He wouldn't have harmed anyone," I say with confidence that I know I shouldn't bear. "Your Omen Marks only indicated him as an enemy because you believe him to be an Accursed. But I assure you, he is not. He is a Sentry."

Odessa shakes her head. "Interesting, that you'll trust a beast known for its ability to deceive, yet you wouldn't trust Seer Josiah—who has all but raised us in Father's stead—to discern the truth of whatever it is that the Oracle said to you."

I huff. Of course, this couldn't simply be about Echo. I ready myself to remind her that part of the reason I neglected to involve Seer Josiah was for his own protection. I would have needed to tell him who the Oracle truly was, or at the very least, risk him discerning it himself once I brought up the subject.

But Odessa fires off a question before I can get the explanation out.

"What *did* the Oracle say to you, outside of trying to get you to follow him? You never did say."

Every word of my conversation with the Oracle cascades through my memory, as clearly as if it transpired yesterday. Yet every time it washes over me, I seem to walk away with a different feeling—ever wavering between rejecting his theories on principle and thinking they make more sense than anything ever has.

"It doesn't matter what he said," I say, despite my unstable position on the subject. "Not until I've spoken with Seer Ariellis in Raevre."

"He's my father, too, Calden. I think I deserve to know what he said to you."

I turn my mug from side to side, avoiding looking at her, though I can feel her sweltering glare. If I tell her, she'll only doubt me more when she notices my stance is so uncertain.

"Please, sister, not on the ship," I plead. "I can't think about this on here—it's too dangerous."

Odessa slaps her palms against the worn tabletop. "Ridiculous. First, you avoided me until our departure, and now you're making excuses."

"Would you like to see what becomes of us if I trigger an episode?"

Her mouth shuts, though disagreement swarms in her eyes.

"Just give me more time, Dessa," I say, cracking under her disappointment. "Once I've calmed my mind on the matter and can think about it without wanting to scream, I'll pull you aside."

Odessa purses her lips, but after a moment, she waves me toward the door. "Fine, then. Go back to whatever it is you were doing. I want to be alone."

I grab my empty mug, rising without argument, and return to the main deck.

Water gushes behind the stern as the ship surges through the tides, driven more rapidly than usual by Alani's Talent. I tighten my hold on the back rail, shaking my head at the recollection of how Odessa had provoked our captain. But I restrain the urge to tell Alani to calm herself. That will only fluster her more.

With a weighty sigh, my thoughts return to my concealed conversation with the Oracle, my breath hitching when I recall again his explanation of my episodes. *Destruction.* That's all they've ever caused. Physically, emotionally, relationally—perhaps even mentally and spiritually. How can I see them as anything besides a curse? To do so feels as impossible as trying to claim that a fellion means no harm to a deer clutched in its teeth.

Yet to accept that explanation would be to accept as truth something else the Oracle said—to nudge myself one step closer to believing that Toaph Elbara is the corrupt Empyreal Guardian in Silvirdia, not Ta'Nathel.

But what if that is the truth? What harm would I cause the world by discarding the Oracle's warning?

"Your mother has always spoken so fondly of you."

I jump at the sudden voice, though it's soft as the first blossoms of Diatûm, but I don't find the strength to turn before she continues.

"One thing in particular I recall was how she envies your bravery in trying the untested."

I peel my hands from their tight grip on the railing and face the woman standing behind me. Zamirah, of course. I thought I recognized her voice.

Her ivory dress reflects the sunlight, creating an angelic aura around her presence as she beams up from a whole head shorter than me. She must not have grown much in height since she achieved Mastery at age fourteen, but what she lacks in height, she makes up for in spirit.

What kind of person would El-Alam award Mastery to at such a young age? Surely, someone most impressive in His sight—someone truly upright.

What might she think of the Oracle's words?

I blink away my question and call to mind what she said.

"I sincerely doubt my mother would praise what she'd sooner label rebellion," I say, and though I mean it as a joke, pain sours my every word. I forcefully lighten my tone. "But if that's true, thank you for sharing. It's comforting to know some part of her appreciates it."

"She said it more than once," Zamirah affirms, yet I feel little relief. If Mother admired my methods of handling things, why did she use that as her excuse to keep the truth of my father's downfall hidden from me?

"Strange," is all I can think to say.

The blustery air flaps Zamirah's hair away from her bronze-toned cheeks as she studies me, like she's evaluating a sculptor's handiwork, and I can't help but watch in her in kind. What compelled her to come share that information with me? And shouldn't she be turning in after being up all night for her shift?

"I hope you know we all believe in you, Calden," she says, but with the sincerity in her tone, she might as well have only said *I.* "Even if we don't find Toaph Elbara in Raevre, we know El-Alam will guide you to the right place, and He won't let this trip be a waste of time."

I lower my chin, though courage seeps into my chest like a first breath after being underwater. "Thank you, Zamirah. That means a great deal to me."

Her wide smile curls even higher, almost childlike, yet her eyes are mature and wise. "Is there anything you need?"

I shake my head, but just as she's stopping herself from curtsying, my brows lift.

"Actually," I blurt, and she stills, "is there anything else my mother said about me that seems noteworthy?"

The question feels overly self-absorbed, but an aching part of me hopes to learn what other good things Mother might have spoken about me when I had no way of hearing them. Maybe that will help soften the pain of her betrayal.

Or it will make it worse.

Zamirah cradles her pointed chin, thinking. "We've spoken a good deal about your episodes. She was determined to stop them and had scholars across the lands searching for answers. I've been the one sending messages to the High Wardens about any developments on the matter."

A burst of laughter from the crew covers my sharp inhale. *She* is the one Mother uses to inform Wardens across the world about my condition and all the destruction I have caused?

Empyrean. Then she must have known, possibly more than the others in the crew, the danger of boarding this ship with a monster of his own sort. And yet, here she is.

Was she offered any choice?

"You must be well acquainted with it, then."

"I am." Somehow, the tone of her simple reply feels like a reassuring squeeze on the shoulder.

"And yet you set foot on this ship."

Her soft expression doesn't so much as flinch. "It is my pleasure to be here. *Truly.*"

I swallow her words—the same as she said to me in our first conversation—but still I struggle to believe them. They *must* have ordered her to board this ship, and this kind sentiment of hers is nothing more than her paying her respects to my status.

"There is another thing your mother said," Zamirah says, as if to yank me from the depths of my mind before I can sink too deeply into them. "She told me the rumors were true."

"Rumors?"

"About your eyes." Her arm sways toward the ocean. "They are bluer than the sea."

I smile, though my gaze dips at her notice of my most prominent feature.

"Where I'm from, people said it's because you've been blessed. You've been given something that no one has had before," she says, and I cringe at the word *blessed*. That is the furthest from how I feel.

"They didn't happen to suspect what that something is, did they?" I ask.

She looks toward the sky. "Everyone had their guesses. It was fun to imagine, but there's nothing helpful to our silly theories, I'm sure. It was more to raise morale and bring hope than anything." Her attention returns to me. "But I don't doubt that you are blessed."

"I wish I could say the same," I mutter before I can think better of it.

Her shoulders droop, as if pulled down by my statement, yet her eyes flood with a renewed intensity. "Even the greatest blessings can come with consequences. But that doesn't mean they aren't still blessings."

My brows pinch. *Blessings with consequences?*

Then is that what she considers my episodes, even with all she must know about them and their great horrors? Would she still say the same if she witnessed one herself?

I'm tempted to press her on the matter, but her words hold me captive as they weave through layers of steel and into the flesh of my heart. And instead, I'm left gaping at her with nothing to say in reply.

She smiles, and as if El-Alam had sent her to impart those words to me and she's now deemed her task complete, she drifts away as quietly as she came.

I watch her pausing to talk with her crewmates—wishing them a goodnight, though it's morning—then she dips beneath the main hatch. I stare at it long after she's gone. Confused, yet grateful, and somewhat more healed than I felt before we spoke.

Don't get attached, Calden, I tell myself.

Yet when I turn back to my overlook, her soul-soothing words are all I can hear.

NORIELLE

"You really don't have to stay in here. I can take care of myself," I say, swallowing another nauseous wave. I shouldn't have tried to eat breakfast this morning. "Go enjoy some fresh air."

From across the small dining table in the deckhouse, Elias gives me a disapproving look. But whether he means to suggest I can't take care of myself or that he wouldn't leave me even if I could, I can't quite tell. I take a sip of yet another peppermint tea he's made me. It must be the twentieth since my seasickness started the other evening. When I set it down, Elias is still staring at me, eyes partially glazed over. For three days now, he's stayed at my side, faithfully tending to my every need like he's a male, more handsome version of Rhiana.

And I've admittedly enjoyed every minute of it—nausea aside.

"Or maybe go get some sleep?" I suggest when he doesn't readily reply to my first suggestion.

He lifts his starroot tea, slurping it before slouching against the backrest of his chair, as if to prove his intention of staying. He nods toward the grimy windows, shining with morning light. "Too late in the day for that now. Would throw off my whole sleep schedule."

What is he doing? Trying to earn my favor? I frown, for once not at the sickness in my stomach. Maybe if I hadn't made him feel like he *had* to earn it, he wouldn't be trying so hard.

"I just don't want you to feel trapped in here," I say with a glance around the space. Our Bind quarters are bigger than what I was expecting. Still, the low ceilings and cabins crammed a few feet away behind a wooden wall provide little space to walk about.

"It's fine, Nori. I don't want to be anywhere else."

I scratch the handle of my cup with my fingernail. "You're avoiding people."

"Wouldn't you? I don't know any of them, and all anybody ever sees when they look at me is the lyre on my hip. If I go out there, they're all going to expect me to entertain them, like I'm just Cal's little monkey that he brought along for the fun of it."

I bite my lip, trying not to laugh at his answer that I know he doesn't intend to be funny. "But you like playing?"

"Well, yeah." He looks away for a while, as if struggling to form his thoughts. "I don't know, Nori. This is the Kieran in me, I guess. I still don't like crowds. I'm just better at pretending I do now."

"Yet you like the attention."

"As much as I like to be left alone." He smirks at the contradiction. "Makes no sense. Honestly, I don't know what it is. Maybe I'm tired of being *the bard* and never just *Elias*."

I take another sip of my tea, glad that this topic has mostly distracted me from the uneasy feeling inside. "So, you're avoiding people because you don't think anyone really cares about you. They just want you to entertain them."

He points a finger at me, as if to say, "That's it."

"But when people are around, all you ever do is play that role," I say. "The charming bard. The overconfident smart-mouth."

"Your point?"

"How can anybody care about the real you when you never let them see who that is?"

My question seizes him for a long time, almost too long, because I notice the rolls of the waves again and feel a pinch in my stomach. I quickly sip my tea and convince myself that the beverage is a magic elixir, working instantly to stop the nausea.

"Those roles *are* part of who I am now, Nori," Elias finally says. "And no one seems to want to look any deeper than that. They are perfectly content to have me for a little show then send me on my way. Besides Ila and Cal." The last part comes out in a grumble, and he looks at his Bind Mark again like he's considering something, or maybe remembering when Calden asked him to join the Bind. Was this part of why Calden chose Elias? Did he notice that Elias longs for something more than the life of an entertainer and scout?

"Everybody likes that version of me, anyway," Elias adds while I'm still pondering. "And you and I both know how people received *Kieran.*"

I hold his steady gaze, the memories of our youth seeming to replay in his dark irises. Landon was so cruel to him, always mocking him and making him feel small. It's no wonder he hated being around most people back then with the way Landon's influence poisoned all our peers' perception of him. He was so disdained for his small stature, foreign-looking appearance, and respect for authorities—not to mention his family's many misfortunes, from poverty to death—that people started treating *me* differently for associating with him.

Is that why he feared I wouldn't spend time with him back then? Why he played along about that dumb rabbit?

"Kieran was my favorite person in the world," I say, hands clutching the thick fabric of my coat beneath the table.

Elias frowns but covers it with a chuckle. "*Was.*"

I gulp, having not considered what I intended as a compliment to be an insult of its own kind. I chew my bottom lip, searching my heart for the truth of how I feel on a subject that still feels layered in fog.

"Forget it, Nori," Elias says before I can respond. "I understand. You want me to be Kieran. They want Elias. But I'm somewhere in between, and that's the guy nobody wants."

I squint. "No—"

The groan of the door opening causes me to break off before I can spew my unfiltered response: *That's exactly who we want.* Elias and I both turn as Odessa steps inside, tightening her curly ponytail.

"Feeling any better?" she asks, closing the door behind her.

"A little," I say, but as if in protest, acid creeps into my throat. When will this end?

"Good. Don't forget you have training to complete." She faces Elias. "I need to talk to you."

Elias straightens in his chair. "What about?"

"Not with her." Odessa flicks a sharp look my way.

My head jerks back. Why can't I be around for their discussion?

An argument seems to well up inside Elias, but while he's still holding it in—probably because of her status—I stand.

"It's fine. I need to lie down again," I say, hoping to spare Elias from getting into trouble. He'll tell me what it's about afterward, won't he?

"Thank you, Norielle," Odessa says.

I exchange a long look with Elias, trying to read any guesses regarding what this is about on his face, but he looks as confused as I am. Odessa clears her throat—a command for me to hurry—and I slip behind the wall to where our cabins are, hoping they'll stay at the table so I can overhear the conversation.

ELIAS

Odessa sits in Nori's chair, and a second later, a smoke-like energy blooms from her hands, surrounding us in a foggy sphere. My face scrunches as I look over the field enveloping us and back at Odessa.

"It's a *Master* Ward," she says with such superiority in her tone, she might as well add "peasant" at the end. "Our conversation will now stay inside this field. And I'd like for it to remain that way."

I gulp my tea. *What* is this about?

"Understood," I say.

She leans to one side, the windowlight falling over her. The woman's face could have been chiseled and polished by an artist. Inhumanly flawless. And absolutely nothing like Nori's gentle features that I'd rather still be looking at.

"I need you to tell me, *honestly*, if Calden seemed tempted to follow the Oracle when you two encountered him in the crypt," she says.

My throat clenches. How didn't I guess she'd corner me about this?

"You were there when they spoke, were you not?" she presses in my delay.

The whole scene replays in my head from the moment the Oracle stepped out from the crossroads to his final words to Cal, "*My son.*" I'd be lying to Odessa if I said I wasn't nervous when Cal started probing for the Oracle's theories or when his counterarguments slowed. And our conversation before we boarded the canoe for the underground river is still cropping up in my thoughts like an unwanted guest.

But this is *Cal.*

"He seemed *curious,*" I finally answer, probably just in time to spare myself a kick in the shin under the table. "But he didn't act on anything, besides to ask questions."

"And how openly did he receive the Oracle's responses?"

I narrow my eyes. Cal hasn't divulged the full conversation yet, has he? And now she's trying to whittle it out of me.

"I think this is a discussion we should have with your brother present."

She scowls. "I've tried, but he subverts every attempt I've made. And I'm not asking you to tell me every word they exchanged. I'm asking for your opinions about what you witnessed, on how receptive Calden seemed."

I incline forward, noticing the slightest waver in her composure, as if the topic actually scares her. *Her. Lady Odessa.* The woman known by all the Wardens to be virtually fearless. Is she nervous about how the Wardens could withstand Cal's level of power if he turned against us? Or is this more personal—a fear of losing the brother she doesn't even seem to like?

"You're scared," I prompt.

Her gaze flicks sideways. "I am *concerned.*"

"Because you care about him or because you think he could kill us all if he joined the Oracle?"

"Both." Her nails tap the table again before she draws her hand into her lap. "Not to mention that the entire world's fate rests on my brother's decisions. I think it is wise that, as members of his Bind, we remain vigilant. Perhaps it is for reasons like these that El-Alam saw fit to call a Bind together, rather than leaving Calden to carry out this mission alone."

I turn my Bind Mark into view again, briefly tempted to ask the great Lady Odessa what she thinks of her brother bringing me in and tying a lowly scout's destiny to hers. But her insinuations about Cal ensnare my focus. What is it about him that has her so sure we need to be nervous about this? Even after his hesitance with the Oracle, the Cal I know has too much moral integrity to surrender to defection.

Or that's what I've been convincing myself of since we returned from the crypt.

"Well, what makes you think Cal would defect?" I ask.

Her arms cross. "Have you not noticed his rebellious tendencies?"

"That's not enough to convince me. Bucking against a few rules and willingly walking into eternal damnation are two very different things." I lift a brow, catching the way she presses her lips together. "There's more to it than that, isn't there?"

"The rest is only mine to know."

I raise my Bind Mark into her line of sight. "Are we a team, or are we all just trying not to bump shoulders while walking in the same direction?"

She only glowers.

"What we're trying to do is hard enough," I add. "The last thing we need is members of the Bind keeping secrets from each other."

"You talk as if you've been in the Bind from the beginning," she says, a warning edge in her tone that I decide to ignore.

"Well, so far, no one else seems to care about actually being a team. You just want to be left alone. Cal wants to *do* everything alone. Alani's too busy batting her eyes at her first mate, and Nori is too new to all this to know any better. At what point do we all come together to figure things out?"

"What do you think I'm doing right now?" she snaps.

"Taking an awfully small step for such a prestigious Second Lady," I challenge, hoping a poke at her pride will get her to spill. "But you could make that a leap by telling me what you know, so I can help you decide if we should be legitimately worried about Cal or not. Do that, and I'll give you my full take on what happened in the crypt."

Her lips suddenly swivel into an amused smirk—the last expression I anticipated. I half expected to get slapped for that. "I see now why my mother sends you to pry information out of the Hunters about their plans. You're annoyingly persistent."

"Nice deflection, princess," I say, folding my hands on the tabletop. "Tell me why I should be worried about Cal."

She stares at me for a long time, seeming to debate whether she'll cave or walk away right now. But slowly, her harsh expression wilts, and a heaviness weighs on her eyelids. "What I am about to share, you cannot repeat to anyone. My brother especially, do you understand?"

I nod.

Odessa's eyes narrow, like she's analyzing how trustworthy I am. "I'm worried because Calden is scared and desperate. And that was the folly of the Sovereign before him."

I tilt my head. "What do you mean?"

Rather than explaining, she seems to fade into her chair, sitting like a motionless specter in front of me.

"My lady?"

Her glazed gaze lifts no higher than my chin. "He was looking for a way to save Calden from his curse."

"He *what?*"

"That's what made him fall."

I watch the swirling fog behind her as her words sink in. The Oracle—the last Sovereign—defected *for* Cal? Trying to *help him?*

Then he wasn't lying when he said everything that he'd done was for him... *to save him.*

Nerves prickle through my limbs. If Calden found out that the Oracle didn't lie about that, how much more susceptible to believing him would he be?

"How do you know?" I ask.

Odessa's words come out lifeless. "My mother told me. Apparently, my father's faith broke beneath Calden's curse. He'd tried every ward to help Calden and prayed on his knees until they bruised, begging El-Alam to free him. Supposedly, he loved Calden more than even Mother did, and when El-Alam failed to provide relief from the curse, my father deemed the Creator wicked and started experimenting with different sources of magic."

I hold my tongue, chills racing down my arms.

"It wasn't for evil that he forsook us. It was for love." Black flames seem to flicker in her deep irises. "*That* is why Mother has never found the nerve to order my father's execution. And why I fear for Calden. If my father could fall into such methods due to his desperation to help Calden, why wouldn't Calden fall into them to help the world?"

The muscles across my chest contract. We both go quiet, the muted noises of footsteps and waves filling the void between our words.

"Cal's not like your father." Yet my voice wavers when I say it. "El-Alam wouldn't have chosen Cal for this mission, knowing he'd turn on us."

Odessa's stare lingers on me for a long time before she finally inhales again. "Everyone is capable of corruption."

"Sure," I affirm. "But not everyone chooses it. Cal won't."

"You really believe that?" Her question comes out softly, like she genuinely needs my reassurance—*the* Lady Odessa, looking to me for comfort.

I slap on a smile, burying my own fears beneath my ready-made mask. "Cal doesn't follow any man's lead. Your father's included. He's too much of a rebel to take directions from anyone but his own heart and El-Alam. And neither of those are going to lead him into the pits."

Odessa smiles—barely—before she heaves another sigh. "Then is that your verdict based on what you witnessed?"

"That's what I saw," I confirm. "The Oracle made his offers, and Cal sent him away. If he wanted to follow him, he'd have done it then. I certainly couldn't have stopped him."

Odessa holds my gaze for a long time, then nods, as if finally receiving my words. "I hope you're right."

"I tend to be," I bluff, as if portraying confidence in my conclusion might help the situation.

She stands, looking around at the mist. "Tell me if he says or does anything that makes you suspicious. It doesn't hurt to be on our guard."

"Order received, my lady."

The field vanishes in a puff, and she leaves me with a headache I didn't need.

NORIELLE

The door shuts, and I peer around the corner again, in time to see the last of the mist dissolving around the table. What was that? Some kind of Master Ward no one has taught me about?

Elias still sits in his chair, rubbing his temples with his head hung so low, the tip of his nose almost touches the tabletop. I wipe the nervous sweat off my palms, ashamed of spying. But why would Odessa need to talk to Elias in private? Why couldn't I be part of their conversation?

I curse the spark of jealousy I feel toward Odessa, with all her perfect beauty, stealing a private moment with Elias. I shouldn't care. It's not like they even got close to each other, and yet, I can't deny the way my stomach twisted the whole time she was here.

Is this how I've made *Elias* feel every time I'm around Calden?

I step out, boards creaking under my feet, and Elias looks up. "Thought you were going to lie down for a while?" he says, but his grin reveals his lack of disappointment.

I reclaim my chair. "What was that about?"

Elias blows a long sigh that tickles my arms as I rest my elbows on the table. "She's worried about Cal."

"What do you mean?"

He looks around, reminding me that without magic like Odessa's, our conversation is open to anyone who cares to listen in, should they be pressing an ear to the deckhouse door. "I don't want to stress you with it, Nori. And she asked me not to tell anyone else."

I give him a hard look, like I might have when we were children. He knows better than to think that will work. "Well, I'm already stressed about it, and you saying that makes it worse. So, tell me what's going on."

He ruffles his hair, and I watch every wave find its new place, chiding myself for having the presence of mind to notice how the added shadows from the window's partial lighting somehow make his bold features more striking.

Did Odessa think that?

"Please, tell me," I say when his silence only perpetuates itself.

"Skies, Nori," he groans. "There's a reason the Second Lady excluded you from the conversation."

"Well, luckily, I'm talking to my best friend, not her."

A smile flashes on his lips. *Best friend.* That's the first time I've called him that to his face since we reunited. But his expression falls as he rakes his fingers through his hair again. "You're not gonna like this."

A muscle in my arm twitches. "What?"

Finally, a look of defeat precedes his reply. "She's worried about Cal defecting because apparently, he's the reason his father fled into the shadows."

"*What?*"

"I guess the last Sovereign was so desperate to stop Calden's episodes, it motivated him to turn against El-Alam and seek other forms of magic. That's what led to him inventing Blood Wards."

I lower my voice. "Does Calden know this?"

Elias shakes his head. "The Oracle implied it, but otherwise, no. No one has confirmed it to him yet. I think, for now, it's best he doesn't know."

Every motion of the ship feels sevenfold stronger than it did before, like the sea is held inside a bottle that a child is sloshing back and forth.

"Odessa is also worried that Cal will get as desperate to save the world as his father was to save him—leading him down the same path," Elias adds.

"And..." I clutch my hands together beneath the table. "What do you think?"

"Cal's not that way." His eyes hold a hint of uncertainty, quickly replaced by resolve. "He'd never defect. He's too loyal to El-Alam, and there's evidence for that."

"Evidence?" I ask, and Elias recoils. "What do you mean?"

His eyes and mouth squeeze shut, as if he could squash the words he just said out of existence. "He's still not told you?"

"Told me what?"

"Why am I everyone's middleman?" he grumbles, wiping a hand over his face. "Nori, you need to ask Cal how he healed you."

"What does that have to do with anything?"

He drags his cup over to check for a last drop of tea before frowning and pushing it away. "Just trust me," he says. "He thinks you don't remember anything about being healed, which is probably why he's not brought it up. But I think you should know. It might bring you some peace about all this."

My body goes stiff, despite how long I've contemplated asking Calden about my healing, especially after my discussion with Rhiana and Alani. Is Elias hinting that Calden used whatever this other method of healing is?

"I'll ask him," I finally agree.

Elias's gaze drops, and I wish I could see inside his mind to know why. He stands a moment later, ceramic skidding against wood as he drags his cup off the table's edge.

"I need more tea," he says, pausing with his boots pointed toward the door. "Do you want something, or are you going to talk to him now?"

My toes curl against the cold floorboards. Impatience and curiosity prod at me, urging me to race onto the main deck, pull Calden aside, and demand answers—if for nothing else, then to know what evidence stands against the possibility of our Bind leader defecting. But Rhiana's voice returns to me:

"What does the affection of one matter, if it's the other your heart longs for?"

"Do you know who your heart longs for, miss?"

While something much more important is now at hand, her words slow me down. I can't ask Calden until I *know* how I want him to answer—and not just for the sake of knowing his integrity still stands.

"I need a little time first," I say, hoping Elias doesn't argue. "I'd like to be completely over my queasiness so I can focus on what he's saying."

Elias lifts a brow—why I thought I could deceive him, even with such a logical excuse, is beyond me. But his expression relaxes without rebuttal. "When you're ready, Nori."

I thank him and watch as he exits our quarters to replenish his tea. But by the time the door closes at his heels, the answer to Rhiana's question blooms in my heart as if already there, like a blossom that had budded at my ball and just needed time to realize itself before it opened.

I hold it up in my mind, inspecting the honesty of its composition—the strength of its stem, the luster of its petals, the depth of its roots. Finding no fault or weakness, I finally accept it for what it is: the flower planted in the soil of my heart when I was a little girl.

CALDEN

The galley door whines as I open it in search of Norielle. It's been four days since she's left the deckhouse for more than a couple of minutes, but Elias claimed she is up and finally on the mend from her seasickness.

The pungent smell of onions and broth prompts a quiet rumble from my stomach as I step into the small kitchen. As Elias assured me I would, I find Norielle inside, washing a pan, her hair pulled back with a wide bow. Across from her, the daytime cook, Orto, nurtures a soup—oblivious, like Norielle, to my entrance. Foamy water spills from the mouth of the pan Norielle attends to, and she gives the inside another scrub before holding it toward the gleaming crystal wall sconces for inspection. A drop of water plops onto her pale dress, leaving a momentary stain. She rinses the pan in a separate pail before setting a cloth to it. As she dries it, she checks the small counter beside Orto, as if looking for something else to wash.

Is she filling in for the galley stewardess? I wonder before taking another step inside.

"Smells delicious, Orto," I say.

Norielle yelps, dropping the towel and pan at the sound of my voice. The metal *tings* against the small countertop, leaving a sustained ringing sound in the room. Orto only grins and gives a small bow to me in thanks. The older man has been mute since birth, I'm told. Not even a Healing Ward from his own mother could grant him a voice. But he's found other ways to express himself, one of which is through food—much to our delight.

"Sorry," Norielle says, retrieving the pan and towel. "I didn't hear you come in."

I dismiss any need for an apology with a smile. "Lias told me you were feeling better."

She looks down, and it's strange to not see her hair fall into her face.

"I am. Mostly," she says at last, hanging the pan on a deep hook.

"I was hoping we could continue your training soon. When you're recovered, that is. I'm not nearly as concerned as my mother was about a single point, but it would be wise to make sure that you are fully prepared before we reach Raevre."

She sets the towel aside and, with a surveying glance, she seems to find her work finished for now. "I feel well enough. Did you want to start today?"

I consider my now wide-open schedule. No councils. No random errands requiring someone with my specific skill set. No standing around seeking the other mind, since to do so on a ship would be utter lunacy. And it would be nice to have something else to do today besides thinking about how similar the ship's railings feel to the bars of a prison cell.

"If you're sure you are ready," I say.

"I'm sure," she says, but her expression shifts, as if suddenly thinking of something else—or possibly receiving a fresh protest from her stomach. "Though... there is a problem."

"What's that?"
"The ward I failed was the Vitality Ward."

I squint against the setting sun as I draw a fresh Shroud Ward on the mainmast. Though invisible, its shield will cover the entire ship for several hours, blocking any nearby Accursed from sensing our use of magic aboard the ship.

With the ward ignited, I lead Norielle to the widest space we can find on the main deck, bringing Elias and Odessa also to help me wall in our temporary arena. Of all wards, the Vitality Ward is probably the worst one to practice on a ship, lest we blow a hole in the vessel or take out a sail. But Norielle must learn, and this is arguably the most important ward she needs to know before we set foot in Raevre.

I swat away a momentary regret for not at least *asking* which ward cost Norielle her final point, then I backhand the intrusive thought that Mother may be right to be concerned over it.

At my command, Elias and Odessa activate their own Vitality Wards and channel them into shields that form staticky blue walls around what little of the deck we can claim for ourselves—a barrier, much like what imprisons Ta'Nathel in Northspire. The cool glow emanating from their walls casts a blue sheen onto the deck and flickers in Norielle's eyes as she turns to me.

"What did Alani teach you about the Vitality Ward and how it works?" I ask.

Norielle peers at Alani through the semitranslucent wall. From the helm, Alani waves at her and sends an encouraging smile.

"She said that in order to use it, I have to pull energy from myself—my own *vitality*—and control it with my will to do what I want." Norielle thinks a moment before adding, "She also mentioned before that how many spheres someone can launch with one ward is contingent on their skill, and that *you*"—a hint of challenge enters her tone—"can launch thirteen of them with a single ward, which is triple what most people can."

She admires me as a child might their older sibling or a hero of theirs, and yet something shifts in her eyes the longer she looks at me—as if a concern snuck up on her like a sour aftertaste.

What is it that troubles her? Is she realizing that the atmosphere between us has shifted? Have my recent actions cost me some of her respect?

"I've had much practice," I say before my pause stretches too long. "And in time, who knows? Perhaps you'll launch fourteen."

Norielle smiles. "I doubt that."

"Well, let's focus on getting one well-controlled sphere out of you for now," I say, grabbing my pen to draw the ward upon my palm. As I etch the sunlike glyph, I continue. "It sounds like Alani taught you well about how to activate the ward, but there may be a gap in your training regarding how you keep said ward under control."

I wave my pen toward Norielle to signal that she should draw the glyph on herself as well. She retrieves the pen that Elias lent her from her belt and etches the Vitality Ward, having mastered that part of the practice well since we sat together at Ila's table.

"Since the energy you are conducting with the Vitality Ward is your own, managing it is about self-control. Typically, those who are good at keeping themselves—their emotions, reactions, and such—under control have an easier time handling it because it comes from that same part of you." I allow her a moment to process, then I shift into a defensive posture. "I want you to try launching a sphere at me."

She shudders.

"I'll block it, of course."

Norielle glances around again, seeming to relax a little when she sees the crew isn't standing about, watching her. Odessa holds up her part of the shield, but otherwise, seems more interested in staring out at the sea, while Elias looks on with full investment. His gaze urges Norielle like he did at her induction ceremony, when she hesitated to give the announcement. And, like before, his small contribution seems to be exactly what she needs to find her courage.

She turns her palm toward me, and I ready my shield, a blue force rippling from my hand. The ship bobs over the waves in her pause, then a spark ignites from her palm. It nearly flickers out before swelling into an orb the size of an apple. It launches, only to dissipate in the air between us, several stretches away from me.

"Wonderful," I comment, despite the failed effort. "Try it again, and this time, make sure you are willing it to hit my shield."

She wets her lips, checking her palm to see that the ward already needs to be redrawn. I wait for her to do so before igniting my shield again. This time, when the sphere spews from her hand, it flies above my head. It hits the barrier, sizzling as it dissolves in Elias's and Odessa's more powerful energy.

"Better willing," I say. "Now focus on both willing and aiming at once."

Norielle tries it again from the beginning, but it launches to my side. And again, it shoots for the deck, and I barely rebound it before it would have blown a hole in the ship.

With a frustrated breath, she draws the glyph again and aims, but the ward vanishes after only the slightest spark.

"Norielle," I say as she's reaching for Elias's pen to redraw it. "That's enough for this session. You could hurt yourself if you keep trying once you've completely exhausted the ward."

She frowns, fingers slipping away from the pen. "I'm sorry."

The barrier around us drops, and I take a few steps nearer to her so I'm not shouting for the entire ship to hear. "You're doing incredible," I say, making sure she holds my gaze. "The Vitality Ward is one of the most challenging to wield of the standard wards. Don't be too hard on yourself. We have plenty of time yet before we reach Raevre, and something tells me you wouldn't struggle with it if you really needed to use it. Sometimes it's easier to get out of our own way when there's no time to overthink it."

She smiles, though the disappointment still hangs in her gaze.

"We'll try again tomorrow."

She stares at the wooden deck beneath us, seeming to contemplate arguing with me before apparently deeming it pointless. "All right."

"Don't feel bad. You might not have defeated Elias's record, but you're still leagues ahead of most—"

"Sea heller!" a man suddenly cries from the crow's nest.

I barely twist my red Omen Mark into view before Alani shouts from the helm. "Drop the sails!"

NORIELLE

"Take Norielle belowdecks," Calden orders Elias as the deck swarms with moving people.

Elias surges to my side, snatching my arm with a firm grip. A rebuttal stutters in my throat as he tugs me across the main deck, but terror chokes the words before they can fully form. I look over my shoulder to see what this *sea heller* is. Through the darting crew, the sea looks calm and empty.

But so did Lake Daleia before it pulled me to the bottom.

"What's a sea heller?" I ask as we reach the hatch to the lower deck.

Elias releases me to pull it open, hinges crying out, as if to accuse me of cowardice. *Fleeing. Again.*

"They were stormcatchers—giant, Empyreal mantas," Elias says, urging me toward the ladder. "They used to follow ships to protect them from sea storms."

I steal another look across the deck at Calden, finding him and Odessa flanking Alani. Calden glances back at me, his eyes seeming to demand I go where he sent me. I swallow the temptation to argue for my right to help, but how much help could I offer? I couldn't even launch one successful vitality sphere, and now I've depleted myself. Not to mention nausea is already swimming up my throat at the thought of trouble at sea.

A warning tingle from my Omen Mark reminds me to move, and I swing myself onto the ladder. Footsteps rumble from overhead as I reach the bottom and look up through the hatch at Elias. His contemplative gaze lingers on Calden before he follows me down the ladder.

"Sea heller!" he hollers toward the crew's sleeping quarters like a crack of thunder. Squeaks and stirrings from the bunks ensue as the late sleepers from the night crew awaken. Elias's voice is almost a whisper when he shifts back to me. "Find something to hold on to. And stay away from metal."

"What?"

"They don't stop storms anymore, Nori. They *are* the storms."

Deckhands, still dressed in their pajamas, dart past us, ascending the ladder to the upper deck.

"Can they kill it?" I ask, ashamed of how quivery my voice comes out.

Elias hesitates in his reply, and one last crew member steps out, short enough to find no need to duck under the low ceiling. Her alert green-gold eyes, faintly lit by a dim crystal sconce on the wall, are set on Elias. *Zamirah,* I recall. I've crossed paths with her once in the galley, but since she works the night shift and I mostly stay tucked away, I've not seen her since.

"Sea heller?" she asks Elias. "Is that what you said?"

Elias nods, but hardly glances at her; instead, he pulls me toward a wooden beam. He pats it, as if to make sure I register it as my anchor if the ship tips.

My side cramps at the thought.

"Are you going back up?" I ask him.

Elias casts a long look at the hatch, and suddenly I realize how quiet it is. No shouts, no footsteps, nothing but the creaks of the ship. I shift closer to him, silently conveying my wish for him to stay, and he wraps an arm around me.

Zamirah, still with us, unlike the rest of the crew, glances at the deck above. Then she lifts her Omen Mark, casting a soft light from her opposite palm to better read it with. I watch her expression like someone awaiting a physician's verdict, since it's too dark where I stand to see my own mark. "It's circling the ship," she says, twisting her wrist to show us. The middle arrow, a darker shade of red than I expected, rotates as it tracks the beast. "That's what they do to build up electricity."

I gasp. *Electricity?*

"Why aren't they shooting it?" Elias asks, his hold on me loosening, as if he's planning to release me and go attack the sea heller himself.

Zamirah shifts her arm to show how the arrow points down when the Omen Mark is upright. "It's too deep."

Elias's hot breath puffs against my hair. "You've encountered these before?"

"Only once, and we narrowly survived it."

"*Comforting.*"

"There weren't six Masters on the ship," she says.

I mentally tally the Masters aboard—Calden, Alani, Odessa, Willian. Who are the other two?

"Though, they've ordered me not to go up on deck in a crisis unless desperately required," Zamirah adds.

She's a Master Warden? She looks hardly any older than me.

Zamirah eyes Elias. "And it seems they've charged you to stay belowdecks as well."

"I'm not a Master," he says, speaking low, as if shame has stolen a third of his voice. "What's your Talent?"

Zamirah's lips quirk to the right. "Singing."

I slant my head at the joke, something unpleasant stirring inside me when Elias responds, "Cute," even though his tone is dry. But before I can fully assure myself Elias meant it sarcastically, Zamirah's attention snaps toward the hatch, as if someone knocked on it.

"Where is the Sovereign Prince? Shouldn't he be belowdecks also?"

At her mention, I realize she's right. Calden *should* be with us. If not because of his importance as the Sovereign Prince, at least for his connection with Toaph Elbara.

"He's where he always is," Elias says. "In the heart of danger."

Zamirah smiles, an odd contradiction to her next words. "And no one thought to insist he step away from it?"

I grimace at how quickly my fear of the water overcame my ability to be rational. But then again, after all I've learned about Calden and what I witnessed in the cedar forest, I'd only feel like I did as a child when I was trying to convince Papa not to return to war—foolish and small.

"He doesn't listen well," Elias says.

Zamirah's gaze returns to the hatch with a spark of determination, like this information has inspired her to disregard her own orders and go up to help. But then, as suddenly as Lake Daleia came alive beneath my canoe, the sea seems to awaken beneath us, and with it, the yells of the people on deck.

CALDEN

Waves slap against the sides of the ship as it teeters back down, like Alani lifted the entire vessel with her Talent, only to drop it. Everyone on deck staggers, some sliding several feet from their original positions as the massive creature below glides back into the depths, hidden after the slightest sighting of its winglike fins.

I scan the sloshing water with the tip of my conjured arrow, but a stillness follows, long enough for the sea to resettle almost entirely. Alani steps ahead of Odessa and me, her loose hair flicking in the breeze. Across the deck, her ready crew pivots their attention between her and the water. Still, silence ensues.

I slacken my bowstring. *Did it move on?*

Perhaps it sensed, even despite my Shroud Ward that should still be active, that this ship has too many Masters for a single beast to take on alone.

No, I realize with a glance at my Omen Mark. It's circling us again...

Charging its electricity, as Alani said. Pity we don't have a lightning-wielder aboard the ship, considering we have wielders of wind and water already.

I draw in a slow breath, watching my Omen Mark. Under the dimming sky, its hue is growing harder to discern, but the red arrow's tip favors the north, suggesting the sea heller either moves away from us in that direction or it is traveling toward us in the opposite.

Toward us, I conclude by how the shade brightens, a heartbeat before the sea swells into a tidal wave mastered by the colossal creature inside it. The pale underside of its diamond-shaped body catches in the sunset, flaunting the wide span of its angular fins—at least half the length of the *Celestella.* Aiming for its slitted gills, I loose my arrow, but the beast dives, evading my attack and a series of vitality spheres alike. I conjure another arrow but haven't time to steady it against my bow before a massive wave ripples under the ship, rocking it. I fight for stability, only for the sea heller to rise on the opposite side and repeat the motion, throwing everyone off-balance.

Three times, it aggravates the sea in this way until the waters surrounding us are tossing the vessel with such aggression that I must cling to the mizzenmast to keep from toppling over. Alani holds one hand toward the sea, the other clutching the same mast. With her Talent, she fights to resettle the water, but it hardly calms to a wobble before a spidery spark ignites beneath the now-blackening sea. I re-form the arrow I abandoned so I could hold on to the ship, watching the lightning build on the circling creature. Its fins flap in slow, concentrated motions as it glides around and around our vessel. Several arrows and vitality spheres launch after it, all missing.

I grit my teeth, fearing what it could do to this ship with this festering lightning. An array of horrors flash through my mind of lightning-filled waves splashing across the deck, electrocuting everyone in their path, or buzzing white tendrils splitting the masts, or bolts reaching something combustible and blowing holes in the ship's body.

The sea heller rises again, conducting the largest wave we've yet seen. Within the water, magical bolts of electricity flash in chaotic pulses, eager to attack. The heller lifts higher by the second, the rate barely granting me the chance to comprehend its motives, let alone fire an arrow—which only sticks between its gills like a thorn.

It means to dive over the ship—throwing that lightning-infused wave across the entire vessel.

"Alani—" I yelp, only to find she's already stepping toward the creature with both palms outstretched.

The sea heller shifts to surge over our heads, but Alani's Talent holds it back with equal force—suspending the beast overhead. The bolts intensify, professing the creature's rage at being opposed.

No, being *trapped*.

Now that precision and longevity are no longer my priorities, I abandon my weapon and ignite my Vitality Ward instead. My sphere launches alongside a score of others, colliding with the heller's white underbelly. Red burns mar its skin, but the water surrounding it lessens our impacts.

A branch of lightning extends toward the ship, spurring yelps from the main deck. I twist in time to see the lightning fizzle out, barely missing the mainmast. Then Alani's whimper swivels me toward her. Her heels slide back an inch, as if pushed by the beast itself as it gains control over the water again, inclining itself and the wave closer to us.

But just when I fear the beast will overpower Alani, Willian steps ahead of us, approaching the very edge of the stern. He draws the air around him like a whirlwind, and with a hand aimed at the flashing wave, he conducts the roaring gust into the beast. The wind slams against the water, spraying it and pushing both beast and wave backward. Still, the sea heller contends with both their abilities, suspending itself once more over the sea.

I reach for my power, coalescing it into a vitality sphere three times the size I'd normally use. The blue glow shines across the wet quarterdeck, like a brilliant star held between my encircling hands. I strengthen it as orbs launch all around me. Their petty sizes are not sufficient...

"Calden," Odessa chides between her own attacks.

But I ignore her, a weakness entering my knees as I draw out even more of my life force to grow the sphere. I hold the powerful mass, my hands trembling at the thought of the damage I'd cause to the ship if I misfire.

Ten normal spheres' worth of vitality finally satisfies me—the last of what I can produce without redrawing my ward. I carefully ease away from Alani and Willian, carrying the large orb with sweeping motions of my hands. Then, at last, I focus my aim on the sea heller, and with a slow exhale for concentration, I launch the glowing mass.

My body goes rigid as the orb arcs overhead like a blue sun and smashes into the sea heller's center, causing it to vault rearward. The beast's smooth back slaps against the sea, the wave it carried crashing down with it. Water surges from the impact, thrashing the ship once more as the lightning sizzles out.

I grip the ship's rail, feeling the temporary loss of my life force yet the upwelling adrenaline of victory as I watch the sea heller drift lamely in the waves. A celebratory ovation explodes from the crew the moment our Omen Marks turn black, and I turn to check on Alani. Her frame slouches like a battle-weary soldier, but she smiles at our triumph. I return the expression, the applause too loud to speak over, but I hope she can feel every ounce of pride I feel toward her. Power and resilience like that is why El-Alam has her in my Bind.

To my alarm, Odessa is the first to reach Alani's side, offering support as she prompts Alani toward the deckhouse. Alani's mouth opens, as if to protest, but Willian quickly asserts, "I'll take it from here, Captain."

Alani meets his gaze to nod both her agreement and thanks. Then she and Odessa descend the stairs, and the cheering crew quiets once Odessa shuts the door behind them.

"Well, that went better than my last encounter," Willian says, voice raspy and weak from his exertion. He looks down at his nightclothes, as if suddenly recalling what he came dressed in, then he dismisses himself to change, leaving the third mate to steward the helm.

I find the nearest place to sit—the top of the stairs to the quarterdeck—where I collapse, shoulders heaving. What would have come of us had we not been equipped with masters of the wind and sea? How do any ships survive out here with such beasts roaming these dark waters?

A sudden creak from the stairs raises my gaze to find Zamirah ascending the steps. She stops a few paces shy of me, donned in a loose, pearlescent nightgown. Stray strings along the gown's frayed lace trim flick in the breeze, a few inches above her tan ankles—an odd sight for such a composed woman.

"Thirsty?" she asks, extending a flask of water toward me as though assuming my answer before she even approached.

Doesn't she know better than to come near me when I'm weary?

I hesitantly take the flask, wondering if someone sent her or if she came of her own volition. But I pull the stopper and guzzle down half the water without inquiry.

"I thought Sovereigns and heirs were supposed to stay belowdecks when we're attacked?" she asks, yet as I lower the flask, I find a grin dimpling her cheek.

"Seems like a waste of resources to me," I say, wetting my throat again when I hear how hoarse my voice comes out. "El-Alam didn't grant me this power for me to hide away, thinking myself too important to be put in danger."

"And now I see why your mother worries about you so." She giggles. "Maybe we shouldn't mention this to her?"

Even with how tired I am, her statement curls my lips. "I was just thinking the same."

I take another sip from the flask and seal it, but the echo of our words reminds me of how much Mother has kept *from me* all these years, and my spirit dims within.

"I better dress for my shift," Zamirah says, with a quick glance at the darkening sky. "Is there anything I can bring you from the galley when I return, or would that put to shame the legs El-Alam thought to give you?"

Her unexpected joke pulls me right out of my inner darkness, and I can't help sending her a puzzled look for a moment before attempting to return the jest. "Indeed. It would be a disgrace for me to not walk over there myself."

She holds a hand toward me, and I freeze, thinking she means to help me stand, but then her gaze flicks toward the flask I'm holding. "Best you give that back, then. You don't want to dishonor El-Alam by drinking another sip of water you didn't retrieve for yourself."

I gape, not sure how to respond, and instead, catch myself musing over the sight of this young woman, standing on the stairs in her bare feet and in nightclothes, stumping me—who just defeated a beast half the size of our ship—at what to say in reply.

"Ah, never mind," she says, touching her ear, as if to listen to something more closely. "I just heard from Him now. He says it's good to accept a bit of help now and again. Especially from those whose lives you just saved."

I clutch the flask tighter, turning my smile toward my lap. If I weren't so fatigued, I'd like to think of a better reply, but the best I have is, "Well, thank you. I'm already feeling much better."

She smiles once more before clutching the skirt of her billowy nightdress. "I really should change. Willian will—" She cuts herself short at the sight of him stepping out from the sailors' quarters across the deck. "*Oops.* Too late. Now he's going to give me trouble for standing around down here, rather than up there." She points to the crow's nest.

I open my mouth to assure her I'd take the blame in that case, but she waves goodbye and rushes away before I can speak. My mouth shuts, and I raise the flask she left me with, drinking the rest of it as a celebration begins on the deck.

39

ZAMIRAH

Blue coats the bristles of my sleek paintbrush as I dab it into my freshly mixed paint. I hold it toward the lantern hanging over my bunk, inspecting the shade in the brilliance of my Glory Ward. Satisfied by the vibrant color, I set the brush against the wood of my cabin wall, streaking a highlight along the petal of a soulcast flower.

The blossom is one of several that embellishes the long, silver shaft of a swordstaff. The sharp blades, which I finished detailing shortly before the sea heller's attack yesterday, stand out as a peculiar contrast to the delicate flowers. But the decorated weapon fits perfectly between my array of paintings, filling the final gap on my wall, as if I'd planned for it to be there from the beginning.

I wet my brush once again, steadying my hand to add one more highlight, but suddenly, the ship dips, and I smear the paint—ruining the last petal.

Before I can groan, a throat clears behind me, and I startle, the brush dropping from my hand and staining the pale skirt of my dress in blue.

"*Sea's breath,*" Willian says, his head ducked beneath the low ceiling of the 'tween deck. "Don't tell me you're awake. Here I thought you'd overslept."

I cringe as I snatch my fallen brush. *Is it night already? Am I late for my shift?*

But rather than carrying on the reprimand he seemed to intend, Willian tilts his head, as if to gain a better view of the newest addition to my wall. "Is that... the Sovereign Prince's staff?"

I wipe the excess paint from my brush on a stained cloth, avoiding his gaze. "It's Toaph Elbara's, thank you."

"And that is why you've covered it in the prince's soulcast flowers?"

My lips skew sideways. After our seven years at sea together and having known him even prior to that, Willian might as well be a brother to me. Still, I hadn't anticipated anyone—even him—to pay any attention to my walls besides a casual glance, let alone notice a minor detail like that. But what other flowers would make sense to decorate the swordstaff with, if not those casting the soul colors of the prince?

"How do you know his soulcast colors?" I inquire.

Willian tugs senselessly at the cuff of his sleeve. "I asked the captain to tell me about the Bind, and she gave me a whole dissertation—soulcast flowers, and all."

I shake out my hair, satisfied that my question provided a worthy distraction. "Oh, and how I'm sure you savored every moment of it." I toss a sly look his way, and he promptly raises his chin, as if to declare himself above this conversation. But his sheepish smile displays his heart like an item for sale in the market.

And our captain is surely the buyer.

"Your shift, Zamirah," Willian says, layering on a tone as formal as his wool coat.

I giggle at him before turning again to my wall and recalling my mistake. I suppose I'll have to fix it later. The trouble will be finding the right mixture of pigment to get the colors to match exactly again. But alas, duty calls.

As it so often does.

I rinse my brush in a cup of water and return all my brushes and paints to a small box with faded vines painted on the outside. The box has held my art supplies since I was a little girl, still wondering about my place in this wide, dying world. It's one of the few items I brought here from home all those years ago.

"I'm coming," I say, turning to lace on my boots—the only part of me that isn't ready to go besides my heart.

"Excellent." Willian smiles. "See you up deck, little bird. And make it quick, will you? Valrone is going to start throwing peanuts at us again if he's not relieved from the nest."

I quicken my motions, laughing at the imagery of Valrone and Willian's insertion of the nickname he gave me when his uncle, Captain Theos, made me one of the designated lookouts. I was only fourteen then, and Willian found the nickname apt for a tiny girl who happened to enjoy singing from her perch. His uses of it have thinned in our adulthood, but it never fails to warm me like a sip of hot apple cider.

Willian heads up without me as I finish tying my laces. Then I whisper an apology to my imperfect painting and race after him.

The dark sky greets me with its vast sprawl as I step onto the main deck. To my shame, the rest of the night crew is already up here, enjoying the music Elias provides. I struggle to maintain my quick gait, entranced by Elias's incredible gift with his instrument and enticed by the opportunity to join in the dancing.

I could have, had I come up sooner. But that painting—

"Pardon me."

I lurch back, and the man before me does the same. My spine snaps straight as I register that the person I nearly collided with is the Sovereign Prince himself.

"Oh, Zamirah. I'm sorry. Do excuse me," he says, as if his initial request for pardon wasn't sufficient. His eyes—the shade I was attempting to match for the highlights on my painted flowers—shift toward the deckhouse where he must have been headed, and back to me.

"How dare you," I tease, and he flinches. "I was the one not watching where I was going. How dare *you* apologize."

He trades his alarmed expression for a smile, alleviating my worry that I made a mistake in speaking to him in the same manner I do with the sailors. He studies me, as he has in our previous conversations, like I've perplexed him—or maybe even intrigued him—and I do the same to him. After all these years, hearing about him from his mother and in passed-down stories, he's right here. And while he lives up to what I've heard, he's so much more human than I expected—in the best of ways.

"Is that... paint?" he asks, gesturing toward my dress.

The blue stain from where the brush fell stands out even in the dimness of nightfall. I brush it—dumbly—like it might fall off, but all that does is smear it onto my fingers that were already decorated in stains.

"Ah, yes." I chuckle, wiping my fingers dry with the back of my skirt. "I was painting the walls around my cabin. It's a bit dreary down there otherwise."

A silly part of me wonders if he'll notice the shade of blue matches his irises, though now that he's before me, I see it still isn't quite right. If only I had more opportunities to see his eyes in the daylight...

"You're an artist," he says.

I can't help but beam at his notice. "Only when I should be asleep."

He laughs. "Of course. That's the best time to be an artist, isn't it?"

"It's the only time there is some days." I glance toward the nest. Valrone peers over the edge, wagging what must be a peanut in his hand. I squeeze a laugh inside my throat and quickly return my attention to Calden. "But you say that as though you understand. Is that another of your many titles?"

"It's not one I'm blessed to claim. Not anymore, at least." He looks down, sadness dimming his tone. "I used to sketch. Past my bedtime, even. That was before this appeared." He shows me his Bind Mark, now completed with all four arrows.

I smile, pretending not to know this detail about his old hobby, though his mother shared it with me when she discovered my love for painting. "I hope you find time for it again soon."

He shrugs, the usual solemnity I've seen on his face reappearing, and I scold myself for imposing on the matter.

"Are you going up there?" Calden asks, glancing up the mainmast.

I withhold a sigh. "I should be."

A complex series of notes sings from Elias's lyre in our pause. I almost mention Elias's skill to extend our conversation, but right then, something *tinks* against the deck. I spy that something—a peanut, now cracked from the long fall—and throw a distraught look toward Valrone.

What if that had hit the prince?

Calden's face scrunches at the sight of the peanut, then he looks toward the nest, but Valrone has already dipped from sight.

"He's complaining," I supply.

This only serves to further contort Calden's expression.

"Obviously, the quartermaster needs to have a discussion with Valrone about how he handles his rations," I add with a laugh. I take another step toward the mainmast, to signal to Valrone that I got the message, but I pause there. "Say, there's not much to do on a ship. You might come across some blank parchments in the roundhouse in need of a little character. If you find yourself bored, that is."

Calden's gaze drifts toward the deckhouse with a spark of genuine consideration. I beam but resist the urge to request he show me his handiwork afterward—Empyrean forbid he asks the same of me and sees his soulcast flowers on my wall.

"See you around," I say, walking backward toward the mainmast. "Hopefully with charcoal stained on your hands."

With that, I rush toward the mainmast to ascend the rigging.

Valrone begins his complaints before I've even climbed into the nest, but his smile once I'm standing on my feet, looking up at his great height, declares that all is well.

We trade places, and a moment later, I'm alone, scanning the starlit sea with my spyglass. Finding nothing of concern, I cast my gaze to the inky firmament.

"Just you and I again, El-Alam," I whisper. His eternal presence has proved a steady consolation for the loneliness of this position. That, and the beauty of the night sky.

A flickering purple dot amongst the stars catches my eye, and I turn the spyglass toward it, enlarging the small sphere by a petty amount. Still, the sighting of it stirs an old feeling of standing on my tiptoes with my father pointing toward the sky, telling me what it is. *Dwephyn,* one of our neighboring worlds. Little is known about it besides that it's inhabited, knowledge which we gained through the insights of Seers.

What would happen to them if our world was destroyed? Would they even notice we were gone?

A sudden motion startles me back to attention. I whirl, glimpsing a dark wing before a large bird dips behind the mizzensail. An unsettled feeling tingles in my chest. I should have seen a bird of such size coming...

The bird glides back into view for a wink. Its wide wingspan and scallop-shaped tail make me gasp. *A windcrier.*

I collapse my spyglass, quickly igniting my ready-drawn Conjuration Ward, and a bow and arrow fill my hands. Without hesitation, I nock the arrow on the bow, turning each way for the bird—a spy for King Arlo's Warden Hunters.

But after a moment, the bird seems to have dematerialized into the wind again. My Omen Mark turns black, hardly a second after its subtle tingle became noticeable on my skin. I remain on watch, ready to strike down the windcrier upon the next sighting.

But it doesn't show again.

What is one doing way out here? I've never seen a windcrier over the seas. Not once.

I relinquish my weapon and look over the railing of the nest, spying Willian and Captain Alani chatting with one of our navigators on the quarterdeck. No one seems aware of the spy.

I think to use my Talent to alert them, but everyone would hear the noise of it—even if not the message itself—and that, too, may cause alarm. I opt for the next best option, waving until Willian freezes in what looks like mid-sentence to furrow his brows at me.

I motion with hand signals like we use to communicate with Orto, informing him of what I saw. Then I raise my spyglass to better see his reply from such a distance.

A windcrier? he signs back, as if unsure he interpreted me correctly. He pulls out his spyglass, and I wait for him to peer through it before signing my reply.

Yes. A windcrier.

He turns to the captain, saying something I can't hear from so far away, and they both leave the navigator and rush up the mainmast.

"You're sure that's what you saw?" Willian asks as he climbs into the nest.

The boards squeak as Captain Alani joins him.

"I only saw it for a moment," I answer. "It seemed like it was circling the ship, then it vanished into the air again."

"Why would King Arlo send a spy out to sea?" Captain Alani asks, but she directs her question toward Willian. "What does he care about Wardens that aren't presently in his kingdom, or even close, for that matter?"

Willian shakes his head.

Captain Alani turns back to me. "Could you tell which direction it was headed?"

"Westward, I'd say," I conclude after a moment's reflection.

"Same as we are," Willian notes.

"Did it come from Raevre?" the captain asks, raking back her curls. "Do their Hunters also use them as spies?"

I wish I had an answer for her, but the best I can do is shrug.

"I've not been to Raevre in years," Willian answers. "Since the wars started, the Lady Sovereign has felt it too dangerous to risk visiting the High Warden there very often. But I'd imagine their Hunters operate similar to ours."

I look down, recalling that Willian was not altogether excited when he discovered the Sovereign Prince's intentions were for us to visit Raevre. But he agreed to the mission, no less, sensing the risk was worth the potential reward should the Bind find Toaph Elbara in Raevre as Calden hopes.

"The crier was alone?" Willian asks.

"As far as I could tell."

"That's odd. They usually travel in flocks." Captain Alani ponders awhile before addressing me again. "Well, keep a steady watch. I've never heard of Hunter fleets on the seas, but we can't be too careful. I'll let Calden know that we'll need to be extra cautious when we reach Raevre in case Hunters are waiting on us."

I nod, but regret sags my posture as though it were my fault that Calden will now have something else to trouble over. And here I'd hoped he'd spend his evening revisiting a lost passion of his, not troubling over new threats of danger.

"Thank you, Zamirah," Captain Alani says before rushing down, likely to inform Calden immediately.

Willian follows in kind, and I set my focus on the seas, scanning the waters with added vigilance.

CALDEN

I pace the deck, a spirited wind tossing my hair across my face. The crew tends to their business with little more acknowledgement than the occasional smile or wave. It's been a week since Zamirah's peculiar sighting of the windcrier, yet nothing has come of it. Alani wrote it off as a coincidence—a rogue windcrier seeking Raevre's warmer climate because of the cold spell falling over Alémor. Willian concluded that King Arlo's Hunters likely sent the crier to scout the seas in case Raevran Wardens were fleeing the wars to join our underground. But Odessa and I developed a much less pleasant theory—since even an ambush of Hunters would be better to accept than our idea.

Our father's Talent was shape-shifting—and a windcrier was among the forms he could take. Has he found a way to access even his Talent by corrupt means?

Could the Oracle himself be who spied on us, and that is why the bird was alone?

I go still at the ship's bow where the carved wooden wings of the Toaph Elbara figurehead spread over the sparkling water, as if Toaph were soaring above its surface. The sight of it, mingled with the possibility of the Oracle spying on us—following us, even—twists my insides.

Raevre draws nearer every day, and with it—hopefully—our encounter with the lost Empyreal Guardian. Yet I still can't get the Oracle's beliefs about him out of my head. What if Toaph Elbara truly wishes to use me for evil? What if Ta'Nathel really came to save us?

What if we've gotten everything backward?

"You're not meditating, are you?"

The crew's banter as they tend the sails nearly drowns out Norielle's quiet voice behind me.

I smile to disguise the black depths my mind was exploring and turn to face her. "Empyrean, no, not on a ship."

"Then you must be thinking," she says, approaching the bow to stand beside me.

"I do like to do that on occasion."

She chuckles at my lame joke, and the late morning light catches in her eyes, drawing up the green usually hidden in the brown of her irises. "Is it anything you want to talk about?"

"Not really." My lip twitches at the lie. "Is there something on *your* mind, Norielle?"

She looks away, hesitating. "Actually, yes. There's something I've wanted to talk to you about for a while."

An icy feeling pours down my arms. "Oh?"

She draws in a breath, looking out to sea for an immeasurably long time before continuing. "You explained to me before how the Healing Ward works—that healing someone from the brink of death would require an incredibly deep care for them."

I nod, urging her to continue when she pauses.

"Well, when you all found me in the crypt, I was dying. I could tell I had only minutes, maybe seconds, left. Yet somehow, you healed me, and when you did, I—I *felt* something." She shifts, as if wanting to run away from me; instead, she turns back, more resolve filling her tone. "I need to know what it was I felt. What healed me."

My mouth hangs open and the brisk air falls, tasteless, on my tongue. All this time, I assumed by her silence on the matter that she'd not been conscious enough when I healed her to have felt anything, or maybe that she had discerned for herself the nature of the power which entered her. But if that's not the case, then what has she been thinking since? That it was purely *my* heart she felt?

Empyrean, why haven't I told her the truth? Was I so afraid of this conversation and all the roads it could lead us down?

Shame shadows me. What a wretched thing I've done—inadvertently taking credit for something I did not do.

"Norielle, tell me, what is it you felt?" I ask.

She recoils. "I-I don't know. It was... warm and... powerful. The only way I can think to describe it is that it felt like I finally found a place where I belong." Her lips seal for a moment before she turns back and adds, "When you anointed me, I felt it again."

My throat parches, and a temptation squirms to the surface from some pit in my being, encouraging me to seize my chance to test her, just to know if I'm worth it to someone. *Anyone.* Would she choose me with all my burdens, mistakes, and episodes if I claimed I loved her, and by that love had saved her life? Is she wishing right now, at this very moment, that I would pull her close—even though she knows the danger I present?

It doesn't matter. I rebuke the foolish temptation.

I'm not in love with Norielle, just as I assured Elias.

I'm in love with an *idea.*

And all I would do by testing Norielle is lead all three of us down a path of confusion and heartbreak which is paved by lies, reckless desperation, and blasphemy toward El-Alam.

Despicable.

"I care for you very much, Norielle." I swallow hard, uncertain what reaction I will elicit from her, but I fill my voice with certainty as I add, "And I am so grateful to El-Alam, because He has granted me now *three* sisters."

Norielle receives my words with unflinching stoicism. No smile of relief to show me that was the answer she hoped for. No wince to suggest she's longed for something more between us. Instead, she leaves me to wonder if it even mattered to her either way how I felt about her.

"But Norielle," I say, finding it easier to speak than before, "it was not purely my care for you that you felt that day in the crypt."

A crease forms between her brows.

"It felt like the anointing, because much like then, it was El-Alam's power that entered you. I channeled *His* deep love for you to heal you from the brink of death."

Her eyes widen, her pursed brows slowly softening as confusion seems to transform into awe. "El-Alam?" she whispers, almost too quietly for me to hear.

"He's who loves you that deeply," I confirm, touching her shoulder to keep her gaze from fleeing mine and missing the honesty in my eyes. "All I did was use the care I have for you as a conduit to channel His."

Moisture beads along her eyelids, and she flutters her eyes, as if to dry them. Still, a single tear escapes, and she backs away, drying it on the long sleeve of her sweater. When she finally faces me again, a smile fills her face, yet she delivers no response.

"I'm so sorry I didn't tell you sooner," I say, also casting a silent apology toward Elias for the temptation I felt and how deeply that would have wronged him.

Norielle flinches, as if annoyed by my failure to bring the subject up, but the knowledge of El-Alam's affection for her seems too great to allow the irritation to last more than a few seconds. "I'm... I'm honored you'd consider me a sister," she says, wiping another tear.

Then her emotions seem to overwhelm her, and she sprints toward the deckhouse, disappearing inside.

I pivot again toward the sea, directing a prayer of repentance toward El-Alam for my selfish actions and thoughts. Then I shut my eyes, awaiting His divine response, but all that answers me is a strong wind, carrying in it the scent of a brewing storm.

NORIELLE

El-Alam healed me.

I hear Calden's explanation repeating again and again as I cry in the privacy of the deckhouse. That incredible warmth, that feeling of belonging—it came from the Creator Himself, not a man. Not Calden.

How couldn't I tell the difference with how pure it felt?

I turn my heart toward El-Alam, but I don't even have words to express all my emotions, besides to apologize for assigning to a person what was done by the power of God, and to thank Him for noticing me, for saving me, and for loving me.

But a pop from the door handle cuts my reverent weeping short. I dab my eyes as a cabin steward steps in, a boy, maybe fifteen at most. Anders. He balks at the sight of me.

"Oh, miss, I'm so sorry," Anders says, reaching for the door again. "I can come back later to tidy up."

I don't know what *tidying* even needs to be done, considering Elias has made it his personal duty to ensure not even one pillow is out of place in here, but I shake my head.

"Actually, it's fine. I was about to leave. Have you seen Lady Odessa or Elias?"

The boy glances as if toward the forecastle. "They're in the galley; last I saw, miss."

I thank him and quickly slip behind him through the door.

The burble of boiling water and the sound of a spoon ringing against a pan bloom in my ears as I open the galley door. Orto stands at the hearth, billows of steam wafting around his broad-shouldered form. Helina, the galley stewardess, delivers a cheery greeting from behind a metal plate she's drying. I return the greeting in kind before a third person turns around—Elias—with a tea in hand, just as I suspected. But the small space, crowded before I even arrived, lacks the other person I sought.

"Elias," I say as he's squinting at my face, likely noticing the puffiness around my eyes. "Have you seen Lady Odessa? I need to talk to her. Both of you, actually."

He signals toward a small set of stairs, leading to an eatery below Orto's culinary space. I follow him down, and we find Odessa sitting at the sole table, alone.

She lowers a slab of cheese from her mouth as she notices us.

"Lady Odessa. I have something I need to tell you."

She glances toward the stairs, as if to ask if this is something safe for Orto and Helina to overhear.

"In private," I whisper.

She lays her cheese on her plate, and with a quick scribble to her palm, she draws a ward that I barely get a glimpse of—something round and surrounded by swirls. A second later, smoke puffs from her hand, forming a sphere that encases the three of us.

Odessa meets my gaze. "What's this about?"

I fidget. "Your brother."

"If you're going to ask if he's in love with you—"

"He's not," I snap, alarmed at the irritation in my tone, but she did say it in front of Elias, which she must know is careless of her. "And I'm tired of you assuming I have feelings for him."

She blinks like I slapped her. Yet instead of reprimanding me, she gives an approving nod. "Then what is it?"

Elias gawks at me, but whether it's because of my outburst or the implication that I don't have feelings for Calden or both, I can't tell.

I gulp, sitting down at the table as I answer Odessa. "I asked Calden how he healed me."

"And?" she asks.

"And he said he channeled El-Alam's love into me to do it." Hearing myself say it out loud sounds absurd, sowing doubt again where I once felt assured. "Is that... possible?"

Elias sits down beside me, saying nothing.

Odessa purses her lips. "It is. We consider it an advanced healing technique. Very few Wardens have ever been capable of it."

My doubts flee back into the shadows. Then this *is* the method Rhiana mentioned—the method that allows someone to heal beyond their normal capacity.

"But it only works if the healer's heart is aligned with El-Alam's. Which I am struggling to believe could be the case for Calden of late."

"How else could he have healed me?" I ask, pivoting my gaze between Odessa and Elias. "He barely knew me, so he couldn't have cared for me as much as was required to save my life. So how else am I still here if not for El-Alam?"

Odessa taps her nails across the galley table, offering no reply for so long that I straighten my posture, marveling that I've proven my point that easily. But suddenly the clicking of her nails stops, and she looks up. "There is also the possibility that he may have used a Blood Ward out of desperation."

I flinch, and Elias raises his hands, as if to deflect her words.

"Cal would never," he says.

"And yet that would so easily explain his recent behavior," Odessa counters. "One use of a Blood Ward is enough to taint a soul, even if slightly. Maybe that's why he returned to the citadel an obstinate madman."

The dried tears on my cheeks, cried in wonder of El-Alam's love, suddenly sting on my skin. I recount every moment from the time I awoke in that haven to the last time I saw Calden during my training. He *has* been so different from the man who rescued me from Lake Daleia. But he wouldn't use Blood Wards, would he? After all that he's said about them corrupting people's souls and the pain he's felt from losing his friends to defection?

"Cal told me what he told Nori," Elias says, his tone so sure and calm, it silences my worries as though he'd shut a door on them. "I know he's not been himself lately, but come on. The man hardly sleeps. He barely eats. He just found out he's the only person who can save this world, and now his father is our biggest enemy besides King Arlo and Ta'Nathel. Not to mention his mother"—he shoots Odessa a hard look—"*and sister* have been keeping secrets from him for twenty years. I'd be a mess, too. I don't think it's fair to accuse him of something like that just because the man is having a hard time."

Odessa folds her arms and leans against the back of her chair.

"And wouldn't his warding pen have dimmed if he was misusing his power?" Elias adds. "I've not inspected it closely, but I haven't noticed it looking any different."

I perk up, recalling Alani teaching me about this. Even if Calden had used one of the Blood Warden styluses instead of his own, his pen would dim, signifying El-Alam was revoking his power to use regular wards because of his disobedience.

But, if anything, Calden has seemed even *more* powerful than I'd thought him before. And what I *felt* was far too holy to be something so tainted.

"When he healed me, it felt the same as it did when I was anointed," I say, my confidence in myself and Calden both returning. "He did not use a Blood Ward. I'm certain of that. It *was* El-Alam."

Odessa looks away, staring toward the curling mist around us. I check Elias's expression, hoping to find him just as resolved as I am. He smiles, giving me a small nod, but his gaze lingers on me, like he's still trying to read how I feel about all this.

"I'm sure you're both right," Odessa finally concedes, then she smiles at me like I might do to Cas when trying to reassure her. "Forgive me for sowing distrust. I just... don't want to lose my brother any more than I already have."

I startle at her apology, but as our eyes meet again, something occurs to me. She's like Calden and Elias—wearing a mask to uphold some image she must think is expected of her as the Second Lady.

"More than you already have?" I press, taking my chance while her guard seems down.

She wets her lips, and I can practically hear her internal debate regarding if she'll elaborate before she says in a resigned voice, "Ever since my mother told me what happened to the last Sovereign—my father—I've had to hide it from Calden because of my mother's fears about him. Withdrawing from my brother seemed the easiest way. But I suppose I didn't anticipate the consequences of him returning the distance, avoiding me as well. I wish now that my mother never told me. I'd rather have found out when he did than be held accountable for keeping the secret all these years."

She looks at Elias, whose gaze falls, as if regretting his rebuke a moment ago.

"I suppose I shouldn't have told you both that," Odessa says, shaking her head.

Why? Because then someone might see you have a heart under all that armor?

I withhold the statement, which is so obviously confirmed by her uncomfortable expression.

"You know, it's okay for you to disagree with how your mother handled this," I say instead. "It's not wrong to believe something different than her, even if she is the Lady Sovereign. That's not being rebellious. That's called having an opinion."

Her lip twitches, but instead of giving any reply, she waves her hand, the foggy sphere around us dissipating. "Thank you" is all she says before she marches up the stairs.

Elias sips his tea, giving time for Odessa's footsteps to fade before turning to me. "You okay?"

I glance at the stairs leading back to the kitchen, wishing Odessa could have left the privacy field around us. "With what part?"

His voice drops even lower. "The part where it wasn't really Cal who healed you."

My chest swells again, recalling the tender feeling of the Creator's love. "Yes," I say with certainty. "I am."

Elias studies me like he is scanning for evidence of a lie. A corner of his lip slowly turns up, but rather than affirming he believes me or challenging me any further, his gaze turns away. "I need to go talk to him. You want some tea?"

I shift to stand. "I can get some my—"

He pushes his steaming cup across the table, and my words break off. Lemon wafts from the cup as he withdraws his hands, surrendering his barely touched tea to me. Then he rises from his chair with a wink and turns for the stairs, leaving me to steep in the wonder of how my life was spared.

ELIAS

A strong westward gust fills the sails and thrashes against me as I step out from the galley. The dark tips of my hair bob in and out of my vision as I inspect the sky for clouds. A late morning sun glares from above, but in the distance, a wall of gray appears to be stacking from the sea to the Empyrean. The howling wind hauls the storm toward us like horses pulling chariots into war, and by the looks of it, we're in the middle of the battlefield.

Alani delivers a shrill order for the sails to be bound so she can propel us out of the storm's range with her Talent. The crew responds without delay, rolling up the white sails like giant scrolls. As soon as the crew finishes securing them, Alani holds her hands out toward the sea, and the *Celestella* jostles as she takes command of the water and impels us ahead.

I stabilize myself and stand, entranced by Alani's Talent for longer than I mean to be. Will El-Alam ever make me a Master? Why did He even allow Cal to bring me into the most important Bind in history when I have nothing special to contribute besides tea recommendations and a bit of entertainment?

Is He up in the Empyrean right now, frowning upon another of Cal's horrible decisions? Or is Cal's heart so in line with His that the Creator knew Cal would make the same choice as Himself and that's why He placed the decision in his hands?

I push my tousled hair from my eyes and survey the ship for Cal until I find him overlooking the bow. I stride his way, receiving an extra whip from the wind as I approach him.

"Hey Cal!" I call.

His hair, twice the length of mine, thrashes across his face when he turns around. But he barely looks at me long enough to blink before casting his gaze back to the encroaching storm. A tendril of lightning spiders through the dark clouds, sending a rumble of thunder into the loud wind.

"You think she needs Willian?" I ask.

"She'd know better than me," he says, nodding toward Alani. "If she needs him, I'm sure she'll send for him. Though he may be too worn out to be of much help. From what I hear, there was another ship nearby last night, and he had to propel the *Celestella* for hours just to keep them from detecting us."

I wince, recalling the windcrier sighting. "You think it was Hunters?"

"It doesn't seem so, since they didn't pursue us. Willian said they appeared to be coming from Alémor, so I'd guess King Arlo is sending more soldiers into Raevre."

More soldiers. More men leaving families behind, and some forever. How many kids will end up like me before King Arlo ends this invasion?

I shake my head, not wanting to think about it too long.

"Cal," I say, my sudden shift in tone pivoting him back to face me. "Nori said you told her what happened."

He squints before seeming to gather my meaning. "How is she taking it?"

"She seems fine."

"It's much more special, I imagine,"—he adjusts the buttoned collar of his shirt—"hearing that the love of the Creator who hung the stars healed you, rather than that of some man."

Some man, as if that's all she's ever seen Cal as.

"I guess." A clap of thunder buys me a moment to prepare myself for my next question. "How are *you* feeling?"

His expression twitches twice before he can hold a steady smile. "Same. Fine. I'm glad she knows."

"*Cal.*" I rest an elbow on the rail and give him my best "I'm not an idiot" look.

"It's not *her* troubling me," he reassures me. "I feel better now that she knows the truth of what happened and after clarifying how I see her."

I tense. Nori didn't mention that.

"Which is like a sister," he adds.

I hesitate but can't squash my curiosity. "What'd she say to that?"

"She said she was honored that I considered her as such."

Is that true? Or did Nori just say what felt appropriate in the moment to spare herself the embarrassment?

I force my thoughts away. I came here to check on Cal, not pry information about Nori out of him. "So, if that went so well, then what's wrong?"

"Well, there's that," Cal says, pointing toward the storm with his thumb. "And the fact that Raevre is drawing near, which is full of its own threats, and I'm not sure how their Elders will receive my questions or how to ask them without it seeming like I've turned completely against my mother."

He looks down, mouth hung ajar a moment before he seals it shut.

There's more. Doesn't he know that, as a scout, I'm trained to read people?

But the thought of us nearing Raevre shoots a cold feeling through my chest. *The land my papa died in.* Even with the war and untamable wildfires, to me, that's all Raevre will ever be.

Will it change anything once I stand on that earth? Will it make the loss of him hurt less? Or will it only make it more real?

"On that note," Cal says, having turned before my face might have given away my inner turbulence. "We're running out of time to train Norielle."

My memory casts back to the past several days. Cal, Nori, Odessa, and I have gathered to help Nori learn her Vitality Ward, but each day has gone the same as the first—minus the sea heller attack. She's too nervous. I can tell by her hesitation, and the way she watches Cal like he's Toaph Elbara himself, testing her to see if she's worthy of helping find him.

"You're making too much of a to-do of it," I say. "The big barriers. Most of the Bind standing around. She doesn't like to feel like people are watching her."

Cal seems to think awhile before his expression lights, as if a Glory Ward erupted in his mind. "You should train her."

I start. "What? I thought only Masters—"

"Why?" he interjects. "You know Norielle better than I, and obviously my method isn't working. *You* train her."

I force myself not to smile at the idea. "The Warden Order clearly states that trainers should be Masters."

"*Should* be. But does it clearly state that they can't be otherwise?"

A light drizzle dapples my face as I consider it, and I notice a thin section of the clouds has crept over us.

"The Order does not directly forbid a non-Master from training. It only recommends they be so for maximum efficiency."

I laugh. "You know the Order just well enough to break it, don't you, Cal?"

"There's always a fault in it somewhere, unless it's a rule decreed by El-Alam Himself." He side-eyes me. "Besides, you could never convince me you wouldn't want to train her."

I debate a few seconds before I slide my elbow off the rail. "I'll do it. For Nori's sake."

Cal draws his pen from his belt. "Let her use this so you can keep yours."

I take it, the presence of the stylus reminding me of my conversation with Odessa and Nori. I turn back toward the galley, admiring the moonlike glow inside the glass shaft as I walk. His pen is as bright as mine, if not brighter, since he's a Master.

That's what I thought, I think with a nod to myself.

Cal is not like his father. He might rebel against the Order, but he would never rebel against El-Alam.

And he would never turn on *us*.

I return to the galley, finding Nori right where I left her, sipping my tea with fresh tears glinting in the corners of her eyes. But she smiles as she sees me, like she's genuinely glad that I came back.

For a second, I consider stealing this moment to probe her to see what all this means to her. Is she truly happy that Cal's labeled her a sister and told her El-Alam is who loves her enough to save her life? Or is the latter overpowering her ability to be upset about the former?

I reject the idea of asking in favor of giving her more time to process and raise Cal's pen.

"Look what I got."

Nori tilts her head. "Is that—?"

"Cal's pen," I say, bringing it closer so she can see how well lit the stylus still is. "Looks normal to me. Just like I said."

Nori sighs, as if something in her still doubted her stance, even though she sounded certain when she addressed Odessa. "You didn't tell him, did you?"

"No, actually, Cal handed it over for a much different reason. He wants me to finish your training." I set the pen next to the mug. "That's for you to use."

To my surprise, a laugh cheers her face. "You're not talking about breaking the rules, are you?"

I shrug one shoulder. "I mean, with Cal in charge, rules are apparently off-deck, so..."

She smiles wider, then lifts her cup. "Does this mean I can't finish my tea?"

That's my girl, I think, pulling out the chair across from her. "There's always time for tea."

NORIELLE

I aim my palm toward Elias, a Vitality Ward drawn and ready for my command. Gusty, frigid air chills my fingertips as I steady my arm. If I miss, my sphere will most likely launch into the sea at Elias's back. Still, the thought of accidentally sending the orb into a mast makes me hesitant to ignite the ward. But Elias insisted we try it this way, rather than gathering up the Bind to make a barrier. I hope he doesn't regret that decision.

"Okay, Nori," Elias says, holding his Vitality Ward toward me so he can block mine. "Ready."

"What if I knock you overboard?" I ask.

A snicker slants his lips. "Then it's a good thing we're not trying this at the bow."

I grimace.

"It'll be fine," he says, more seriously. "First, I won't let you do that. And second, even if you somehow did, it's just water."

Just water. After what happened to me in Lake Daleia, that statement doesn't bring much comfort, especially when he flinches after saying it like he had the same thought. What if, upon sensing someone in the water, the sea awakens like the lake? Would the Peace Wards on the keel be enough to quell it?

"*Nori*," Elias reprimands me playfully. "I appreciate you bothering to worry about me, but stop it."

I give him an annoyed look but correct my posture and turn my focus to the ward drawn on my palm. Energy kindles against my skin, declaring the ward ready for use, but when I will it to launch toward Elias, nothing happens.

"I don't know if this is going to work," I say, lowering my arm. The tingle of energy fades as the ward deactivates. "How am I supposed to tell it to do something I'm nervous about doing?"

Elias drops his defensive stance. "Pretend I'm Landon or something."

The bully's name makes me scoff. "You look nothing like Landon."

"Hey *Freckles*, where's your stupid boyfriend?" Elias says, shifting his voice to sound like a twelve-year-old Landon. He flips his hair, and though the wind knocks it right back, the motion is disturbingly similar to Landon's. But instead of the anger Elias must have thought he'd provoke, I laugh. *Freckles*. That used to feel so insulting when I was younger. Now, the only thing insulting about it is how uncreative the nickname Landon gave me was.

Elias's smile tightens like he's trying not to laugh; then, after recomposing himself, he tries his impersonation again. "Little Fairy-Fingers is off hiding in the woods with his harp, isn't he? Bet you couldn't tell that twig from the trees."

"Elias, stop." I'm laughing so much, the words hardly make it out. "How am I supposed to concentrate?"

It's made funnier when I imagine Landon turning up to see Elias now. He'd be hopeless at recognizing him. Though Landon would still be taller, Elias looks at least twice as strong, and I can imagine the contempt the bully would display seeing Elias already has a full beard when all Landon could grow was patches of stubble.

I'd like to take Elias back to Behria just to witness Landon's reaction to him.

"What's so funny, Freckles?" Elias continues while I'm still trying to calm myself.

"Stop," I say again between my giggles. "Be Elias again."

"Who's that? Another of your dumb little friends?"

Something—maybe the way the pressure lifts off me the more I laugh—implores me to play along, and I forget the burden of my lesson. "I'll have you know, Landon, Elias could snap you in half."

Elias's smile grows before he seems to remember his act. "Yeah, right. Lemme see him try. Then I'll go whine to my papa about him and get him in big trouble, because I'm too much of a baby to handle it if someone is better than me."

"You'd better go find a nice crib to lie in then."

Elias cackles but waves his hand with the Vitality Ward. "Aren't you supposed to be doing something, Freckles?"

"I would be if you weren't making me laugh so much, *Elias*."

He finally switches back to his normal voice. "You were supposed to turn red and throw something at him like you did when you were ten."

Unwanted images of me hurling pinecones at Landon—with about as embarrassing of an aim as I've had with the vitality spheres—emerge behind my eyelids. "Let's not think about that."

"What? Those are some of my favorite memories," Elias says, then his tone sobers, settling me back down with him. "It's good to see you laugh again."

"It's good to have a reason to." My gaze lingers on him, old and new memories seeming to dance around us like the people at my ball. Is his presence here another of El-Alam's displays of love toward me?

"For real now, Nori," Elias prompts while I'm still musing. "Give it another try."

I reel away from my thoughts and raise my hand toward Elias, meeting his gaze to be sure he's prepared before I try reigniting my Vitality Ward. After he readies an energy shield, I send the mental commands to my ward and do my best to align the rest of myself with it. The tingle awakens on my skin; then, after a few quickened heartbeats, a blue orb forms and spits from my palm directly toward him—as perfectly as when I practiced with Alani and Odessa before.

My sphere collides with Elias's translucent shield. Our energies fizzle against each other, and the blue reflection cast across Elias's face fades, quickly replaced by sunlight as Alani's efforts finally pull us under the patchy outskirts of the storm.

"Knew you'd do it when there wasn't so much pressure." He gives a short round of applause before urging me on. "Let's see how many more you can do."

I try not to envy how he doesn't need to redraw another ward yet or that, even with a new one, I will still exhaust my ability to use the Vitality Ward before Elias uses up his first ward.

"Ready?" I ask, though a shield already shimmers around Elias's hand.

"Launch it."

I draw in a slow breath. I've already done this once today—I can do it again.

The vitality swells against my palm and blasts toward Elias, strong enough to make him stagger backward a step. We both grin like fools at my success, but before I can scribble another ward, footsteps creak up the stairs behind me.

"Empyrean, Lias, if I'd known it would go this well, I'd have asked you to train her from the beginning," Calden says as he steps onto the quarterdeck.

Elias straightens. "I don't think the Elders would have smiled upon that decision."

"Well, I see that's another rule that needs amending once I'm Sovereign." Calden turns to me, digging into the pocket of his coat. He withdraws a warding pen, wrapped in a purple-tinged leather case. "I believe a trade is in order."

My eyes widen as I grasp his meaning. *I passed.* I finally passed.

I hand him the pen he lent me and claim my own, squeezing it tightly.

"Congratulations, Norielle," Calden says with a proud smile. "You are now *officially* a Warden."

CALDEN

The sky is still dark when I exit the deckhouse, neck slick with sweat from a tormented night trying to sleep. I had to wake. The distress of my nightmares was threatening an episode, and even if not for that danger, I'd rather suffer exhaustion than see what other ways my uncontrolled mind would like to torture me.

I'm surprised to find Alani already at the helm rather than Willian, and I stride toward her, giving a raspy greeting to the night crew as they tend the ship under the starlight.

"You're up early," I comment as I reach Alani.

"Hardly," Alani says with a nod toward the slight glow over the horizon. "I thought I would return Willian's favor. He's traded shifts for me early several times now. I thought he might like to catch some extra sleep."

Alani's attempt to sound indifferent as she talks about her first mate makes me smile. I'm tempted to tease her for it, but I decide to limit my response to an agreeable, "Ah, I see."

"Why are you awake already?" Alani asks.

"I wasn't sleeping well. Feeling restless..." I turn my back to her, watching the crew. One man swabs the deck, the slopping of his mop nearly matching the rhythm of the water underfoot. Others tend to the sails, and even with the door closed, I can faintly smell a savory breakfast cooking in the galley already. "It's odd having nothing to do."

Alani tucks a ginger coil behind her ear, despite what little it does to clear her face from her curls. "Well, if you want something to do, you only need to ask. I'm sure I can come up with something for you."

"Please," I say. *I need a distraction.*

Alani's lips twist sideways as she thinks, probably only now realizing I have zero skills involving sailing a ship, and shamefully, I've not even had to handle a mop in my life. She suddenly perks up, her focus ascending the mainmast. "How about I put you up in the crow's nest for a while?"

I shrug. It's not as engaging of a task as I hoped for, but it's a contribution, and I have wondered what the sea looks like from up there.

"Sure."

"Zamirah is up there now," Alani says. "Just ask her what to do. She'll be happy to fill you in."

The mention of Zamirah sends a pulse of nerves across my chest. Our fleeting conversations are still fresh in my ears, and I'd be a liar to claim I haven't replayed her encouragements to me a hundred times since she spoke them, particularly between my nightmares whenever they trouble my sleep.

"What is it?" Alani asks.

I turn back to her after a long gape at the crow's nest and find her eyes narrowed at me.

"Nothing," I say, but my unconvincing tone causes Alani's brows to lift.

"Oh, come now, Calden, what kind of fool do you think I am? Is something wrong?" Her question and her smile do not quite add up.

"No," I say. "I learned recently that Zamirah is the one my mother has long used to deliver updates and inquiries about my... condition... across the kingdoms."

"Ah. I see." The way she echoes me is most unsettling.

I turn away from her, deciding I'll only draw more attention to the matter if I refuse to go up to the nest. "I'll holler if I see anything."

With an order to myself to keep my distance from the woman above, I approach the long rope ladder and begin the wobbly ascent. The air seems to thin, growing colder the higher I climb. It bites at my knuckles and slithers beneath the gaps in my shirt. Though, the chill is refreshing and far preferable to the deckhouse. It's suffocating in there.

As I near the top, I register a quiet sound—a sniffle from above. But the wooden crown of the nest blocks my view of Zamirah, and likely, her view of me. *Is she ill?* I wonder. Though she showed no signs of feeling unwell yesterday.

A solemn hum follows her next sniff as I reach the nest. I hesitantly climb through the wood frame, the floor squeaking beneath my steps and provoking a gasp from her. She dabs a handkerchief at her face before she twirls around with a smile that flinches when she notices me.

"Oh, Sover—" She catches herself and tries again, "*Calden.* I wasn't expecting to see you up here."

I glance at the handkerchief she squeezes in her paint-stained hand, and she tucks it behind a ruffle in her floral dress. In an instant, my command to myself to remain distant dissolves. "Are you well, Zamirah? You look troubled."

Her smile widens, as if to make the expression more convincing, but her gaze evades me. "Oh, I've been sending messages to my family, and I... miss them. It can be lonely speaking but hearing nothing in return." The first light of dawn illuminates her eyes as she faces me again. "I can feel when they receive my words, though, which is comforting. At least I can trust they know that I'm thinking of them."

I step further into the nest, the great height reminding me of the citadel's balcony. Only here, an expanse of water surrounds us at every angle rather than trees and cliffs, and the wobble of the ship is nothing like the stable ground of my old overlook. "It's a blessing with consequences, as you'd say."

Appreciation fills her countenance. "Exactly. Though I'd never dare compare my loneliness to your experiences."

"It's all relative, isn't it? Pain, that is." I look toward the glistening sea as dawn speckles it with light. "And I'd say loneliness is a silent killer, as vicious as any other curse."

My lip twitches once I realize I've again called my episodes a curse, and to the woman who asserted they are a blessing.

But instead of correcting me, she studies me with compassion. "Your mother said sovereignty is lonely. And how much more so when you're afraid to let anyone close lest they get hurt?"

The chill in the air suddenly feels glacial. Does this woman see right through me?

I shake the thought away. Zamirah was the one upset when I came up here, so why are we talking about me now?

"Where is your family?" I ask.

The long look she gives makes me wonder what she thinks of my deflection, or if she's only alarmed that a member of the Sovereign household would ask her a personal question.

"My family lives on the northeast coast of Alémor. They are safehouse keepers," she says, fiddling with her handkerchief.

No wonder she has such an inviting presence—hospitality is the trademark of those El-Alam chooses as safehouse keepers. Her parents must have raised her in their likeness.

"Do you have siblings?" I ask.

Her chest swells, but she takes a long moment to reply. "Yes, an older sister. She's who I was sending a message to."

I tilt my head, curious about her lengthy delay. "You must have been close with her before Captain Theos claimed you for this ship."

Again, she pauses, only to answer with a deflection of her own. "Actually, it was your mother who decided I should join the *Celestella*. After I achieved Mastery, my parents sent me to the citadel to see what use my Talent might be to her."

"You came to the citadel?" I ask, doubting I could forget meeting her—the youngest Warden to be dubbed a Master, and admittedly, a beautiful one.

"You were away at the time, and your mother had me on this ship before I'd the opportunity to meet you." She pays the sea a thorough inspection, as if suddenly remembering her duty. "I do confess, I was disappointed. I really was curious about those rumors."

It takes a moment before I remember which rumors she means. The ones about my eyes.

A sudden ache in my facial muscles alerts me that I'm smiling, and much more than I have in some time. *Distant, Calden. Stay distant.*

"I'm glad to have you here, Zamirah," I say, laying on a more formal tone. "And when we return to Alémor, I'll arrange a visit home for you."

She turns back to me, a hand pressed over her heart. "Thank you. That means the sea and sky to me."

"It's the very least I could do in thanks. You've apparently been trying to help me for years, and I didn't even know." My throat tenses as I hear my own words, recalling again the implications of her relaying the information about my episodes. And here, she's sought me out more than anyone else on the ship besides my Bind and Willian. The forced formality unwittingly drops from my voice. "Yet even with all your knowledge of me, you say you *want* to be here."

"Oh, Calden..." Her smile slips. "I'm not afraid of you or your dangerous blessing."

The world seems to go quiet, except for the echo of her words. I've heard statements like this before—uttered from Corene. But they proved false as soon as she witnessed an episode.

You're dooming yourself to disappointment, I tell my heart. And again, repeat the command I carried up here. *Stay distant.*

Yet Zamirah takes a step nearer, seeming to pass through the smoke of my dark memories and fears. This subtle action calls to mind my temptation when speaking with Norielle yesterday, my wish for *someone* to draw closer to me not *after* my episodes were over, but *despite* them.

That will never happen.

Nor should it. It would only put that woman in danger.

"Fear doesn't lead to understanding," Zamirah says when I offer no response. "I have long thought the reason we don't know how to help you is that everyone is so afraid."

I look down, my hair brushing against my chin. "They have every right to be afraid of me. You may have heard many things, but you've never seen with your eyes how much damage I can inflict."

"But it's not really *you*." Her tone grows so bold in speaking to me, one might think she's a member of the council. "You yourself are not a dangerous person, Calden. You cannot attach yourself to what happens when your mind is not your own. None of that has ever been or will ever be your fault."

I turn a shoulder toward her, fighting to keep my expression from exposing the way her every word seems to wrench my heart. But it's as though she's twisting it into place, not out of it. How does she know exactly what I need to hear?

"I'm sorry," she says, a hint of timidity returning in her voice. "I've wanted to say so many things to you for so long. I hope I'm not overstepping."

My mouth opens and shuts twice without speaking. "You haven't overstepped," I finally say. "It's just easier to hear these things than it is to believe them."

She smiles. "Then I'll be sure to keep saying them until they reach your heart. With enough arrows, one is bound to hit the target, isn't it?"

"At least once." I linger in her bright gaze, as though if I looked away, I would see all the surrounding darkness again. And yet, a part of me senses that even if I did, I'm now better equipped to face it than I was before this conversation.

She twists away, her dress fluttering in the light breeze. Her hand lifts toward her eye—*is she wiping away a tear?*—then a long sigh lowers her shoulders before she turns back again, beaming in the sunrise. "Was there something you came up here for? Do you need me to send a message?"

I scrunch my brows, my mind so far from where it was when I ascended the crow's nest that I can hardly recall why I did. "Alani," I say as I remember. "She sent me to relieve you from your post. I wanted something to do."

She taps her chin with a finger. "A prince on lookout duty?"

"I'm not a prince on board, remember?"

She chuckles. "That's right."

"She did suggest I ask you to give me some instructions before you go. If you don't mind."

"Oh, it's *very* hard." Her sudden lively tone catches me off guard. "You must keep your eyes on the sea the whole time. Not even one blink, you understand?" She leaves no space for me to answer before she's snapping a spyglass to its full length. "And every so often, you must remember to look through this.

It's quite tricky to pull off, though, I warn you. You have to squint one eye. Like *this*."

Her exaggerated demonstration is unfairly adorable, and it wins yet another face-aching smile from me that reminds me I'm failing—epically—at obeying my own orders.

"Here." She shoves the spyglass toward my hands. "You show me you can handle that."

I wrestle my smile into something milder and take the spyglass. "Does it matter which eye?" I ask to keep the jest going despite myself.

"Well, they don't call it the *right* eye for nothing," she says, but as soon as I'm raising the spyglass toward my right side, she adds, "Your *left*, of course."

I trade sides with a snort. "And I close the eye I put the spyglass to. Correct?"

"Definitely." She giggles. "You want to be sure you can't see a thing."

"Perfect. I think I'm getting the hang of it."

She laughs again as I genuinely peer through the spyglass, marveling at the details I can now see on the distant waves. Every direction I turn toward, the sea looks the same. Infinite and empty.

I lower the spyglass to my side, finding Zamirah calm and poised again as she regards me.

"Well, if you're sure you've got a handle on this very difficult work," she says, blinking a fond expression from her eyes, "I probably should retire for the day."

Something tempts me to tell her "No, I don't have a handle on it" so she'll stay a little longer, but the sounds of the other crewmates changing shifts below remind me to be considerate. She must be tired. I shouldn't keep her—nor should I be allowing myself to enjoy her presence so much.

"Your paints are waiting for you, I'm sure," I say instead.

"Ah, yes." She tilts an ear toward the deck. "I do hear them calling for me. Though, that reminds me. Have you found the time to visit those parchments?"

I rub the smooth metal casing of the spyglass with my thumb. "I found the time, yes, though not the inspiration."

She beams, as if I told her I filled every page in the round-house with magnificent artwork. "Keep showing up. Inspiration doesn't like to be chased. I often find it only comes to me if I sit still long enough for it to feel safe approaching me."

Her answer conjures a memory of holding my hand toward Echo, waiting to see if he'd attack or allow me to pet him. And suddenly, I know exactly what I'll attempt to sketch once I have the moment for it. My furry friend.

"It does seem to find us, doesn't it?" I say, and after a pause, soaking in the pleasant atmosphere between us, I add, "Thank you for your excellent training."

"Thank you for promising to let me see my family again soon," she says, climbing onto the rigging. "Goodnight, Calden."

I glance at the steadily rising sun beyond her. "Goodnight, Zamirah."

CALDEN

The sharpened tip of my charcoal pencil scratches against parchment, shading in one of Echo's pupils. The sketch resembles the canyx better than I expected, though my slow progress and uncertain pauses reveal my lack of practice. I can't recall the last time I sat to draw anything that wasn't a ward, besides when copying a map.

But the inspiration that came to me this morning while chatting with Zamirah in the crow's nest, along with my dire need for a distraction as Raevre nears, keeps me seated at the Bind's private table in the deckhouse, filling the page while Odessa braids her hair at the vanity. The old feeling of a pencil in my hand while my sister sits nearby reminds me of our youth—and how different things were between us when we still preferred to be in each other's company rather than away from it. Yet I can't muster the willpower to attempt a conversation with her. The sour way our discussions so often end suggests it would only spoil both of our peaceful moods.

I'm just filling in Echo's second pupil when the door flings open, hinges squealing as Elias hollers inside, "You in here, Blondie?"

"Good thing no one was asleep," I chide him.

Elias glances at the bright window, but rather than commenting that it's the middle of the day, he stops in front of the table to squint at my picture. "Didn't know you could draw."

"I didn't think I still could," I admit, setting my pencil down.

Elias swipes the page off the table, nodding as he inspects my artistry. "*Hmm.* Still looks like a spy." He winks as he returns the page to me, but his expression and tone turn serious. "If you're not too busy, I need to talk to you."

Through her reflection in the mirror, Odessa gives Elias a questioning look. Elias's lips slant, but when he says nothing, Odessa shrugs and continues braiding her hair, as if to proclaim she will not leave on her own accord.

Elias hesitates but finally pulls out the chair across from me and plunks into the seat.

"We could go upstairs to the roundhouse?" I suggest before recalling that Alani and the navigator are in there.

Elias shoos the suggestion away before I can mention using a Privacy Ward as an alternative. "It's fine. It's nothing I shouldn't be saying in front of her, too."

Odessa sits taller. "So, you mean to say I should pay attention?"

"I mean to say you can, if you want. We're a team, after all." The way he eyes her suggests a conversation happened between them I'm not aware of. But Elias's heavy demeanor keeps me from probing.

"Look, I was talking to Nori the other day," he starts, the usual confidence in his tone already wavering. "And she got me thinking. I haven't been the most honest person with you."

I fold my hands, giving him my utmost attention. "What do you mean?"

Elias looks anywhere except at either of us. "I hid a lot of things about myself when I joined the Wardens. I was..." A smirk cracks on his face that doesn't match the feeble way he carries on, "I was afraid, I guess. Afraid to talk about it. Afraid of what people would think of me. And I... I thought if I pretended my life before this didn't happen, the memories might fade. You know, stop hurting so much."

Odessa goes still in my peripheral vision, but Elias stops speaking, almost as if losing focus—something I've rarely witnessed him do.

"You're from Behria, like Norielle," I offer, a guess based on their history. Though years ago, he told me he hailed from Bridgewood, a town off the coast facing the Western Isles.

Elias stirs. "Yeah, that's where I was raised. I was born in the Western Isles, but my parents migrated to the mainland when I was a baby. They didn't even name me Elias; they called me Kieran. But they'd both died by the time I was twelve, and I ended up with my grandparents back on the Isles. That's how I got separated from Nori. My grandparents died not even two years later."

My posture curls, mirroring his. All these years, he's not shared this even with me?

"Is that when you became a bard?" I ask.

He nods. "Not exactly by choice, like I've made it sound. That Warden recruiter swept me off the streets only a couple of months into it."

Elias scratches at the tabletop, the scraping noise filling a long recess in his story. I wait, expecting him to share something worse based on his behavior, like he became a thief or accidentally harmed someone. But he remains quiet until Odessa swivels around again.

"Why *Elias*?" she asks.

Elias shuffles in his seat. "It was the name my mum wanted to give her next son, if she had one. And since Kieran let her down, I guess I hoped Elias might make a better son. Even if she wasn't around to see him."

I resist a frown as memories of the fourteen-year-old boy I met those years ago resurface. He was always on edge—making jokes to dodge questions, playing things down, only for me to find him hacking apart the training dummies in the arena. I often sensed something was wrong, but he's always been swift with his deflections, and I've never been one to impose on someone's privacy—lest they try to do the same to me.

"You were twelve when she passed?" I ask, and when he confirms I'd heard him right, I lean back into my chair to look him over better. "How could you have possibly let her down so greatly as a child?"

He casts an uncomfortable look toward Odessa, barely keeping his face stoic. "She died of the same venom that almost killed Nori. And just like then, I couldn't save her. But even before that, I could barely fill in for my papa. I didn't know how to comfort her. How to make her stop hurting or silence the rude people in Behria and their condescending comments, claiming that if my papa was a good man, El-Alam would have protected him. It ate her alive." Elias draws in a long breath, looking around the table, as if a cup of tea might be there to offer him some comfort. "I did everything I could to make things easier for her. But obviously, it didn't matter."

I lower my gaze to my sketch, staring emptily at the little lines that constitute Echo's fur until they seem to lose their meaning. The offense that I suppose I should feel about Elias keeping all this a secret can't find soil to take root in. It's too easy to imagine myself doing the same, seeing a chance for another life and wanting to blind myself to the pain of all that came before it.

And here I've been so jealous of his simple life—never realizing all the hardship he endured before he joined us. I always assumed he was angry with his family, and that's why he didn't talk about them. I never considered the true reason might be that it hurt too much.

"Anyway." Elias attempts a chuckle, but it dies two notes in. "I didn't come to tell you some sob story. I just wanted you to know the truth and to say I'm sorry. There are a lot of things I should have told you sooner. And I really messed things up by not doing that, especially once Nori showed up. I still don't know why I didn't at least tell you about her. That would have made things a little less complicated."

I hide my hands beneath the table, wringing them together. Indeed, it would have spared us both much trouble if he'd at least spoken up about Norielle when he arrived at Ila's house. But now I can see why he wouldn't, even if he hasn't realized it yet. He'd have needed to tell me all this right then. And with Norielle not recognizing him, he probably wanted to spare himself the embarrassment of me knowing they were so close before. Plus, my impolite reaction to his arrival in Aldrian didn't help the situation. That alone was enough for me to lose my right to know his sensitive history.

"So," Odessa draws out the word until Elias turns to her. "Is Auden even your last name?"

"It is," Elias says. "Didn't want to disown my family name. Just wanted to feel like I was starting over."

Odessa absorbs this for a moment before she stands.

"Well, good to know you're only half of a liar," she says in an inappropriately chipper tone. She gives Elias her best attempt at a sympathetic look, then she exits to the main deck.

"You know what's most offensive about all this?" I ask when the door shuts. Elias goes stiff, but I smile. "All this time you've been giving me trouble for not sharing what bothers me, yet you've been carrying all *this* alone."

He releases a dry laugh. "Well, I'm not the prince in charge of saving the world. My problems are only me-problems. You're carrying all Silvirdia on your shoulders."

"That doesn't matter."

He shrugs.

I sigh, looking across the low ceiling of our quarters. "I won't lie; it was rather frustrating to learn about your history with Norielle from *Alani*—as it was. But I understand why you'd protect that information, and I can't say I'd have done much better in your position, all things considered."

His brows purse, but he holds his mouth closed. My attention drifts to my drawing, a brief recollection of Zamirah imploring me to rediscover this lost part of myself softening my heart even more to the situation at hand.

I meet Elias's uneasy gaze. "I'm rooting for you with Norielle," I say, relieved when the statement stirs not even the slightest doubt within me. "I hope you know that."

"Not sure if it matters, but thanks." He scoots his chair back. "You're a good person, Cal."

"I have good friends," I counter as he stands.

He raps a knuckle against my drawing, right atop Echo's nose. "I still think that one's a spy."

I laugh as he exits the deckhouse, and after a long moment of staring at the door, processing our conversation, I retrieve my pencil and set back to work.

CALDEN

"Meeting on deck!" Alani calls at next sunrise, upon my request.

Most of the night crew already joins us, some standing, others perched on crates and barrels. They await my words with sharp anticipation, and I can't help but wonder if any of them are chewing on doubts about me, like that supplier. If any are, they've disguised it well thus far.

Of the night crew, Zamirah is the last to reach us, descending from the crow's nest with her dress fluttering in the wind. Despite having been up all night, she lands with a catlike *plop* and sends me a heartfelt smile as she joins the others. I watch her, admiring how she seems to grow more lovely at every sighting, until I reprimand myself.

After all that I've been through, why must it be so hard to blot her from my thoughts? Have I not learned my lesson yet?

The day crew filters in with sluggish steps and yawns. Elias leads the pack, the only one who looks fully awake besides Willian. He stops at a crate and sits, raising his cup toward me in a greeting. I respond with a nod before Odessa and Norielle drag themselves over with drooping eyelids. I smile at them both, but only Norielle finds the energy to return it.

"We're almost to Raevre," Alani announces once everyone is with us, and a half-hearted cheer resounds from her crew. "There's only one full day between us and land, so the Sovereign Prince would like to give you all some direction for what to do when we arrive."

I smile at Alani, always impressed to hear how authoritative she is when addressing a ship of people at her command compared to the way she is in other conversations. It's as if the sea swept her insecurities away and left behind the woman she is meant to be—a leader.

I refuse to give Odessa any credit for that after the way she provoked her, even if Alani has projected even more confidence since that day in the roundhouse.

"Good morning, friends," I say, stepping ahead as Alani sits.

An array of greetings rolls through the group.

"I'm sure you all understand the potential dangers of setting foot on Raevre, as both Wardens and people of Alémor." A mental image of my mother's disapproving glare slows my words, but I force them to come out stronger as I go on. "However, the Raevran Wardens have a hidden cove by which we will enter. The watchmen should be ready to receive us, thanks to our messenger." I wave a hand toward Zamirah, who gives a meek smile at my recognition of her. "They will lead us into their underground routes, so you may seek shelter in their base. My Bind and I will meet with the High Warden to plan our next steps in searching for Toaph Elbara."

I pause for them to absorb my words, though most of them should know this information already. Then I venture into the main purpose of my address to them.

"But, of course, everything always sounds far simpler than it often ends up being," I say with a light laugh. A few of them smile or nod. "While nearing shore and especially once on it, we must be sure to remain vigilant and swift. If Raevre's coast guards detect us, they may think we are soldiers of Alémor or spies. If we get past them, Hunters may still find us. And even more, we'll need to be wary of Blood Wardens and the Accursed... and the wildfires."

Several sets of shoulders sink, and I try not to do the same. For the next ten minutes, I delve into various courses of action we should take if things don't go according to plan, and by the time I've completed my briefing, my throat is dry. Alani hands me a flask of water, which I gulp down while the crew murmurs about everything I said.

I shift away from them, silently praying to El-Alam that my plans aren't utter rubbish. Every person on this ship is under my care, and should I lead them astray—

"Well, that was a lot to remember," Elias says, downing the final drops of his tea as he approaches me. How his tea lasted to the end of my lecture astounds me. He must have truly been paying attention.

"And I hope no one will need to." I watch the crew disbanding behind him, some turning in to rest, others splitting off to their unique posts per Alani's commands. A mixed atmosphere of enthusiasm and unease fills the ship, much like what brews inside me. But I fight to hold on to my optimism about the rest of the journey to the Raevran Wardens' base. We've made it this far with only the sea heller and a few close encounters with storms to threaten us. Maybe we'll make it safely ashore and into the underground with just as few complications.

"You're still set on finding Toaph?" Elias asks once most everyone but our Bind has moved on. He gives me a look that fills in what he's not voicing: *To help him, that is?*

"I wanted to talk to you about that." I look toward Norielle and Odessa, who are engaged in a quiet discussion I can't hear. "All of you, actually."

"That sounds bad."

I think back on my promise to Odessa. I told her I would share my full conversation with the Oracle once I had calmed down about the matter, and though I'm still unsure if I'm ready, Elias's recent bravery to share his secrets convicts me that it's time for me to do the same. We are a team after all, as he'd said. And I'm supposed to be the *leader* of it, not the coward.

"The Bind needs to know," I say, palms turning clammy. "And I... I've changed my mind about holding off for their input until Seer Ariellis can discern the truth of the Oracle's theories."

Elias smiles, as if proud of me, before looking into his cup. "Might need a fresh tea for this. When's the Bind meeting?"

"Now," I say, deciding as I speak. Any delay, and my nervousness might creep up to dismiss the meeting before I've even called for it.

Elias glances at his cup again before asking over our cabin steward, Anders, to take the dish back to the galley for him. The boy readily grabs the cup, and Elias offers to let him try his lyre sometime, as if the young steward requires additional payment for such a small errand.

As the boy rushes off, beaming, I holler for the rest of the Bind. "Alani. Odessa. Norielle. I need to speak with you all."

A few moments later, we seat ourselves around the meeting table of the roundhouse above our cabins. Sunlight pours in from behind me through windows along the curved back wall, illuminating a map pegged to the center of the table. A series of red dashes roughly mark our voyage so far, and nerves twinge through my chest at how close that line has come to Raevre's conch-shaped landform.

Once everyone settles in, I retrieve my warding pen, swiftly drawing a swirled glyph on my palm. I cast the Privacy Ward into the space, enclosing the entire Bind inside a foggy sphere that will entirely mute our voices. Alani releases a nervous laugh as I tuck my pen into my belt.

"In case anyone thinks to eavesdrop," I say, but my tongue seems to adhere to the roof of my mouth. *How will they all respond to this?*

"Well? Let's hear it," Elias prompts, resting his elbows on top of the table so he can prop his chin against his hands.

I inhale, holding my air long enough to make Alani stir before releasing it into my words. "I've been debating for a long time whether to share this with you all, but it seems this isn't something I can sort through on my own. And perhaps I shouldn't try."

The three women in our Bind exchange questioning looks.

"When I encountered the Oracle, there were many things he said to me outside of informing me of his true identity." I catch my hand fidgeting with a button on my coat and lower it to my side. "He suggested something about Toaph Elbara that has made me apprehensive about helping the Guardian once we find him. I... I've tried my best to convince myself it's all lies—trickery—yet the consequences of assuming so only to be wrong would be... devastating."

I expect at least Odessa to offer some comment about how long it's taken me to bring this up or a chastisement that I'm taking the Oracle's words into consideration, but even she holds her tongue.

"His suggestion was that Toaph Elbara became corrupt, and that Ta'Nathel came to rescue us from him. However, the Wardens misunderstood the event, and trapped Ta'Nathel after Toaph fled. The Oracle claims a curse is not responsible for the chaos and destruction spreading across Silvirdia, as we've assumed. Rather, it's through Toaph Elbara's rage toward the world now that his soul is corrupt, as though his corruption were poison spreading across the world, eventually to destroy it."

I picture the cedar forest we passed through—the barren, wilted branches and blanched bark of the ancient trees. The sickness appeared to be spreading, sapping the life from tree after tree, just as the Oracle insinuated Toaph's corruption has done.

"The Oracle also believes that Toaph Elbara is incapable of defeating Ta'Nathel—hence why he went into hiding. He thinks Toaph is hoping to use me, or possibly all of us, to rise against Ta'Nathel. But doing so—should the Oracle be right—would mean striking down the Guardian El-Alam sent to save us and leaving the world in the control of a Guardian who would likely turn against us the moment we served his purposes."

I pause, inspecting their tense expressions. Alani's head lowers into her hands, her soft groan the only response for the longest time. But finally, Odessa straightens her spine. "And you... believe this, brother?"

"No," I say too quickly. "Well, I haven't completely discarded the possibility."

"What makes you uncertain?" Norielle asks.

I take a while to form a proper answer. "I suppose it was the way he explained my episodes. They *seem* like a curse. They cause violence and destruction and fear—all things that make no sense if Toaph were still good and trying to reach me."

My words slow as I recall what Zamirah said: *Even the greatest blessings can come with consequences. But that doesn't mean they aren't still blessings.*

But consequences like mine?

No. There can't be anything holy about that.

"The Oracle thinks Toaph is trying to channel some sort of power through me," I continue, my certainty waxing and waning by the second. "And because the Guardian is corrupt, his power would cause destruction."

There's another lengthy pause that makes me wonder if they are all actually considering the idea.

"Have you any other evidence?" Odessa asks.

"The Accursed," I say, even more of my mind being won over to the idea as I recall this detail. "The Sentries are tied to the Empyreal Guardian's soul, like the world. If he became corrupt, so would the Sentries. How could Ta'Nathel turn Toaph's own Sentries against him if Toaph lives? How could his curse overpower the bond between a Guardian and their most loyal servants?"

"Didn't you just say Ta'Nathel is stronger than Toaph Elbara?" Odessa asserts.

My mouth hangs open for a moment. "Yes."

"Then his curse would be stronger than the bond, especially if that bond was severed through Toaph's weakened, hidden state."

My argument cracks, and I seek Norielle's and Alani's gazes again—the two members of my Bind who haven't yet taken a side on this matter. Alani avoids my eyes, but the pitiful way Norielle looks at me feels very different from the way she used to admire me. Does she think I've officially lost my mind?

"What are you thinking?" I probe.

Norielle's lips press together as she ponders. "I'm not sure," she finally confesses. "Your argument *is* strong, but where does the Oracle get his information? From Ta'Nathel, wouldn't he?"

I nod, not knowing what other source he could have.

"Wouldn't Ta'Nathel like to convince us he's the one trying to help us?" Norielle says, echoing the same concerns Elias expressed before.

"And Seer Josiah has already affirmed that Toaph Elbara is communicating with you," Odessa puts in before I can respond to Norielle.

"He has," I say, drawing in another slow breath. "But recent events have made me question his discernment, as I've mentioned before. Could it be that Seer Josiah's desire to receive this good news caused him to make a mistake? Perhaps all he truly discerned was that Toaph Elbara lives, and he assumed the rest to be true without proper consideration?"

"Calden..." Alani's hands drop from her face, and she looks up at me. "I can't say this isn't at all convincing, but can we really take the Oracle's word above Seer Josiah's? I know he's your father, but..."

"You only want to believe him because you're angry at Mother," Odessa supplies, and whether or not that was Alani's intended direction, Alani's sympathetic smile suggests she's at least considered the same.

"That is not true," I counter. "And I don't *want* to believe him."

Elias shifts, reminding me he's still here despite his uncharacteristic silence. "You do," he says, but his tone is not accusing. "Because you can't reconcile your episodes otherwise."

His statement draws me into my heart, inspecting its dark corners and avoided halls. "It's just hard to believe they are good after all the damage they've done." My eyes meet with Alani's, and a long quiet propagates, as if my words hold every tongue in the room hostage.

Again, Zamirah's statement about blessings and consequences echoes within me, like she'd engraved it into my heart.

Why do I still wonder what she might say about this matter? A woman of such great faith in El-Alam, whose knowledge of my episodes may well be vaster than everyone else's in this room, besides myself and Odessa?

"What about my other theory?" Elias prompts. "About Ta'Nathel cursing you to keep you from hearing from Toaph?"

My spirit seems to awaken at this mention, even as it conflicts with Zamirah's sentiment. In my distress about Mother, I've forgotten this theory Elias briefly proposed on our way back home from the crypt. "I could believe that," I say. "Though that would bring us back to needing to find a way to break the curse if we don't find Toaph in the Valley of the Four Winds."

"That's a good theory, Elias," Alani comments.

Elias nods to her in thanks before returning his focus to me. "I'd rather think you're cursed and Toaph is good than believe we've got this twisted around just because the leader of the defectors said so."

"Agreed," Odessa says, eyes seeming to plead that I respond in kind.

I look again to Norielle for her verdict, but she diverts her focus to Elias as she speaks. "Elias must be right, or at least on the right track. There's nothing in history to suggest that Toaph was slipping into corruption. I'd think that would be a gradual process."

She would know, after all her studying in the Seer's library.

I shut my eyes, letting their reasoning fall upon me like rain that slowly seeps through my skin and into my spirit. "Okay,"

I finally submit. "I will still present this to the Seer of Raevre, but until then, we will consider Toaph Elbara pure."

47

ELIAS

Boots drum against the deck in almost perfect rhythm as the crew sings an old melody in one—somewhat disharmonious—voice. Across from where Cal and I sit, a crewmate who I usually see swabbing the deck attempts to carry the song on his cittern, but one string is out of tune, and his fingers seem to chase the beat rather than riding it.

And now I understand why everyone on the ship prefers I lead the entertainment.

But they'll have to wait. I have a tea to finish before I put the cittern player out of business for the night.

"Do you think the Raevrans have starroot? This is the last of mine," I say, turning my attention back to Cal. He's been dry-washing his hands for the past five minutes, like if he rubs them together long enough, whatever is troubling him might be eroded from existence.

But now, his gaze is stuck on a group of women from the crew who are dancing along to the "song." He doesn't even glance my way, as if missing my question altogether.

Has he blanked out in their direction, or is he watching them?

One woman says something to the others that I can't quite hear, and a burst of laughter sounds from the group. When I look back at Cal, he's smiling.

I lift a brow. "You keep looking at them like that and one of them is going to come ask you to dance."

Cal shudders and gives me a weary look. "Looking at them like what?"

"Like you're picking out your Lady Sovereign."

Cal nearly chokes on the sip of morning brew that he shouldn't even be drinking right now. The shanty almost drowns out his quiet retort. "*Empyrean*, Lias."

His mug *clunks* against the small crate we're using as a table. I laugh, inspecting the women again to figure out which one he was watching. There are four—the galley stewardess, then two women who look just a few years older than Cal, and the gold-eyed girl who accompanied Nori and me during the sea heller attack. Zamirah, was it?

That's the one. I've seen her lingering around him every time their paths cross, and he always watches her like she's a storyteller who never finished the tale.

I draw my conclusion a moment too late, and one woman pauses, noticing my eyes on them. She throws me a wide smile that I hardly return before checking if Nori has come out from our cabins. She claimed to have a book from Seer Josiah to read and return once we got back, as if I wouldn't know that's her way of saying she wants to be left alone. By the looks of it, she must mean for the entire night.

I turn back to Cal, only to find him staring at Zamirah again. I try not to feel selfishly relieved by this development. He really meant what he said about Nori.

Now, if only I could convince myself that Nori meant it when she told Odessa she didn't have feelings for him...

"She's pretty," I comment.

Cal shoots me a foul look. "Stop."

"What? You don't think so?"

"That's not what I was thinking about."

"But you've thought it before."

He rubs his forehead. "She's my mother's messenger. The one who's been charged with sharing information regarding my episodes with the other lands."

"Funny how you knew exactly which girl I was talking about." I smirk before his words catch up with me. "So, what?"

Cal reels his gaze back to me. "It's strange that she's here on this ship, knowing all she does. You'd think she'd be too afraid."

The shanty ends before I can answer, and a loud cheer erupts from the crew. Laughter and clapping fill the gap before Willian shouts out the name of some nautical song I've never heard of. The men of the crew respond with a low note that vibrates in my ears.

I finish my tea, setting the cup aside so I can ready my lyre to intervene the moment this song ends. If I have to listen to that flat string on the cittern much longer, I'm going to hurl it into the sea.

"Please tell me you plan on finishing out the night with that." Cal nods toward my lyre as I pull it from my satchel. "I can't take much more of this."

I snicker. If Cal can tell the music is terrible, then it must be even worse than I thought.

"I've got you," I say, propping my instrument upright. A couple of crewmates notice, and their faces light up. I lean closer to Cal. "Maybe you can *accidentally* disintegrate the cittern, you think?"

He laughs—a strange noise to hear from him after how solemn and detached he's been. It settles me. Maybe he will be okay. Maybe, somehow, everything will.

"Perhaps you could help him tune it and that may prove sufficient," Cal mumbles, leaning further away from the cittern player.

The song finishes, far shorter than the others, and I pluck a string before the cittern is done humming out its last note. Immediately, heads turn in my direction, and a round of applause welcomes me to relieve us all of the cittern player's *valiant* efforts.

I start with a peppy song that used to require all my skill to play, but now, it's so instinctual for me, I hardly have to think about it anymore. The rapid notes stir up the crew, and in seconds, lively motion spills across the deck. I settle into the song, watching the strings blur as they vibrate from my quick plucks and strokes. They barely have a chance to still before I'm striking them again.

"It's much more fun if you join in."

The sudden voice almost causes me to fumble my strings. I look up from my lyre, startled again when I see Zamirah standing in front of me, but her eyes are on Cal.

I strangle my smile, dialing my eyes back on my instrument, but my ears tune in for his response. This is the first time he's even stuck around for more than a couple of minutes during the nightly merriment. Serves him right to get pulled into it. Especially by her.

"Perhaps for everyone else," Cal says after a longer than normal pause. "I'm sure watching me blundering around would be quite entertaining for all but me."

I shoot him a disappointed look. After all that staring, *that* is how he's going to respond?

"Oh, skies," she giggles, holding a hand toward him. "All you have to do is stand there and spin me around."

Cal stares at her hand like he might light her on fire if he touched her, but the girl maintains her smile despite his delay.

I bump into him. "Don't be rude, Cal."

He elbows me back, knocking my hand off the strings, and I miss a full set of notes. I huff as he stands and lets the girl lead him toward an open space on the deck. He gives me a betrayed look over his shoulder, as if accepting a pretty girl's invitation to dance is the worst thing that could happen to him.

Yet as soon as he must think he's out of my range of sight, he's smiling again.

Don't mess this one up, I think toward Cal and his twirling partner before I return my gaze to my lyre and drift into my memories of dancing with Nori at the ball. For once, I don't feel guilty for reminiscing about it. I just enjoy recalling the way it felt to hold her—the girl I thought I'd never see again—returned to me even more incredible than she was when my misfortunes ripped me away from her.

"I thought you weren't going to play tonight?"

The memories vanish at the sound of Nori's voice.

She sits where Cal was as I force my hands to remember every last note of my song. The crew applauds my musicianship, and I begin something easier so I can play while talking.

"Well, the former entertainment was giving me a headache," I mutter, looking up to meet her gaze. But her attention is drawn away from me to Cal and Zamirah.

Nori's lips part like she wants to ask a question, but she seems to think better of it. Instead, our conversation ceases until I start the chorus.

"I thought you had a book to read," I say.

She finger-combs her hair so that it covers the right side of her face, as if trying to hide from everyone on deck. "I heard you playing,"

I smile, plucking my strings with an added sense of purpose. "That's what lured you out of the cave?"

She twists a satchel into her lap that I'd not noticed her wearing. From it, she draws her book—a record log that she mentioned included her Warden grandfather. Though, last she updated me, his name hasn't come up yet. The spine crackles when she opens it.

"Remember when we used to sit by the lake, you practicing your songs while I read?" she says, flipping to where a striped feather marks her place.

The comfortable memories flash by me like it was last week. The musty lake air. The mild breeze. The feeling of her hair tickling my arm, since we always shared the same tree as a backrest.

"Yeah, Nori," I whisper.

"I wanted to feel that again."

I breathe her words in. "Well, I'm here anytime you want to pretend you're home."

She shifts a little closer, and my hands ache to set down my lyre and run my fingers through her hair instead of across these strings. Would she let me if I tried? Or is she only happy to sit here in the familiarity of my presence, thinking about who we both used to be?

"You'll come back with me, won't you?" she asks, stroking her feather bookmark.

"Back home?"

She nods. "To teach Milo how to play music."

It hurts to not have a face to put to her little brother's name, but I conjure an image of a boy who looks like a male version of how Cassia did when I left. "I'll show him everything your papa taught me. All his songs, too."

She smiles, though she looks ready to cry. "He'd love that."

"Me too."

She turns down to her page, and I transition to a song her papa composed, wishing the melody could carry us back to the man who wrote it.

CALDEN

Zamirah's dress blossoms like a yellow flower as she spins away from me, only to collide with the galley stewardess. I wince, even as they chortle at one another. *That was my fault, wasn't it?*

Zamirah whirls back toward me, nose crinkled from her smile. "I wasn't supposed to let go, was I?"

"I thought *I* had," I say, offering my hand for her to reclaim, should she dare.

Without hesitation, her gentle grip takes hold of mine again, and I try not to notice the tingling on my skin that her touch incites or how she draws closer than Norielle ventured at her ball. Maybe even as close as Corene once did.

"I've been told I'm a rather clumsy dancer," she says as I take her other hand and move us in time with Elias's song. "I should have warned you."

I laugh. "I'm certain that was my fault, not yours. I'm not exactly known for being great at this, despite how many balls my mother insists on hosting."

Zamirah's eyes sparkle at the mention of the citadel balls, something members of the naval sector usually miss.

"All right then," she says, "that one was your fault. Better?"

"Actually, you are the one who pulled me out here. Maybe that makes everything thereafter your fault," I tease before I notice I'm about to bump shoulders with Willian. I dodge him with a sharp turn. "Except for that," I add, glancing back at Willian, but he's too fixated on his partner to notice our near collision. And she is too fixated on him to see me, either.

Not that I'd expect anything less from Alani.

I return my focus to Zamirah, slowing us to a standstill. "Perhaps one and a half songs is plenty participation for one night?"

"Only if you've at least had a little fun?"

"For someone who despises dancing, I'd say this was one of the better times I've had doing so," I confess.

She surveys my face, as if trying to decide whether I'm only saying that so it will end, or if I mean it.

"Truly, thank you," I add. "Sometimes I need a little tug to get out of my head for a while."

She glances down at our hands, which are still enclosed around each other. I release her to rub the back of my neck, glancing toward Elias with intent to return to him, but I notice Norielle has taken my place. My gaze veers to the bow—my regular post where I can pretend to have privacy without having to hide myself away in the stuffy deckhouse—but a trio of crewmates occupy it, guzzling ale and cackling.

"Are you worried?" Zamirah asks, her uncomfortable shuffle alerting me to my rude behavior. Here, she's gone out of her way multiple times to encourage and help me, and I'm looking for a place to run from her to at the earliest opportunity that presents itself.

But it's for her own safety—that much, she of all people should understand with her extensive knowledge of my episodes.

Or is it for my sake that I run?

The question alarms me, as if it didn't come from my own mind at all. And suddenly, I recall Odessa's accusation in the cedar forest. *You're afraid you'll get hurt.*

"I'm sorry," I say, shaking off the chill the conviction left on my arms. "I suppose I am worried. It's just that we'll be in Raevre tomorrow..."

Empathy swathes her bronze-toned face as she waits for me to expound on my concerns. Instead, I fall quiet, admiring her in the moon's glow. *Pretty* is the word Elias used, but it falls short. Yet I can't seem to find one worthy of describing her. How does one define a beauty that is more than just on the surface, but radiating from one's very soul, enveloping another in her presence even under such less-than-ideal circumstances?

But the thought only entangles me in a web of fear. What if something happens to her in Raevre? What if I get her and everyone else killed on this foolhardy quest of mine?

"We all know where we're going, Calden," Zamirah says after a prolonged stillness. She stands taller, as if trying to match my eye level from her shorter height. "We've known since before we set sail for the voyage. No matter what happens ahead, we chose this. Even if we all died in a storm tonight, that would not be your fault. You did not force a single one of us to board this ship."

Something stirs in my core. "Are you a Grand Master, Zamirah?"

Her head inclines to the side. "Why do you ask?"

"Because I swear you're reading my thoughts, as if blessed with another Talent."

She giggles, clutching her hands together in front of her chest. "No, it doesn't take a Grand Master to guess the troubles of a future Sovereign, even whilst he pretends, for a time, that's not who he is."

My lips part, yet I'm not sure how to respond.

Her expression turns serious again. "I don't for a moment believe El-Alam brought us here to die. He is with us, and that, too, is why this isn't all on your shoulders."

Despite her encouragement, my smile falls away completely, and a bitter taste crawls up my throat. "If I could confess something," I say, checking around us, only now realizing that we've drifted apart from the others and into a lonely space on the deck. "I'm not sure if El-Alam led us here or if it was my pride."

Elias transitions from one song to the next as I await her answer. I don't know why I said it, but now I'm fighting not to tell her everything that led us here, as if doing so will grant me the response I deserve—her to take back her reassurance and march away from me, calling me a fool.

"Oh my," she says, her smile more nervous than before. "You say that as if His plans were so easily thwarted by our own."

My throat clenches, preventing me from swallowing or even asking for her explanation.

Fortunately, she sees the request in my eyes.

"If He allowed it, then there's a purpose to it," she says, stepping closer once again in a moment where I'd expect someone to be backing away. "El-Alam is not unsuspecting of our humanity, you know. Even yours, *Sovereign*."

My heart flutters. "I'm not—"

"But you are," she insists. "You *are* the Sovereign. Maybe not in title yet, but in heart. I believed that upon hearing of this quest, and even more so while listening to you this morning. You are already the man El-Alam needs you to be. Who *we* need you to be. There are not expectations you need to strive to meet. You are already there, and we are with you."

I try to inhale, but the air seems to snag in my throat, never reaching my lungs. The ship sways—or perhaps I do—and the briskness of the breeze hardly registers against my skin, even as it brushes my hair into my eyes.

"But if I told you I have doubts," I say, voice dropping to a whisper. I chide myself the moment the words slip out, but now it's too late. Now I *need* to know how she'll respond—this wise woman who's given me far too much credit than I should be allowed. "Doubts about the other Elders. Doubts about who our real enemies are. Doubts about... myself."

Her mouth closes, and she looks down. Ashamed, surely. Ashamed to have placed such confidence in me before cracking me open to see what's truly inside.

"Do you doubt El-Alam also?" she asks after a long while. "His goodness?"

I consider my episodes and all the devastation they've caused. Then the world, all the pain—the wildfires, the storms, the wars. All this destruction happening right under our Creator God's watchful gaze. Yet His hands seem so unmoving, so distant, outside of leaving mere men, such as myself, to deal with the catastrophes that He could end with a snap of His mighty fingers.

My voice is timid when I reply, "Sometimes."

"Good," Zamirah says, her expression flickering between the joyful girl I just danced with and the sage woman who belongs amongst the Warden council. "Because I'd retract my former claim that you are human if you'd said otherwise." She takes one of my hands, holding it between both of her own, and my pulse escalates. "We all doubt ourselves, each other, and even our Maker, Calden. And I can only imagine how much more so when in a position such as yours."

A temptation to spill everything, every argument I have for why she shouldn't be so confident in me, rises and falls with my chest. *Receive it,* something inside me says. *Receive this grace.*

Because she's right. I am no more than a man—a man who's been given more than my mortal hands can carry. And yet every eye still watches me, leaping to judge me at even the slightest teeter of my balance.

My eyes, especially.

"You're allowed to be unsure," she adds in my silence. "You're even allowed to be afraid and make mistakes. You are facing something no one in history has ever had to face, and if you ask me, you are doing a remarkable job."

Her hands gently squeeze mine, as if she is trying to impress her sentiments into me by force. The action bewilders me—first, because she's both declared me Sovereign and yet treated me as her equal, and second, because she should know not to lay a hand on me when I am obviously distressed.

Did she truly mean what she said in the crow's nest? That she isn't afraid of me?

Am I now the one who needs to not be so afraid?

The thought conjures an image of Mother standing with me on the balcony. *There are ways to protect others from your episodes that do not involve cutting yourself off from everything that makes life worthwhile,* she said. And even after all that has come between us, I still feel Mother's care for me in those words.

How can I let one horrible mistake erase a lifetime of her love and devotion? Especially knowing it was done, in part, to protect me?

"Thank you, Zamirah," I whisper, holding her gaze until the guilt for the way I left Mother grows too great to be ignored. I gently slip my hand from Zamirah's grip, twisting my face away to recompose myself before asking, "Would you please send a message to my mother?"

A fleeting look of confusion crosses her face before she nods. "Of course. What would you like me to tell her?"

"Tell her we're nearly to Raevre, and that I'm sorry. She'll know what for."

She examines my face, like she wants to ask more, but her chest swells and she shifts away from me. I watch, uncertain what she must do to send the message. Is it as simple as thinking it in my mother's direction? Must she say it out loud?

A sustained note leaves her mouth; the purity of her voice seems to mute the music behind us. She follows it with a wordless melody, so beautiful it turns my body hollow. The sound fills my ears and stops my lungs from breathing until it fades, drifting away from us, as if her voice literally swept across the sea.

My mouth hangs open as I recall the song Elias often sings, the one he learned from Norielle's father. Could a Warden with a gift like Zamirah's have inspired the lyrics?

Zamirah faces me again, her speaking voice seeming more radiant after I've heard how she sings. "Your apology has been sent."

I only gape at her. It's like she isn't even real. Did the Empyrean open up and drop her on this ship?

She turns, as if someone called for her, before whirling back with a wider smile. "And received."

Mother.

I sigh at the thought of Mother hearing those words. *We're close. I'm sorry*, in whatever eloquent way Zamirah sent them. I hope Mother knows I mean the apology for my behavior, even if I'm still shattered by hers.

"Thank you," I say, groping for the present moment before it's gone. "I confess, I wasn't expecting you to sing."

She laughs. "Sorry, I thought you knew how it worked."

I shake my head, disappointed in my memory for not clinging better to the details about her. "Well, it was absolutely ethereal."

"Why, thank you." She curtsies. "Though I will say, it was strange to send a message from you to her rather than about you from her."

My eyes narrow at the thought of Mother and Zamirah standing here on this ship, discussing me. How much has Mother revealed to her about my episodes, truly? Is it even as much as I've assumed, considering how unbothered Zamirah seems by the knowledge that I could turn violent any second? Or is she simply so optimistic that she falsely believes she's safe with me?

I want to ask, but before I can decide on my phrasing, Zamirah glances at the crow's nest.

"I really should be going up there before Valrone starts throwing peanuts at us again," she says, and my blood turns cold at the thought of her leaving—abandoning me to the troubles that have wracked my mind all day. "Not that I haven't had an excellent excuse to be late."

I swallow the disquieting feeling, not wanting to expose how quickly my anxiety strangles her efforts to encourage me. "Please do blame me," I say, smiling to disguise my unease. "I'm sorry I've kept you."

"I'm not," she says, stepping toward the mainmast. But she slows, meeting my gaze again like she senses something is off with me.

I force more serenity into my expression. "Is there anything I may do to repay you, Zamirah?" I ask, hoping the unexpected question will both buy me another moment with her and distract her from probing me about my slip of composure.

"For what?" she asks.

"Your kindness." I want to add more details, but I think better of allowing my heart full reign of my tongue.

"Kindness that requires repayment isn't kindness at all. And you have been no burden to me. One simply being human is not a burden." The color of her cheeks turns ruddy as she smiles at me. "And I quite like talking to you. Troubles and all, you're lovely company. I'm grateful for this chance to have met you outside of your mother's stories."

So Mother has shared more about me.

A warm feeling, like a freshly stoked fire, floods my chest, even as fear hovers nearby, threatening to stomp out the flames.

"I've enjoyed your company, too," I say. I bid my lips to stop there, but they fail to obey with the way she lights up at my words. "I should have accompanied my mother years ago, so I could have met you sooner."

She looks down, almost bashfully. "El-Alam crossed our paths right when He meant to."

"I suppose He did."

I spy Valrone peering over the crow's nest again, shaking his head at her. The good-natured man likely means little by it besides to tease her, but we can't leave him up there forever.

"You really should be going up," I insist. "I'll see you tomorrow for our arrival in Raevre."

She nods, seemingly resigning herself to her responsibilities. "I'll see you then."

She carries on, and I bow my head, smiling despite the jumbled feeling in my chest. But the longer I stand alone, the more my fears build within me—as if she were only a shield blocking an oncoming assault, and I sent her away a moment too soon.

Should we even be going to Raevre? Could we turn back now, spare us all the danger?

I could seek Seer Josiah's guidance, with Mother's blessing, and we could face this all together, the way we were meant to as Elders.

The squeal of a door turns me toward the galley, quickly enough to spot the quartermaster dipping in. I dash after him, entering the small kitchen as he's retrieving a tray of ales to pass about.

"Sir," I start.

The middle-aged man stills, ale sloshing onto his rubber boots. "Would you like one, my lord?"

I wave the offer away. "Actually, I need to ask you something."

He lowers the mugs, giving me his full attention.

"How much food do we have left?"

His forehead crinkles. "Plenty to reach Raevre with. We planned to restock there, assuming the Raevran Wardens would be so kind as to help us."

"Ah, I-I see." I wipe my sweating palms against my pants. "So, there's nothing extra?"

"Well, we always bring more than we need, if we can. I'd say there's enough to stretch us another week if we had to, though portions would be slim."

Then there's no backing out.

The ship wobbles underfoot, but only I seem to notice it.

"Are you wanting to forfeit the expedition, my lord?" the quartermaster asks, quieter than he last spoke.

I force a smile. "No. I—" But I can't find the clarity of mind to think up another reason I'd be asking. "Well, I was just curious. Thank you for the information."

"You're welcome, my lord."

The man watches me as he inches toward the galley door. I step out of his way, and I'm left standing in the otherwise vacant galley.

El-Alam, protect us in Raevre, I pray, before the taste of dust salts my tongue.

ELIAS

As I shift from melody to melody, the laughter and dancing perpetuate across the deck as though the crew were controlled by my fingertips. It is a magic of its own—to have the power to change an atmosphere without needing to say a word. And even if the constant pestering for me to play is like a thorn in my foot sometimes, when I'm in the mood for it, it's one of the more satisfying parts of my new life. Maybe there's more to it than people just wanting to be entertained. Maybe it's a need. Something I need, too.

I give the cittern player a small nod of thanks, though he doesn't see it. He's too busy throwing back a mug of ale. If it wasn't for his untuned string and lackluster skill, I probably wouldn't have decided to play tonight, and then I'd have missed out on remembering why I wanted to learn music in the first place.

For people. To bring them together.

And to spend time with the girl who's still sitting beside me, reading her book.

But with my fingers cramping from playing for so long, I finish my current song and declare that was the end of my services. The crew applauds me as I tuck my lyre back into its satchel and stand.

"Wait," Nori says, closing her book and stuffing it into her bag. "Can we talk?"

A chill rushes through me. *Why does that sound so serious?*

I make myself smile. "Of course, Nori."

She glances around at the people still lingering nearby before turning toward the mostly unoccupied quarterdeck. "Can we... take this up there?"

I shrug and lead the way. We wave to Willian, now at the helm, as we pass, but the man hardly seems to notice us, since his attention is on Alani as she laughs with the crewmates. The air feels even colder at the highest point on the deck, where the breeze is completely unobstructed. The sensation revitalizes me, but Nori is puffing air into her hands to warm them within seconds.

"What's going on?" I ask.

Her gaze wanders from the ship to the sea before resting on the star-flecked horizon. The moon's glow stripes the darkened water like a beam of light that dissipates before it reaches the *Celestella*.

"I-I know things between us didn't get off to the best start since we met again," Nori says.

I suck in a breath, only to hold it until she continues.

"But when we were on the way to the citadel, you said you wanted to see what you and I could have..." She faces me, her hazel eyes scanning my features, as if reading them on a page. "And... so do I."

My jaw falls open, but skepticism holds me silent. Is she only saying this because seeing Cal with Zamirah finally convinced her he's truly not an option? Or is that my own insecurity refusing to believe even *Nori* wouldn't choose me over someone as all-around great as Cal?

"What made you decide that?" I try to laugh, as if I'm asking her as a joke, yet I can't help but plead for an honest answer with my eyes.

"What do you mean?"

"A lot has changed since we were kids, Nori," I say. "Things have happened to us. *New people* have stepped in. What made you decide you still want to give me a chance after all this time we've been apart?"

Her hand runs across her hair, and her silence only multiplies my doubts.

"Nori..." I hesitate, part of me wanting to ignore all my unease and dive straight into this—forget everything except the fact that my Nori has come back to me, and she's wanting to find out what we could become together. But I can't. I can't jump if I don't trust that there'll be something real to land on, because if there's not, we could lose even what we have now. And I can't handle that. Not after losing everyone else that I've ever loved from my life before joining the Wardens.

"Listen, I don't want to be your backup plan," I say. "If you're only saying this because Cal's not interested, then maybe we shouldn't be having this conversation."

"You're not my backup plan," she says, her voice stronger than before. "I knew you first."

I chew the inside of my cheek as I study her expression. "But you still have feelings for him."

"No, I don't. Not the kind you think I have."

I lean closer to see her better in the dimness—checking for all the signs I've been trained to notice that might indicate a lie, but the only thing I find evident in her shortened breaths and tensed jaw is frustration.

"I've just been confused," she adds, calmer now. "Elias, he saved my life. He satisfied a desire I've always had—to meet a Warden—then he offered me a place among them, a place to belong. And his hands were the ones used to heal me from near death."

I try not to flinch. *His hands.* Not mine.

Even knowing it was El-Alam who truly performed the healing, the reminder that I failed Nori still stabs me in the chest.

Nori inches closer to me. "Calden *represents* things to me. My purpose. My acceptance. El-Alam's care for me. Not to mention he's our world's hope. It's hard not to feel *something* toward him."

"Exactly." I recover the distance between us.

"No." She steps after me yet again. "What I'm saying is that it was easy to confuse my gratitude toward him with something else."

I close my mouth, all the noise of the sloshing waves and blabbering crew fading away. Does she mean that, or does she only *think* she does? Because there's still no trace of a lie on her face.

She tugs at a long strand of her hair, looking at the sea beyond me as she continues. "Calden is a great man, Elias. I respect him, and I want to help him fix our world. I won't pretend that I didn't start seeing something more than that, but... it's not like it is with you. You don't know how heartbroken I was when I lost you or how long it took for me to feel like *me* again. And even then, I don't think I ever did, not until we met again."

I shut my eyes, struck by how easily her statement could have come from my lips instead. Still, the sentiment seems to get stuck outside my heart, knocking on the door. She can't mean all this. She's tricked herself into thinking this. She practically *hated* me upon meeting me again, and she didn't start opening up to me until she figured out who I was.

Who I *was.*

"Tell me this," I say, fighting a glance down at her lips. Putting an end to this would be so easy. She could make me believe her with a single kiss, and then it would be over for me. "If you never found out I was Kieran, would you be saying any of this? Because I'm not just Kieran anymore. I'm also Elias. *This*"—I gesture to myself—"is all that comes with Kieran. The person you met at Ila's table."

"The one who complimented my nightgown?" She summons a smile, and even though I can see it reaching her eyes—another sign that she means every word she's said—I can't silence that voice of doubt inside me, the one telling me I'm not good enough for her. That she deserves better.

She deserves *Cal*.

I turn away, failing to give an answer as all the insecurities I've trapped and buried inside seem to spill out like ink from a shattered cartridge. The black stain spreads, so thick, I couldn't wipe it away to pretend it wasn't there, even if I could reach into my heart to try.

That's what's been wrong this whole time, isn't it? I want the *best* for Nori, and I've always known that's not me. Even back in Behria, I knew that. But here it's been so much plainer—Cal can save the world and hand it to her.

What do I have to offer her? What have I *ever* had?

A sharp sting swarms my eyes, and I turn away from Nori, not wanting her to see them turning red. "I'm sorry, Nori," I say, cursing how my voice breaks. "I'm not trying to make this hard."

I just don't know how to accept a good thing, even when it's being handed to me.

Because as soon as I'm holding it, it will disappear, won't it? Everything always does.

Everyone does.

The floorboards creak behind me, and Nori's hand lays against my arm. But her touch only makes it harder to breathe, like she's an enemy who's captured me and now I'm about to meet my end.

But she's not. She's my dream. My Nori...

So, why can't I turn around?

"Elias, I can see you," she says, so gentle and yet so strong. "I can see you through all the pretenses you uphold because—somehow—you got convinced that nobody would like you if they saw your true heart. I can see Kieran hiding behind your feigned confidence, like he used to hide behind trees in Behria. I see his funny quirks and sense of humor and hardworking spirit and his loyalty, all poking out between your new layers. But that little boy has been through so much. He's lost so much."

She pauses to catch her breath, and I tilt my face toward her but still can't muster the courage to fully turn.

"I'm not asking you to be the person you were before everything got broken. I'm telling you I see who you became after it all, and even if you don't know who that is, I do. And that's the person I want to be with—the person who makes *me* feel whole. Because we've *both* changed, and even though we grew up apart, we somehow grew into pieces that I think fit together like El-Alam Himself designed us that way."

She finds my hand, clasping it. With the softest tug, she beckons me to turn and meet her eyes again, which are now streaming with tears.

"I don't need to pretend I'm home with you," she says. "I *am* home."

Her gaze drops to my lips, as if asking.

"Nori," I whisper, and though I'm smiling, I feel scared—like a kid unsure whether to laugh or cry when caught doing something wrong. "Don't do this to me unless you're sure."

She drifts even closer, the cloud of her breath dissipating right below my eyes.

I raise my free hand, pressing my fingertip against her soft, quivering lips. "*Please*. Not unless you're sure."

She hesitates for another breath before she grabs my other hand and pulls it down, resting it against her heart. Even through her thick layers, I feel her pulse hammering as she holds my gaze. Then she presses her lips to mine, and electricity surges through me like I've been touched by the sea heller. The bolts clash—a flash of emotions and desires arcing inside my chest. The feeling overwhelms my senses until all I'm aware of is *her*. Her lips. Her heart. Her words. All swirling around me like a whirlwind that sucks the oxygen from my lungs.

She pulls away, leaving my lips tingling as our gazes realign.

"I'm sure," she whispers, a fresh tear slithering down her cheek.

But I can't speak. My mind feels like it erupted and everything that was once in it is now drifting in the air, unreachable. I watch my breath puffing between us, my fingers still shaking in her grasp.

"Nori—"

But that's the furthest I get before a woman's scream rips from across the deck.

I jerk my head around, air hissing through my clenched teeth when I find the cause for the cry.

Cal, standing just outside the galley—his eyes glowing white.

NORIELLE

The white glow in Calden's eyes appears and disappears with his every blink. He's fighting it. Resisting. Yet each time, the white lasts longer. His face suddenly convulses, and a loud bellow explodes from his throat. The wretched sound is like a war cry, but it ends with an agonizing whine, as if someone stabbed him.

"Stay back!" Elias yells at the crew as he vaults down the stairs to the main deck. The few people who hadn't already dispersed to the borders of the ship draw back as Elias charges toward Calden.

"*Elias,*" I whisper into my hand, a feverish shake overwhelming my body.

Odessa lunges for Calden before Elias can reach him. But Calden deflects her with a buzzing wave of vitality that throws her backward. Her spine slams against the deck, and she skids until she collides with a barrel. Another of Calden's screams rattles my ears as Elias charges him from the other direction. He grabs Calden's wrist, but by the time I realize what he's doing—trying to pin him with a Snare Ward—Calden has blasted him with energy, tossing him nearly as far as Odessa. My heart twists as he smashes to the floor with a loud grunt.

I start after him, but Calden's next scream freezes me at the stairs leading down from the quarterdeck. Suddenly, all the power I've marveled at feels terrifying. The man who can heal cedars or disintegrate them with his touch, who can channel three times more vitality than an average Warden, has now turned against us.

Is anyone on this ship even powerful enough to stop him?

Odessa and Elias gather themselves as Alani approaches Calden, whirling a rope with a loop on the end. She tosses it like she's trying to lasso a bull, but Calden grabs it, disintegrating the entire line. A second later, a swell of energy flings her back. Her shriek tears across the deck until she lands in Willian's outstretched arms.

Calden's glowing eyes seal shut, his hands curling into his hair. He wails, writhing like he's trying to pull the *other mind* out of himself. He's still there, then—a little.

Resist it, Calden. Please resist it.

I force myself to take a step forward, but right then, Calden jerks his head back, yelling, and a blast of energy explodes from him. The dome-like pulse surges across the entire deck, knocking over every person and cracking every piece of wood in its path. Just before it reaches me, I duck. The power collides with me, weakened so that it only tosses my hair and sends a hot wave across my skin. But when I look up, the mainmast holding the crow's nest is split.

A shrill yelp echoes from above, and I glance up to find Zamirah clinging to the rigging she must have been climbing down.

"Calden, s-stop," I try to shout, but fear strangles the sound to an inaudible whisper.

What if he destroys the ship? What if we all end up in the *water?*

Horror nearly stops me from realizing that Calden's glaring white gaze is set on me. His brows twitch between agony and rage as illuminated tears streak down his face.

With quaking hands, I reach for my warding pen, dreading the thought of using it—making Calden the first enemy that I fight. But before I can even retrieve the pen from my belt, three bodies leap at him, blocking any strike I could dare to attempt.

Alani and Odessa each snatch one of his arms, pushing Calden toward the deck. Elias wrangles Calden's other arm, but somehow, Calden's strength is magnified, and he withstands all three of them. They get him no lower than a kneel before he hurls Odessa away from him again, screaming a word that sounds like it's from the Empyreal language. Their movements are too fast to process—tumbling and rolling, shouting and slamming. Then, suddenly, there's a loud slap, followed by a hiss, like raining sand, and dust clouds the air. A crash ensues, and several deckhands race toward the hatch.

I stand from my crouch, knees wobbling. Alani is gone, and now there's a massive hole in the middle of the deck where Calden must have disintegrated the timber.

Calden rises, and Odessa charges him again. Her hands coil around his forearm, but he twists, tossing her into the hole. Another clamor rattles from below as she falls into the lower deck. Without pause, Calden turns his attention to his final opponent, Elias, and fires a blue sphere toward him. Elias ducks, the sphere zipping just over his disheveled hair and toward the crew. They leap like waves in opposite directions, and a sphere collides with the starboard side, blasting a large hole in the ship.

Saltwater splashes onto the deck. My breaths turn shallow as I look across the sea, stretching endlessly beneath the dark sky.

Elias charges after Calden again, shouting his name with pleas for him to return to himself, and the two lock in a brief hand-to-hand wrestle. The sight is nauseating—Elias and Calden fighting each other. My best friend and my leader.

Do something, Nori!

Yet I still can't move. *The water.* We're all going to end up in the water. Is this how Papa felt when his ship was sinking in this same sea, taking his brother with it? How he felt when Lake Daleia tugged him under?

Flashes of the lake invade my vision. What if the sea comes alive? What if it pulls us to the bottom? It's so deep—

So deep.

Calden's ear-buzzing scream reels me back to the battle in time to see him clutch Elias's throat. I squeal, my cry lost in the uproar below. An emptiness fills Calden's face, though his eyes remain lit. Finally, the crew abandons their orders to stay back and rushes to Elias's aid. But before a hand touches Calden, Elias charges a Vitality Ward and punches it into Calden's chest. Calden stumbles back, and Elias hits him with another, making him crash into the mast Calden previously cracked. The harsh collision evokes a loud *pop* from the pole. The fissure snakes up several feet higher, and the whole shaft tilts. The ship teeters with the weight, and nausea swims through my stomach and into my throat. *The water.*

I can almost feel it, snatching me, pulling me down into even deeper depths. Seaweed entangling me—

I should never have boarded this ship.

51

ZAMIRAH

The tension in the rigging gives way, ropes sagging as the cracked mast stoops toward the water. I cling to the loosened cords, anticipating my plunge into the cold, angry waves. But just as I am holding my breath, the tipping ship pulls upright, and the sea drifts from my field of vision. The broken mast whines at the sudden shift of position, but it holds up—though slanted—dangling me several stretches above the chaotic deck.

Directly below, Captain Alani—returned from the 'tween deck where she fell—extends her bruised and bloodied arms toward the sea to force the vessel straight. All around her, saltwater surges toward the drain holes, pushed by her Talent, soon aided by Willian's mighty gusts.

The Second Lady emerges from the lower deck, just as disheveled as Captain Alani. She races to reinforce Elias as the fight moves into my view. Elias catches one of the Sovereign Prince's battered arms, and Lady Odessa snatches the other. With extra hands from the crew, they wrestle Calden against the deck, his wretched screams filling the skies, surely to be heard from the Empyrean to the pits of Gehenna. The fury, terror, and pain in his voice is so visceral, I feel it on my skin like burns.

Can they not see they are making it worse? Does no one realize that the more they fight him, the more frightened he becomes, and therefore, the more volatile?

I scold myself for taking so long to decide to come down. With all the Lady Sovereign's tales about Calden's episodes whirling through my mind, it took an endowing of bravery from El-Alam to get me to move, even after my self-proclaimed fearlessness. And just as soon as that bestowed courage mingled with my compassion for Calden, the mast fractured, obstructing my path to him.

A *pop* jerks my attention back to the ropes before the line supporting my right hand and foot breaks from the crippled mast. I swing, grappling for another source of support, but the moment I clutch it, my weight proves too great for the weakened rope, and it snaps.

All at once, the mast creaks and my other support breaks, and before I can so much as look for another line to snatch, I'm plummeting. I thrash in midair, hoping to catch myself when I land, but I don't complete the turn in time, and my shoulder smacks against the wet deck.

Yelled orders and panicked shouts blot out the noise of my yelp. Yet I don't hear Calden among the voices. *Is his episode over? Is he back?*

Cringing from the pain, I twist, hoping to find the prince's eyes returned to the stunning blue I've heard stories about since my youth. But the moment I see they are still as white as lightning, another dome of vitality erupts from his hands, knocking everyone around him to the deck. He rises, and his face finally comes into my full view—red, bruised, streaked with tears. The pain from my fall temporarily flees, replaced by a sharp agony in my heart. For years, I've heard of Calden's suffering, even wept over it as I pleaded with El-Alam on his behalf. But my imagination failed to capture the full misery of it.

I shouldn't have left him. I could tell he was still distressed. Why didn't I at least offer for him to join me in the nest?

Lady Odessa and Elias regain their feet, dashing after Calden with Snare Wards on their palms. Once more, madness fills the deck as the crew follows their lead.

"Get up, Mirah," I command myself, yet every effort stabs my shoulder like an arrow.

I grit my teeth, pushing beyond the pain to sit up. I rub my shoulder with my opposite hand, then test if I can move my injured arm. When it cooperates, I urge myself to my feet, quickly scanning for the rest of the Bind. Captain Alani remains near the hatch, focusing all her efforts on keeping the ship out of the sea's thrashing arms. Near the quarterdeck, Norielle staggers toward the mayhem, face pale and chest pulsating. She stops, clutching a rope, as if she cannot move even one more step closer.

The water. Willian told me about her lake back home, what it did to both her and her father.

I send her an empathetic thought, but leave her, setting my focus on Calden at the center of the ship. Clouds of dust puff from every non-sentient thing he touches, powdering the air. I sprint toward the fight as Lady Odessa blasts her brother with a wave of vitality. He crashes into the ship's port side, his tortured scream raising the hair on my arms.

Through the wobbling tears in my eyes, I see blood saturating Calden's white shirt over his abdomen before he turns his back. His hands clutch the railing of the ship, and in a blink, dust swarms from underneath his hold. His power eats away at board after board until water is gushing into the ship, now on both sides.

"No!" I yelp as the ship teeters, groaning like a woken giant.

I glance back to Captain Alani, finding her face redder than her hair as she strains to save her beloved vessel. Somehow, she musters the strength to push the water back and straighten the ship—but there's no way she can keep on.

This has to stop. They *have to stop.*

"Calden!" I yell, and to my alarm, he turns toward me, his expression still terrified, as if unaware that he's the one causing this destruction. Or perhaps witnessing it, yet being physically unable to stop.

But he heard me. *He heard me.*

From all his mother has told me, that doesn't happen—not unless he's returning to himself, but judging by his blazing eyes, that doesn't seem to be the case.

Then what is this?

I open my mouth to assure him we are on his side, but Lady Odessa races after him, shouting for reinforcements. And like a flame dropped onto crisp leaves, Calden's rage reignites, and he releases the most grievous cry yet as he materializes his swordstaff into his hands.

I withdraw the step forward I just took as screams split across the deck. Everyone but Lady Odessa and Elias retreats at the sight of his weapon—the one I so delicately painted beside my bunk.

"My Lady Odessa!" I shriek as she conjures her sword.

She surges after him, even though Calden has yet to begin any attack with his swordstaff. I gulp, regretting my next action before I take it—

Then I launch a weakened vitality sphere into the Second Lady's torso, pitching her sideways to keep her from reaching him.

My hand shakes as she skewers me with a stunned glower that grows more furious by the second. Then she directs her rage toward Elias in a bellowed command: "Grab him!"

"No, don't—" I whip around, only to see Elias racing after the Sovereign Prince.

I cry the prince's name as he swivels his swordstaff to attack and—

Elias catches it by the shaft.

The weapon turns horizontal, forming a bar between them. Shadows etch along their strained muscles as they contend with each other's formidable strength. Calden's heels slide, and he backsteps as Elias gains the upper hand.

I fill my lungs, the rising of my chest shooting pain through my shoulder yet again. Water slops over my ankles as I dart after them, but another loud groan from the ship stills me. The *Celestella* tilts even more fiercely than it did before. I glimpse Captain Alani, collapsed on the flooded deck yet still reaching for the sea, still fighting.

She's going to kill herself. The painful realization wrenches a cry from my throat, and yet, what can I do? Not even a Healing Ward can restore a person from overexerting their vitality.

Norielle stumbles to the captain's side, her long hair dipping into the water. She wraps herself around the captain, quaking.

"Water in the hold!" Helina shouts.

My breaths turn rapid and shallow. The entire ship is going to go under—and what will happen to our savior prince then? Our *world*?

A loud splash pulls my attention back to the port side where Calden was, but now he's gone, as is Elias. Lady Odessa clings to the wrecked railing, screaming toward the open sea.

Calden. Did they fall overboard?

"Abandon ship!" Willian cries—a broken sound.

My fists squeeze when he repeats the call, even more shattered. *Willian*, my sweet friend. *Hurting.* I twist to find him beside Norielle.

The captain hangs limp in his arms.

El-Alam, no. More tears well up in my eyes. *Don't let her be lost. Please, no.*

But there's no time—no time for reassurances or grief. For the sea's hunger does not relent, and it will not be satisfied until this ship lies in pieces on the ocean floor.

"My lady," I say, turning to face the same woman I knocked over only moments ago. "Come with me."

ELIAS

Freezing water hits my face, stealing my chance to catch my breath, and the current knocks me back under. I thrash my arms, kicking, fighting though I've already exhausted myself, until I crest the waves again. The muted noises become clearer—the screams and shouts of the crew, the creaking of the ship.

Gasping, I twist each way, searching the teetering waves for Cal. I knocked us both overboard, having not realized how close we were to the hole in the ship's side. But now where is he? Is he conscious? Can he swim in his present state?

I look back for the ship, alarmed to find it so far away. Another roll of the sea sweeps me even farther from it. Boats—I see them in the water, but they're all so distant. And Cal. Where is Cal?

A horrid, gurgling roar jerks my attention to the far left, and right before the sloshing water drags him under again, I spot Cal's pale hair and blazing white eyes.

Empyreal Skies. When will this episode end?

"Cal! Calden!" I yell, though it's worthless because he slides back underwater the next second.

I dive after him, swimming harder away from the ship. With every wide stroke of my arms, I bob under the surface and back out. Saltwater spills into my mouth, and coughing wrecks my opportunities to breathe. But I swim and swim, and I never reach him.

Where is he? Under? Is he sinking?

I look back at the ship. The sea has already swallowed half of it. I can barely see the boats beyond it. Is anyone going to come back for us? Do they even know where we are?

My breaths staccato into short puffs that hardly seem to reach my lungs, but I force myself to peel my desperate gaze from the boats. I'm not going to them without Cal. He's somewhere—somewhere close. If I swim away now, I may never find him.

I remember my Bind Mark and check it for his direction, then plunge beneath the water. The cold surrounds me, the currents driving me away from my hope of survival. I open my eyes, keeping them wide despite the sting of saltwater, then I awaken a Glory Ward and channel its light through my palm.

But the light is dim, half the strength of a flame torch. I curse it. This won't last long. I'm running out of energy, which also makes me nearly defenseless against Cal.

If I ever find him.

My faint light illuminates specks and murk and the occasional fish, but I don't see Cal. I swim deeper, following my Bind Mark. My pulse throbs in my neck. There could be something else in these waters, something that doesn't want Cal to escape. Could it sense he's the one Toaph chose? Is that where he's gone—dragged under like Nori in Lake Daleia? How could I ever reach the ocean's depths?

A need for air forces me to the surface, and I pant, checking again to see how far I am from the others, but water spills over me, sending me under again. When I fight my way back up,

I'm facing the other way, and there I glimpse him—Cal, limply bobbing in the waves before he's sucked under again.

"Cal!" I call, my frantic, jerky motions propelling me after him.

I ignite my Glory Ward again, but the light depletes before I reach him. Luckily, his wide, glowing eyes are shining in the water to guide me. But they stare aimlessly at the surface.

Like he's dead.

Cal, don't you dare.

I swim even harder, expending more of my energy reserves. This is the future Sovereign of the Wardens. Toaph's chosen. The leader of the Bind I never should have been allowed in. The hope for our world.

But he's also my friend. One who never knew Kieran and still took me as I am today. Who mentored me when he never had to. Who put this mark on my wrist and decided I deserved to be part of saving this world.

Even if his dead body is all I have to take back with me, I'm not leaving him.

I follow those gleaming eyes deeper beneath the water until he's finally within reach. I stretch out, kicking until I can grab him—

His whole body convulses at my touch, a muted scream causing bubbles to surge from his mouth that glint in the light of his eyes. I recoil, but then his eyes drift shut, and he goes completely still. With nerves buzzing in my hands, I grab for him again, this time seizing him without retaliation.

I heft him under my arm and beg my body to find strength enough to get us back to the surface, and that by some Empyrean-sent miracle, a boat will be there waiting.

The return to the surface takes an eternity, like we've sunk into the chasms of Gehenna itself, and by the time my head is above water, I don't have enough strength to hoist Cal up for air.

Between slaps of water, I suck in oxygen. Then I look around for the miracle I hoped for.

No. No miracle. No boats—

Wait.

I blink the saltwater from my eyes. Is that—? Am I hallucinating?

"Elias!" a female voice shouts, but my ears are too full of water to tell who she is.

"I got him!" I croak.

After a few more rapid blinks, I see it's not one woman, but two. By the dark, slender features of the one, I recognize Odessa. But the other? All I can tell is she's smaller. The women paddle toward us, sparing me some of the swim, and finally, hands are reaching down to take Cal from me. The identity of the other girl becomes clear—Zamirah—as they hoist Cal into the boat, barely keeping it from tipping over. His dense body thumps inside, and Odessa reaches for me, cuts marring her arm and her usually flawless face. She tugs me aboard, and I collapse into the boat. The vessel rocks violently for several seconds before steadying itself against the sea's troubled motions. I remain where I flopped in, holding myself up by the elbows, panting.

I made it. I'm on a boat. I got Cal.

I got Cal.

Please tell me he is alive.

"He still has a pulse," Zamirah says. "But he's not breathing."

I urge my exhausted self to sit up. Cal's eyes are sealed shut, his head lying in the girl's lap. She clutches his shirt with one hand and strokes his hair with her other, as if she witnessed none of what he just did—like she's oblivious to how dangerous he is. But I know she's not. Not even close to it.

"Should we try to heal him?" Zamirah asks, turning her attention to Odessa.

Odessa stares vacantly for a while, like she's not sure. I don't have an answer either. Will healing him restore his consciousness enough for him to attack us again?

When no one answers, Zamirah tries to roll Cal onto his side, but she releases a moan of pain. Realizing she's injured, I reach out to help her. My fatigued muscles hardly muster the strength to tug him off her lap and to the base of the boat. I eye the girl, too worn to say anything, but I gesture for her to slap his back to help clear his lungs. She seems to understand and obeys—she probably knows to do it anyway, but maybe since this is the Sovereign Prince, she had apprehensions about hitting him.

Or maybe she is more afraid of him attacking her than it first seemed.

Odessa paddles against the waves, fighting to catch up with the others as Zamirah smacks Cal's back. I turn my attention to the ocean. Despite the moonlight, I can hardly see the other boats, let alone tell which faces made it onto them. And the ship is gone.

Nori.

El-Alam, please let Nori be on one of those boats.

The thud of the girl's hand whapping Cal's back is the only sound besides the sloshing of the paddle for a time. Then, finally, Cal coughs. All three of us still, eyes honed on him, waiting. Several moments of quiet pass, then a raspy cry makes us jolt.

Cal's eyes open—blue, then glaring white.

Not again.

Zamirah stiffens, but rather than scooting to the far side of the boat, she leans over him, her wet clumps of hair sweeping off her shoulders and hanging near Cal's face.

"*Shhh*," she whispers, stroking his cheek with her quivering hands. "Everything is all right, Calden."

Cal's cry breaks into a whimper, and he doesn't move. Doesn't attack. Only cries at the base of the boat.

Zamirah wraps her arms around his head, offering him more reassurances. "You're on a boat, Calden. You are safe. We are all safe. You can see what you need to see."

I gape at the scene. No one has ever dared get close to him when he's like this, unless it's to wrestle him down. We've always jumped into defensive mode, binding and suppressing him until it's over. Would this have worked from the beginning? Could this girl have subdued him with a comforting touch if she'd been able to reach us?

In the stillness, I finally notice all the blood and bruises covering Cal. His white shirt is torn in the arms and stomach, stained red. His blood seeps into the girl's yellow dress as she holds him, tears slipping from her eyes. Cal quiets, though his eyes remain lit. Slowly, Zamirah peels away from him, looking between Odessa and me.

Odessa's lips tighten, like she's trying to resist the urge to join in with the weeping—Odessa, the fierce and often stoic Second Lady of the Wardens. She keeps paddling. I stare down at my hands. They look like Cal's whole body, torn up and bleeding. I'm still shaking, and my pulse feels like it will never slow again.

"Do you need healing?" Zamirah asks.

"If anyone's getting healed, it's him," I say. "I'm fine."

Am I? The longer I sit here, the more aware I become of every injury I sustained. Something stings across my side, and my face is pulsing over my right cheekbone.

Zamirah gives me a doubtful look, but Cal whines, drawing her focus back down. She inspects the bleeding wound on his stomach.

"Lady Odessa?" she prompts more urgently. "Shall we heal him?

Odessa trains her focus on the boats in the distance. "I can't heal my brother." The words are quiet, like she didn't want to admit them.

Zamirah looks at me next.

Could I? Even if I had any power left to heal with?

She shakes her head before I can respond, as if realizing I've depleted my energy. Her hands move to Calden's face, brushing salty clumps of hair away. "I can manage it."

I raise a brow at her. *She* means to do it?

"He's losing too much blood," she presses, already lifting Cal's head back into her lap. "If we don't heal him now, we might lose him."

"Be careful, Zamirah," Odessa says. "I don't know how he will respond."

Zamirah nods, unbuttoning a pocket in her dress and retrieving her pen from its depths.

CALDEN

Violent gusts whip my hair against my face as I struggle to stand without being blown over in the wind. My feet, once booted, are now bare, toes sinking into the dense blanket of gray dust. It surrounds me on every side, stretching from one end of the horizon to the other like the sea. Tiny particles swirl in the air, sprinkling my sleeves and tickling the back of my throat. I cough, shielding my mouth with my cloak. My eyes squint through the turbulent, grimy air at the gray world around me. Even the sky above is gray, sheeted in dark clouds.

"I'm going to heal you, all right?" a voice says, as if trapped inside the howling wind. "Please don't be afraid. No one is trying to hurt you."

I spin a full revolution, searching again for who is speaking to me, but I find not even a tree or stone. The dust is all there is. Yet the terror that I felt moments prior has fled, as if banished by her voice. Where is she? *Who* is she? I recognize her voice, but her identity feels lost beneath the layers of dust underfoot.

I've been here before. The thought strikes me like an arrow piercing through fog, and upon its impact, the haze over my mind clears.

The other mind. I'm in the other mind.

"It's going to be okay, Calden," the voice speaks again, so far away and yet so close.

Calden. Yes. That's my name. And the voice—is that not Zamirah?

I gasp—a mistake, for it makes me choke on the dust—and adrenaline buzzes through my limbs. I remember. I actually remember.

I know why I am here.

But I no sooner think it before something launches overhead, colliding somewhere beyond my vision with a thunderous *crash*. The noise rumbles through the atmosphere, obstructed only by the whooshing of the wind. In the sky, a trail of light dissipates into the gray.

"Toaph?" I whisper, but the sound doesn't escape my lips.

Where is my voice?

A figure emerges from the dusty haze, wings spread as wide as the *Celestella*'s sails. I can hardly see more than the silhouette, but the double-sided swordstaff the being clutches gives him away. It *is* him—*Toaph Elbara*. Our Empyreal Guardian.

I *found* him.

Another blast rattles the sky as something like a Vitality Ward fires directly at the Guardian. He deflects it with a spin of his staff, and the red orb's path redirects straight toward me. Another soundless yelp escapes me, and my heels slide back in a pointless attempt to evade the massive sphere of energy. I raise my arms before the orb strikes—

But its red glow only passes through me and explodes against the ground, kicking up more dust into the wind. When I return my gaze to the sky, the silhouette of another winged figure looms in the distance. It rushes toward Toaph Elbara, wielding a massive sword. I hardly have a moment to comprehend that this must be Ta'Nathel before he sweeps his sword and a wave of fire shoots from the thick blade. Toaph turns, but the flames catch on his left wing, blazing from orange to blue as it eats at the feathers.

Toaph returns the attack with a blast of cerulean energy, then the two Guardians shift from magic to weapons, blades clanging in the sky. My cloak flaps as I stand, staring like a statue at the battle overhead.

What is this? Is this happening now? Is it a vision of the future? Or the past?

The Guardians' voices are like thunder that surrounds me as they close in. They grunt and shout in Empyreal words—accusations and orders to leave, from what little I can interpret. The angrier their voices grow, the more violent the wind stirs until its thrashes are too much for me to remain standing.

I crouch, shielding myself with my cloak. Even on the ground, the aggressive gusts rock my body, and I have to fight to maintain my balance. Still, I peer over my covering at the fight. The Guardians are close enough now for me to discern their armor that shields every inch of them besides their glowing eyes. Blasts and rumbles, flashes and bolts, accompany their furious attacks, filling the atmosphere like a terrible storm is upon it. Then, suddenly, a loud cry—as beautiful as it is agonized—ruptures the noise, and the wind slows.

I flutter my dust-salted eyes as the Guardian I deemed to be Toaph falls toward the ground like a bird shot in flight. Ta'Nathel bounds after him, webs of glowing red igniting across the blade of his sword as he aims it toward Toaph.

"No!" I yell, jumping to my feet like I might defend the Guardian. But again, my voice has no sound. As if I don't even exist here.

Ta'Nathel's blade, charged by the velocity of his flight, pierces the breastplate of Toaph's armor. From this distance, I can't tell if it makes it through, only that Toaph screams again. Utterly despairing.

Ta'Nathel's sword brightens, the red webs spidering over the blade like lightning. The bolts spread to Toaph, sizzling across his armor, then his wings. His cries vibrate the ground beneath me, as if it was from his voice that landquakes were formed. A loud crackling noise drowns out his bellows, and the dust on the ground starts to slip into the earth. Then I see them—the fissures in the ground. It's breaking apart. From Toaph? From Ta'Nathel?

I leap away as a crack slithers beneath me, only to land on another. But the dying notes of Toaph's scream distract me from caring about my safety—if it even matters in this place—and my full attention turns to him. His swordstaff, I finally realize, is not in his hand. It's in the shifting dust, being dragged away by the motion.

Could I bring it to him? Can I help?

All my former efforts have proved worthless, but how can I just stand here watching this?

I lunge forward, only for a dome-like explosion to swell from Toaph, thrusting Ta'Nathel back. I freeze, expecting Toaph to rise, yet he lies still, and a second later, Ta'Nathel soars toward him, his malevolent sword aimed to finish what he began. He thrusts it toward Toaph's chest again. I wince and shrink away, ears ringing with the expectation of hearing Toaph scream once more.

Instead, silence.

I look back through the blond streaks of my wind-tossed hair. Toaph is gone.

He's *gone*.

What happened? Did Ta'Nathel slay him? Did he vanish beneath Ta'Nathel's blade?

There's a long pause, enough for me to notice the damage done to Ta'Nathel as well. A tear on his right wing, cracks in his armor.

The intruder Guardian writhes in each direction like he's searching. A furious roar explodes from him, then his blazing gaze turns toward me, as if suddenly sensing me here.

I retreat a step. But in my next blink, the world of dust disappears, and I find myself somewhere else.

NORIELLE

Silent tears stream from my eyes as I scan the boats. Elias isn't on any of them. No one knows where he went. And I don't see Odessa either.

Will they turn up as lifeless bodies floating in the sea?

I twist my Bind Mark into view, checking that Willian is still rowing us in the direction of Calden's faded arrow. *Faded.* Dying. Our Bind leader, my rescuer, our hope for the world, is *dying*.

Just like our precious captain—my friend—lying at our feet.

"Willian, more to the east," I say, showing him the arrow.

Willian nods and paddles with more effort in the adjusted direction. Behind me, Orto joins in with the other paddle. If only the Bind Mark could tell distance like the Omen Mark. How far are we from Calden? What state will he be in when we find him? Underwater? On a boat?

El-Alam, tell me he's on a boat and that Elias is with him. Alive. Let Elias be alive.

The thought that the kiss we shared could be both our first and last at once produces a cramp in my side. I'm still not sure if he even fully believed me—that I chose him. That I love *him*. Just as he is.

Did he die not knowing how much I meant that?

Alani's quiet moan draws my hands back to her. I stroke her ginger coils away from her blood-smeared face. Willian's Healing Ward sealed her wounds, but apparently, nothing can cure a Warden who has overextended their energy besides time and rest—should they survive long enough to recover. Alani drew from her own life force to sustain the vessel as long as she did.

And still the sea devoured the *Celestella*—the ship she was so excited to captain.

I avert my gaze, too pained to look at her. But the sight of the black water around us only renews the trembling in my core. I shut my eyes, wishing for somewhere to flee to in my mind, somewhere safe. But there's nowhere to go that doesn't hurt. No pleasant escape in my imagination or memories like I found while dying in the crypt. Everything I try just reminds me of Elias and his absence or how far away I am from my family. I don't even have Papa's sword to cling to for comfort. I'd forgotten it in the chaos, and now it's going down with the ship—hopeless to be recovered unless I become a Master someday and can use that Conjuration Ward on it to summon it into my hand.

I grip the strap of my satchel which contains the only belongings I have left since I was already wearing it. But the record book inside is surely waterlogged, just like my notetaking journal and snacks inside.

A low sound suddenly rumbles, as if from the depths of the sea, and my eyes open to find the water rippling.

"W-Willian?" I stutter as the sound fades.

Willian goes still, then Orto. I look up to the dark sky, expecting a thunderhead to have appeared over us, but all I see are stars.

What was that?

The sound repeats with more ferocity, vibrating the boat. Willian turns around as the deep resonance fades beneath the slapping of the waves, and the sight of his pale face shortens my breath.

"There's something in the water." His voice is hollow, thin.

I shake my head, as if I could simply reject this reality and it would pass from us. "What something?"

Willian peers over the edge of the boat as another rumble quakes the dark sea. "I-I can't see. I don't know."

He retracts his paddle, directing his attention across the bumpy stretch of water to the nearest boat. The passengers—all members of the crew—are already looking our way, visibly horrified even from so far away.

Fear crawls across me like a million tiny spiders, paralyzing me. Alani is barely alive. Willian drained most of his power. Our other three Masters are missing. Who knows if Calden has regained consciousness, and even if he has, *he's dying*.

Tears swarm my eyes. *No more, E-Alam. Please, no more.*

And yet another rumble quakes the sea.

CALDEN

A forest full of evergreens surrounds me, much like the woods where I found Norielle, only here the trees are much denser. I lay my hand against one's bark, testing to see if I can feel it. The rough texture satisfies my fingertips, but my pulse throbs through my body.

Where is Toaph? Dead? Is this now Ta'Nathel's world? Where am I?

"Hello?" I attempt to call, but my voice still doesn't work.

I tilt my head back. Stars peek through a canopy of silhouetted trees, and a crescent moon shines its fragile light through the branches. An owl hoots, and a small creature skitters into the brush near my feet.

Everything seems so... tranquil. So very different from the place where I last was.

The faint sound of voices turns me to the left, and I register the soft crunching of footsteps against dried pine needles and crispy leaves. I shift behind a tree trunk, attuning my ears to their voices. One figure is male, with a bag slumped on his back and a basket hanging from the crook of his arm. The other is a female with a smaller pack on her back. Both have bedrolls hitched to their luggage.

Travelers, but where are they going?

I sneak a look around the tree, spying them as they pass me. I miss my chance to glimpse their faces, but the man's hair seems light—blond, maybe. A velvet cloak shrouds the female, but she is carrying something close to her chest.

My brows press together as I watch them. What am I doing here? What are *they* doing here?

Should I follow them?

My curiosity answers for me. I creep behind them, careful to stay close to the trees, though I'm not sure if they'd see me even if they looked. My footsteps, much like my voice, don't make a sound.

The couple—I realize they are so when the man wraps his unoccupied arm around the woman—continues their chatter as their path winds toward a massive lake. A musty smell mingles with the freshness of pine, growing stronger the closer we get to the water.

The number of places to hide dwindles as the trees thin along the lakeshore, and I'm forced to stay back too far to hear anything but the murmur of their exchange. The woman stops, turning toward the man, and finally, I spot what she's carrying.

A baby. A small, peacefully resting baby, wrapped in a warm blanket.

The man turns to face the woman, and though dimly lit, I glimpse his face. His extremely familiar face...

He looks... like me?

Only, his hair is a couple of inches longer than mine, and a full beard fills his jaw.

Is he me? Is this a vision of the future?

With a gentle hand, the man nudges his wife's chin so that she tilts her face toward him. From my angle and with her hood,

I still can't see any of her features. The man kisses her forehead, then both their gazes turn down to the baby. The man's smile stirs a cold feeling in my chest.

Such a happy father. Something I've never fathomed becoming. Yet he looks so much like me...

Suddenly, the man gasps, and the basket falls from his arm, food supplies spilling into the grass. He draws his wife and baby close, and I follow his wide gaze to a blue wisp jittering toward them through the trees. Its light flickers like a dying flame fighting to stay alive, but the blue of it... it's the exact shade as the energy Toaph wielded.

Is this him? Is this how he fled Ta'Nathel—as a spirit?

It must be.

Whispers riddle the air, growing louder as the wisp approaches. The Empyreal words are barely discernable, but I register it is requesting that the people not be afraid. I sneak from my hiding place as the wisp stops, hovering a short distance from the small family. The woman twists to look at it, but again, her hood hides her face. From the orb, a thin mist stretches like a vine toward the baby, and the whispers intensify. Through the lengthy Empyreal utterances, a sentence becomes clear in the Silvirdian common tongue.

"Lay down your child."

Yes. That's the same voice—the one whose words have echoed through my mind incessantly for weeks. *I fled. I failed.*

The wisp *must* be Toaph's spirit.

But the man doesn't move, his knuckles turning white as he clutches his wife even tighter.

Toaph's spirit repeats the demand, but then another noise draws our attention toward the deep woods—a guttural rumble that causes the pebbles on the ground to tremble. The spirit's glow flickers again. When it steadies, the light is dimmer than before.

"Lay down the child," Toaph's spirit repeats through another chorus of Empyreal whispers.

The man exchanges a look with his wife. After another long pause, he lowers the infant to the ground, almost as if they realize who this spirit is and feel compelled to obey him.

"Stand aside," the spirit orders.

The father pulls his wife back, and the wisp dissolves from its orb-like form into a smoky, luminescent vapor. The mist slithers around them, passing over both their faces, and they collapse. I lunge a step forward, but freeze as the mist glides toward the child, seeping into the baby's mouth and nose, as if breathed in.

I cover my lips, though my shout makes no noise. And for a moment, everything is like me. Silent. No hooting owls. No rumbles from the deep woods. Not even a cry from the infant.

Then a shrill noise splinters the quiet—the baby screaming. His eyes open, brilliant white, like Toaph Elbara's. Like mine, when I am overcome by an episode.

Me. The baby is me.

The realization tightens my hand's clasp over my mouth, and I back away until I bump into a tree. This is a vision from the past. A memory.

Those are my parents. *My* parents. My blood father and mother—lying in the dirt, unconscious.

And this is the moment Toaph Elbara chose me.

NORIELLE

T he roaring noise ceases, leaving behind only the whispers of the sea, but my Omen Mark is still glaring red.

Does whatever is beneath us not realize we are here? Or is it just readying its attack?

My lips tremble as I look back at Orto, seeking his reassurance, but he's watching the water, skepticism deepening the lines on his face. "Orto," I whisper.

He swallows hard as he faces me.

I don't know what I want from him. He can't promise me we're safe—he couldn't, even if he had a voice to speak with.

"We're too far apart," Willian mutters, reluctantly lowering his paddle toward the water. I hold my breath as it dips below, fully expecting something to snatch it from his hand like what happened to me in Lake Daleia. But Willian manages three gentle strokes without even a groan from the deep.

The crewmates nearby mimic Willian, turning their dinghy toward us. But why does it matter if we are apart? Will us being closer together somehow help us if whatever we heard attacks? Or will it only make it easier for it to kill us all at once?

Calden, why aren't you here? We need you.

I steal another glance at the mark. It points in the same direction as before, toward where the moon hangs. But is it... darker than before?

My heart flutters. *Darker.* Then he's improving—which must mean someone found him. Someone *healed* him. Was it Elias? It had to have been—

Or Odessa, I realize as I recall that my last sighting of her was her searching the water, just before Orto dragged me to the lifeboats. She must have gone after her brother.

A sting fills my eyes despite my relief about Calden. *Where is Elias?*

The boat dips and dunks along the rolling waves as Willian and Orto propel us toward the other dinghy. The other boats are lost from sight now. Willian ordered them to continue toward Raevre while we searched for the others. But now I'm wishing they hadn't left us. There's only a handful of us if the beast below should—

A bassy moan, like an amplified whale call, interrupts my thoughts, and everyone freezes. Close. The noise was so near, I felt it shaking my bones. I grip the edge of my seat as the water suddenly pulls us in a new direction. But the current only tugs us for a short stretch before relenting, as if something moved the water as it swam past us.

I squint in the direction it seemed to travel in, watching the nightglow teeter on the disturbed waves. Then, suddenly, the moonglade on the water splits, a dark mass rising where the moon once reflected. I jump back, covering my mouth to mute my yelp as what I realize is a massive, scaled head dips beneath the water again. Its back spines poke up from the waves just before it dives lower. Three fierce heartbeats later, its thick tail whips over the surface. And then it's gone.

Gone. It left us.

I peel my hand from my mouth, ready to breathe a sigh of relief, but then I glimpse my Bind Mark again, and the air jerks back into my lungs.

Calden. It's heading toward Calden.

CALDEN

I stand over my parents, weeping soundlessly, as I watch their chests rise and fall. They are alive—in front of me—and yet, I can't will my weakened knees to bend and lower me any closer to their unconscious bodies.

I study their moonlit faces as the infant-me's cries dwindle, the light dimming from his eyes. My father's features are truly my own, though now that I am closer, I can spot the slight differences in the shape of our cheekbones and the angles of our eyebrows. My mother, who I can at last see, has soft features—muted brown hair and lightly tanned skin. In her sleep, she looks so at ease. What will she do when she wakes?

A moth flutters between us, white wings humming before it lands on my mother's still hand. I crouch at last to shoo it away, but I freeze, spotting a familiar marking on her wrist, nearly hidden by her long sleeve.

An Omen Mark.

I gasp and twist to look at my father's limp arm. Sure enough, another Omen Mark peeks from beneath the cuff of his sleeve.

Wardens. My parents are—*were?*—Wardens. But why haven't I seen them before? Do they die here beside the lake? Or—

My attention returns to the bag strapped to my mother's back, and understanding coalesces. A young baby. Two traveling Wardens.

They must be journeying to the citadel to have me blessed and endowed by the Elders, as all Wardens do with their young.

But where are they from? Somewhere in Alémor that's too far from the citadel for them to attend our balls, like Zamirah's family? Or could they be from another kingdom altogether?

I lean closer to further inspect their features. With their light skin, they aren't likely to hail from Schillon or Raevre, but perhaps Ashtera? The kingdom known for its mighty mountains and violent storms?

Their features *do* align with the common characteristics of the Ashterians...

Something crunches to my right. I jump to my feet, fearing that I'll find Ta'Nathel approaching between the trees with his massive blade at the ready. Instead, I meet a pair of moonlike eyes, staring at the infant-me who is lying, now quiet, in the grass. I have hardly a chance to register the eyes' familiarity before the wolflike creature leaps from the brush, the glimmers on its midnight fur twinkling like stars.

"Echo?" I ask, but still no sound exits my lips.

The canyx pays me no notice, his focus fixed on the infant-me. A sorrowful whine rises from his throat as he stoops near my small form. His head turns each way before his gaze lands on the fallen basket. With a flick of his tail, he creeps toward the basket and digs out what few supplies didn't spill when my father dropped it. Once it's empty, he paws the basket upright, then he turns to the baby, ears tucked back and tail low.

I ease a step closer to watch as Echo gently takes the blanket wrapped around infant-me in his teeth. He lifts me from the ground, gingerly carrying me toward the basket. The little-me coos obliviously as Echo sets me inside the basket. Then, with more adeptness than a trained household dog, the ancient Sentry tugs on the blankets to better wrap me. My tiny hands reach out for him, chubby fingers fumbling until they reach Echo's muzzle. He nudges me back, just as he did in my recent encounters, then his teeth clamp around the basket handle and he lifts me, carrying me along the lake's edge.

What is he doing? Why is he taking me away from my parents?

I shift to chase after him, but a realization pulls me up short.

He's taking me to the citadel to surrender me to the Sovereigns.

Because he saw where Toaph's spirit went.

Inside *me.*

I stumble backward, only to trip on a root and fall. But when I hit the ground, my eyes open to a treeless, star-flecked sky and a pair of teary green-gold eyes staring down at me.

I blink, everything that transpired in my mind fading like a dream disappearing upon waking. I clutch my fists, internally grappling for the visions—but only fragments remain.

Still, I catch hold of one sight above all others: the blue mist sinking into the baby.

Into me.

"I know where he is," I croak without taking a moment to process where I am or why Zamirah is leaning over me, crying. "I know where Toaph Elbara is."

At my rising, Zamirah scoots back to help me sit up, and I realize I was lying with my head in her lap. Blood saturates her yellow dress, and by the red-stained rip in my shirt, I presume it's mine. I hold her wide gaze for a moment, noticing I hardly feel any pain. Was she *healing* me? While I lay in the other mind?

The utter exhaustion in her eyes and how she holds her abdomen in the same place the blood stains my shirt answers my questions a moment before I notice the dark water glinting in the moonlight right behind her.

Why is it so close?

I jerk my gaze around, finding that I'm surrounded by the ocean, and ahead of me, in the longboat, sits Elias, looking like he lost a terrible fight, and Odessa, clutching a paddle.

A paddle. A boat. My heart stammers. *Where is the ship? Where is everyone else?*

What happened to Elias?

"Calden," Odessa says urgently. "You know where Toaph is?"

I shift my focus back to her, but my mouth only hangs open. How could I claim such a thing out loud? Will anyone even believe me?

"He's—" *This can't be possible.* "He's inside me."

"What?" Odessa and Elias spew the question at once.

"What do you mean?" Elias adds.

Air swells in my chest but remains there for several bobs of the boat before I can muster another word. "I saw him and Ta'Nathel fighting, but then Ta'Nathel slayed him or... *something.* The next time I saw Toaph, he was but an orb, a wisp. He found me as a baby with my blood parents..." Sorrow wells up inside me, washing away my ability to speak. *My parents.* What happened to them after Echo carried me away? Why didn't Echo leave them to finish the journey if they were already taking me to the citadel? Did he sense they wouldn't after what they witnessed—or at least, that they wouldn't agree to leave me with the Sovereigns?

Was it not their choice to abandon me after all?

"Calden?" Odessa presses again, jerking my thoughts from my parents and back to the Guardian. "Tell us what happened."

"Toaph's spirit..." Every word comes out slowly, taking a force of will to form each syllable. "It entered me."

Zamirah sucks in a breath, her face out of my field of vision. But Elias's and Odessa's mouths open wide, eyes boggling at me. I turn my gaze downward, wanting to hide from their reactions, from everything. What does this all mean? An *Empyreal Guardian's* spirit is inside of me? I'm not *cursed*. I'm a *vessel* harboring the soul of an immortal being.

How am I even alive?

Questions about this revelation bombard me like fists pounding into my head, but I'm too mentally weak to even begin answering them. So, I turn my focus back to my location. This boat is not where I last was. I dimly recall being inside the galley, regretting ever turning us toward Raevre, when the waves of the other mind began crashing over me. I rushed out to the main deck, thinking I might ready myself to jump overboard should it prove necessary.

But the dust overcame everything one step outside the galley.

"Where is the ship?" I ask.

Everyone stares at me, leaving a long quiet in response to my question. A long and telling quiet.

A jagged breath stutters in through my nose. "I–I destroyed it, didn't I?"

Elias's lips form a frown, offering no reply. Behind him, Odessa gives the slightest nod.

"I destroyed it." My voice cracks, and my lungs seem to collapse inside my ribs.

"It wasn't you, Calden," Zamirah whispers, a steady stream of tears glistening down her cheeks.

She repeats her reassurance twice more—*it wasn't you*—reminding me of her promise in the crow's nest. She'd say it until I believed it. Yet how can I? How can I not blame myself as we float, alone, in a boat with our ship surely sinking to the sea's depths—if any of it even remains?

"Where is everyone else?" I ask. "Alani? Norielle?"

"They went ahead," Zamirah answers. "Odessa and I came after you and Elias. He's the one who retrieved you from the water."

Retrieved me from the water?

I look again at his battered face, only now realizing what must have happened to him. *Me.* I did that. What if I had killed him?

"Calden, it wasn't you," Zamirah says again, laying her hands on my arms like an invitation for me to return to the place where I was when I woke—with her.

I lean toward her, succumbing to both my physical weakness and my inability to resist my need for someone's comfort. She wraps her arms around me, and at the sound of her weeping, I surrender my inhibitions to reciprocate her embrace.

But even in her arms, my mind returns to Toaph. His spirit—inside of me. Why hasn't the Guardian left me? Can he not? Or does he mean to use me to face Ta'Nathel?

My muscles seize at the thought. *Me*—facing Ta'Nathel. No. That can't be Toaph's intention. Why would he limit himself to my mortal form?

But why else would he still be within me?

"We're going to figure this out together," Zamirah whispers over me, as if I asked my questions aloud. "You're not alone in this. Everything is going to be all right."

But she no sooner finishes uttering the words when a deep roar shakes the sea.

Zamirah jerks away from me, and I sit up straight, turning to look toward where the noise came from. I clear my bleary vision in time to see a black-scaled beast surging from the waves.

NORIELLE

I pull the paddle from Orto's insistent grip and plunge it into the water. Despite his resistance, the elderly man thanks me with a pat to my arm, though I only claimed the paddle to propel this boat faster. Whatever that monolithic beast was, it's heading toward Calden. Calden, and possibly Elias and Odessa. I don't know what we could do if we find them, but we can't leave them.

I can't leave them.

The other dinghy gains the lead, occupied by four crewmates. Helina, Valrone, a burly man whose name I never caught, and the man who played the cittern.

I steal a glance at my Omen Mark. The red tinge is still dark, but it looks slightly more vibrant than the last time. Maybe the beast slowed?

Or it's found them already.

"On track?" Willian asks between pants.

I look at my other wrist to check my Bind Mark. "On track."

How I wish we weren't. I wanted to see Calden's arrow and the Omen Mark no longer pointing in the same direction.

My arms are just starting to shake from my efforts when, suddenly, the boat launches forward. I retract my paddle from the water, twisting toward Alani to find her eyes barely open and her quivering fingers pointed toward the sea. *Alani, stop,* I think, but I can't make myself say it out loud, because we need her. We'll never catch the beast otherwise with how quickly it swam.

Willian turns back, giving his captain a grieved look. But same as myself, he withholds any opposition. Nothing—no one—can be placed ahead of retrieving Calden.

Even if this must be the death of us all.

Alani's magic current tugs us along for several minutes before a thunderous rumble blares through the night. This time, the noise is clear—no longer muted by the water.

And far in the distance, I see the monster's dark figure cresting the waves. A blue light launches after it, and another storm-shaming roar bursts from its wide, toothy mouth. Then it dives below the surface again.

I set down my paddle, hands trembling as I double-check the wards I drew on my arms while Orto was paddling. Will I even be able to ignite them?

I swallow hard, assuring myself I don't have a choice.

Alani's propulsion suddenly gives way, and our boat slows a fair stretch from the other dinghy. Her hand falls limp again, but she's still breathing. Still hanging on. *Stay with us, Alani.*

I squint through the darkness, desperate to see who the figures are on the vessel just up ahead.

Odessa. Calden. Zamirah...

"*Elias!*" I shriek, an utterly foolish thing to do with a monster below.

He turns, smiling wide enough that even the distance between us can't obscure it, but his face quickly falls, fear thinning his voice as he yells back. "Get away! Go back!"

But before I can shake my head in argument, the beast's large snout reemerges, thrashing its pointed teeth toward their boat. A current of blue energy from Odessa smashes into it, and the monster recoils beneath the water with another raucous growl.

"Orto." Alani's weak voice is hardly audible; still, I'm alarmed to even hear it. "Pull me up."

The man delays for a moment, but with a deep frown pressed on his lips, he reaches past me to hoist Alani upright. He supports her wobbling form as she seems to fight her eyelids to open wide enough to see Calden and Elias's vessel. Again, she reaches for the water, this time using it to tug their boat toward us.

But before they are more than a few feet closer, the monster blasts from the sea again, tossing their boat out of the water. The dinghy flips, discarding all four passengers in midair, and they drop, screaming, into the sloshing waves. The beast's massive head jerks each way, as if searching for which one it wants to devour first. Then it lunges after someone with dark hair.

Is that Elias?

I stand, knees wobbling as I force myself to balance on the teetering boat. My ready-made Vitality Ward tingles to life on my arm, and I aim it at the beast. But another blue sphere launches, its speed creating a trail of water as it zips across the surface. It collides with the flat top of the beast's head, and the creature yowls, twisting away from its prey a moment before its jaws might have captured them.

The beast turns toward its attacker—Calden—bobbing in the chaotic current, and I spy Zamirah's face behind the beast's tail right before she's pulled under by the waves.

I pivot my aim as the monster charges after Calden. His palm raises toward the beast, like he'll defend himself, but nothing comes out this time. My hand trembles as I reignite my Vitality Ward—

Come on, Nori.

The sphere spews from my hand and blasts the beast straight in its slanted black eye. Saltwater sprays from its mouth as it roars, the noise crackling in my ears. Its head whips in my direction, and terror represses any pride in my strike.

What have I done?

The monster plunges under the water, and Willian sets down his oar. He splays his hands in front of him, and a howl resounds as a powerful gust pounds against one side of the bow. Water sprays as the wind pushes our dinghy, throwing us into a quick spiral. I crouch, gripping the edges of the boat.

Scales and teeth rise from the dark waves, missing our vessel by inches, and Orto blasts the beast with a sizzling orb. The force of his vitality knocks us back and cracks the scales of the beast. Then, just as it's rerouting toward our spinning boat, an orb smashes into its side, shot from afar. The monster yowls again, writhing toward what I now realize is the four crewmates' boat, finally caught up with us.

One crewmate—Helina, I guess by her stout form—clutches a rope. I follow its slithering line to a circular buoy bobbing in the waves. Someone's dark arms hug it tight.

Odessa, I register.

Helina reels it in, hauling the Second Lady toward her vessel, but not nearly fast enough to contend with the beast's strokes. A pair of orbs shoot from the other two crewmates, one bursting against the monster's saggy neck skin as it attempts to twist away. The other collides with its thick, armor-like back. But it resumes its attack within a second, as if its fury numbed it to the pain, even as blood seeps from its neck.

My heart hammers in my chest as I target the beast again, igniting another pre-drawn Vitality Ward. Miss, and I might hit the boat or waste what could be my last offense. Strike, and I'll likely lure it back to us.

And the boat is still rocking from the burst of wind Willian used to save us.

I squeeze my eyes shut as the energy leaves me; the force pushes our boat even farther away. The beast's snarl opens my eyes again in time for me to see it twisting its wide face toward us. But instead of charging our way like before, it only growls its frustration and returns its focus to the crewmates' vessel as Odessa is struggling aboard.

Orto aims another sphere, but he stills at Willian's shout, "Wait!"

Orto and I turn, following Willian's pointing finger to where Calden swims toward us, pulling Zamirah along with him. Orto snatches the paddle and, with six mighty strokes, he closes the gap between us and them. Willian stretches out his hands. The boat teeters, and Orto and I send our weight the opposite way. Alani, now unconscious, flumps into Orto's shoulder, but the lurch of her shoulders reassures me she's still alive. At least, for now.

"Take her," Calden orders.

Calden hoists Zamirah toward Willian first, despite her protest, and the first mate pulls her into the boat. Her sopping dress, doused in faded blood and saltwater, slaps against the deck as she falls from Willian's weakened grip, landing on her hands and knees. I reach for her, intending to help her sit up, but she twists from my grasp, crying Calden's name before even taking inventory of who else is here. She joins Willian, forcing me and Orto to lean further back to compensate for their weight. Over the rim of the boat, Calden grapples for their outstretched hands. The waves thrust him away, as if by intention.

"Orto," I say, and he sets his paddle back to the sea, closing the gap again.

Then, finally, Willian grasps Calden's wrist and reels him closer. Zamirah grabs Calden's other arm—whining in pain—and they heave together. The boat slants again, water leaping in and swelling by our feet. Then the three of them topple inside, collapsing into a mound of bodies. Willian rights himself, attention snapping back to the stretch of water far away from us, where screams and blasts of energy ricochet over the roars of the unyielding beast. Behind the creature's mounting attacks, I can hardly see anything besides that Odessa launches most of the defenses. I suddenly recall her Master Talent that increases her vitality. But even with it, how long before she depletes her ability to draw energy from the beast?

I twist around as Calden pushes himself off Zamirah, coughing and heaving. Despite his convulsing chest, he reaches for Zamirah and pulls her upright. I vaguely hear him saying Alani's name and Willian giving some report of her state as I scan the undulating water for Elias. Wood shards and bits of supplies nod in the waves, but I see no trace of him.

My entire world seems to swirl, as if a vortex opened up beneath the boat. Why is it every time I think I have him back, something else takes him from me?

"Elias!" I scream his name, not even caring if it draws the beast's attention. "*Elias!*"

Calden jolts and holds up his Bind Mark. The main arrow, once pointed at me, shrinks and a lighter arrow stretches out, pointing behind him.

Faded. It's faded. Hardly even visible.

I stand, holding my arms out for balance, and scan the black water again. The sea rolls, knocked around by the massive beast that the others are still battling on their own.

But amid the waves, I still see nothing more than splintered pieces of boat.

"Norielle?" My name doesn't properly register until Calden repeats it. "Norielle, do you see him?"

I cover my mouth, trying to clamp in the wail I want to release as I violently shake my head at him. *No. I don't see him. Elias. Where is my Elias?*

But then, just as my vision starts flickering, I see him drifting in the water. Unmoving. Not even trying to fight the waves that crash over his face.

My hand slides from my lips. "There!" I say, jutting a numb finger toward him.

Orto and Willian take up their paddles, batting at the water again. I crouch but refuse to sit. I can't lose sight of him. The boat rides over a watery hill and glides down its slope. As Elias rotates in the water, the moon shines upon his battered face. He's clutching something—a large piece of wood. It keeps him afloat, yet he seems otherwise lifeless. Not even looking up to acknowledge the boat.

But we're closing in. We're going to get him. And as soon as he's aboard the boat, I am going to heal him, every single wound on his body.

Including the ones I left on his heart.

"Elias!" I shout again, desperate for his response, but a high-pitched yowl from the beast drowns out my cry. Distant shouts of warning fire at us immediately after, and I turn in time to see the monster thrashing away from Odessa and the crewmates and redirecting its course for us. Willian and Orto set down their paddles to prepare their defenses.

I freeze, courses of action splintering through my mind. I nearly attempt to try my last prepared Vitality Ward before an impulse turns me back toward Elias again. I have to get him. I *have* to.

But the fear of submerging myself in the sea—into waters nearly as alive as Lake Daleia—paralyzes me until the beast crests the waves again, spit and water dribbling off its sharp fangs.

Orto fires the first attack directly into the roof of its mouth. But the energy pushes our boat back. Away from Elias.

No.

My heart seems to restart, and adrenaline erupts with my next inhale. Before I can form another thought, I twist toward the water.

"Norielle!" Calden yells at my back as I dive into the frigid sea.

I ignore him, swimming with all my strength toward Elias. Thoughts lash at me like the icy waves.

That's the last time you'll hear Calden's voice or see Alani.

We're all going to die. All of us.

We should have never set out for Raevre.

My exhausted arms beg for rest that I can't grant them. The crown of Elias's dark head is all that I can see through the currents. But it's just enough to guide me—

Just a little farther.

The beast releases an agonized sound behind me, unlike any I've heard yet—a *weakened* sound. Hope flutters across my chest, and I steal a glance over my shoulder.

Calden. Of course, *Calden* stands in the boat with a hand stretched toward the wriggling beast. He fires at it again, and the beast ducks under the water.

Where is it going? Retreating?

Oh, let it be retreating...

I shudder, realizing I've slowed, and in my distraction, Elias drifted even farther from me. With wide strokes, I pursue him again, ears ringing in the sudden quiet. As I close in, I count down the estimated strokes I have left before I reach him. Twenty-five. Twenty-four.

I hear the slap of oars against the water—Willian and the others coming after me.

Twenty. Nineteen.

Elias's face winks into view when the waves dip. His eyes are open, brows scrunched. He's conscious. I forget to count when he looks at me with weak eyes. A smile twitches on my face. *I'm coming,* I think, wishing I could say it aloud. His eyes shut again.

I restart my counting from another guess.

Eleven. Ten. Nine—

A guttural moan dissolves *eight* from my mind, and water tugs underneath me. My eyes widen, but I don't have a chance to even scream before the beast's snout blasts from the sea with its jaws stretched wide. A current sucks the water toward the beast's mouth, and I flail backward, resisting the pull.

But through the splashes of my frantic kicks, I see it—almost a moment too late—

Elias inside a cage of teeth.

CALDEN

Norielle is still screaming Elias's name when Willian and Orto pull her aboard. I can't move. I can't even speak.

Lias. The beast *swallowed* Lias.

He's gone. My best friend is *gone*.

My lungs threaten to hyperventilate, pulsing in aggressive, quick punches. This cannot be happening. I can't lose him—I can't.

His arrow, I recall abruptly, and I twist my Bind Mark into view. The large arrow that once pointed to Elias has vanished, and now only three small arrows remain.

I stare at the mark, cursing it, cursing myself for inviting Elias on this voyage, for making him part of this Bind. What kind of cruel trick was this? Letting me choose my last member so he can die on a quest I should have never even taken us on?

I suddenly feel Norielle's gaze burning against the side of my face. I tilt toward her as the sorrow in her expression transforms into something furious, red blazing around her swollen eyes. Without a word from her mouth, I can hear her shouting at me.

This is your fault. You did this to him. Elias is dead because of you.

But the return of her harsh weeping cripples her searing glower, and she turns away. Orto draws her into his arms, and she falls against the elderly man's chest, as if he were her grandfather. On his other side lies Alani—my next dearest friend—unconscious from overexertion trying to save the ship *I* destroyed.

Zamirah's arm wraps around my shoulders, holding me yet again. She whispers reassurances that contradict Norielle's silent accusations. But her arrows miss their target, again and again.

All of this is my fault.

We're shipless. Separated. And now Elias is dead because of *me.*

60

ZAMIRAH

Something bobs in the sea, catching my attention as dawn crests the horizon. Orto's steady paddling brings us closer, and I squint at its angular shape. My sad wish for it to be my box of paints dispels when the box turns in the water, revealing itself as an empty, broken crate.

I sigh, feeling foolish for my hope—my heavy art box would sink to the sea's depths, not float to the surface. Just like the rest of the *Celestella* that served as my home for the last seven years. The nest I used to pray from, the deck I danced across, the ropes I tied and rails I polished, the cabin wall I painted as though it would always be mine. All lost to the sea that once carried it.

But my loss feels insignificant—like someone crying over a broken vase while a man lies dead beside it. As far as I am aware, none of my personal losses contained a heartbeat. Not like the loss Calden and Norielle now suffer.

It's all relative, isn't it? Pain, that is.

Calden's statement from the crow's nest finds me just as it did then—right when I need it. Still, it feels wrong to mourn material things in the wake of Elias's loss. And even though he was little more than a stranger to me, my heart still bleeds for him. He gave his all to save our prince, and now, he's gone. Lost in a single blink.

Would he have survived if he'd let me heal him? Should I have done so without his blessing?

Is this loss partially on my hands?

A fresh wave of heartache seems to well up in Norielle like the waves surrounding us, prompting a fresh cry just when I thought sleep had offered her some relief. I cast a sorrowful look toward her. She lies beside Alani now, nestled against our unconscious captain's shoulder. Her cries ease a moment later, and she squeezes Alani's limp hand.

Against my right arm, Calden shakes in random convulsions. Sharp inhales often accompany the judders, suggesting he's sucking in cries of his own and swallowing them before anyone but me can notice. I remain stiff beside him, having put to bed my attempts to comfort him with words. Nothing I say will fix this or make it hurt less. All I can do now is hope that somehow, knowing someone is close is enough.

It's all I've ever wanted in my moments of deepest despair.

When the sunlight swells enough to illuminate the edges of the waves, Calden shifts, turning his Bind Mark into the light. But seeing no change, he drops his arm into his lap and another suppressed cry escapes through staggered puffs from his nose.

I lean closer to him, and he turns toward me, moisture brimming in his eyes. Never have I seen a man cry so much, even if silently. The men aboard the *Celestella* never wept in my presence, and my father always contained his crying to a few tears in sparse appearances that he always tried to hide.

And yet, I'm not sure if I've ever respected a man more than I do gazing into Calden's teary eyes, seeing the heartbreak in them that only the deepest love and devotion can cause.

Elias was not Calden's friend.

He was his brother.

Calden smiles—as best as he can—as though to show his appreciation. Then he settles deeper into the boat, allowing more of his weight to land on me. Despite everything, gratitude buds within me that amid the horrid circumstances, at least there's *this*. Our newfound friendship.

Calden and Norielle finally go quiet—relieved, at last, by sleep. Willian gestures to me to gather my attention. Then he signs his question with his hands, so as not to wake Calden or Norielle, *"Are you all right?"*

I nod, careful not to disturb Calden, then flick my gaze toward Captain Alani before returning the question in kind.

Willian stares at the captain for a long while before responding. *"I'll be better once she wakes."*

"She will," I promise, though I can't guarantee it. I've seen it before, though—Wardens expending their energy to the point of losing consciousness.

In fact, I've done it myself, and it took me a full day to come around.

Willian smiles, though it doesn't light his eyes. *"Maybe we'll get an even nicer ship after this."*

I lower my chin, hiding a secret wish that my sailing days will end after this voyage. I want to go home and see my sister and parents. Though the thought of separating from Willian, a brother-at-heart like Elias was to Calden, only deepens my empathy for the prince.

Had I lost Willian—

I can't even complete the question in my mind.

"Though I think the prince may not want to put you on it," Willian adds, more of his usual levity returning to his weary face.

My chest flutters at his implication, but my hands curl rather than forming a reply when I recall what Calden discovered just before the beast attacked us—something we've yet to inform Willian of.

"Toaph Elbara's spirit is inside the prince," I sign.

Willian flinches, mirroring my statement back to me in question. I affirm he understood me, and he petrifies, staring at Calden like the man is on fire.

"We don't know anything more," I add. *"Or what that means for him."*

My breath comes short as my fears from when Calden relayed this news return afresh. What does Toaph mean to do with him? To send him and his Bind against Ta'Nathel? To take over him completely, claiming Calden's body as his own? Have all Calden's episodes been Toaph gradually trying to take more and more control over our prince?

Why would Toaph do such a thing to him? To a *baby*?

A sudden lightheadedness makes me feel like the boat is caught in a storm. I don't have answers for my questions, only prayers that I've misunderstood the meaning of this, and that Toaph will soon leave Calden—freeing him—and face Ta'Nathel himself.

But why wouldn't he have done so already? Is he not able?

I turn to Calden, wishing I could press him for more details about what he saw, but I wouldn't even if he were awake. He needs time to grieve and recover. Hopefully, Raevre will soon offer him that.

Willian takes up his oar, signaling to Orto to rest.

"Would you like me to take a turn?" I sign toward Willian.

"No." Willian musters another smile. *"Your prince needs you, little bird."*

I swallow hard, wanting to appreciate Willian's bold assumptions, but my heart only twists inside my chest. *My prince,* Willian calls him.

And yet something tells me I'll lose him—one way or an-other—by the time he fulfills his mission.

NORIELLE

Someone pats my shoulder, and I stir, blinking my tear-crusted eyes to see Alani's hair blazing red under a brilliant sun. I lift my head from her shoulder, checking that she's still breathing in her sleep before turning to see who tapped me.

Orto. He gives me a half-hearted smile, and foolish hope deflates in my chest. He's not Elias.

Elias is *gone.*

My nose burns and fresh tears well in my eyes. Why didn't I jump the moment I spotted him?

Would it have even mattered?

Orto's sympathetic gaze flicks ahead, signaling for me to look beyond our boat. *Have we reached land?*

I should be happy. Relieved. But the thought of stepping ashore without Elias is sickening. Still, I urge myself to sit up, body aching from the uncomfortable way I lay beside Alani. In the distance, beyond Odessa's boat ahead of us, a pale landmass blares in the midmorning light, a thick cloud of smoke hanging like a giant storm over it.

Raevre. Elias's papa died in Raevre.

I bet he never imagined his son would die hours from the shore.

A swell of nausea draws my gaze back to the other passengers in the boat. Willian paddles with whatever embers of energy he has left. His eyelids sag even as he attempts to smile at me. The expression is like Orto's—the look of someone who is afraid to make eye contact with you in case you fall apart right in front of them.

I swallow hard as I swivel my attention to Calden. He slouches across from me with his shoulder pressed against Zamirah's, as if they are using each other for support. His head hangs, eyes sealed shut but tilted toward his Bind Mark like he fell asleep staring at it. But his other hand covers my view of the mark.

Fury rises in my chest the longer I look at him. He didn't know this was going to happen. He didn't intend for it to. Yet it's hard not to see him as the face of the disaster. Could Elias have escaped if he hadn't spent all his energy wrestling with Calden and rescuing him? Would he be on this boat right now? Alive?

Zamirah's weary gaze suddenly catches mine, so empathetic, and yet I can't help but glare at her after watching her console the man whose actions led to Elias's death. She shifts, disturbing Calden. His eyes slowly open, a dazed look crossing his face before the color and life drains from it again, as if all the memories of what happened a few hours ago slapped him at once.

He jerks his Bind Mark into view, staring at it a long while before looking at me, then Zamirah. "It's... back."

"What?" I gasp, rocking the whole boat with how I lurch toward him to see it.

As claimed, the fourth arrow, now larger than the others, has returned, though faintly. I wipe my eyes and lean closer to it, as if our grief has made us both delusional. But when Calden twists it into Zamirah's view, her jaw falls, confirming she sees it, too.

Alive. Elias is alive.

I slap a hand against my mouth. In an instant, tears I once thought exhausted are trailing down my face in steady rivulets. How is that possible? It was *gone*. *He* was gone.

"W-where is he?" I stutter.

Calden studies the mark again, relief leaving its wet tracks on his face. His gaze pivots between the arrow and the landmass in the distance.

"Calden?" I press in his delay.

"It's pointing toward Raevre," he says.

"*Raevre?*"

He shows it to me again so I can follow the arrow's point to Raevre myself.

Impossible.

"I think the beast came from Raevre," Willian says, our heads turning toward him at once, as if pulled by a string. "It looked like a *leviathus*. A former *Grand* Sentry. They live in grottos beneath landforms, but no one has sighted the one underneath Raevre since before Toaph's disappearance. I didn't realize it was even still alive."

"We must have woken it with all of our energy," Zamirah supplies.

Calden's chin lowers, and I guess he's thinking the same as I am. *He* woke it. Not *we*.

Willian nods at Zamirah's suggestion. "It may have carried him to its lair. Little is known about their nature as Accursed. Maybe they don't... feed right away?"

My stomach knots.

"But..." I can hardly muster a sound, let alone finish my words. "H-he was... *dead*. How could he survive?"

There's a long pause before Willian replies. "Maybe the Raevran Wardens took notice and rescued him? Or the beast's injuries got the better of it on its way home, allowing his escape, and someone retrieved him?"

"It was so dark out here last night," Zamirah addresses Calden. "Perhaps the arrow was still there, but too faint to be seen without the sunlight."

All eyes turn to Calden, awaiting his thoughts on the matter, but all he offers is a furrowed brow before setting his sights toward Raevre. I follow his gaze. All the worries I should have about entering an enemy kingdom hang like distant stars behind the gleaming moon of knowing Elias is alive and close.

I take the paddle from Willian's exhausted hands and propel the boat with every fiber of energy I have left.

CALDEN

The boat bumps against soft sand, and my breaths shorten. A horde of regrets and anxieties swarms me, demolishing any peace I have about arriving on land.

My gaze sweeps across the pallid beach. Odd spindly plants and tall, branchless trees capped with broad leaves decorate the landscape—foliage I've never seen before. Beside Odessa's newly arrived boat, three abandoned dinghies from our crew rest on the shore, near enough to the sea for the thinned waves to slosh against their sterns. The crews' footprints indent the sand, leading inland, suggesting they followed my orders from yesterday morning, and headed directly to the Warden base.

Yet where are the Raevrans? I thought their watchmen would be here to meet us. Did they assume the crew that made it here were the last of us that remained alive?

Willian climbs from our boat first, paying the cove and his Omen Mark a full inspection before turning back with a hand stretched out toward me. I accept his help, and my boots squelch against the damp sand as I exit the boat. After weeks on water and in my unrecovered state, even the few strides I take are sloppy and weak, like a drunkard. Willian assists

Zamirah, Norielle, and Orto next, leaving only Alani inside, still unconscious. Her deep breaths flutter the disheveled curls around her pallid, bloodstained face. When I say her name, she doesn't even flinch.

I check her arrow again on my Bind Mark—still light gray, but far darker than Elias's hardly present arrow.

"Let's set her on land," I say to Willian.

He nods, and we meet beside the boat to hoist Alani out together. Willian scoops his hands beneath her arms, and I grab her by the boots, my elbows trembling from exhaustion even with the shared weight. We fumble a few steps sideways, then lay her in the warm, pillowy sand. Willian steps back, addressing the crew from Odessa's boat, but I crouch beside Alani, squeezing her limp hand.

"I'm so sorry, Alani," I whisper.

She doesn't stir, and a knot forms in my throat, cutting my apology short. If she survives, will she ever forgive me for this? Was not what I did to her when we first met enough?

The need to check on my sister draws me back to my feet, and the moment I'm standing, Willian returns to Alani, his knees thudding against the sand as he drops to the ground beside her. As if unaware that I'm still watching—or not caring that I am—he leans over her, planting a kiss between her expressionless brows.

A deep ache spreads across my chest. *El-Alam, let Alani wake to know she's finally found a man who cares for her the way she's always longed for.*

I pull my focus away and stagger toward Odessa, noticing her unraveled braids and the cuts and bruises that mar her typically pristine skin. Apologies swell in my heart, and I reach to hug her. But she turns from me, lips quivering like she might cry. For a blink, I see her as a child again in her wardrobe, hiding from me—from her brother. Scared to even meet my eyes lest they turn white again.

A sting pricks my eyes, but I bat the feeling away and force my breaths to steady. I can't be seen like this—emotional and devoid of my wits. Not here. Not now. No matter what has happened.

No matter what I have done.

"Zamirah," I say, finding her kneeling beside Willian, consoling him.

She stands, dried blood crusted on her skin and faded red stains on her tattered dress. I can't help but remember when it was only paint blemishing her. When she smiled. When Valrone was on the crow's nest, tossing peanuts and laughing at us, not standing behind us with a gash in his arm, fatigued and silent.

"Can you try sending Elias another message?" I ask.

Norielle swivels toward Zamirah, breaking her long inspection of the cove.

"Of course," Zamirah agrees. She tried twice already while we paddled to shore, but she never felt the message reach him. She did at least manage a successful message to Mother, informing her of our dire situation.

Zamirah walks a few paces away from the lapping waves. The torn edges of her yellow dress flap open, revealing bruises on her calves and knees. More injuries. More pain that *I* caused.

Zamirah's quiet song emerges from her in a whisper, but it swells into a warm melody that sweeps over me like a Soltûm breeze as it glides across the beach toward the thicket ahead. Zamirah stares in the general direction she sent her voice, waiting, waiting. Then, a long moment after the resonance of her song has completely vanished, her chin lowers.

"Nothing," she says, casting Norielle and me each an apologetic look. "He may still be unconscious. He won't be able to receive my message until he wakes."

I stare at Elias's arrow on my wrist again, then at Alani, imagining Elias must be in a similar state, though worse given the lightness of his arrow. At least he isn't at sea, but neither my Bind Mark nor Zamirah's song can indicate where he is *exactly*. Is he aboveground? In the Warden base? In the grotto?

"The Wardens must have him," Willian insists again.

"If they didn't, Elias would be dead," I agree.

"It's at least a two-mile hike to the base entrance," Odessa interjects. "And unless something has changed in the past decade since Mother and I last visited, the only way in is down a rather long ladder. Someone should stay behind with Alani until she's strong enough to make the hike and climb down herself."

A sharp breath jerks into my lungs at the thought of abandoning Alani here. The cove is said to be safe—kept secret through protections granted by ancient Masters—and is allegedly undiscovered by Hunters or commoners in Raevre. Still, defectors would know of it, should there be any nearby.

"No one here has the strength to carry her all that way, let alone haul her down the ladder," Odessa asserts in my silence. "But maybe the Raevrans can help us get her if she doesn't come to on her own."

I submit to this with a bow of my head, but before I can ask who will stay, Willian is speaking out from Alani's side.

"I'll watch over her."

"I'll stay with you," Valrone says hardly a second later, and Orto quickly chases his offer with a confident hand gesture toward Willian that I take to mean the same.

The three other mates—Helina, the cittern player, and a burly man—all add their pledges to stay. Then my and Willian's gazes turn in unison to Zamirah. She looks between us, as if unsure who to grant her presence to.

"Go with the prince," Willian decides for her with a soft smile. "Six of us is plenty to look after the captain."

I withhold my sigh of relief as Zamirah accepts his command. She steps toward him, and he rises to embrace her. The tight hug they share reminds me they've been at sea together for seven years—roughly a third of Zamirah's life.

"We'll meet you there soon, little bird," Willian promises.

Zamirah's only response is to press her head against his chest. When she releases him, Willian retrieves a map from a sealed compartment hung on Alani's waist, passing it off to Odessa's eagerly awaiting hand.

I cast one last glance at Alani, still lying limp in the sand. *She'll be fine,* I tell myself as I turn my party toward the thicket. *They are all going to be fine.*

I hang my head as we walk inland, feeling my own presence as if my soul itself were ablaze. Every step I take, I'm carrying Toaph Elbara with me. What would happen to him if I were killed? Would that set him free? Is he trapped? Or would he die with me, taking the whole world with us?

I deflect that thought. There's no way an Empyreal Guardian would put himself—or Silvirdia—in that fragile of a situation.

Right?

I step around another spiky shrub, following Odessa's lead through a lightly worn, yet hardly noticeable path through the foliage. Norielle chases at my sister's heels, focused ahead, as if Elias might race out to meet us along the way.

If only.

I check my Bind Mark yet again, frowning when I see the shade of his arrow hasn't changed.

But it's still there, I reassure myself. Whatever the Raevran Wardens are doing, they are at least sustaining him.

Behind me—per her insistent request that I not be at the back of the line—Zamirah trails, scanning the surroundings with a mix of intrigue and suspicion. The sight of her, even discouraged, bruised, and bloodied, offers me a soft comfort, as if I still lie in the boat with my head resting in her lap. Though I have little physical memory of it, I can recall the secure feeling of her tender presence, even whilst in the other mind. Without it, without *her*, would I have ever settled enough to witness all I had? To discover where Toaph is?

The path through the barbed vegetation opens up enough to allow us to walk in pairs. Norielle embraces the opportunity to cling to Odessa's side, spying on the map in my sister's hands. But Zamirah remains behind me.

I turn to her, finding her gaze still roaming the landscape. She glances back toward the sea, which is shimmering between the gaps in the towering trees. Tears glint in her eyes as she faces forward again, though she keeps her head down, as if to spare me from noticing her sorrow.

"Zamirah," I whisper, beckoning her to join me at my side.

She stops walking, and my muscles stiffen. Has she now had time to process how frightened of me she should be? To register that I am responsible for destroying the ship that's been her home for the past seven years?

But the smile that finally reaches her damp eyes suggests otherwise as she steps toward me. I wrap my arm around her shoulders, hoping to offer her the same comfort she gave me in the boat.

"Thank you for coming with me," I whisper.

She smiles again but says nothing. And it's only now, in this moment of quiet, that I completely register the implications of what happened on the boat. This woman healed me. Uninhibited. After witnessing the longest and most destructive episode I've ever had.

Then everything she's said to me is true; they aren't empty words of consolation, or some forced view held in her mind but not her heart. She *truly* meant it when she said she wasn't afraid, and all the many times she's proclaimed that none of this is my fault. Otherwise, she'd have been unable to heal me, let alone have come close enough to try.

The realization spills a deep peace over me, washing away—for mere seconds—the troubles of where we are, what I've discovered about Toaph, and the unstable states of two of my dearest friends.

El-Alam has *not* denied me everything. Some things, I have only denied myself.

And He's done more than send me a woman who accepts me even with my episodes.

He's granted me one who can tame them.

CALDEN

Odessa stops ahead of us, inspecting the dirt between two large ferns.

"This is it," she says, passing her map to Norielle so she can retrieve her warding pen.

I retract my arm from Zamirah to check Elias's arrow on my Bind Mark again. "It still appears he's down there," I affirm when Norielle catches me looking.

She clutches the collar of her dress—the only clothing on any of us that isn't bloodied or ripped. Yet I know the heart beneath it is in more disrepair than anyone's, besides maybe my own.

Odessa kneels, drawing a Key Ward into the dirt. A ring of light ignites on the ground, like the floor in Ila's spare bedroom, and in seconds, a hatch forms. Dirt grates inside the hinges as Odessa opens it. She peeks inside, shining a light from a Glory Ward into the blackness below.

"Wait a moment," she orders Norielle, then she climbs onto the ladder.

Almost a minute passes before her voice resounds from lower down than I expected to hear.

"The passage is clear," she says. "Come on."

Norielle looks to me for confirmation, but I seal my lips, gaze returning to the coast, now nearly hidden by the brush.

They'll be fine, I tell myself again, then I send Norielle and Zamirah ahead of me.

Once they are safely below, I descend the lengthy ladder into the underground. The familiarity of the jagged stone walls settles my nerves with a sense of home, or rather, something akin to visiting the house of distant family members. But the tunnel is silent and empty, besides the noise from those accompanying me. How deep into their passages are the others? And why aren't there guards or a guide of some kind awaiting us? Shouldn't they have sent someone at least this far in case anyone else survived the sea?

I step ahead of my small company, igniting a Glory Ward of my own, and follow the winding shaft until crystals transform the passage into something even more familiar. Except unlike the crystals that grow in clusters or those that sheet the ceilings back in our kingdom, these crystals are dispersed along the ground, as if planted.

We follow the multihued path for several minutes before the mostly dirt tunnel converts to one made of putrid limestone bricks, similar in appearance to the walls of an Alémor tomb. The clamor of our gear and footfalls echoes down the lengthy shaft, and the walls amplify our every slight utterance. Our path ends with a door that stands nearly as tall and wide as the tunnel itself.

I peer at my companions behind me, unable to muster the smile I'd normally send to encourage them, then I rap my fingers against the wood. A long silence follows the sound, and a sense of disquiet rustles within me.

After a second knock, I try the door, expecting to find it locked and disintegration to be the only means of getting through. But the latch opens without protest. I look inside the dim yet colorfully lit room within—a foyer of some kind. Three other doors with grimy windows lead off in different directions. In the center of the space, a labradorite statue of a canyx sits, looking toward the raised ceiling.

I ease into the foyer. Zamirah and what remains of my Bind follow suit, our gazes all shifting from door to door. Norielle raises the map, but just as she's declaring where the door on our right leads, the center door opens.

A woman with hair nearly as long as Norielle's steps through, but her older and deeper-toned features carry no other similarity. "Greetings," she says, her red-brown dress fanning as she curtsies. She rises, eyes set on me. "We've been waiting for you, my lord. Our High Warden apologizes for our inability to meet you at the shore. The ancient protections over the cove have deteriorated, and Hunters have recently discovered our presence there, so we had to stay back. We have received the others from your company."

My thumb twitches, and I visualize, with horror, Alani, Willian, and the others who stayed behind being ambushed by Hunters. "There are more," I say, struggling to sound half as formal as this woman. "One of my Bind members is injured and unconscious. A group from the crew stayed back to watch over her until she could make the hike here, unless you might send aid to them."

The woman glances toward one of the other doors, gesticulating a silent command to a man whose face suddenly appears behind its dusty glass. She smiles as she returns her focus to me. "Help is on the way."

"Thank you," I say. "May we reunite with the others?"

The woman studies me for a moment. "The High Warden would like to meet with you immediately, my lord. However,

I would be pleased to lead the rest of your party to the others once I have escorted you to him."

I resist the urge to shuffle my feet in discomfort. Mother has often warned me to be wary of those who seek to isolate others, and now, knowing it isn't merely my body standing here, but also Toaph's spirit, to not take extra precautions seems foolish.

"I would prefer to bring them with me," I say. "They are some of my most trusted companions. There is no discussion between me and the High Warden that they should not be part of."

She eyes each of the women with me. "Are they all members of your Bind?"

I almost agree, so that Zamirah won't be left in here alone, but they would unearth my lie too quickly, thus sowing distrust. "This is my sister, the Second Lady, Odessa, and Norielle. They are both members of my Bind."

I pause too long, and the woman presses, "And the third?"

My mind races, trying to determine what would be the wisest title to give Zamirah to ensure that they allow her to come along. *Advisor?* No, she looks too young. *Betrothed?* She'd have a ring.

I could claim she lost it in the shipwreck?

"She's my Consoler," I say, as the idea strikes me. "She can subdue my episodes. As such, she is required to remain with me at all times for everyone's safety."

Zamirah hides a smile at this, but confusion twists the Raevran woman's face. "Is this... a Talent, my lord?"

"More of a blessing," I say, not finding a better response.

Our guide ponders a long while before shaking her head. "Well, the High Warden was quite clear. He wanted to meet with you privately before you go any further, as is our custom." She signals toward another door, and a man with a pointed black beard steps out to receive his orders. "Bring the *Consoler* behind us. We will keep her close, should there be trouble with the Sovereign Prince's... episodes."

The man strides toward Zamirah, offering his arm with a polite smile. But she delays, turning instead to me with an inquiring look.

"Can the others not wait with her outside of the High Warden's court?" I ask, only for Norielle to clear her throat and shoot me an impatient glare.

Elias. She needs to get to Elias. Who knows how long I will spend with the High Warden? And if anyone else can heal him, it is Norielle. Even with her lack of experience, her devotion could at least start the process until I am able to reach him myself.

"It's fine, brother. We will honor their customs," Odessa says, settling some of my nerves.

If she is submitting, then this must be how it was when she visited Raevre with Mother. The High Warden must always seek a private meeting with the Sovereign, or the person closest to him, which is presently me.

"Forgive me," I say, returning my focus to the long-haired woman. "Please, take me to him."

The woman leads me along a lengthy corridor. Zamirah and the bearded man follow a small way behind. I study the unique architecture as we walk—the wards carved into the walls as designs, the patterns and images formed by the intentionally placed crystals. It's a far cry from our underground, which is only maintained enough to be livable. Then again, we have the citadel. The Wardens of Raevre have nothing aboveground—nothing in the sunlight. Their entire kingdom exists below.

The woman pauses in front of a double door flanked by two guards. "The High Warden is within, my lord," she says before curtsying a final time.

I glance back at Zamirah and find that her guide stopped her farther away than I expected. The worry in her eyes sends a tremor across my chest, but when I smile to reassure her, she returns the expression with mirrored confidence.

The guards open the doors without a word, and a light from within spills over me. My eyes adjust in rapid blinks as I step inside. Sheetlike crystals like those from Alémor cover the ceiling, except these are not only white but red, gold, blue, and silver, and they appear as though a skilled artist painted them across the ceiling in a spiral.

Beneath the radiant sheen, an extravagant rug sprawls across a polished moonstone floor, which, like in our ballroom, spans from one column-lined wall to the other. And at the center rests a dais, arguably more elegant than Mother's with its gold trimming and the shining crystals embedded into the chair's tall back and curved armrests. A man rises from it, his regal robes a deep emerald, but he turns his face down before I can see his features. The door shuts, and a brief glance around makes me aware that I am now completely alone with the High Warden.

Why aren't there advisors? Guards? Attendants?

"You've made it," the High Warden says, and a breath jerks into my lungs at the familiarity of his voice.

He turns, smiling at me, his angular face clear of the black-painted mask I expected to see. But his eucalyptus-green eyes confirm what I didn't want to believe.

The windcrier. It *was* him.

He steps from the dais, and my muscles seize tighter across my chest with his every stride toward me.

I project my voice, loud, hoping that Zamirah will hear it through the door. "What are you doing here, Oracle? Where is the High Warden?"

"There is no High Warden in Raevre anymore. There hasn't been for some time, not that I would expect anyone from Alémor to notice after a decade of negligence." He stops two paces from me. "I see you must have a lead you are following to Toaph Elbara. Tell me, what is it you intend to do upon finding that traitorous Guardian, if you should?"

I clench my teeth. Even with his powers of perception, he doesn't know where Toaph is—that he's standing right with me, *inside me*. And he mustn't.

"I intend to do as I've been called to do," I say, keenly watching his reaction. "I will aid Toaph Elbara in defeating Ta'Nathel, in whatever way he requires me to."

"I feared you would say that." His chest expands with a long inhale. "Have you not considered what I shared with you in our last discussion? That you will sentence the world to its complete devastation if you restore Toaph to his former state?"

"I have considered it thoroughly."

"And yet you've discarded it. Based on whose opinion? Your own? Or those who think themselves wiser than you?" He strokes his gray-streaked beard, considering me when I don't reply. "A part of you knows that what you've long believed makes no sense—not with the suffering you endure from your curse or the destruction it causes."

It's not a curse, I want to say, now that I know it with such certainty. But I withhold the retort. Should I speak too much, I might accidentally divulge Toaph's location. And what would the Oracle do to me then?

"Even blessings can have consequences, but that doesn't make them any less of a blessing," I counter, wielding Zamirah's words like a weapon. Though in the face of what I did to the ship, I can hardly maintain my confidence as I say the words aloud. "My suffering will not be in vain once Toaph

Elbara reigns as Empyreal Guardian over Silvirdia again, and Ta'Nathel is defeated."

The Oracle leans toward me, his gaze intensifying. "Or would that only be the beginning of the worst suffering you've ever known? Could you stand for your eternal soul to look upon a world you've led to destruction forever? To see its remains floating in the universe for all time—knowing it was your decision that led it to such a fate?"

I turn away, wishing they'd allowed Zamirah to enter with me, so I'd have someone to look to for encouragement. But now I see why they were so insistent on bringing me in alone. The woman's brief consideration of allowing the others to attend was merely her gathering information from me.

Fool, I chide myself. Now what will happen to them?

"You are already on the path of destruction, son. Can you not see that? Or is what happened to your ship insufficient in proving such to you?"

My jaw tightens. How does he know I destroyed the *Celestella?* Was he there? Soaring, unnoticed, in the night sky? Was it a vision that revealed what happened? Or was the information simply pried from the mouths of those who made it here first?

Elias. What is to come of Elias if none of us can heal him?

"Your means of getting home is destroyed. Friends are dying," the Oracle continues. "All because of the devastating power of a corrupt Guardian surging through you—untamable, unstoppable, uncontainable power. And do you not see how it grows stronger yet? What more will Toaph do by your hands?"

My muscles spasm in my chest as his words stir Zamirah's constant affirmations back into my mind. *It wasn't you. It's not your fault. None of this has ever been or will ever be your fault.*

And she's right. It *wasn't* my fault.

It was Toaph Elbara's.

Toaph Elbara is who nearly killed Alani when I was retrieving her to join the Bind. Toaph Elbara is who scared Corene and so many others away from me—trapping me also in a prison of fear of myself. Toaph is who destroyed the ship, nearly killing Alani *again*, and hurting everyone aboard. Toaph is who awoke the leviathus that stole Elias from us.

All the destruction. All the pain. The fear. The torment. It's all because of Toaph Elbara.

The Oracle's hand grips my shoulder, and his brows tilt up, as if in compassion. "My dear son, Toaph is our enemy. *Your* enemy. If you release him, you *will* doom the world."

I pin my gaze to the ground, blurring the Oracle from my vision. "What is it I am to do, then?"

His hold tightens on my shoulder. "You must find Toaph's location and deliver it to Ta'Nathel. Call down the barrier. Release the Guardian who El-Alam sent to save us and let him finish Toaph Elbara. That will end all the destruction—the curses—both on you and the world."

The room falls silent as I consider the words, turning them over and over until something catches.

The Guardian who El-Alam sent to save us. El-Alam.

Why would El-Alam revoke the powers He endowed His Sovereign with if the man still honored him? He wouldn't. If anything, had the Oracle's pursuits been holy, El-Alam would have increased his power—made him a Grand Master. Supported his plans.

But as it stands, El-Alam has revoked the Oracle's divinely gifted ability to ward and has surely sentenced his soul to Gehenna for his continual rebellion against Him. For the Oracle has done more than turn against the Wardens; he's turned against the Maker Himself.

So, why then would the Oracle serve an Empyreal Guardian whom he believed was sent by the Creator he rejected?

"Please, Calden." The Oracle's voice trembles. "You must trust me in this, for the sake of our very world."

I straighten my spine, my confidence restored in at least one thing. Whatever Toaph's alignments, *El-Alam* is where my loyalties lie, and an enemy of El-Alam is an enemy of mine. For it was by His hallowed hands that my life was given, and to Him my life belongs. Even if He has imprisoned me in this purpose of mine, taking from me the pleasantries of a common life, I will surrender to His far greater sovereignty. For I am foremost His vessel, whether the Guardian inside me is wicked or pure.

And I will not fall prey to the temptations Mother and Odessa feared I would. I am not that man.

I am not like the last Sovereign.

"How can I trust you?" I question, rupturing the silence. The Oracle's hand slides off my shoulder. "You were the *Sovereign*. The man El-Alam chose to lead the Wardens in righteousness. You were supposed to be my Venerate, my mentor, my *father*, raising me in how to follow in your virtuous footsteps. But now what have you become?" I meet his gaze with firm resolution. "The leader of those damned to eternal darkness."

His kind expression flinches, a flash of anger threatening his amiable mask. In his eyes, I swear I can see all the faces of those he's taken from me and my people. Corwin. Corene. Those two young girls who captured Echo. Hundreds more. All of them, now fated to spend the everlife apart from El-Alam, suffering forever for their continual choice to follow this man into corruption.

This very man who should be the one in my place, yet here he stands, an obstacle. An enemy.

"My son," the Oracle's voice struggles to sound as gentle as it did before. "If you will not listen to me, I will be forced to take actions that are most regretful."

I knot my fists, imagining a plethora of vile tactics he could try to persuade me with. But I hold my stance. "I will not take advice from the mouth of a deceiver."

His glower darkens, the lines of his aged face deepening. "Then you force my hand."

His words no sooner leave his mouth than something latches itself to my ankles. I jerk, but my feet are held fast to the ground, black tendrils of energy crawling up my legs. The buzzing webs wrap around my torso, pulling my arms down despite my resistance. They climb to my throat, where they stop, but not without constricting my breath.

The Oracle frowns in a way that almost seems genuinely troubled. "I truly wished you would be reasonable. I did want to have my son back."

He leaves no space for my response before facing the doors with a shouted command for the guards outside to open them. The doors are flung wide, and the Oracle's nostrils flare as he delivers his next order.

"Seize the rest."

TO BE CONTINUED...

WARD GLOSSARY

About Wards:

Wards are what Wardens use to wield their magic. The symbols are derived from the Empyreal language which is written in glyphs rather than letters. To use wards, one must first be endowed with power from El-Alam, the Creator God. Wards are broken up into various categories, such as Standard, Master, Conditional, and Consequential Wards. How much a Warden can use a ward before it "expires" (meaning, it fades and must be redrawn) is dependent on that Warden's skill level with that ward. All Wardens can access Standard Wards, but only those who have excelled to a Master Warden status can use Master Wards.

The following is a list of every ward that has appeared in the series so far. More wards will be revealed throughout the saga as they become important.

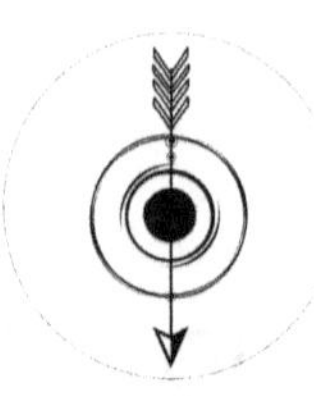

BIND MARK (MEMBER'S)

Sustained, Conditional

A Bind Mark may only be drawn by a Bind leader onto a member of their Bind. The arrow moves on its own accord, always tracking the Bind leader. The Bind Mark will vanish if the Bind leader dies. It cannot be controlled by anyone once drawn, not even the Bind leader.

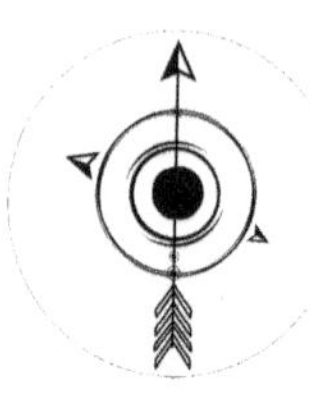

BIND MARK (LEADER'S)

Sustained, Conditional

A leader's Bind Mark is a divinely imparted mark, placed on the wrist of El-Alam's chosen Bind leader. As members of the Bind are selected by El-Alam, arrows will appear on the leader's Bind Mark. The arrows point to each Bind member independently. However, a Bind leader can choose one member to track with precision. This appears as the largest arrow. If a Bind member dies, their arrow will disappear.

CONJURATION WARD

Master

The Conjuration Ward allows a Master Warden to conjure the weapon of their choosing into their hand. This includes conjuring arrows for use with a conjured bow. No one else can wield the weapon. If dropped or claimed by someone besides the Master Warden who conjured it, the weapon will dissolve.

GLORY WARD

Standard

A Glory Ward is used to generate light which is drawn from the glory of El-Alam. This is most often used to power lanterns but can be wielded directly from one's hand. This ward is off-limits to defectors (because El-Alam is the direct source of the light).

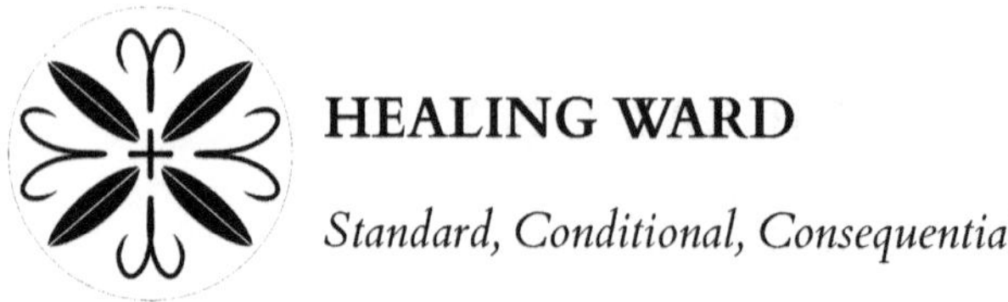

HEALING WARD

Standard, Conditional, Consequential

Allows a Warden to heal someone who is injured or sick, but they must bear the pain of the afflicted. The Warden must care for the afflicted and hold no bitterness or unforgiveness against them. This ward cannot resurrect.

KEY WARD

Standard

A Key Ward is used to seal or unlock the Warden's hidden doors or passages. This ward requires minimal energy. It cannot be used to create new passages or doors.

OMEN MARK

Standard, Sustained

Omen Marks are permanent wards that turn red when an enemy is nearby. It also points to an enemy's general location. A Shroud Ward can negate the effectiveness of this ward if wielded by a Master Warden.

PEACE WARD

Standard

The Peace Ward is used to calm forces of nature, including, but not limited to, storm crystals, raging seas, and fires. To work, this ward must come into direct contact with the force needing to be quelled or its source.

PRIVACY WARD

Master

The Privacy Ward creates a foggy dome around the user which traps all voices inside the barrier, allowing a space for private conversations.

PURIFICATION WARD

Standard

The Purification Ward is used to cleanse water of impurities and make it safe for drinking. Water treated with this ward is blessed with purifying properties allowing it to be used for ridding infections, cleansing wounds, and even hygienic uses.

SEALING WARD

Grand Master, Sustained

The Sealing Ward is a high level ward, only usable by those who have attained Grand Master status. This ward allows a Grand Master to create hidden doors that can only be revealed by a Key Ward. These wards are what are used to close off the Warden's underground passages and other secret places.

SHROUD WARD

Master

A Shroud Ward can be applied to a small area to help prevent detection by enemies. This ward keeps the Accursed from sensing a Warden's use of magic in the marked location and blocks defectors from detecting them with their Omen Marks. This ward must be applied directly to a major surface in the area the Master Warden wishes to shroud and cannot be worn for use while traveling. The effects last for a limited time (dependent on the skill level of the Master Warden who wields it).

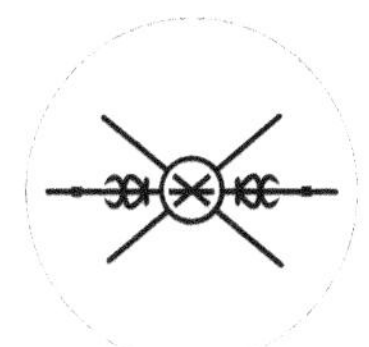

SNARE WARD

Standard

A Snare Ward creates tendrils of energy which will hold any one or thing captive until the user releases the ward (or dies). Snare Wards cannot be released by anyone but the person who drew the ward.

VITALITY WARD

Standard

The Vitality Ward allows a Warden to pull from their own life-force (vitality) to create and manipulate raw energy. This ward can be used to create shields, explosive balls of energy, and more.

ACKNOWLEDGMENTS

I couldn't have written this book without my Savior, Jesus Christ. This story took me into the deep waters of my own struggles, doubts, and insecurities, and yet, in those same depths, the Lord brought me more clarity than I've ever had—both for the story and for my own life. So above all, I thank my friend, Jesus, for the healing work He did in me as I wrote this novel, and for His companionship and guidance as we composed this story together.

To my husband, Rob—I've said it in every book I've published, and I'll continue to say it: I couldn't have done this without you. All your encouragement, the sacrifices you make, the council you give, and the ear you lend to my long rambles are the difference between this being a dream and being a reality. Thank you for being my Elias—ever looking out for my needs, cracking jokes to make me smile even on the worst days, and reminding me not to do things alone—*and* my Calden—ever sacrificing for me and our family, leading us with utmost integrity, and giving me a chance all those years ago, when we were both afraid of what might happen if we opened up our hearts. I love you, and I'm so grateful for the decade we've spent together so far!

To my editor, Jasmine—oh, my friend. You waded into a battle with me on this one. We fought hard through the mires of my indecision and mixed feelings, and while I know it was a rough go at first, I'm so grateful for all your wisdom that helped me make the final calls on this story. There are so many aspects of this finished story that I can point to and say, "Jasmine inspired that" based on the feedback you gave and our many email chats. So, thank you *dearly* for the amount of time, effort, and passion you poured into this, not to mention all the amazing ways you've been a friend to me over these past few months! I am so blessed to know you. (And I'm sorry about your ship haha!)

To my proofreader, Amanda—I am so grateful for you offering your help and for all the enthusiasm you have for this story! Even for the short length of time we've known each other, I have been so blessed by your encouragement, vulnerability, and kindness. Thank you for helping me hunt down those pesky typos!

To my alpha and beta readers—Hannah, Chloë, Melody, Elyse, Jenni, Gabriella, Katelyn, Julia, Bailey, Lilly, Ashlyn, Caroline, and Nathan—wow, there were a lot of you! Thank you all so much for stepping in, sacrificing your time, and helping me work through this story in all its various stages. Your feedback and encouragement were priceless and paid such a key role in pulling the threads of this story together.

To my Bind, aka my street team—thank you all for all the many ways you've helped me spread the word about my story and all the other ways you've supported and blessed me. I never in million years thought I'd have such a loyal, enthusiastic fanbase for my stories. It genuinely blows my mind. I am so thankful for each one of you.

To my friend, Kristee—thank you for being one of the biggest blessings in my life and for stepping in to be the hands and feet of Jesus in so many ways. I can't put to words how deeply grateful I am for all the time you've given me by watching my kids and for the many other resources and aids you and Mark have provided to help my family. For all the times I doubted if God really saw me in the past, I know now, just by your presence in my life, that He does. I pray you know how seen and loved you are by Him, too.

And lastly, to the rest of my family, friends, and readers who have supported and encouraged me—thank you for believing in me, rooting for me, and helping me in so many "unseen" ways. You have no idea how far just a little bit of belief in someone's dreams can go. Thank you for believing in mine.

ABOUT THE AUTHOR

A. M. Daylin has a deep passion for connecting with others' hearts through the power of stories, and hopes that her words will help others experience healing as they go on thought-provoking, imaginative adventures. When not writing (or daydreaming about writing), you can find her drawing past her bedtime, spending time with her family and Jesus, going for long drives whilst blasting cinematic music, and occasionally writing a song or two. She and her husband currently live in Arizona with their two young daughters. Connect with her on Instagram (@a.m.daylin) or at amdaylin.com.

If you enjoyed this book, please consider leaving a review on Amazon and/or Goodreads.